To Philcstick:
With admirati[...]
respect. Honest. Bo[...]
have been known to lie.
Tom Dunne

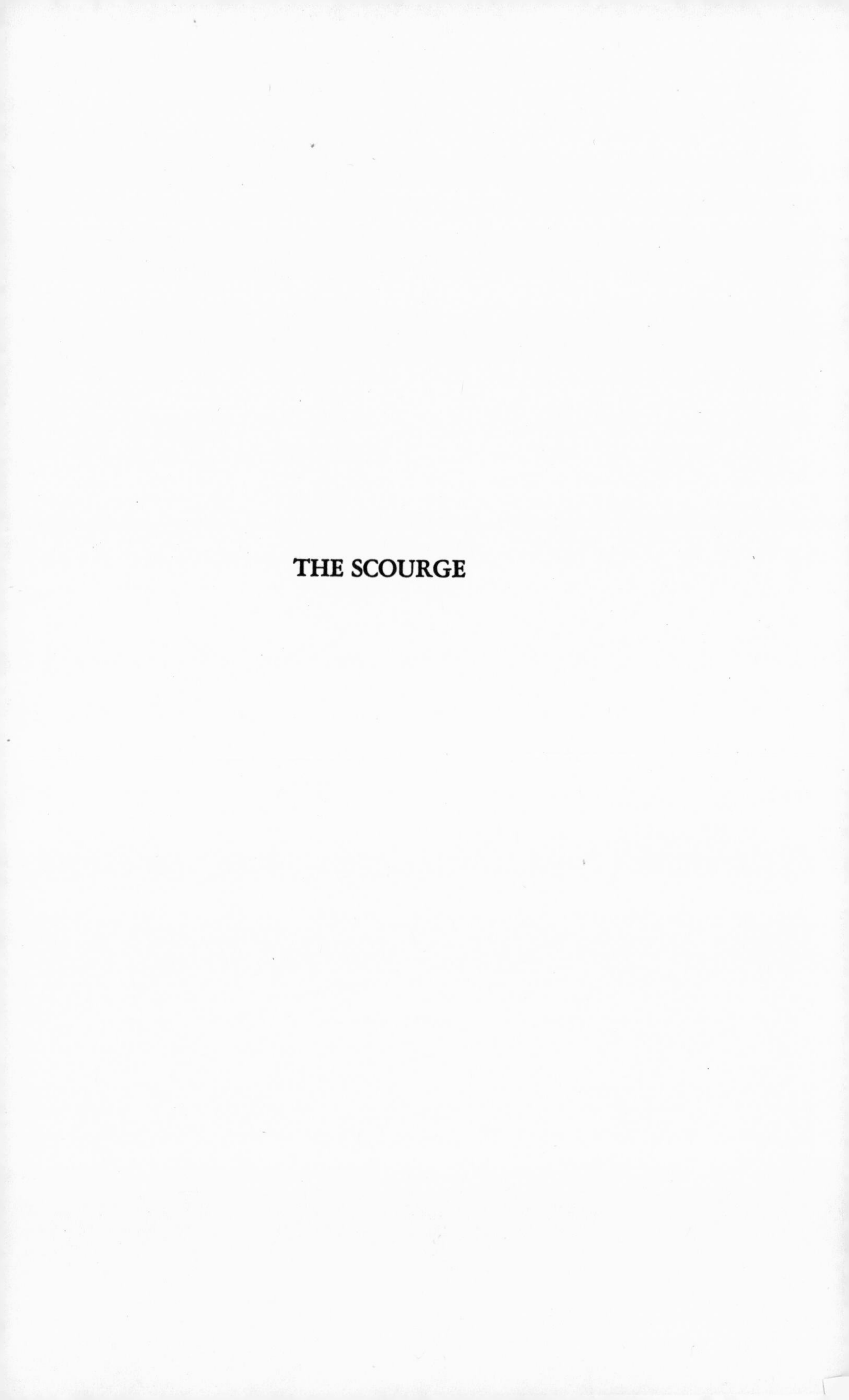

THE SCOURGE

THE SCOURGE

Thomas L. Dunne

Coward, McCann & Geoghegan, Inc. New York

Published on the same day in Canada by Longman Canada
Limited, Toronto.

Library of Congress Cataloging in Publication Data
Dunne, Thomas L
The scourge.
I. Title.
PZ4.D9238Sc [PS3554.U4936] 813'.5'4 78-597
ISBN 0-698-10893-0

Printed in the United States of America

This One's for Mary

THE SCOURGE

1

Brooklyn, New York

Marcia Spaguolo's funeral was simple and dignified.

She had planned it that way. The two-evening wake was limited to the family and a few close friends. Flowers were discouraged and a contribution to St. Catherine's Church recommended as an appropriate substitute. Father John Leone, a popular young priest, agreed to celebrate a brief and simple funeral mass and burial service. Marcia was glad that the Long Island cemetery which catered to firemen and their families, among others, forbade monuments; a simple brass plaque for everyone, nothing more. When Marcia was certain she was going to die, she asked Joe to take her to the cemetery. At first she thought it was part of a golf course–a lush green meadow rolling down to Long Island Sound. The densely packed obelisks, weeping angels, and mausolea of Greenwood, and most of the city's other graveyards, had always reminded her of the subway at rush hour, their marble passengers eternally crammed together, stranger jostling stranger. She was glad she would not be buried in such a place.

For almost twenty-eight months, Marcia Spaguolo fought the

disease. When she had begun to cough up blood, her first thought was of tuberculosis. *Nobody gets TB anymore,* she told herself. She was right. Her doctor diagnosed esophageal cancer. Day by day the malignancy relentlessly grew. It constricted her esophagus until she could no longer eat or drink. Eventually, bypass devices were inserted into her throat so she would not die of thirst or starvation, and as an aid to breathing. But the clawing, living growth refused to be hindered as it clutched at her throat like an indolent strangler.

She was in great pain.

Chemotherapy slowed the course of the disease, but after each treatment she was so nauseated that even the smell of food would make her sick to her stomach. Each new series of drugs produced a new set of side-effects. One caused her to turn a pale shade of yellow, and another covered her entire body with a fiendishly itchy rash. But Marcia Spaguolo was no coward. She was willing to submit to any therapy, however slight the chance of recovery might be.

All her hair fell out.

With remarkable courage, she faced the cancer and fought it with all her strength. Even one of her nurses commented on her bravery, which was high praise coming from one who had worked for years in a six-hundred bed hospital entirely filled with cancer patients, many of whom were dying and not a few of whom were children. But when death finally came, she recognized it, and was happy the struggle was over. Three days before the end, Marcia returned to her home in Brooklyn, and with her husband, sister, daughters, and Father Leone standing by her bedside, she quietly died.

For Joseph Spaguolo, grief was tempered with a deep sense of relief. As a New York City fireman, he'd found his medical bills were largely taken care of by his city and union health plans, and there could be little doubt that Marcia had received excellent care. But there had been more than a few times when he guiltily wished the inevitable would come more swiftly. He watched helplessly as his pretty, rather plump wife was whittled down to an eighty-three-pound mannequin. He had always believed that being burned to death was the most terrible death possible, but now he realized that being slowly eaten alive was far, far worse.

The wake and funeral went exactly as planned. Joseph immediately recognized that the mortician's art had been unable to restore his wife to anything resembling her former self, and he had the good sense to order her casket closed. At the wake and funeral he accepted condolences and mass cards with great dignity. He almost cracked the first night when his two daughters came into the funeral home and, seeing him, burst into tears. But he held himself together and was even able to comfort his sister-in-law, whom he despised, whenever she broke into sobs and shrieking, which was often. He had seen death before and had buried both his parents. It was a matter of personal pride that he be composed and in complete control while everyone else was so vehemently—even violently—mourning. All agreed that Joseph Spaguolo conducted himself very well.

The Shannon Bar and Grill is about as unusual as its name. Its somewhat grimy front window faces the busy traffic on Atlantic Avenue and sports several neon beer signs, including one for a brand defunct for five years. It is the kind of bar that from ten in the morning until one at night never has fewer than two patrons or more than ten. The Shannon is by no means filthy, but it is not especially clean either. If food were served (despite the "Grill" appellation, the only food available is beer-nuts and jerky), the facilities would probably be cited by the health department as unsanitary. Six feet above the bar is an enormous color television, installed by its owner, a retired fireman named Mickey, at great expense in a futile attempt to lure new business to the Shannon. But that November, business was largely confined to a handful of regulars as it always was except for St. Patrick's Day and the evening of December twenty-fifth, when it seemed that every man in the neighborhood sought release from relatives, children, and the endless repetition of Woolworth's $3.99 "Great Christmas Carols." Most of the regulars thought of the Shannon as a home away from home. In the months after his wife's death, Joseph Spaguolo came to think of it as home, period.

On some evenings, Joe would quietly drink his Rheingold with an occasional shot of Dewars and, aside from intermittent comments to Mickey or the television, quietly stare out at the Atlantic Avenue traffic. But when one of his special friends, like Francis X. Feeley, was at the bar, he would joyfully boom out his comments on sports and politics. Feeley, the lowest-paid reporter on the *Daily News,* had an opinion on just about anything, and he loved to argue. Joe treasured his company.

"The thing about the Jets," Joe said, pausing and looking around the room, "I mean the thing is that they got no *guts.* A pick-up team from a convent could push 'em off the field . . ."

"Bullshit," murmured Feeley.

"Bullshit to your bullshit," shouted Joe. "You watch that game on Sunday? The fucking *Rockettes* could field a better defensive line."

"Make for a good game," said Feeley.

"Better'n last Sunday, that's for sure. An' that sissy quarterback. Can't run, can't throw, can't take a tackle without sendin' for a team of surgeons. . . ."

"You, my Sicilian friend, are wedged beyond belief," said Feeley. "The Jets got a terrific team. . . ."

"Terrific, he says. Terrific. Lose four outta six and they're terrific."

"It's not the team," insisted Feeley, "it's the management. Those guys. . . ."

"At last you're makin' some sense; they haven't learned anything since Pop Young died." Joe paused. His expression reflected the surprise he saw on Feeley's face. For the previous few minutes, tears had been rolling down Joe's cheeks. At first he brushed them away and blamed the cigar smoke of a patron two stools down the bar, but they continued to come, steadily coursing from his eyes onto the bar. He tried to continue, but in the middle of his next sentence, a sob unexpectedly escaped. He looked confused.

"Let's get outta here," said Feeley, "car's right outside."

"I can walk. 'Snot far."

"Lemme drive–it's on the way anyway," Feeley lied.

At the first traffic light, Joseph Spaguolo, who had not cried in twenty-three years, began to sob uncontrollably.

"It shunna happened, I mean, why her? She lived clean. Went to church. Ate good. Never smoked. *Never."* He emphasized the word by punching the dashboard. "Then wham!" He punched it again. "Cancer . . . rotting before you're dead. Cancer." He pronounced the word like a vile obscenity. "Knowing you're rotting. Shunna happened."

"Joe," Feeley began softly, sympathetically.

"Sorry, Frank, I dunno what . . ." He mumbled something inaudible. "But it shunna happened. Why? There's no reason." He continued to sob quietly to himself for the rest of the ride.

Feeley led his friend into his neat frame house. It was small, and the rooms smelled as if they had not been aired for months. He made Joe drink a very large whiskey. Then he helped him undress and tucked him into his bed, much as one would a small child.

Feeley decided to spend the night on the living-room couch.

2

Bethesda, Maryland

On the rare occasions when Dr. Henry Rogers attended a cocktail party, he would answer the inevitable query concerning his occupation with the words "suffering and death, particularly death" and a menacing grin. Perhaps it was his unprepossessing appearance, or the grin, or the maniacal glint in his eye (he thought of it as a twinkle), but this rejoinder was more often than not a conversation-stopper. A surprising percentage of his questioners would abandon the stance of cocktail camaraderie and suddenly discover the need for another drink or spot a long-lost friend across the room. Rogers was ambivalent about this reaction. On the one hand, he had an anarchic streak that allowed him to enjoy disrupting the flow of fraudulent good will. He fancied himself an eccentric, a curmudgeon, one not-to-be-fooled-with, a teller of Truth. But he wanted to be liked. Though he was neither loud nor rude, he would often ask what seemed to him an obvious question in the middle of a discussion, only to be met with a particularly attentive and calculatedly blank stare from his hostess or her guests.

Dr. Henry Rogers was a thoroughly unhappy man. He longed to

be surrounded by friends who admired his wit and intelligence. But because he was an intensely private person, he was also an intensely lonely one. For one thing, he *looked* unhappy, a fact that discouraged a great many people from ever really trying to get to know him. He was an odd combination of fastidiousness and slovenliness. At 5′ 11″ and 198 pounds, he was easily forty pounds overweight. He typically draped around his portly frame one of three lightweight sport coats–two were bilious shades of green, the other a bilious shade of brown–which he combined with shirts of dark, nondescript colors and one of several thin, dark neckties. His slacks were cheap and his shoes even cheaper. Worst of all, a long habit of parsimony prevented him from using the services of a dry cleaner in all but the more dire emergencies. His wrinkled and stained clothing belied the fact that he was personally very fastidious. He often bathed twice a day. He was particularly proud of his good teeth, which he brushed after every meal, and the immaculate nails on his small, plump hands. Nevertheless, he was distinctly out of place at dinners and cocktail parties given by prosperous physicians or government officials.

Though a great many of the elegantly tailored men and beautiful, tanned women at such gatherings were professionally familiar with the medical facts of life, it is not hard to understand that when the disheveled Dr. Rogers slipped like a dark virus into the nucleus of their glittering cell, conversation often broke down. Dr. Henry Rogers was respected, and a few people admired him, but though he had read almost every self-help book from the works of Norman Vincent Peale to *I'm OK, You're OK,* he sadly knew that he would never be popular.

Henry Rogers' office contained the requisite square footage appropriate for the rank of a GS-16 who oversaw the work of more than three hundred government employees, but it looked quite small. For a man whose job was, by its very nature, precise, careful and accurate, the room was so chaotic that, had it been photographed, it could have led to a taxpayers' revolt over bureaucratic inefficiency. Rogers found it extremely difficult to throw anything away. Heaps of yellowing medical journals and National Institutes of Health publications lined one wall and entirely covered the couch. He had strictly forbidden his secretary to remove *anything* from his desk without his permission (though she regularly did so on the sly), and the effective work space was reduced to roughly one square foot. The office had long ago been christened "Fibber McGee's Closet" since Henry's search for a particular document or file would typically send an avalanche of papers, books, and articles cascading to the floor. It was, in sum, a mess, and Dr. Henry Rogers' superiors would never have tolerated it except for the fact that the man was clearly a genius. As head of the statistical division for the National Institutes of Health, he was recognized as one of America's premier statistical analysts, the author of several articles on data retrieval and theoretical mathematical models that were justly considered scientific classics.

Only one area of Rogers' office was perfectly tidy: a ten-foot-long bank of electronic equipment resembling that found on the bridge of an atomic submarine. He had spent several years assembling the hardware by wheedling, begging, borrowing, and in one instance, outright thieving from another department. The centerpiece of this collection, a multivarient display screen capable of three-dimensional representation, cost almost $100,000 and was one of the few available outside the Pentagon. Technically, it *was* owned by the Pentagon, but Rogers had been able to trade several months of his free time, working on an analysis of the domestic impact of a biochemical war between Russia and China, for the "loan" of the unit. "Off the books," so to speak. The brass at Arlington were pleased with the deal. They had hardware to spare, so Rogers' work had been effectively free, though they could not know that the eccentric statistician had also learned how to tap into the Pentagon's computer time-sharing capacity on a priority basis whenever he wished.

As he reviewed the monthly figures cataloging the national ills, he lit a cigarette and turned, as was his habit, to the lung cancer statistics He heard, as always, the whistle of the disease's relentless scythe through the lives of thousands of other middle-aged smokers. Henry Rogers had helped prepare the Surgeon General's famous report linking smoking to cancer, but he had been unable to give up the habit himself. Several of his superiors did not appreciate his chain-smoking, but it was a common enough vice, and hence tolerated, if not encouraged. His monthly summary of sickness and death was routine paperwork, but he always glanced through it just to make sure it had been correctly drafted. Even a small error could lead to a call from a sharp congressional assistant or, worst of all, an inaccurate and embarrassing newspaper story. Quickly flipping through the pages, Rogers almost passed over the stomach cancer figures, but then he paused.

"Too high," he muttered aloud. The total reported cases for the previous month was 4,151, a fraction of the figure for lung or breast cancer, but still disturbing. He squinted thoughtfully. The normal figure should have been about half that.

He rose and went over to the computer. He knew most of the retrieval codes from memory and punched out the numbers that would display on command all the data available on stomach cancer. Rogers played the computer "typewriter" with the casual, almost caressing touch of a great pianist performing Chopin. He was capable of absorbing a great deal of information at a glance, and the screen presented him with a multicolored choreography of flickering tables, graphs, charts, and maps.

Incidence.

Prevalence.

Mortality.

Case-Fatality-Ratio.

Each flickered, danced for him, and dissolved until the cigarette in his mouth almost burned his lips. Rogers sighed and made a note that the one-month rate for cancer of the stomach was up by more than 100 percent. Worse, the case-fatality-ratio, the deadliness of the disease, was extraordinarily high. He suddenly realized it was very late in the day, and that the only light in his office was coming from the screen before him which flashed in an eerie green light the question: ANY FURTHER QUESTIONS SIR. *Later,* he thought.

Rogers switched on his desk lamp, an ugly "colonial" model he had bought in college and kept for over three decades; he wished it would burn out so he could get rid of it. He checked his calendar for the next day. It was a good day except for a meeting at 3:00 P.M. with Undersecretary Potter to begin planning the departmental budget for the next fiscal year. "Ah, shit," Rogers muttered. Potter was one of his least favorite superiors. Rogers granted that he was an efficient enough bureaucrat, though he doubted Potter could read an article in *Scientific American* without the aid of a dictionary. What was most annoying was the sign on the front of Potter's desk that read: *Thank You for Not Smoking.* The Undersecretary ensured his visitors' courtesy by having no ashtrays in his office. After two hours of deliberation Rogers knew he would be in the clutches of a vicious nicotine frenzy, and he also knew he would be forced to retreat to the men's room for a quick fix.

The morning schedule, however, was clear. He set aside time to look more closely at the stomach cancer figures. A random pattern search would determine if the victims had anything in common medically, ethnically, socially, or geographically. Henry Rogers did not expect to find any pattern, however. One did not need a Ph.D. in statistical theory, let alone an M.D.–and he had both–to understand that statistical "bumps" were quite common. An average was simply that, and fluctuations were not unusual. As he left his NIH office and walked to the parking lot, his mind was more occupied with the probable traffic jam on Rock Creek Parkway than with the sudden jump in stomach cancer. The figures were probably just a statistical anomaly.

3

Providence, Rhode Island

Dr. John Blanchard found autopsies boring. Some of his colleagues at Rhode Island General were devoted detective-anatomists, while others were slightly sickened by the procedure, even after years of medical practice. To Blanchard, only paperwork was more tedious. The hospital required that a staff member be present at, and preferably conduct, the examination of any patient who died unexpectedly. Even when there was no indication of malpractice or any other sort of liability, the hospital's insurance company required the investigation, and Blanchard was usually willing to take on the task: it was easy money and the diagnosis was often obvious.

As he cut through the chest cavity before him, Blanchard thought of his wife. Lillian was rarely out of bed before noon, and though she was not often falling-down drunk, it was also rare not to smell the thick-sweet odor of bourbon on her breath. From the beginning, theirs had been a marriage of convenience: her parents had been ecstatic that she was being courted by a doctor-to-be, rather than the feckless young men she usually fancied, and Blanchard had found her almost as attractive as her father's willingness to finance his medical education. Blanchard regretted that he had not divorced her before he had begun to earn a substantial income; a settlement now could cost him dearly. And the taxes he had to pay. . . . He sighed and removed the liver, slicing off a fragment for further tests.

Dr. Blanchard did not really believe there was always a "cause" of death, or at least one that could be determined with any precision. Like many physicians, he was convinced that sometimes people just *died.* For reasons unknown. Nevertheless, families, hospitals, and insurance companies preferred any explanation to none at all. The former patient on the slab in front of him was not willing to part with any answers, however. He had been given no medication of any strength before he suddenly died, and tests indicated no pathogens in the blood.

As he probed the upper intestines, Blanchard noted with pleasure out of the corner of his eye the arrival of a particularly good looking intern. "Glad to have you," he murmured absently. *Like to have you,* he thought to himself and felt a stirring in his groin. Blanchard liked to think of himself as omnisexual, and though the great majority of his pre- and postmarital affairs had been with women, he occasionally found himself attracted to an exceptionally handsome younger man. The intern, Bill, was tall, trim, and broad shouldered. His hair was jet black and his fair skin and intensely blue eyes caused the heart of more than one nurse to flutter. At thirty-six, Blanchard was in good physical condition and not unattractive himself, and he had "taken a special interest" in Bill shortly after his arrival on the hospital staff.

Blanchard carefully removed one of the kidneys for further tests and was happy to realize the procedure was nearly over. Perhaps the younger man, who looked more than a little queasy at the bits and pieces of the corpse laid out before him, would want to have a few drinks afterward. Blanchard recalled the time he had had several beers with Bill and offered to help him avoid several particularly onerous hospital duties. He had even listened sympathetically while Bill told him of his arguments with the girl he lived with. When Blanchard excused himself to go to the bathroom, Bill had said, "Me too," and followed him. He noticed that Bill did not stand almost hugging the urinal; rather he stood back a bit, exposing himself. Not blatantly, but enough to catch his companion's eye. At the time, Blanchard had thought him either very well endowed or slightly tumescent, but he lacked the nerve to stare. Still, he had thought of the incident often, and the prospect of another encounter and its possible result excited him.

John Blanchard was a well-trained and highly competent doctor. He was also an honest person. He did not skip any of the required steps in the dissection, and it is unlikely that anyone but a very careful and very suspicious pathologist would have caught it. The tumor he failed to notice was very small, at the base of the brain, near the pituitary. "You look like you need a drink or three, Bill," he commented as he scrawled his name and observations on the hospital form. "Three would be nice," Bill said, and smiled.

A dozen pages of early test results and notations were attached to the file on which Blanchard worked, as a nurse and an orderly removed the remains of the body from the examination table. Below the name, Jonathan Patrick Taylor, and the age–three days–he wrote in the box labeled *Cause of Death:* "Unknown. Probable respiratory failure. Crib death." Perhaps further tests would turn up something.

He signed the final page and looked up with a bright smile at the pale young intern. "C'mon, Bill. Time to wash up." They left the operating theater and headed for the scrub room.

4

Bethesda, Maryland

As Henry Rogers maneuvered his TR-8 through the morning traffic on Wisconsin Avenue on his way to work, his mind was not occupied with thoughts of budgets or the upcoming meeting with Undersecretary Potter. The Triumph was singularly maladapted to the six-mile run from his apartment on Connecticut Avenue to Bethesda and back. He was always gearing down from stoplight to stoplight, and the engine growled continually: a powerful animal only rarely allowed to run flat out. Rogers knew it was not sensible to own such a machine and not use it properly, but sports cars were the only luxury he allowed himself. He had grown up in a family of five who were members of what could be called the "strapped middle class." There were always clothes for the children, and food was good and plentiful, but there was almost no money for extras. Henry was never able to think of his boyhood home in Alston, a Boston suburb, without a combination of sentimentality and claustrophobia. The Rogers' home was invariably neat, but filled with his parents, brother, three sisters, and grandmother; there was hardly a place to sit quietly, let alone have any privacy. He and his brother shared a small bedroom into their early twenties. They fought often, as brothers always do, but with a peculiar passion unique to children fighting for *Lebensraum:* he and his brother were both in their thirties before they were able to become truly close. His sisters, packed three in a room, would never like one another, though they worked very hard at it.

When Henry Rogers graduated from Boston University, he was presented with a Phi Beta Kappa key from the dean and his first car, a used MG midget, from his father. John Rogers was proud of his son. The boy had a natural aptitude for science, and spent a great deal of his free time in the library. His father could not have known it, but Henry had started "hanging out" at libraries for much the same reason other boys congregated at the local Dairy Queen: to flee the claustrophobia of home. As a science teacher, John Rogers worked hard at interesting all his children in the subject. Every new exhibition at the Boston Museum of Science became a family outing, and he was truly talented in explaining a complicated bit of physics or chemistry to children of almost any age. But only Henry took more than a polite interest in his father's passion. The elder Rogers believed that each of his children should follow any chosen career and he also told himself he loved them all equally. But when Henry had asked for a chemistry set for his ninth Christmas, he almost wept; from that point on, the boy became his favorite, and before Henry was a teenager, John would take him each Saturday to the school in which he taught, where they could tinker with levers and frogs and delightfully smelly chemicals. When Henry Rogers graduated from Boston University, Phi Beta Kappa, *summa cum laude,* to begin his studies at Harvard Medical School, his father did indeed cry.

John Rogers died two years before Henry graduated from medical school with more than his share of academic honors. The Rogers family was left not exactly poor, but badly straitened. Harvard generously increased Henry's fellowship to cover all tuition, but the cost of books, living expenses, and occasional financial aid to his family left him $8,000 in debt by the time he received his M.D. degree.

A brilliant physician-to-be is considered a good risk in banking circles, but to Henry's orderly and cautious mind the loans assumed gigantic proportions. Several years of internship and residency would probably double the sum, and it could take years to pay back while he established his practice. Upon graduation, he had accepted a research position at Bell Labs and within three years had paid back the loans, saved some money, and bought himself a bottle-green Alfa Romeo. But, having been raised by survivors of the Great Depression and having survived years of money worries, Dr. Henry Rogers was security-obsessed. Even well-financed, progressive Bell could, conceivably, decide to cut back or eliminate the costly research division should there ever be another depression. After almost five years and the acquisition of a Columbia Ph.D. in mathematics paid for by the Labs, Dr. Henry Rogers decided to accept an offer from the National Institutes of Health. The salary was somewhat less than he was then earning, but it was more than enough for his needs. And the security of a civil service job lured him to NIH even after Bell offered him a substantial raise. When and if the Crash came again, he would be among the last to go down with the ship. The government, after all, printed the money.

Rogers eased the TR-8 around a bus, and gunned up to the light nearest NIH's Center Drive entrance. The light quickly switched to red.

"Shit," he muttered, braking and shifting down.

Stopped at the light, he thought back to the stomach cancer statistics he had noticed the previous day. His reverie was broken by a honk behind him; the light had changed without his noticing it. Rogers remained deep in thought as he pulled into his parking space and strode to his office. Sitting down at the computer console, he reviewed the statistics he had looked at the previous night. As the numbers flashed before him, he became convinced he was either following a dead-end road or that some correlation was missing from the data. He carefully scanned the occupations of the previous month's victims. As with many carcinomas, cancer of the stomach can be induced by the ingestion of any of several carcinogens. An on-the-job hazard could sometimes cause a sudden jump in one of the hundred-plus varieties of the disease. But there was no geographical pattern indicating a localized environmental insult–an accident–and there was no occupational clustering. The stomach cancer patients ranged from wealthy and professional people to derelicts.

Stomach cancer was a particularly interesting carcinoma. Japan had one of the highest rates in the world. The United States was among the lowest. The night before, Rogers had skimmed some of the literature on the disease. Besides Japan, countries as diverse as Iceland, Chile, Austria, and several Eastern European nations had very high rates compared to the U.S. Among Americans, only immigrants from these countries and native Hawaiians had a high incidence. For the population as a whole, only about five percent of cancer deaths were attributed to stomach cancer, as compared to twenty percent just a few decades before. Here was a perfect detective case for nutritionists, and theories had been put forth suggesting its cause as smoked foods, alcoholic beverages, habitual drinking of very hot or very cold beverages, the consumption of too much fish or too much cabbage. Clearly, something was common to peoples as diverse as the Japanese, Chileans, and Austrians, but no one had ever been able to figure out what.

Rogers punched in the codes for ethnicity and national origins. Sure enough, Hawaiians and Japanese-Americans led the list. All the proportions were just about normal: there were simply too many cases across the board. For ninety minutes, Rogers sought some missing piece of evidence, some correlation to explain the sudden upsurge. Sometimes the numbers spoke to him in an almost audible voice, but this time they were silent. He stared at a map with a case-incidence breakdown for each county of the U.S. and superimposed the typical distribution. They matched perfectly. The map was actually pretty: four colors checkerboarded across the continent flickering ever so slightly. With a grunt of disgust, he typed out ENDIT to clear the machine. The screen flashed THANK YOU–HAVE A NICE DAY. "Pentagon's goin' soft," he muttered, and lit a cigarette. Finally, he went to his desk and started to review the departmental budget he would have to present to Potter that afternoon. But it was hard to concentrate. For the first time in his professional career, a sickening, sinking feeling crept into his mind: something was very wrong. Call it dread. It was irrational, just an intuition, but Dr. Henry Rogers was suddenly very afraid.

5

Scarsdale, New York

It was a beautiful, brilliantly sunny morning. Hope McCormack snuggled in her bed, sipping a third cup of coffee. The children were at school, Jim was at his office, and, best of all, her cleaning woman had called in sick. Every Wednesday morning Hope frantically straightened up the house in anticipation of the arrival of the housekeeper. Every Wednesday she told herself she was crazy to do this—if anything, she should leave the morning dishes unwashed and the toilets unscrubbed. Perhaps it had been her mother's obsession with neatness that engendered the intense fear that her cleaning woman might think her slovenly.

But *this* Wednesday, she could relax and enjoy herself. She sipped her coffee and watched a stiflingly dull French film director interviewed on the *Today Show.* She thought to turn it off, but her bed was too comfortable. She ignored the interview and considered making something really delicious for dinner. Maybe a salmon mousse. When she returned her attention to the television, *Today* had evolved into *For All Sisters,* a program she rarely had time to watch.

"The topic for this week is breast cancer," the host said seriously, "its detection, causes, and treatments. It is a disease which will strike one out of every six women in this country, and coping with it is important for all sisters." The show's theme song began to play, and the camera moved back to reveal a panel of doctors, all men.

"Bummer," she muttered aloud. She had hoped they would have a famous chef making something delicious. She listened inattentively for a few minutes, then rose and went into the bathroom.

Returning to the bedroom, she pulled her nightgown over her head and began to dress. On the television, there was a film of a woman examining her breasts. "Be thorough," the narrator said sternly, "it only takes a few minutes." Impulsively, Hope dropped her nightgown on the floor and began to examine herself. First the right one. Now the left.

She stopped.

In her left breast, just below the nipple, there was a lump. Not a big lump, about the size of a pea. Cautiously, she felt the rest of her breast. There were no others. Her hand went back to the lump. It was still there, a hard marble beneath the skin. Hope McCormack stood very still and listened to her heartbeat thundering. Then she sank onto the bed and concentrated on breathing slowly and evenly. She realized she was sweating profusely. "Go ahead, cry if you want to," she told herself, but the tears wouldn't come. Her mind raced: call Dr. Miller . . . get an appointment *today* . . . be insistent about that . . . call Jim at his office . . . ask a neighbor to pick up the kids at school if she was with the doctor that afternoon . . . go to the library and check out everything they had on breast cancer . . . call her mother–no, wait until she knew more, no reason to frighten her if it was nothing. But it *was* something. Her fingers continued to massage the bump as if trying to make it go away. "Okay, Hope," she told herself, "get on the stick. Get going." She sat for another ten minutes, kneading the lump, otherwise unable to move.

At last, she went into the living room, still naked, and dialed Dr. Miller's office. "I'm sorry, Mrs. McCormack, but the soonest I can get you in to see doctor is next Tuesday," the receptionist said politely.

"I have to see him today," Hope replied.

"That's just not possible, I'm afraid. He's overbooked as it is. I just can't fit you in . . ."

"But this is an emergency," Hope said, realizing she was almost shouting.

"Have you hurt yourself?"

"No, I . . ." she hesitated, unwilling to seem indelicate. "This morning I found a lump. In my breast. I'm afraid I might have. . . ." She couldn't say the word aloud.

"Just a minute," the secretary said. Hope waited, nervously biting her lower lip. "Can you come in at four, Mrs. McCormack?"

"I'll be there," she said, hanging up the phone.

She moved through the rest of the morning like a sleepwalker. Showering, dressing, taking some spaghetti sauce out of the freezer for dinner. She called Jim's office, but he was in court. She told his secretary to tell him she had gone out, and if he got home before her, the children would be next door. She looked at her watch. Eleven. Five hours to kill. She made a cup of tea and a sandwich. She ate it, tasting nothing. "Okay, just get organized," she said aloud. "First the library, then Dr. Miller's."

She was surprised to find that the Scarsdale Library had over a dozen books on breast cancer, and scores of others on cancer in general. *Popular subject,* she thought bitterly, and pulled half a dozen from the shelf. She really wanted to read about the nature of the disease, and particularly the survival rate, but she found herself drawn to two rather old personal accounts. *First You Cry–not me,* she thought–seemed well written. Another bore a rather grim, if descriptive, title, *The Invisible Worm.* She opened it, and read the William Blake poem on the first page.

O Rose, thou art sick!
The invisible worm,
That flies in the night,
In the howling storm,

Has found out thy bed
Of crimson joy,
And his dark secret love
Does thy life destroy.

She stared at the page, and reread the poem again and again. "Thy life destroy," she murmured. *Her life.* She looked up and was surprised to find that several people were staring at her. Hope McCormack realized she was crying. Tears rolled down her cheeks and splattered onto the book in front of her. Hastily, she grabbed her purse and headed for the door. She sat behind the wheel of the car and willed the tears to stop. *Worse than a baby,* she thought, and was reminded of her children, the children who might not have a mother before long. The children she loved so very, very deeply. The tears started again, accompanied by deep, shuddering sobs. She hated herself for feeling self-pity, particularly since she had always been proud of her composure and strength when others were falling to pieces. Finally, she pulled herself together, blew her nose, and put the car in gear.

Dr. Miller's office was only about a mile away, and she would be more than an hour early for her appointment, but she knew that just sitting in his hideous knotty-pine waiting room was preferable to driving aimlessly around the streets of Westchester. *You've had your cry,* she thought, *and that's the last one. So I have a lump—that doesn't mean cancer. And if I do have it, I can take it. Have to cope just as thousands of other women did. Betty Ford, Happy Rockefeller, hell, even Julia Child. Probably be worse for Jim and the kids than me. One step at a time. We'll take it one step at a time.*

Hope McCormack slammed the car door and strode into Dr. Miller's office. "Guess I'm early," she said to the startled receptionist, managing a convincing smile. By the time Dr. Miller saw her, she knew the McCormack guts had triumphed. Whatever happened, she could face it.

6

Scarsdale, New York

Dr. Albert Miller looked up from Hope McCormack's medical record and stared at the pretty young woman opposite him.

"Your last check-up was only seven months ago, so I think we can assume that whatever you've found is a recent development." He smiled inappropriately. Dr. Miller was an excellent internist, but even he knew how inept he was when it came to bedside manner. He very much wanted his patients to feel comfortable with him, but he came across as cold and distant. His rimless glasses and ascetic features gave him the look of a high school principal. Despite his appearance, he felt an empathetic twinge for Hope McCormack. She seemed remarkably calm, but he knew she must be terrified. The sooner he cleared up the problem the better.

"The odds are very much on your side, Mrs. McCormack," he said as he examined her. "Particularly at your age. Women in their early thirties or even younger can, of course, develop cancer of the breast, but it's not typical. It usually strikes at a later age, especially after menopause." He palpated the lump. "Still, there is something there."

"Yes, I know."

"Probably just a cyst. Nothing to worry about."

"But how can I know?" Hope asked calmly. As usual, Dr. Miller annoyed her. His heavy-handed attempts to reassure her were patronizing and useless.

"Oh, that's simple enough. We lance it, rather like a boil, and draw out the fluid. It's an office procedure, and I can do it, though if you'd prefer a surgeon . . ."

"No, that's all right. You do it," Hope said.

She was not overfond of needles, and the one Dr. Miller produced was a wicked-looking weapon. It was long and hollow–its silver finish glistened. Hope gritted her teeth.

"Just lie back and relax. This won't hurt much. All you'll feel is a little prick."

Probably said that on your wedding night, Hope thought, surprising herself with her uncharacteristic raunchiness. She smiled at the doctor and did as she was told. Miller furrowed his brow with concentration. He pinched the lump with his thumb and forefinger and inserted the needle. *He was right. It hardly hurt at all.* Dr. Miller grunted.

"Well?"

"Well, it's not a cyst. There's no fluid. So what we've got is a tumor," he said calmly.

"What *I've* got is a tumor, you mean."

"Look, Mrs. McCormack. . . . You can sit up now. . . . The odds are still very much on your side. Eight out of ten breast tumors are benign, harmless. It will have to be removed, of course, but you'll probably be out of the hospital in less than a day. The scar will be small, hardly noticeable after it's healed. Over the years I've seen more than a dozen of these tumors, and almost all of them were benign." He smiled at her pleasantly, and she felt an urge to slap his smooth, pink face. *Take it easy,* she thought, *listen to him. He's trying to be kind. Give you the facts.*

"You said 'almost all of them.' I assume some were malignant."

"Yes, of course. A few were. You can get dressed now." He turned on his heel and went into his office. Hope pulled on her clothes and followed him. Miller was at his desk scribbling on a piece of paper.

"I'll give you the name of a good man, Dr. Lynd at Markland

Memorial. He's young but very competent," Dr. Miller said, emphasizing the last two words. "He's the best man for the job. There's been something of a backlog of this sort of thing in recent weeks, but I'll call him and try to get you in to see him before the month is out."

"That's a long time to wait not knowing if, if . . ." Hope's composure began to crack; her voice was hoarse.

"Yes, I understand your concern. I'll do my best. I just know he's been very busy lately. You see," he said shyly, "we sometimes play tennis together, and he hasn't been able to get away for weeks now. Been working a six-day week, or so he tells me."

"Guess he's in a growth industry," Hope said, intending to sound grumpy and unintentionally making a pun.

Dr. Miller paused. "That's very witty, Mrs. McCormack. I'll have to remember that. I'm glad you're taking this in the right spirit."

"Taking *what* in the right spirit? Is the lump malignant or not?" Hope asked, her voice trembling slightly.

"I told you, Mrs. McCormack, the odds are very good that you have nothing to worry about. Nine out of ten of these tumors turn out to be benign."

"You said eight out of ten before."

Dr. Miller looked surprised. "Yes, I did, didn't I? Well, the precise figures are readily available. The point is, I want you to realize the simple fact that you have a small tumor does not mean *per se* that you've mammary carcinoma. In fact, it's unlikely. Do you understand?"

"Yes. Thank you. I'm sorry. It's just, well, a scary thing to suddenly discover. And not knowing for several more weeks before I can see this Dr. Lynd . . . Is there anyone else who could take me sooner?"

Dr. Miller looked sympathetic. "Leave it to me. I completely understand your concern. *(Do you,* Hope wondered.) I'll call Lynd at home this evening and let you know tomorrow. There are a number of other men I can recommend. I just think he's the best in this field. He's trained in both surgery and oncology."

"What's that."

"An oncologist is a cancer specialist." Hope's eyebrows shot up.

"But that doesn't mean you have anything to be concerned about. You'll have to have a series of tests, of course, and Dr. Lynd is the perfect person to go over the results and make a judgment. If, I repeat if, something is wrong, he is the ideal person to operate. And in any event, you'll want to have that tumor taken out whatever the test results indicate. So let me talk with him. In a similar situation I'd send my wife to him, Mrs. McCormack."

For the first time that day, Hope felt reassured. Dr. Miller's voice was soothing, and though she knew she would worry until she found out whether or not the tumor was malignant, her panic receded and almost disappeared. "Thank you, Dr. Miller. You've been very kind. And I'm sorry if I seemed testy. I'll wait to hear from you." She rose to go. She was surprised when Dr. Miller extended his hand.

"Of course, of course. I understand," he said, smiling. "But believe me. You probably don't have a thing to worry about."

"Where the hell have you been?" Jim McCormack looked up from the stove at his wife. Hope stood at the kitchen door with a pile of books in her arms. "I think that sauce is about to burn; better turn it down," she said dumping the books on the kitchen table.

"Shit," Jim muttered, adjusting the flame. He hated cooking, even heating up something as simple as frozen spaghetti sauce. "I waited as long as I could, but the kids are hungry," he muttered accusingly. He stirred the sauce vigorously and splattered some on his tie. "Jesus Christ! Will you *please* take over while I change?" He stalked out of the room. Hope turned the gas down to simmer, took down a large pot, and filled it with water.

"You still haven't told me where you were," Jim said, returning to the kitchen. "At the library all this time?" He eyed the books on the table.

"Didn't you get my message?"

"Just that you were going out and the kids would be next door."

"Well, I was at the doctor's," Hope said quietly.

Oh, God, Jim thought, *she's pregnant again.*

"I didn't know you had an appointment today."

"I didn't. Something came up. I examined my breasts today, and I found a lump. At first, Dr. Miller thought it was just a cyst, but it turns out it's not. It's a tumor."

Jim McCormack's expression evolved from anger to disbelief to sympathy in a matter of seconds. "A tumor. . . ." he spoke the word gingerly. "Does that mean that you have . . ." he struggled to finish the sentence.

"Sit down, Jim," Hope said calmly. He sagged onto a kitchen chair and stared at her, his mouth slightly open, as she recounted everything the doctor had told her. She left out of her account the scene she'd made that morning at the library. Her tone was flat, dispassionate, as if she were relating the results of a golf tournament. At last, she noticed that the water was boiling. She rose and dumped a box of spaghetti into the pot. ". . . and so Dr. Miller seems to think I don't have much to worry about. There's a chance it's cancer, of course, but he said that nine times out of ten things turn out to be benign."

Jim said nothing for several moments. "Well, he's supposed to be a good man, and if he thinks this Lynd guy is tops, that's certainly encouraging. But darling, you must have had a terrible scare. I'm so sorry I snapped at you when you came in. I didn't know. . . ." He put his arms around her waist. "If there's anything I can do. . . ."

"There is," Hope said seriously.

"What?"

"Set the table and tell the kids to turn off the damned television and come to dinner. Oh, and open a bottle of wine. It's been a rough day, and I could use a bit of relaxing." She smiled at her startled husband.

"Sure thing, baby," Jim said. He set about his tasks and marveled at Hope's composure. *She really has guts,* he thought, opening a bottle of chianti. *She's one tough cookie.*

It was a quiet evening. Dinner was typical. Kate and Denis bickered while wolfing down the spaghetti, agreeing only that they had learned "nothing" at school that day. Hope had three glasses of wine and really did find herself relaxing just a little. The children returned to their television, Jim sat at his desk and looked over some briefs, and Hope started one of her library books on breast cancer. After the kids were in bed, Jim wanted to talk more to her, but he sensed Hope was enjoying the peace and quiet as she intently read her book. The telephone rang.

"It's Dr. Miller."

"Yes, doctor, I was hoping you'd be able to call. Did you ask Dr. Lynd about me?" Hope's voice was calm.

"Yes, I just got through to him. He was working late at the hospital. He said he couldn't see anyone else for at least two months." Hope's heart sank. "But I asked him to take a look at you as a favor to me. He's really frightfully busy, it seems–has a lot of surgery backed up. But he agreed to see you on the afternoon of the twenty-second." Hope glanced at the kitchen calendar. The fifth. Seventeen days. Dr. Miller continued. "I made a date for you, but I also called a couple of other good people–seems like everyone I know is overloaded right now. One can see you on the nineteenth, but for the difference of a couple of days I'd recommend Lynd."

"Of course. I agree. And thank you for all your trouble. I guess I'll just have to wait," Hope replied.

"Well, remember what I said today. The odds are very much in your favor. And even if it turns out to be a malignancy, you caught it right away. A couple of weeks shouldn't make any difference at all."

She thanked Dr. Miller once again and hung up. Jim looked up as she came into the living room. "Is the appointment set up?" he asked.

"Yup. The twenty-second of this month, and that apparently took some string-pulling. I guess tumors have suddenly become fashionable in Westchester County," she said cheerfully. She took her book and went into the bedroom. She undressed, and took her prettiest nightgown out of the dresser. Then she paused and stood naked before the mirror. *Not bad,* Hope thought. *Could lose five or ten pounds, but not bad for an old lady of thirty-three.* She looked at her breasts and resisted the temptation to touch them. She knew it was silly, but she felt that massaging the tumor might make it spread. She turned sideways. *Thighs could use some exercise.* Then she faced the mirror again and tried to imagine her left breast missing, a long scar running from the center of her chest and up to her armpit. She shuddered, hastily pulled her nightgown over her head, and got into bed.

"You can leave the light on if you want to read," Jim said, unbuttoning his shirt as he entered the bedroom.

"No, I've read enough for tonight. Not exactly light reading," Hope said.

Jim grunted in agreement and pulled off his pants and shorts. He was a good-looking man, slim-hipped and broad-chested. Except for the fact that his hair was thinning he could have been a model. As he slid under the covers beside her and turned out the light, she wondered if he would want to sleep with her if and when she was mutilated by a mastectomy. With his looks, he certainly wouldn't have any trouble finding other women. She dismissed the thought. Jim was short tempered and a little self-centered, but he was also decent and loyal: he would stand by her. *And,* she thought, *he loves me.*

"I love you, darling," Jim said, as if reading her thoughts. He kissed her cheek. "Try not to worry. You'll be all right. You'll have the best care. . . ."

"It's okay, Jim," she interrupted. "God knows I'm worried, but I can take it. Whatever happens."

"I know. And so can I. I love you very, very much." He kissed her on the mouth, a long, passionate kiss. She felt his body against her. His hand caressed her hair and strayed to her right breast. Suddenly, she stiffened. Jim's hand moved to her left breast, and for a few moments she allowed him to stroke her. But she couldn't stand it any longer. She tore his hand away.

"No!" she howled, her scream echoing in the silent house. "No, no, no, no!"

7

Washington, D.C.

"It's an extremely important position." Undersecretary Potter folded his plump hands in front of him and smiled. "It's an outstanding job, one with real authority in any number of policy-making divisions. You'd be the youngest man in many, many years to hold such an important HEW post. But I think you're the man for it. Your work has been outstanding, for the most part."

"For the most part?" Eric Zimmermann did not readily accept criticism, and he interrupted Undersecretary Potter somewhat abruptly.

"Well, you *have* had more than a few, uh, disputes with some of your colleagues out at Bethesda, but," he raised his hand to cut off Zimmermann's reply, "I'm sure you just wanted to get the job done efficiently. And your work has been outstanding. Outstanding."

Potter beamed at the handsome young man sitting across from him and instinctively disliked him. If it had been up to him, Zimmermann would have been fired months ago. Potter hated troublemakers, and Dr. Eric Zimmermann apparently found it impossible to get along with any of his colleagues at NIH. It was,

Potter thought, idiotic to give a job as sensitive and important as Deputy Director of the Center for Disease Control to this snotty bastard.

"You know, Eric," Potter said, "I'm personally delighted you got this job. Joe Elkins will be retiring in about two years and you should have a good shot at the top slot in Atlanta when he does."

Zimmermann studied the Undersecretary for a moment. He was confident that Potter was not pleased with the appointment, and he had never been able to restrain his contempt for the mentality Potter represented. The successful bureaucrat, plump, smug, and secure, far more interested in budgets and departmental politics than in public health. Eric relished making him uncomfortable.

"I'm glad to have your support, Sam. Things may need some shaking up down there, and it's good to have a friend back home," Eric said brightly.

Potter repressed a cringe. "Of course, of course. But remember, this is a much more, uh, *exposed* position. You'll have to try to be more shall-we-say discreet. Just give me a call before you do anything impulsive, OK?"

"Sure, Sam. You don't have to worry. I'll be a good boy."

Zimmermann rose without being dismissed. He smiled, shook hands with the Undersecretary, and left before Potter could offer more advice. *I'll get that arrogant punk one of these days,* Potter thought. *One of these days he's going to step into a big hole and I'll be there to bury him.* His anger turned to a sense of intense pleasure as he thought of the prospect of being the agent of Zimmermann's humiliation, and whistled softly to himself as he turned to the paperwork on his desk.

Dr. Eric Zimmermann was also whistling as he left the massive HEW headquarters on Independence Avenue. Clearly, he had it made. At thirty-one, he already had a brilliant medical career behind him: a Yale A.B. at barely twenty, an M.D. at twenty-four, followed by postdoctoral research in immunology and epidemiology at Rockefeller University. During his years at Rockefeller, he had published several widely acclaimed research papers and won some lucrative research grants. Obviously a young man with a future, he stunned many of his colleagues when he accepted a post with the National Institutes of Health overseeing certain research programs around the country. It was a very important position, but one that allowed little time for him to pursue his own work. But Zimmermann had long before learned at his father's dinner table that the control of money was very often the most negotiable kind of power. The government, he reasoned, distributed the great bulk of the medical research funds in the United States, and by the careful selection of programs to be funded, he could not only further investigations of interest to him, but he could also cultivate the most powerful and distinguished researchers in the country. Zimmermann had no intention of spending his life in the service of his country. He fully expected to win the Nobel Prize and had even said so publicly once or twice. A few years at HEW and NIH would secure him the position and facilities he needed. He dreamed of setting up a well-funded (by the government) research institute and then resigning from HEW just in time to be appointed its director. Failing that, he was confident he would soon be able to write his own ticket at one of several major institutions. Like those Pentagon generals who, upon retiring, found themselves on the boards of the same defense contractors who'd been soliciting their favor.

Zimmermann was not surprised that Potter disliked him–most people did. Some colleagues were simply jealous. He was brilliant: the rare combination of a careful scientist and intuitive thinker. And he was handsome. His 6′2″ frame was in nearly perfect condition, though he exercised only occasionally. Even white teeth set off his broad, pleasant face, particularly when he was tanned, which was most of the time. Besides brains and looks, Zimmermann possessed the third prize for which so many of his fellow men hungered: substantial wealth.

When John P. Zimmermann died, he left a fortune of close to four million dollars. Eric's share produced an annual income of about $90,000 without ever diminishing the principal. A good portion of this money was carefully reinvested in stocks and municipal bonds. But while Eric lived well, he was not obviously a young man who possessed a fortune and who was steadily enlarging it. John P. Zimmermann had truly loved his wife and Eric, but they saw very little of him. The creation and protection of his fortune demanded long hours. Eric's mother, everyone told him, was a very beautiful woman, a woman of great style. But she found it difficult to maintain interest in anything for more than an hour or two. She had tired of her pregnancy four months before Eric was born and had tired of Eric before he was two months old. She was hardly ever unpleasant or intentionally cruel; she simply did not like the responsibilities of parenthood. Eric was her first and last attempt at motherhood. It had seemed, she often thought wistfully, like a good idea at the time.

So Eric had learned to live alone from the time he was a small child. His parents were distant, if listlessly affectionate, and they tolerated most of his boyhood pranks and accidents in much the same way a well-paid baby sitter would. The only exception to this fond disinterest involved Eric's education. Both his father and mother firmly believed that, as their offspring, Eric would have to be an exceptional child. They carefully selected an immense variety of educational toys and bought him hundreds of books. John P. and his wife were pleased, if not surprised, to discover that Eric was indeed exceptional and their interest in his intellectual development became a hobby for them. They were determined their son should become a remarkable human being, a genius. And Eric obliged by becoming, to all intents and purposes, a genius.

At an early age, he had learned that the only way to please his parents was by his academic achievements. The converse was also true. The only time he ever saw his mother weep was when he received a C– in arithmetic in the sixth grade, and this was the only occasion when his father showed more than mild annoyance at his actions, abandoned his distracted air, and administered the only spanking Eric ever received. Eric was distraught–he had come to treasure the moments of sincere approval when he presented his parents with a good report card or a composition with a big red "A" on it–and his next report card produced an "A" in arithmetic and all his other subjects. For the next fourteen years of formal education, Eric never received a grade below "A."

So Dr. Eric Zimmermann had made it. He was tall, dark, and handsome. He was rich. He was brilliant.

Dr. Eric Zimmermann was also emotionally stunted, arrogant, and driven by a desperate need to please his permanently disinterested father and still distant mother, to show them he was worthy of their attention. That he was–though he would not have thought of it in these terms–still an exceptional child.

When the news reached his NIH colleagues that Eric had been promoted to the number two job at Atlanta, they were delighted. They would be glad to be rid of him.

8

Westchester, New York

The lab technician was a pleasant-faced black woman who for some reason hummed "Pop Goes the Weasel" over and over again, as she set up the equipment. Hope McCormack sat in a corner of the room and tried not to let the song's constant repetition annoy her. *Just be thankful you finally made it here,* she thought to herself. Her original appointment with Dr. Lynd had been postponed twice, and it was now almost seven weeks since the morning she had first found the tumor in her breast and rushed to Dr. Miller's office. Miller was obviously embarrassed by the delays, and continued to reassure her that it was likely benign. Lynd himself had called the second time and quickly apologized for yet another delay. He had to perform emergency surgery. Again.

This time, though, she was finally going to meet the great healer. First she filled out a twelve-page questionnaire that asked some expected questions: *Do you smoke? If so, how much? Is there any history of cancer in your family for the past three generations? Give all details. Have you ever taken any form of birth control pills for more than three years? Are you now?* And there were some unexpected ones: *Have you been under unusual stress any time in the past two years? Have you grieved for a close relative or friend in the past year? Would you describe your marriage or relationship, if any, as generally happy? Have you recently been divorced?* Hope dutifully filled out the questionnaire as thoroughly as possible. The final page had only one question: *Please describe in detail your own estimation of the state of your health starting with your earliest memories. Use back of sheet or additional sheets if necessary.* Hope thought for a minute and wrote:

> In complete honesty, I can say that I have enjoyed nearly perfect health for my entire life. My mother was something of a health-food freak, and Carlton Fredericks and Adelle Davis were her gods. I was stuffed with fresh vegetables (organic only) and wheat germ, brown rice, and brown sugar throughout my childhood. Surprisingly enough, this seemed to work. Though I had most of the typical childhood illnesses, they were extremely mild cases. I still take large quantities of vitamins, and though my diet is now somewhat more "junky" than my mother would like (she is a vigorous woman of 68) I am still very healthy. My last cold was more than two years ago, and my last serious illness was over four years ago—the Panama flu. I have never taken any medication regularly, nor do I drink much alcohol. Both my children were born using natural childbirth techniques, and both deliveries were comparatively easy. In sum, I can say I enjoy very good health.

She looked at her essay and was dissatisfied, thinking that if her health was so perfect, what the hell was she doing here listening to a lab technician hum an idiotic children's tune.

"Okay, honey, I'm ready for you," said the technician, whose nameplate said "Mrs. Brown." "Now just ease yourself up against this and we'll take some pictures." Hope placed her breast on a metal slab and Mrs. Brown slowly slid down another one, sandwiching it. The metal was cold.

"Breathe out . . . hold it . . . breathe in . . . hold it." This routine was repeated several times, and then the same procedure was repeated for the other breast. "You did very good, darlin'," Mrs. Brown said, smiling. "Now let's make us some nice carbon copies."

"What?"

"Thermograms. They measure the heat pattern in the breast."

"Oh yes, I know."

"I just call 'em carbons 'cause we don't have any film to get developed. The print comes out over here." She pointed to a slot at one end of the machine.

"Well," said Hope after the thermograms were finished. "Anything on there?"

"I can't say for sure, dear–that's for your doctor to decide. But don't worry. Even if the news is bad, us women know how to cope. I lost mine, both of 'em, almost ten years ago." She pointed to her full chest. "And I thought it'd be the end of the world. But life goes on, and I'm still here, ain't I?" Mrs. Brown said, chuckling.

Hope stared at Mrs. Brown. "Thank you. That's awfully nice of you to tell me. Is that why you decided to do this work?"

"I don't rightly know. I've worked in the hospital for over twenty years. Twenty-three to be exact. After my operation, a friend of mine in personnel told me there was going to be someone retiring, and if I took the right courses–there was a hospital program that'd pay for most of it–then I'd probably get the job. So I took the courses and here I am. I think it's fair to say, though, that I take a little bit of *extra care* since I've been through this myself."

As Hope was leaving, she turned at the door and thanked Mrs. Brown. "Good luck, honey," the big black woman said, "and remember what I told you. Good luck."

Dr. Lynd greeted Hope McCormack as warmly as he was capable. "Hello. Please take a chair. Sorry I had to delay your interview." Hope looked at him and said nothing. The brilliant Dr. Lynd whom she had waited all this time just to meet looked about twenty years old. He had a round, baby face and wore the same sort of rimless glasses Dr. Miller favored. "*You're* Dr. Lynd?" she asked.

"Yes, of course, now please sit down." He was very tired. For the past three months he had examined and treated a staggering number of cancer patients. He'd even gone as far as to call the N.Y. State Public Health Department, which admitted they had several other similar inquiries about an increase in cancer incidence, but that the national statistics showed only a very slight increase overall. Dr. Lynd sat down at his desk, removed his glasses and rubbed his eyes. Then he spoke abruptly.

"I know I look very young, Mrs. McCormack. Despite appearances, though, I am thirty-four years old, and will be thirty-five next month. My father looked under thirty until he was well into middle age, and then he almost overnight looked like a candidate for a rest home. Now. Dr. Miller tells me that he had a negative on fibroadenoma . . . a cyst."

"That's right."

"Well, I've gone over the results of the very thorough physical Dr. Miller gave you and the battery of tests. There's nothing out of line there," he said, tossing aside the folder. "Now, when I get the pictures from the xeroradiomammogram, along with the thermograms, we'll be able to make a judgment." He paused.

"You mean you're not going to let me know today?" Hope was furious. "What is this, a social call? I've been waiting two *months* for this appointment, and now you tell me I have to wait for tests to come back. And then wait for you to get around to looking at them?" She started to get up.

"Sit down. If you insist, I will be happy to examine your breast. But I think we're all agreed you have a lump, a tumor, in your left breast. Am I correct so far?"

"Yes."

"Then you don't need me to tell you that. Now this is what I consider a most important meeting. I want to explain to you what your options are *if* the results of the test you had today indicate mammary carcinoma. Because if they do, then we must, I think you'll agree, move quickly. It's important that you know what the procedures are. That's all."

Hope was barely mollified. "Very well. Go on."

"If the tests show that you very likely do not have a malignancy, then there is a simple surgical procedure to remove the tumor. Any surgeon can do it, and I certainly would not be involved since I have a number of surgical cases backlogged already. I assume that you have by this time read all about the alternatives: radical mastectomy, mastectomy, lumpectomy, radiation therapy, chemotherapy, and so forth. I should tell you that I am personally very old-fashioned and if I find a malignant tumor, I believe in a radical mastectomy. That is, taking off the breast or breasts, as well as the lymph nodes up here." He ran his hand along his armpit. "I'm the first to admit I'm conservative by nature. If surgery is necessary then it is the duty of the surgeon to preserve the life of the patient, both in the short *and* the long term. Are you following me?"

"Yes . . . no, not really. What are you driving at?" Hope asked.

"I'm sorry. I'm tired," Dr. Lynd said. "Let me try to be concise. If the tests come back showing no likely cancer, fine, though it is very important that you have the tumor removed, just to be on the safe side."

"Why?"

"Because both the mammogram and the thermogram as well as the other tests you had previous to your visit to Markland Memorial are all flawed. Their results are 85-95 percent accurate. Their results combined are convincing. But not quite. Too many people have had positive results that turned out to be falsely indicative. So even if all the indications are that there is no cancer, we still do a biopsy of the tumor when it's removed. It's quick-frozen and rushed to a lab in the hospital while you are on the table. If it turns out to be malignant, then we remove the breast."

"You mean," Hope said slowly, "these tests could show that I have a benign tumor, but when I have it operated on, I could wake up missing a breast?"

"Yes."

"I see." Neither said anything for a few moments. "So I coul
end up with a mastectomy whatever your opinion is."

Dr. Lynd looked uncomfortable. "Well, that is true, though i
both the mammogram and thermogram show the same result, yo
can be quite confident. It's just not 100 percent certain, and I wan
you to know that. Of course, there'd be a number of other tests an
scans. The results are very likely to be accurate."

"Removal of the breast is the only procedure you'd recommend i
the, ah, results are bad?"

"Unless the cancer has already metastasized via the lymphati
system. At that point there'd be no reason to remove the breast
We'd go right to chemotherapy."

Hope heard Dr. Lynd's voice, but she had trouble concentratin
on the words. She felt cold. "If it's malignant . . . and if I refuse t
be operated on, what are the odds. . . ."

Dr. Lynd spoke quickly. "The odds are terrible. Sooner or later
the carcinoma would spread all over the body. It can move ver
quickly. To refuse the operation would effectively amount to a deat
sentence. Suicide." He rose and put his hand on her shoulder. Hop
noticed that his fingers were short and stubby, and wondered wher
she had heard that all surgeons had long, tapering hands, lik
pianists.

"Very well," she said, "I'm not suicidal. When will you know on
way or the other, and when do I go into the hospital?"

Lynd looked at his calendar. "I should have the results by the en
of the week. Possibly as early as tomorrow, though the lab has latel
been overloaded for some reason. As soon as I examine them, I'll ca
you and let you know. If the tumor is benign, I'll put you in touc
with a surgeon. If it's not, we will meet again, and I'll get you a be
as soon as possible. Markland Memorial is short of beds at th
moment, still I doubt you would have to wait more than anothe
week or two to have the operation. But don't let this get yo
depressed. I'll prescribe some mild tranquilizers to help you throug
the next couple of days. I'm sure Dr. Miller told you the odds ar
very much in your favor at your age. . . ."

"Yes, he did. Thanks. It's just that even one chance, one *rea* chance, in a thousand of this . . . happening . . . can get to you. The waiting without knowing if. . . ."

"I understand," Dr. Lynd said quickly. "Really, I'll get back to you as soon as I have any news. I promise."

Hope left the hospital and walked across the parking lot. She had never taken a tranquilizer in her life, but she knew she would have the prescription filled. She hoped Dr. Lynd would remember his promise.

9

Bethesda, Maryland

The spring was beautiful that year. For the first time in half a decade, the cherry blossoms all came out exactly in time for the Cherry Blossom Festival. In the springtime, Washington is one of America's most beautiful cities. Brilliantly colored azaleas, dogwoods, and a host of flowering trees transform even the most stern public buildings and banal suburban houses with a stunning, postcardlike beauty.

The National Institutes of Health is situated a scant ten miles from downtown Washington on a three-hundred-acre "campus" of rolling hills and winding roads. The NIH buildings are scattered harmoniously, surrounded by beautifully kept lawns and carefully planned landscaping. Visitors invariably find it difficult to believe that the NIH campus is really a small city, employing over 15,000 workers. For this handsome complex is quite literally the heart of America's health research effort, pumping close to three billion dollars into thousands of bioscience investigations across the country and around the world. Dr. Henry Rogers had once commented that a program should be funded to analyze the effects of spring fever, a chronic, if pleasant, condition on the Bethesda campus that afflicted even the most dedicated scientists, himself included. In the spring of that year, everything bloomed simultaneously, and the weather was perfect. But Rogers hardly noticed.

For the month following his fruitless investigation of stomach cancer data, he had occupied himself with his usual duties. Except for paying slightly more attention to the Center for Disease Control's most popular publication, *Morbidity and Mortality Weekly Report,* he succeeded in convincing himself he had simply stumbled over a statistical bump, a temporary aberration.

By the next month, however, he was deeply worried. Something was happening, though he doubted if many of his colleagues had yet noticed a trend. The total number of reported cancer cases across the country was up .93 percent, a very significant increase if it continued for each successive month. Still, it could be just another statistical anomaly. On impulse, he called a friend on the *Weekly* in Atlanta.

"Yeah, I noticed," his friend reported. "I don't think we have anything significant on our hands, for now anyway. Is DHEW going to make some large research grants next fiscal?"

"Not that I know of," Rogers confessed.

"Well, same sort of thing developed in the early '70's. 'The War on Cancer' was so well funded that just about the only sure way to get grants back then was to throw together a cancer program. Lot of universities and research hospitals were close to going bust, what with education and health grants being slashed. Cancer was the only game in town. So state and local health departments started making sure physicians reported every case, every *suspected* case they encountered. It was crazy there for a while."

"Yeah."

"Same thing with crime statistics. More crime, more programs. More loot."

"I haven't heard about any exceptional grants about to be funded. Have you?" asked Rogers.

"No. But I was really just using that as an example. Could be any of a hundred reasons. Lot of hospitals and physicians catch up on the paperwork they let slide during the holidays about now. . . ."

"But you adjust for that."

"Yeah, sure. But, Henry, you *know* that. You helped set up the programs. What're you onto? Is there something in particular we should be on the lookout for?" The man sounded mystified and slightly annoyed.

"No, Bill, that's okay," Rogers said.

"Well, we check, of course, for any unusual distribution or concentration whenever there's an anomaly. There's no new pattern this month with cancer. Perfectly normal. Just some additional cases reported. . . ."

"Nine thousand."

"For Christ sake, Henry, there's a quarter of a *billion* people in this country. Nine thousand extra cases is interesting, but statistically it's meaningless. But you *know* that—you just about wrote the fucking book." There was a brief pause. "Henry, I'll run any kind of program you want, just tell me what to look for. Tell me what you're onto, and I'll get a couple of staffers to. . . ."

"I've got the staff, Bill, and thanks. Sorry I bothered you. I'm sure it's nothing. Just thought I'd check in with you. Not to worry."

The two men chatted for a few minutes, and Rogers dismissed any further questions about the cancer figures for March. He was overreacting. He *had* just about written the book, and he knew he must have sounded like a first-year graduate student. He thanked his friend once again and decided to take a few days off. He could just justify a trip to New York, set up a couple of meetings at Sloan-Kettering, Columbia, and Yeshiva, and, he thought with pleasure, take in the Auto Show.

A month went by.

And another.

By the third month, Rogers knew his instincts had been correct. His call to Bill Abel in Atlanta had piqued the interest of several CDC statisticians, who fed Rogers data from specific locales in the field. But Rogers had already assigned three of his best people to track the course of all reported cancers, and to program all available historical and demographic data into the NIH computers. And he had conversations with several colleagues at the National Cancer Institute just down the road.

To some extent, the staff of NCI did not intermingle with their colleagues as much as one would expect. Also, to some extent, this was understandable. President Nixon had announced his "War on Cancer" in 1971, and for over a decade, billions of dollars had been spent searching for a cancer "cure," or at least an understanding of the fundamental nature of the disease. Whether it was, indeed, a single disease or a hundred-odd abnormal cell conditions that were defined as cancer was still a matter of dispute. The funds had led to some brilliant work in DNA research and cellular biology, as well as a number of successful treatments for specific cancers. But billions of dollars later, there was no cure. The research was still proceeding, as it should have, step-by-step, while scientists tried to understand the most complicated biological problem ever posed. Almost everyone at NIH realized that to understand the nature of cancer was to understand the mechanics of the cell. To define the nature of life itself. NCI officials were understandably a little paranoid over their political vulnerability for not having found the "cure." And at least some of the other researchers at NIH had for years resented the ease with which the cancer researchers acquired huge sums of money while their own divisions had to compete for every governmental dollar.

Henry Rogers was familiar with most of the larger research projects at NIH. He had no personal involvement with specific studies, but as director of the computer services and statistical analysis for all divisions, both clinical and experimental, he was a very important, indeed powerful, man. Access to the computers was essential to almost all the research carried out at Bethesda–from mental health to dental health–and as the arbiter of priorities for the finite amount of computer time available at NIH, Rogers was probably as knowledgeable about the entire scope of research there as the director himself. Of course, Rogers personally had access to the seemingly infinite capacity of the Pentagon, but he kept that information secret, except from a couple of trustworthy and very distinguished scholars like Simon Carey-Ross.

Carey-Ross was a Nobel laureate, one of twelve at Bethesda, and probably the single most brilliant DNA researcher in the United States. Rogers had slipped him the access code to the Pentagon data analysis facilities with all the secrecy of a spy. Carey-Ross had responded by reading it, quickly memorizing the information on the small slip of paper, and eating it. They laughed and became friends.

When the two men almost literally bumped into one another one fine summer morning, it was Carey-Ross who cut through the pleasantries and began to question Rogers on the very subject he was on his way from NCI to discuss with him.

"There's quite a buzz on up there," Carey-Ross said, gesturing in the general direction of the Cancer Institute headquarters.

Rogers raised his eyebrows quizzically.

"I was coming over to see you."

"I was coming over to see *you,"* said Rogers.

"Neutral territory. Have a seat, Dr. Rogers." They sat down in the shade of a large pin oak. "I know it's about the cancer figures," Carey-Ross began. "I have nothing to do with population monitoring, and they've been acting very suspiciously of late. Lots of meetings. Lots of quiet conversations in the halls. The fuckers think I'm some fuzzy-headed crackpot who doesn't notice anything. In love with my test tubes, and so on. Well, Henry, something's up. And I suspect you know what it is."

"Oh?"

"Come off it. We all have our little secrets, but the last three weeks or so it's been like CIA headquarters. I keep expecting to see H.R. Haldeman skulking down the halls." (Rogers had to think for a moment to remember who H.R. Haldeman was.) "But I have my sources. At least enough to have a general idea of what's up. It's the cancer figures, isn't it?"

"Right," said Rogers.

"And something very ... nasty ... is happening, right?"

"Simon, I begin to understand how your Yorkshire ancestors succeeded in coloring my school map pink," said Rogers, smiling.

"Not mine. Most raised sheep, and the only ones I know of in the military tried to keep Ireland pink. Turned green. Now, what's going on? I can be trusted—you know that."

"What seems to be going on, old friend, is a dramatic and totally unexplained rise in the incidence of cancer. The figures are still inconclusive, but not only is there more of it, the case-fatality ratio is way up. Way up," repeated Rogers quietly, plucking a few blades of grass.

"Really bad?"

"Really bad. I first thought I saw something about four months ago, but dismissed it. Now there is no question: lympho-sarcoma, 41 percent above average; malignant melanoma, 93 percent above average; cancer of the colon, breast, liver, stomach ... shit, *all* of them, and I mean every single one, are anywhere from 19 to 163 percent above what they should be." Rogers inadvertently pulled up an entire clump of grass by the roots and then tried to pat it back into the ground.

"How long?" asked Carey-Ross.

"*That,* my friend, is the question. It seems to have been developing over the past couple of months. But the latest figures—and I now see them just about every day—are much, much worse."

"Jesus Christ."

"So you wondered why there was a flutter over at NCI? Hell, they've already begun to rig the figures," said Rogers.

"No."

"Yes."

The two men sat silently crosslegged, like boys on a summer day, idly passing the time. Carey-Ross spoke first.

"I refuse to believe that any scientist here would deliberately falsify data. And the idea of a conspiracy to do it is, well, impossible. You're mistaken, Henry."

"I know I'm not. First of all, remember that keeping track of the numbers around here is my job. Also keep in mind that I've been watching these particular stats for several months. Someone has been systematically tinkering with the historical data for the past quarter. That's for sure. And I've got some pals down at the Center for Disease Control who've been feeding me with figures they've been assembling on their own. Don't look surprised, Simon. I don't blame them," Rogers said.

"How can you say that? Falsifying . . ."

"Look, almost any physician in the country and *every* health department in the country can plug right into any of our statistics. If cancer is starting to go out of control, even for the short run, it's only a matter of days before somebody puts it together. Then boom," Rogers threw his arms apart, "skyhigh. I'm sure accurate records are being kept; they're just not fed into the memory bank. Simon, this could well be the biggest health crisis we've ever had to deal with, so it makes sense for administration, particularly for NCI administration, to keep the lid on and try to figure out what's happening before some hysterical reporter from the *National Enquirer* blows the whistle."

"I see." Carey-Ross looked pensive.

"Even if this continues, it'll take months, maybe a year, before a lot of hospitals and private doctors begin comparing notes and putting the numbers together independently. Each is looking at a small piece of the picture. We see it all and have to figure out pretty fast what the hell is going on and what, if anything, can be done. That's why the bunker mentality."

"Who knows?" asked Carey-Ross.

"Who knows?" replied Rogers with a shrug of frustration. "My guess is most of the key people at the Cancer Institute. Probably some in the NIH hierarchy. I think they're double-checking, making sure, preparing their case, getting it together to present to the director and HEW. Another week or two should do it."

"So there's nothing we can do?"

Rogers lit a cigarette from the stub of his previous one. "Simon, I don't think we can wait. They're just beginning to see the outlines of the situation. It could take a month before everyone's covered his ass and triple-checked his data. It could take weeks after that for HEW to start their wheels turning. Say two months total. Some of the cancers have been increasing at a geometric rate. In two months. . . ."

"I see. What can I do?" asked Carey-Ross.

"I'm gonna goose 'em, Simon, and soon. Just let me know what you hear. You're my first officially appointed spy. When the chips begin to fall, I may have to call on my favorite Nobel laureate to twist some arms."

"Ready and willing, my captain." Carey-Ross smiled and untangled his gangly limbs. Then he looked serious. "Just let me know, Henry, and I'll come in with all barrels blazing."

Rogers shook his hand. "Will do." The two sauntered off in opposite directions, looking to all the world like the classic absentminded professors. They and the Bethesda campus around them looked perfectly normal. But both men knew that would not last very much longer.

Henry Rogers and Eric Zimmermann liked one another. To the younger man, Rogers represented a first-class mind combined with just the right amount of eccentricity. He knew the chaotic office and slovenly appearance belied the fact that Rogers had one of the sharpest intellects at NIH. Both men shared a distaste for the bureaucracy and civil servant mentality, and Rogers delighted in making both administrators and colleagues wince by referring to Zimmermann as "that nice young man."

Zimmermann looked up and saw Dr. Rogers standing uncertainly by the open door to his office. "Going somewhere, Eric?" he asked.

"Yeah, Atlanta, remember?"

"Oh, sure, I forgot. I, well, you're packing up your stuff and I'm sure you're . . . I mean you'll be . . . well, good luck, Eric. I'll be in touch. Anything you need. . . ."

Zimmermann looked at him a trifle suspiciously. "Henry, come in, sit down, and spit it out. You didn't come all the way over here just to watch me clean out my desk and bid me a fond farewell." Eric slammed a file drawer shut. "Now, what is it?"

"When do you start at CDC?" Rogers asked, taking a seat.

"Next week. I shouldn't have waited until the last minute to pack up, but I wanted to take some vacation before I enter the fiery furnace. Now, come on, Henry, what is it? My psychic powers tell me you did not trek all the way across the campus on a hot day to present yourself in person at my door without a very good reason." He stared at Rogers' person and thought that the rumpled man digging through his pockets for a match must be the worst-dressed doctor in the United States. Rogers found a match and lit a cigarette.

"Oh, but Henry," Zimmermann said, holding up a sign which read: THANK YOU FOR NOT SMOKING.

"When ... *how* did you get that?" Rogers asked in astonishment.

"My secret. I really should grow up. Please note that this *objet* was very carefully unscrewed, not ripped out of Herr Potter's fine government issue desk. I'm sure he suspects me—but *proof,* that's what the man lacks. Anyway, I'm sure it's against regulations to screw personal property into government property. Here, I was going to mail it to you anonymously." Zimmermann gave him the plastic plaque.

"My boy, I have stood virtually alone in predicting a brilliant future for you. My faith has been rewarded. Thank you from the bottom of my heart. I shall treasure it." Rogers grinned with delight, and tucked the sign into his jacket pocket.

"Believe me, it was my pleasure. Now. Tell me what you came over here for."

He paused for a moment, and then Henry related everything he knew about the cancer statistics, starting from the beginning up to his conversation with Carey-Ross only two hours previously. He spoke for close to twenty minutes, uninterrupted save by a few grunts from Zimmermann. When he had finished, Eric looked straight at the older man and said, "What you are postulating, you know, is the existence of an epidemic of a series of diseases which are recognized as being noncontagious and generally take years to develop in a given individual. Further, you are postulating that for reasons unknown, large numbers of people are suddenly "catching" these diseases at an unheard of rate. All at once. You imply that cancer in general has suddenly become more virulent, more deadly. And you state, on the basis of no concrete evidence," he held up his hand to cut off Rogers, "Let me finish. On the basis of no concrete evidence whatsoever, that a number of high officials of NIH have intentionally been falsifying national scientific data. Henry, I think you're nuts."

"Sorry to trouble you, Eric." Rogers rose to go.

"Hey, wait. I may think you're nuts, but that doesn't mean a thing. *Convince* me, for Christ sake. There are fewer than a dozen people in this loony bin I wouldn't have tossed out on their ass if they'd come up with this story, I mean theory. You have your head screwed on right. Though I have my doubts about Carey-Ross. . . ."

"Now who's nuts? Listen, I just told you I was on my way to tell *him* what I just told you, not the other way around. That man's a genius," Rogers asserted.

"Okay, okay. I yield." Zimmermann reflected for a moment. "Henry, I assume that you want me to keep on top of this when I get to Atlanta."

"That's part of it."

"What else?"

"We go to Potter."

"Oh, shit, Henry, that asshole wouldn't know a carcinoma from athlete's foot! You can't be serious," Zimmermann exploded.

"I'm very serious, Eric. Deadly serious. If we try to work through channels here, we'll probably be put on some committee and sworn to secrecy. Me anyway. I'm staking my reputation that they are going to keep this thing bottled up until they know what they're dealing with. That's understandable, but I just don't think we can afford the time.

"Our friend, Mr. Potter, whether we like it or not, is in the position to force the issue and get the evidence into HEW, the Cabinet, and the White House. I think we are facing a national catastrophe, Eric. Maybe I'm wrong and maybe the rate will stabilize. But if it doesn't, almost every branch of government will be affected. Potter's one of the most tedious men I've ever met, but if we can convince him. . . ."

"We?"

"Yes, 'we.' You scare him, Eric. He respects me, I suppose, but I'm not very imposing. . . ." Rogers sighed. "With your support though, I think we can get him to budge, or at least make it clear to him that *not* investigating it could blow up in his face. I want you to browbeat him. Pleasantly threaten him." Rogers smiled, but looked pleadingly at his colleague. "Please, Eric."

"Administration will run amok when they find out we went directly to Potter," Zimmermann said.

"They've never intimidated you before, Eric, and you're virtually on your way to Atlanta. I think I can take the heat. So," Rogers leaned across Zimmermann's desk, "will you join me?"

"No," Eric replied, leaning forward to within a foot of Rogers' disappointed face. "Not until I go over all your evidence myself." He stood up. "C'mon, I always wanted to play with those gizmos in your office."

Zimmermann knew most of the basic operations necessary to use Rogers' computer terminal, and the two men worked until nearly eight that evening. For the most part, Eric said little and his colleague simply made suggestions for a more thorough investigation.

At one point, Zimmermann looked up from the terminal in astonishment. "My god, you're hooked into the Department of Defense. I thought this hadn't gotten out."

"It hasn't. And my access to their capacity is my little secret. How did you know?" Rogers asked.

"This THANK YOU HAVE A NICE DAY shit. I helped our warriors with a little problem about a year ago, and each series ended that way. On the top priority programs, anyway. Henry, you are a source of constant amazement to me." The two smiled conspiratorially and returned to work. Finally, Zimmermann leaned back and said, "Where do you want to eat tonight?"

"Hadn't thought about it. Look, I want to show you the age spread on uterine cancer; it's distinctly abnormal as well as unusually high."

"Don't bother, Henry. You win. I'd say it was impossible, but it looks like I'll have to throw away my epidemiology texts. What you've got here is an epidemic in the making, but with no concentration of infection, no demographic or geological concentration, no pattern whatsoever. It's everywhere, all at the same time. Of course, it's hardly noticeable at this point, but the progression's pretty clear. Have you estimates . . . ?" Rogers nodded. "Bad, huh? Figures. I've never seen anything like it. Spread smooth as butter, every corner of the country."

Zimmermann stared at a tangle of multicolored graph lines. They all swooped upward and off the terminal screen. "Bad," he said. "I think we should have a decent dinner tonight, Henry. A lot to talk about, and in my new capacity at CDC I have a nice little expense account. Might as well start using it. How 'bout *Rive Gauche?*"

"Do we go to Potter?"

"Tomorrow we go to Potter."

Undersecretary Samuel Coleridge Potter refused to see them.

"Look, Dr. Rogers, for the second time today I must remind you that this is the busiest time of the year. The final budget proposals are *all* due in this month. I'm sure it is important, and that's why I'll give you all the time you want in two weeks. Listen, I can't argue. Call and make an appointment with my secretary for any time after the twenty-eighth. Good-bye." He put down the phone and smiled. One had to be firm—he wasn't a goddamned guidance counsellor.

Late that afternoon, Henry Rogers and Eric Zimmermann walked into Potter's office and sat down in the two chairs before his desk. The Undersecretary avoided asking them how they got by his secretaries. He simply looked at them pleasantly, and spoke softly.

"Now look, fellas, I know you want to talk about something important, but I just can't see you today. I told you, Henry, that this is one of the two busiest weeks I have each year. I'm seeing no one. If President Wilson walked in here right now, I'd shake his hand, tell him he was doing a fine job, and invite him to leave. Now, I'll call Mrs. Russell and she can set up a time when . . ."

"Potter, if you touch that buzzer, I'll break your fuckin' hand."

Zimmermann was on his feet. He leaned forward, both his hands on Potter's desk, ready, it seemed, to spring. "I mean it, Sam." Potter sat back in his chair, his expression a mixture of outrage, curiosity, and fear. "It is now nine minutes to four," Zimmermann said slowly. "We want those nine minutes, okay, Sam?"

"If it's that important, go ahead," said Potter, resolving to ruin both of them. Zimmermann in particular: he was going to regret this day. He smiled serenely. "Well, now what is so important?"

Rogers did most of the talking, with Eric only occasionally underlining a particularly significant point. The nine minutes passed, and then another twenty. Potter said little and made a few notes. When Rogers concluded, the Undersecretary looked directly at him and said, "That's amazing. Why is it I haven't heard about this?" For another five minutes the two explained why they thought it necessary to come directly to Potter. The NIH leadership would justifiably want to examine all the data and file a complete report, perhaps within a week or two, but time was running out.

"Well, Rogers, Zimmermann, I think you were justified in approaching me. But the numbers are still, comparatively speaking, rather small. This statistical jump in cancer cases is, of course, troublesome, *very* troublesome. But there could be any number of reasons for it. You know statistics can only give a general idea of trends, and the margin for error ..."

"Mr. Secretary," Rogers said carefully, "believe me, I would not have troubled you if I weren't sure. This is a very serious ..."

"Of course it is," Potter hastily said.

"No, I want to be sure you understand. *Serious* is too broad a word. Let me put it on the line, and in one word: *disastrous.* My projections of the statistical trend. ..."

"Projections."

"That's right. As I said, some carcinomas started out ahead of others, but they are all more or less leveling out at the same rate of increase."

"And?"

"Well, I haven't even mentioned this to Eric. It's pure extrapolation, though based on accurate and definite data from the past four months," Rogers looked concerned, almost embarrassed.

"What do you *extrapolate,"* asked Potter, accenting the last word.

"In twelve months' time, at present rate of increase of incidence, bearing in mind that the likelihood for given diagnosis may vary and a certain proportion of these diagnoses might even be incorrect–I have of course incorporated these factors into the projection, but one must also . . ."

"What is the number, Dr. Rogers?" Potter asked testily.

"Roughly fifty-seven million."

"Fifty-seven million cases of cancer?"

"Within the next twelve to fourteen months," Rogers said.

"Now look . . . Dr. Rogers . . . I am familiar with your reputation and I know that you," Potter looked at Eric, "and Dr. Zimmermann are very distinguished scientists and scholars. . . ."

"But you don't believe us," Zimmermann said flatly.

"No, on the contrary, whether you're right or wrong, this must be investigated, and I agree you were right in coming to me. I should have known when you were so insistent, but let's forget that. No, I can see that this is not just a medical, but potentially a national security, problem. I'll get onto this right away, first by calling NIH. I won't mention your names, of course (he would). It's just that projecting this geometric increase over a year . . . I don't know, the short-term statistics are troubling, but . . ."

Eric interrupted. "Sam . . . Mr. Secretary, I refused to believe it myself at first, but the data clearly indicates . . ."

"Indicates, yes, I know. That means suggests, not certainty. Now please," Potter said, seeing Zimmermann tense, "I'm not saying you're wrong, it's just that. . . ."

"Look at these figures," Zimmermann shouted, throwing a thick file folder on Potter's desk, *"babies* are getting cancer. Infants . . . newborns. We're even getting reports of babies with prostate and stomach cancer, tumors, and God only knows what else."

"Okay, I got you. I promise you I'll get on the phone to the Director of the Institutes immediately, and I'll put some people on this right away. I won't argue science with you two. And I also promise to start monitoring the cancer data myself. We'll get to the bottom of this, you have my word."

"The President," Rogers said softly.

"The President will be informed as soon as I've made a preliminary investigation of your reports. That's only fair, isn't it? But I *won't* sit on it, I promise both of you. Now, satisfied? Today's Wednesday. I want you to start calling in to me beginning next Monday. By then I should have some idea where we start. Okay?"

"Fine, Sam," Zimmermann said.

"Excellent, Mr. Secretary," said Rogers.

"Dr. Rogers, have you spoken to anyone else about this? In detail, I mean. If this got out . . ."

"I understand. Just Simon Carey-Ross," replied Rogers.

"Oh." Potter's tone was both surprised and sad.

"If anything . . ." Rogers began.

"Dr. Carey-Ross suffered a nervous collapse. Just yesterday afternoon, I believe. I'm told he was under great stress. A brilliant man, and I'm sure he'll bounce back. He's at the NIH clinic."

"I'll visit him this afternoon," Rogers said.

"As I understand it," Undersecretary Potter said slowly, carefully examining the grooves on his gold-filled Cross pen, "he is under sedation right now. I'm sure that in a day or two," Potter brightly forecast, "he'll be as good as new. I'm told it's nothing too serious."

"What now?" Rogers asked Zimmermann as they left the HEW building. "Do you believe him?"

"No."

"So?"

"We go to Secretary Greenbaum. If Greenbaum bullshits us, we go to our Pentagon friends. If that doesn't work . . ." Eric paused, "we go public. Potter's going to drag his feet, I assume, at least until he finds out a lot more. CYA: Cover Your Ass."

"I should have known. He may have been telling the truth about pressing the investigation," Rogers volunteered as they walked down Pennsylvania Avenue.

"Do you think he was, Henry?"

"No. I don't."

"Then we go to Greenbaum next. Did Carey-Ross seem on the verge of a nervous breakdown when you saw him yesterday?"

"Of course not. The most stable man I know. But Secretary Greenbaum's in England. I read it in the paper," Rogers said, a note of panic entering his voice.

"Then you read yesterday's paper. He arrived in Washington this afternoon. On the Concorde."

"And I suppose we're going to crash into the HEW Secretary's office with all the ease with which we snuck into Potter's?" Rogers asked skeptically.

"Not to worry. We just ring the doorbell. I know where he lives. But first, dinner. I missed lunch because of you. Never face a politician on an empty stomach."

10

Sandpoint, Idaho

Had there been a nationwide contest to find the All-American Boy, Tony Boyer would have been a contender. Sandpoint is a small (pop. 4,800) town perched in the Rockies of northern Idaho. The air is clean, and the small farms of the area are neat and generally prosperous. Tony was an Eagle Scout and captain of both his high school basketball and cross-country teams. An excellent student, he looked forward to attending college in another year.

Basketball is a popular sport in the mountain states, and Tony was determined that in his senior year his team would do its best to become state champions. Though a cold hindered his performance in the first few weeks of the season, he was still the best shot on the team. Only when he was no longer able to run without coughing and wheezing did his coach send him to the school nurse. Though she was an ardent basketball fan, Miss Jackson took her nursing duties seriously.

"Tony, you've got a real bad cough there. Go home and go to bed. With any luck you'll be back on the court in a week, two at the outside. You'll be as good as new before you know it." Though he felt honor-bound to protest, Tony knew he was sick and sadly went home and went to bed.

He remained there for over three weeks. On some days, he seemed almost completely recovered, and he and his anxious parents hoped his 'flu' had finally passed. But after a day or two, the coughing and fever would return. Eventually, he was hardly able to get out of bed without help. The Boyers were very concerned, but they had three other children, and they knew that sometimes it could take two or three weeks to recover from a childhood illness. Still, they were worried.

"If he's not better by Friday," Mr. Boyer told his wife, "I'm gonna take him into town to see Doctor Sawyer. This flu could develop into pneumonia or somethin' if it keeps up. The kid's weak as a kitten. Don't like his color either."

Mr. Boyer did not wait until Friday to bring Tony to Sandpoint's only doctor. Tony had always been a skinny kid: almost 6′ 1″, he barely weighed 140 pounds. But on Wednesday morning, he noticed that he could see all of Tony's ribs. Helping him to the bathroom scale, Mr. Boyer was shocked to discover that his son had lost almost twenty-five pounds. They were in Dr. Sawyer's office before noon.

The people of the Sandpoint area counted themselves lucky to have a physician at all, let alone one as excellent as Bill Sawyer. He had been raised on a nearby farm, but received his undergraduate and graduate education at UCLA. Sawyer liked California, but after a brief period of practicing in Los Angeles, he decided to settle in his home town. His income was good, and he had plenty of time for outdoor activities. Sandpoint is situated near some of the best hunting and fishing areas in the United States. Its residents were usually quite healthy, and except for an occasional violent accident involving farm machinery or hunting, he had comparatively few chronically ill patients. He was, in short, quite happy being among the last of a rapidly diminishing breed, the small-town G.P.

Even before he began his examination of Tony Boyer, Dr. Sawyer knew the boy had something worse than the flu. This diagnosis was accurate, though based on the rather unscientific data of mere observation: Tony looked like hell. As the examination progressed, he found it increasingly difficult to reconcile the symptoms he observed with the likelihood of Tony's having the illness. Fatigue, coughing, intermittent fevers, severe weight loss, tightness in the chest: he toted up the symptoms, but they did not make any sense. After taking several blood samples and an unusually large number of X-rays, he sent Tony home.

"I'm not sure what he has," Sawyer admitted. "The test results should be back within a week, and we should have a pretty good idea then. You'll have to bring him back next week. He may have to go to the hospital."

Mr. Boyer was worried. "But what for? What's he got?"

"Oh, it could be any of a dozen things. I've got to see those test results before I can say for sure. The boy is obviously pretty sick."

"I coulda told you that," said Mr. Boyer, who quickly realized he was being rude. "I'm sorry. We'll just have to wait, I guess."

Dr. Sawyer watched the father and son leave his office and hoped his private diagnosis was wrong.

Most of the way home Tony and his father were silent. Mr. Boyer knew his son was very ill, but he was particularly troubled by the boy's listlessness. Tony was weak, it was true—he'd had to support him out of the car and into Dr. Sawyer's office. But there was something else. Tony's eyes betrayed a sense of sadness that both moved and angered him. Tony'd always been a talkative boy, and though father and son, the two usually chattered like childhood friends whenever they were together. They were very close. But for the past few weeks, the elder Boyer had watched his son drift away, as if he were in a small boat being pulled relentlessly out to sea by unseen currents. Mr. Boyer cleared his throat.

"Buck up, Tony, you'll be better before long."

The boy was silent for a moment, still staring out the window as the car glided by farms and tracts of pine. When he spoke, his voice was raspy. "I hope you're right, Daddy. I just have this feeling, this sense that. . . . Well, that I'm gonna get worse, not better."

Mr. Boyer was chilled by the tone of hopelessness, a combination of fear and resignation, he detected in his son's voice. And Tony had not called him "Daddy" in ten years.

"Of course you'll get better," he insisted. "Why shouldn't you? You're young and strong, and Sawyer's a fine doctor. As soon as he gets all the tests done, he'll prescribe some medicine, and you'll be back in action before long. I know you feel bad right now, but. . . ."

"Dad, I don't feel just bad. It's like there's some invisible puncture in me somewhere and my life is draining out of it. I think I'm going to die, Daddy. I can feel it. I know I sound like a baby, but honest, whatever's wrong with me isn't about to let go." He turned to face his father. Mr. Boyer glanced from the wheel once, and then again. "I don't know if you and Mom know how much you both, I mean how much I . . . love you both. I, I wish I could tell you how sorry I am for the times I've. . . ."

"Stop it, Tony." Mr. Boyer was surprised at how angry his voice sounded inside the small cab of the pickup. He spoke more softly, "Don't let yourself get so depressed. I know it's been hard on you, but believe me, there's no reason to talk like. . . . I mean you have to take the good with the bad. You'll be fine in another couple of weeks. Back in school, probably back on the team. They won last night, you know." Tony nodded and smiled the same brave smile. Mr. Boyer was shocked he hadn't asked the score. "Tony, you've got to promise me you won't let this get you down. Really, I know you feel rotten now, but sometimes we all get sick, and sometimes it goes on for a long time. Promise me you'll hang in there and fight whatever it is you've got, and I *promise* you you'll be better before much longer."

"I promise, Dad."

"Good."

When they arrived at the farm, Mr. Boyer helped Tony up the stairs to his room and watched him slowly undress and get into bed. In a matter of moments, Tony was asleep.

There were half a dozen chores he had planned to attend to, but Ralph Boyer impulsively walked out into the fields, carefully and unnecessarily examining the earth. It was still hard, but before long the deep snow on the mountains would melt and turn the ugly gray-brown landscape into lush green fields. But the dark skies promising more snow that evening and the hard, somber landscape were at one with Mr. Boyer's mood.

When he noticed the bird, he also noticed with surprise that he was almost a mile from the house, a scant hundred yards from his neighbor's property. Despite his expression of concentration as he walked through the fields, Ralph Boyer had seen little as he crunched over the brittle remains of the previous fall's crop. He just walked, walked. But then he saw the bird.

It was a crow. He had no idea where the crows migrated, but they always arrived just before planting and left a few weeks after harvest. So it surprised him to see the large black bird only a few yards ahead of him, idly pecking at the frozen earth. Boyer stood still for a minute pondering the discrepancy of this solitary bird–no others were around–and wondering if it was an early arrival or if it had simply decided not to leave for the winter. As he stood there he realized that he had rarely seen a crow alone–they were sociable creatures, almost always found in groups. Did the birds sometimes cast out a member of their tribe? If so, what could be the crime? The bird was unnatural, out of place, and this annoyed Boyer, though unlike his neighbors he generally tolerated the depredations of birds on his crops, having long before discovered that the remedies often did more harm than good. Ralph Boyer, big, almost brutish in appearance, was really a gentle man. So he surprised himself when he very slowly reached down and carefully removed a stone from underfoot.

The bird walked nonchalantly through the field, pausing occasionally for no apparent reason, rather like a shopper peering into the windows of empty stores. Boyer threw the rock with tremendous force.

It should have missed, overshooting the crow by several feet, but the startled bird took flight at precisely the wrong moment, colliding with the projectile and falling limp to the ground. Boyer hurried to the spot and looked for a moment at the dead creature at his feet. He picked it up. It was still warm, and he half-expected it to recover from its shock and fly out of his hands. He turned it over again and again, minutely and gently examining it. He stood there in his empty brown field, a mile from his home as dusk approached with the body of a dead bird in his hands. He began to cry.

It all happened very quickly. Less than a week later Tony was in the hospital in Idaho Falls.

Dr. Sawyer's diagnosis had been corroborated by the tests. On the morning Mr. Boyer called to report a new symptom, hemoptysis—spitting up blood—the doctor was staring at the results and wondering how he could explain it to the parents. Tony Boyer had lung cancer.

"It's rare, extremely rare," he told them in the hospital, "but these things do happen." Sawyer was telling the truth, but he still could not accept the truth himself. Tony had always been very healthy, an athlete; the mountain air was pure, and neither the boy nor his parents ever smoked. It just did not make medical sense. The next day he explained to Tony why he had to have an operation. The boy listened attentively, and even managed a brave smile. He could no longer talk due to paralysis of the laryngeal nerve.

The operation took almost six hours. Tony's left lung was removed, but it was too late—the cancer had spread. Three days later he was dead.

11

London

"Would you like a little breakfast, dear?"

Arthur Greenbaum, Secretary of Health, Education, and Welfare and personal representative of the President of the United States, sat up in bed with a start. He stared, blinking, at the pretty young redhead sitting on the edge of his bed.

"Uh, no. Thank you." He smiled and tried desperately to remember her name. Jane? June? It had only taken him a few seconds to recover from the surprise of finding someone in his bedroom, but her name eluded him completely. A nice girl. A "date" provided by the embassy. He lay back in the big bed and watched her brush her hair. Jane-June had been a perfect choice for him. American. Something to do with USIA. She understood good wine and enjoyed excellent food. The general disarray of his suite indicated that the previous night's frolics had included more than food and wine.

Now that he was fully awake, Arthur Greenbaum wished she would leave. For one thing, he was moderately hung over, and he preferred solitary suffering. Also, though he had a well-deserved reputation as a ladies' man, in daylight he was almost prudish. Several years before he had thought some distant ancestor might be responsible for the legend of the werewolf. During the day, he was hard working, efficient, courtly: the very model of a Cabinet member. But when the sun set and he sat in a dim restaurant with a pretty (or even not-so-pretty) young woman, his soul began to growl and stalk his prey. Now that the sun was pouring into his room, he wanted to jump out of bed and get to work. For a man who had enjoyed the company of a great many women, Arthur Greenbaum was extraordinarily shy about exposing his naked body in broad daylight. Even in front of his wife. Perhaps it was a bit of Victorian guilt about his nocturnal passions; perhaps it was modesty or embarrassment over his substantial paunch which superb tailors could diminish but which saddened him each morning when he stood shaving before the mirror. For Arthur Greenbaum was an elegant man, a person possessing a sure and exquisite taste, a connoisseur. In an administration whose hallmark was a combination of Johnsonian crudity and Nixonian tough-talking worthy of a convention of high school coaches, Greenbaum stood out. He was welcome in the salons of Georgetown, and even the New York *Times* had exempted him by name from its savage denunciation of Wilson's cabinet appointments, "The Worst and the Dumbest." The fact that Greenbaum's task was to dismantle the HEW colossus which had evolved in the Kennedy-Johnson-Carter years did not escape notice in the liberal press, but Greenbaum, ever-ready with a quip or elegant turn of phrase, was rarely attacked personally.

"Do you brush your hair like this every day?" he asked.

"Try to. A thousand strokes. I'll have to settle for seven-fifty today. I'm late for work." She flashed a brilliant smile into the mirror at him, and even though it was morning and he was hungover, he felt a twinge of carnal desire. She put down the brush and approached the bed. "Is there anything I can get you?" she asked, kissing him on the forehead. Greenbaum felt a definite stirring in his groin, but shook his head. "No. I'm just going to loll here and enjoy the hospitality of the United Kingdom."

She rose to leave, and turned at the door. "See you tonight."

Greenbaum's mind raced. All that wine, and then the cognac; where were they going tonight?

"How about the Connaught Grill? It's comfortable, and the food's superb, which is saying something for UK cuisine," he said.

"I meant the reception." She smiled.

"Yes, of course. The reception. Well, maybe we can get away for a nice little supper . . ."

"Your wish, Mr. Secretary, is my command." She blew him a kiss and quietly closed the door.

The reception. Arthur Greenbaum sighed and swung his legs over the side of the bed. *Another* reception. He started toward the bathroom and paused at a handsome Louis Quinze armchair. A large red blotch of Cheval Blanc '64 stained its fine brocade. He felt a pricking of conscience. The stain would be impossible to get out, and the fabric was beautiful, perhaps irreplaceable. He thought he should offer to pay for it but knew he would be refused. The embassy would never say a word, and the poor taxpayers would have to bear one more tiny burden to pay for his or Jane's—if that was her name—carelessness.

He stood in the shower longer than usual, letting the scalding water steam out much of his hangover and idly anticipating the coming evening's erotic delights. A somewhat more orderly passion, he resolved, as he stepped refreshed from the shower and surveyed the chaos of his bedroom.

Typically, Secretary Greenbaum rose early—often before sunrise—so he could fully enjoy a morning bath, take almost a full hour dressing, and still be at his desk by 8:00 A.M. He dried himself and carefully hot-combed his hair, sprayed it, checked his finger- and toenails, dusted himself with talc, and began the process of selecting, discarding, and matching his clothes for the day. Certainly he was vain, but the results were, as usual, just right. Never overdressed, never foppish. Always elegant.

When he was finished, he studied himself in the mirror, and nodded with satisfaction. Most of the day he was free, and he planned a pleasant few hours on Oxford Street consulting with his shirtmaker and tailor. Refreshed and cheerful, Arthur Greenbaum set out on his stroll, reminding himself to be back by four to dress for the reception.

The reception at Windsor Castle was very lavish and very dull. It was the culmination of almost five days of diplomatic entertainments and speeches of thanks from British officials combined with daytime conferences and meetings between exchequer ministers and treasury officials from half a dozen countries.

"So nice to see you again, Phillip," Greenbaum murmured politely to Phillip Llewelan, a stiflingly dull Conservative MP who had cornered him at a party several days before and lectured for over an hour on the evils of unionism.

"Ah, *Arthur,* so good of you t'come. Have some of the caviar when it comes by. Gift to the King from the Shah. Fellow sent several hundred pounds of the stuff for Charles' birthday. It's absolutely the best Iranian, but the King doesn't care for it and sent it over for the party."

"How nice of him," said Greenbaum, catching a warning look from Amabassador Keeney, who had warned him to divide his conversations equally among Liberal, Conservative, Labour, and National party officials. He nodded slightly and said, "I love caviar. I believe I'll find some."

He started to move away, but the MP grabbed a passing waiter and sent him in search of the Shah's largesse. "You know, Arthur," he began in a low voice, "I have it on good authority that King Charles plans to make a surprise appearance here tonight."

"How nice." Greenbaum smiled and once again saw a warning look from the Ambassador. He diplomatically neglected to mention that he knew Charles' "surprise" visit had been planned over a week ago. "Oh! There's a colleague of mine I've got to give a message to. Do excuse me, Phillip. I hope we'll be able to talk again." Before his auditor could object or attach himself, Greenbaum plunged into the crowd. For the next two hours, he chatted with politicians and assorted worthies of all political persuasions, always smiling, always looking interested, and never giving a hint of the intense boredom he felt.

It had been in the interests of the U.S., EEC, and Japan, of course, to bail out the UK when its financial structure had suddenly and thoroughly collapsed. The Third World had wrested control of the World Bank from the capitalist countries several years before, and that institution was now itself virtually bankrupt. Britain's friends and trading partners had no choice but to step in after the bloody riots in Manchester and a virtual state of siege in Glasgow. The North Sea oil had come too late, due largely to the somewhat sudden nationalization of foreign interests, who simply pulled out all their technicians and much of their support equipment in a matter of weeks. Reports that the North Sea deposits had been greatly overestimated, though erroneous, sent the market in the City plunging to 1932 lows, and the pound slid to eighty-three cents before "the cavalry" (as the *Financial Times* called them) came to the rescue. Most economists had previously believed that a sudden, 1929-style Crash and Depression was unlikely in any developed postindustrial nation, but the Black Spring showed how fragile the economic web could be. In thirteen weeks, there were two changes of government, the collapse of the pound and the Bank of England, and the closing of industries throughout the United Kingdom. Unemployment hit 24 percent and civil disturbances began to spread. Before long, the exchanges on Wall Street, Tokyo, Bonn, the Bourse, and elsewhere began to slide, and gold rose to an incredible $392.50 an ounce. So it quickly became clear to almost all nations in the capitalist world that if England went under, she just might take them all with her. With the U.S. in the lead, pledges of over fifty billion dollars of aid and low-interest loans were secured from almost twenty nations. The cavalry arrived just in time.

But now that England was once again on a shaky but even keel and the oil was flowing at 100 percent capacity, Greenbaum mused, the British were punishing their friends with an endless series of ceremonies, medals, and dinners. Perhaps it was India's sending aid for which he was now suffering. . . .

After what Greenbaum had to admit was a delicious dinner and two mercifully short speeches, everyone, male and female, "retired" to another hall for brandy, port, and cigars. The King, surprisingly, had not appeared as scheduled after dinner, which may have accounted for the brevity of the speeches, which were probably meant to be introductory. In any event, Greenbaum was relishing his second balloon glass of superb, forty-five-year-old Remy, a gift of the French people, when he saw a stunning redhead in a midnight-blue velvet dress gliding toward the door at the far end of the room. *Jan,* he thought, and was pleased that he had at last remembered her name. She looked marvelous and his werewolf heart began to pound. Sir Phillip Llewelan had just caught up with him once again, but Arthur looked suddenly surprised and said, "Aha! There goes a colleague of mine. I've got to give him a message." Flashing an apologetic smile at Sir Phillip, he rushed off after Jan. Only after he had worked his way halfway across the room did he remember that he had used the same excuse on the same man twice in a row. *Fuck it,* he thought to himself and headed for the door. He never made it. The grip on his arm was firm, and the voice pleasant but commanding. "I've got to talk with you, Mr. Secretary. Could you come with me?"

Annoyed, "Sir Nicholas–so good to see you. Can it wait? I've just spotted an associate I've been looking for all evening. Got to give him a message."

"It's really very important," Rawlings replied.

Sir Nicholas' tone was flat, but his expression quickly convinced Greenbaum he was serious.

"OK, where shall we talk?"

"This way."

Nicholas Rawlings was one of the most respected men in the British government. Aside from the brief horror of the National Party's reign, he had served under both Conservative and Labour governments. His scientific credentials were impeccable, and he had once come close to winning the Nobel Prize for his work on recombinant DNA. Rawlings left disputes about National Health to the politicians, and though he was often baited for his apolitical stand, he was respected by scientists and physicians of all political parties in England and throughout the world. His work with WHO had helped eradicate malaria. Despite his administrative duties, he still found time to publish several scientific papers each year. He resembled a tall, willowy Harold Macmillan, with silver-white hair and moustache, and baggy, rather sad bassetlike eyes.

Sir Nicholas led Greenbaum out of the room and down a long hall. At the end of the corridor, he opened a beautifully carved, and obviously heavy, door to reveal a handsome library. The room was enormous, but by the fireplace was an intimate cluster of comfortable leather chairs and highly polished mahogany end-tables.

"Do take a chair," Sir Nicholas said, gesturing to the two nearest the fire. "Let me get you a refill. I think I'll join you."

Greenbaum noticed that he still held the empty brandy snifter he had absentmindedly carried with him on his silent journey with Rawlings. He already felt the effect of several scotches, three dinner wines, and the cognac he had been enjoying before Rawlings had almost forcibly escorted him from the party, but now that he was seated in a soft leather armchair before a fireplace crackling with a five-foot log, he willingly agreed.

"Now there are several fine cognacs," said Sir Nicholas, standing by the bar near the door, "but I think you'll enjoy this. It's very rare. Just an Armagnac. But it has aged beautifully. But if you'd prefer . . ."

"No, no, I'd love to try it," said Greenbaum.

"You see, this Armagnac was probably the best of its time. It seems to get better with each passing decade. Of course there's not a great deal of it still about. For reasons I can't understand, the vineyard went out of business after the war, and no more was produced. I don't believe troops passed through the region, but there it is . . . this is one of the last vintages."

"Perhaps the bombers . . ." volunteered Greenbaum.

"Oh, no, I meant the Franco-Prussian war," Sir Nicholas said as he poured two large drams into two very large glasses. He smiled, crossed the room to hand his guest a glass, and walked to the door and turned the key.

"Just so we won't be disturbed," he said, answering Greenbaum's quizzical expression and taking the chair opposite him.

"Such a beautiful room," Greenbaum observed, "does it have any special name or, uh, purpose?"

"This is the King's personal study."

"I see." Arthur Greenbaum cradled the snifter in his hands and smelled the amber liquid. The bouquet was excellent, and his first sip was delightful. Though he had already had a fair amount to drink, the brandy was a beautiful surprise. Instead of the coarse, powerful taste typical of Armagnac, there were a delicacy and flavor he had never before experienced. Greenbaum was a true aesthete, and he knew he would savor this experience for the rest of his life. "If Wilson got hold of this," Greenbaum thought, "he would've turned the treasury over to England." Only he and perhaps a few other close associates of the President knew of his fondness–some said overfondness–for liquor, particularly brandy.

"This is superb. Where on earth did you get it?"

"It's the King's favorite, and I'm sure he would not begrudge a few glasses to one of our American friends," said Sir Nicholas with a sincere smile. "May I get you another, Mr. Secretary? I'll join you in a refill in a minute."

"Well, Sir Nicholas, I have a long flight home tomorrow; I'll sleep then. Wonderful brandy. And please call me Arthur," he said, holding out his glass.

"Of course," Rawlings replied, "and I hope you will call me," there was just the slightest pause, "Nicky." The two smiled at one another.

"Very well, Nicky, here I am in the King's study drinking his favorite brandy, and talking to one of his most honored ministers. As they say, in my old home town of Boston, 'What's up?' "

Nicholas Rawlings paused, and then leaned closer to Greenbaum with his elbows resting on his knees. "What's up," he said, "is cancer. Cancer of every sort. And we can't find any reason for this sudden increase. The past months have shown almost four hundred percent more cases than normal, and we haven't a clue why this is happening. None whatsoever." Sir Nicholas looked pleadingly into Greenbaum's eyes. "This country has suffered a great deal in the past two years, and if we now are to have some kind of . . . epidemic of all types of carcinoma, I just don't know. . . ." His voice trailed off.

"You're sure of the figures?" Greenbaum inquired.

"Absolutely. One of the advantages of our National Health Service–and don't tell anyone I praised it in any way–one of the advantages is an accurate and immediate reporting of all illnesses directly to our offices. We checked and rechecked, but there can be no doubt. Cancer–*all* cancers–seem to be out of control. I may need your help, but for now I wanted to know if this is something localized in the British Isles or if you have seen any of the same indications in America."

Greenbaum was stunned, and mystified. His room at the embassy was filled with all manner of reports and "urgent" memos from all his division chiefs at HEW, but he had ignored most of them during this "diplomatic mission." He felt a surge of panic, but quickly quelled it, assuming he was reacting to the brandy as much as Sir Nicholas' words. He had never paid a great deal of attention to the "H" of HEW. Education subsidies and welfare chiseling were his special targets, and he was suddenly deeply embarrassed before a man as distinguished as Rawlings–a man who was close to begging for his help–to confess that he did not know. That he might well know if he had only done his homework.

"How bad does it look?" Secretary Greenbaum asked.

"Right now, very bad. I assume from your expression that this is the first you've heard of it?"

"Yes, but you have my word, Sir Nicholas, that as soon as I reach Washington . . . No, I'll call tonight. A day, two at the most, and I'll have your answer. This is terrible. Does the King know?"

"Yes, he knows."

"Good."

"Not so good. The King has cancer of the liver. Rare in so young a man. It's metastasized. I . . . I will have to wait for more tests of course, but I . . ." his voice cracked, slid out of control, "I am almost certain King Charles is dying."

Later that night, Arthur Greenbaum sat in his suite and stared out the window. Just a false alarm: an old man's reaction to the illness of a young king. Or could it be worse, much worse? The call he had promised had been made as soon as he had reached the embassy scrambler. As he looked out the window, the five days of unusually clear and beautiful weather which had characterized his visit to London ended. It began to rain.

Around midnight, Jan called.

He told her he would be unable to see her.

12

Washington, D.C.

The District of Columbia is known, of course, as the seat of government and the site of monuments and public buildings. The city also enjoys, if that is the word, the reputation of being one large ghetto, riddled with rotting housing, poverty, and crime. To a degree, this is true, but a large chunk of the city, Northwest D.C., is one of the most prosperous and comfortable residential areas to be found anywhere in the nation. And in one corner of the Northwest, only half a dozen miles from some of the most disgraceful slums in America, Fox Chase Road meanders through tree-filled countryside sprinkled with imposing homes set back from the road and hidden behind thick, manicured hedges.

Arriving in Washington to take over his duties at HEW, Arthur Greenbaum fell in love with this area. Even Greenbaum, a multimillionaire, was shocked by the price of real estate in the District, and particularly along Fox Chase Road, but he swallowed hard and convinced himself that even a $650,000 house was far from ostentatious in the neighborhood, with the Kennedy family just down the road, as well as the little estate that had belonged to Nelson Rockefeller during the decades in which he pursued the presidency and through his brief tenure as Vice President. The Rockefeller house was now owned by an Iranian businessman who entertained a suspiciously large number of Congressmen, but it was impeccably maintained. With property nearby valued at well over a million dollars, Greenbaum felt positively frugal with his modest 2.4 acres and nineteen-room colonial. It was a house designed for large-scale entertaining, and he and his wife Sara quickly established themselves as the premier partygivers of the stunningly dull Wilson administration. Invitations to their cocktail parties or buffet dinners were avidly sought and not-so-casually mentioned at elegant Georgetown hairdressers or over lunch at Sans Souci. Most prized of all was an invitation to one of the small, "family" dinners, never more than twelve at table, the Greenbaums held three or four times a week. On such evenings, a typical mix would include a network correspondent, one or two diplomats, a syndicated columnist, perhaps a visiting entertainer or financier, and a sampling of powerful Senators or Congressmen from both parties. The food and wines were invariably excellent, and dinner-table conversation at the Greenbaums' was the most sought after gossip in a city devoted to the pursuit of rumor.

Of course, there was not much competition. The "Georgetown Crowd," whose membership also included residents of Northwest, Chevy Chase, and half a dozen other prosperous suburbs, were most comfortable with Democratic administrations, and many had folded their tents to await the coming of the next Carter or, best of all possible worlds, the return of the now-mythic Camelot. President Wilson had offered hope at first: he was after all the first young and energetic Republican president since Teddy Roosevelt. But it quickly became clear that while Wilson could be charming at White House functions, he did not enjoy them and kept them to a minimum.

Wilson's Cabinet appointments made Eisenhower's look like a bouquet of Beautiful People at Régine's. Only Arthur Greenbaum could be counted on for fun. He, and the President's only daughter,

Wendy—the wildest, most lively, and independent White Hous
teenager since Alice Roosevelt—provided the city with most of it
entertainment. The country was prosperous. America was at peace. I
was all extraordinarily dull. Even Carter's nonalcoholic square dance
or LBJ's huge bar-b-ques were now sentimentally recalled as akin t
Louis XIV's divertissements at Versailles.

Rogers insisted on driving that evening, and Eric could see why
He had wondered why a man so oblivious of personal possession
would own a TR-8, but he was flabbergasted when he was led to
brand new Mercedes 290-XL.

"Christ, Henry, when did you get *this?*" he asked, his voice tinge
with awe as he stood by the gleaming two-seater.

"Just last week. I fell in love with it up at the Auto Show
couple of months back in New York. I had to wait awhile to ge
this shade of green." Rogers beamed.

"I don't mean to be personal, but this must cost . . ."

"Just over thirty. I trade a car in almost every year. You'd b
surprised how much you can get for a good year-old sports ca
Anyway, I always wanted a little Benz. Won't depreciate much, an
living alone as I do, I don't spend half my salary. Like it?"

"Love it. Pull up Greenbaum's driveway in this and we'll look lik
the guests of honor. Drive on, my man."

Rogers skillfully eased the car through the light evening traffic
The maitre d' at the small but elegant Georgetown restauran
Zimmermann had chosen looked askance at Rogers' wrinkle
clothes. But he did have a jacket and tie, and the restaurant was no
close to full this early on a weeknight. As they ate, the two discusse
strategy. They would demand to see the Secretary, even make a scen
if necessary. Rogers would explain the situation quickly and i
nonmedical terms. They would insist that the President be informed
and if refused, would hint that the press would hear of it.

"Fine," said Rogers, pushing aside his plate and lighting
cigarette. "That should have us under observation for a 'nervou
collapse' in a matter of hours."

"Good point. We tell him we want to see Carey-Ross tomorrow morning. *And* we tell him we have explained everything to two other people not associated with NIH, who will go right to the *Post* if either of us are in any way 'detained.' " Zimmermann signalled for the check.

"That's an excellent idea, even if it is a lie. If he calls our bluff though . . ."

"He won't. Let's go." Zimmermann paid the bill, and less than twenty minutes later, they were ringing Arthur Greenbaum's doorbell.

Sara Greenbaum had been surprised when her husband had called that morning from London, and suggested inviting several people to dinner. She'd assumed he would be tired after a week in London and a four-hour flight. "Just be sure you invite Dr. Jonas," he said.

"Who?" She had no idea who Dr. Jonas was.

"He runs NIH at Bethesda. You met him once. Be sure he comes."

"It's not much notice, Arthur, are you sure you . . ." Sara sounded doubtful.

"Just use your wiles. If necessary tell him it's important to see him. You shouldn't have to, though—he'll come. Oh, and pick two or three others. Just nobody from HEW. Okay?"

The addition of half a dozen people for dinner was no problem for the Greenbaum cook, but Sara was perplexed. It was unlike her husband to insist on having a specific person at the table, especially on such short notice.

When she answered the door, her smile only flickered briefly when confronted with two strangers, one young and strikingly handsome, the other middle-aged and vaguely familiar. "Ah, Dr. Jonas, right on time," she said, addressing Rogers. "Do come in."

"And you are . . ." She looked at him quizzically.

"Dr. Zimmermann."

"I'm so glad you could come too. Come have a drink." She led them into a large, tastefully furnished living room. Greenbaum was chatting with a correspondent from CBS at the far end of the room, and looked mystified as the two men entered.

"Now, just help yourselves. If there's something you'd like that's not here, just speak up—we've probably got it in the study." She gestured to a portable bar laden with a minimum of fifty bottles. Rogers, flustered, stood with his hands clasped in front of him.

"Please, Dr. Jonas, do help . . ."

"I . . . I'm not Dr. Jonas, Mrs. Greenbaum," Rogers stammered, blushing like a boy caught playing doctor. "My name is Rogers, Dr. Henry Rogers. From the National Institutes of Health. And this is Dr. Zimmermann . . . oh, but you've been introduced."

Sara Greenbaum's bright smile flickered, dimmed, and was almost extinguished.

"I'm sorry for the confusion," Rogers continued. "We took the liberty of calling on you, that is to say . . ."

"We are here to see Secretary Greenbaum on a most urgent matter. It should only take a few minutes." Sara looked from one man to the other and then smiled once again. "Well, help yourself to a drink anyway. Here's Arthur right now." Arthur Greenbaum was approaching his uninvited guests, a pleasant but quizzical expression on his face. The doorbell rang.

"Now, *that* must be Dr. Jonas," said Mrs. Greenbaum pleasantly and excused herself.

"Gentlemen—Dr. Zimmermann, I believe—and . . . ?"

"Dr. Rogers, Data Analysis and Computer Services, NIH. I'm sorry to barge in, Mr. Secretary . . ."

"Ah, yes, Rogers. We've never met, but I have, of course, heard of you and your fine work," Greenbaum said pleasantly. "Now, I insist you let me make you a drink." He took their orders, and humming softly to himself, carefully mixed a scotch and soda and a gin and tonic. "Now," he said, a smile on his lips but his tone frosty, "would you be so kind as to tell me why you have so suddenly appeared in my living room?"

Rogers spoke first. "Mr. Secretary, I'm really sorry to barge in on you like this, but I, we, thought it essential to talk with you."

"I have office hours, Dr. Rogers, office hours. From about eight to about six. Surely you could . . ."

"Mr. Greenbaum, we've come on a matter of national security."

"A very unfashionable phrase, Zimmermann. Much too Nixonian. And if what you say is true, and it can't wait until tomorrow, I really think you should be talking to our friends in Arlington or Langley. Please feel free to have another drink, but I'm afraid our table is already set so I won't be able to invite you to stay for dinner. I hope I make myself clear." Greenbaum spoke evenly, still smiling, but his intent was obvious. He had heard of Zimmermann's reputation as a troublemaker and resolved this stunt would cost him dearly. He started to turn away.

Zimmermann grabbed his arm, ignoring his startled expression. "Now listen, Greenbaum, I know you think we're gate crashers or crackpots or something, but all we want is a few minutes of your time. This country is about to face the biggest health catastrophe, no, the biggest catastrophe *period* in its history. If we are correct, it is possible that as many as sixty million Americans will have cancer in a year's time. . . ."

"Cancer." Greenbaum spoke very softly, very distinctly.

"Look, I know it sounds ridiculous, but if you would just give us half an hour of your time, even fifteen minutes. . . ."

"Please stay for dinner, gentlemen. We can always accommodate two unexpected arrivals. But nothing of this to anyone, mind you, until after the other guests leave. Except Jonas, of course—that's why I invited him here tonight."

"You mean Dr. Jonas has already told you about this?" Rogers asked.

"Hardly. I've just returned from England. I was about," Greenbaum winked conspiratorially, "to tell *him.*" Greenbaum smiled, and left both men for once speechless.

For the second time that night, Rogers and Zimmermann were served an excellent meal. And under the benign but watchful eye of Mrs. Greenbaum, they cleaned their plates.

After the other guests left, Arthur Greenbaum led Rogers,

Zimmermann, and a thoroughly confused Dr. Jonas into his study. It was a comfortable room, filled with floor-to-ceiling bookcases, and large, comfortable leather chairs clustered around a fireplace that was not in use that evening. French doors opened onto a terrace and garden at one end, and a massive mahogany desk dominated the other. A huge oriental rug covered the floor. Zimmermann estimated its value at close to $20,000 and took care not to spill the liqueur the Secretary offered him.

"A superb dinner, Mr. Secretary," Jonas began.

"Please, Arthur," said Greenbaum.

"Thank you. A lovely dinner and a marvelous evening, Arthur, and I hope you will invite me again, but I suspect your summons was not because you lacked an extra man." Jonas nodded at Greenbaum and Rogers and continued. "We seem a bit top-heavy with NIH people tonight, so I assume there's something you want to know. What can I do for you?"

"You're most perceptive, Harold, and you will be invited again, I promise, but I think we should hear first from the gate crashers." Greenbaum smiled.

"I beg your pardon," said Dr. Jonas.

Arthur Greenbaum sat back in his chair and nodded to Rogers, who outlined his findings, broadly at first, and then in more detail. He spoke, uninterrupted, for over fifteen minutes. When he mentioned the sudden "nervous collapse" of Simon Carey-Ross and his suspicions that the scientist was being held against his will, Jonas came close to exploding but was silenced by a wave from Greenbaum. When Rogers asserted that the computer data at NIH was being tampered with, Jonas did explode.

"Mr. Secretary . . ." he said, rising.

"Arthur," Greenbaum reminded him.

"Mr. Secretary," Jonas continued, "if any of this is true–and I am sure it is *not* true–you will have my resignation within twenty-four hours. If your idea of a good time is to invite someone to your house for dinner and then throw out a string of charges of incompetence–of *criminal behavior* for that matter–then I, or rather you . . ." Jonas paused for just a beat, infuriated and tangled in his syntax.

"Please sit down," Greenbaum commanded firmly. "I had no intention of setting you up for criticism. I've already said that Drs. Rogers and Zimmermann came here uninvited and would not be in this room right now if I had not learned of something very serious when I was in England which they seem to have discovered on their own here in the U.S." His tone was gentler, "Please sit down, I assure you that Dr. Rogers' little science fiction story may well be true."

Jonas returned to his chair without another word, stunned. Greenbaum related what he had been told by Sir Nicholas Rawlings.

"Did he give you any specific data?" asked Rogers.

"No, but I'm sure you can have whatever you want whenever you want it. The question is, gentlemen, what do we do? It looks bad right now. I think Dr. Rogers has made the point that this is not just a statistical error. Still, we don't know why the disease suddenly started to blossom. Bad word, I suppose–increase, then. It is still possible it will go no further. For now, we have to begin to plan for the worst while preventing national panic. What we know may be unfortunate public knowledge in a few months, but for the moment, this is the biggest secret since the Manhattan Project. I'm not exaggerating. If the public panics, the ramifications could conceivably mean the end of democratic government in this country. I think this must have occurred to whoever at NIH or NCI decided to keep Carey-Ross quiet–I'm not endorsing the action, but I understand the motives–this has got to be Top Secret until we can organize a plan–Christ, a thousand plans and contingency plans–to deal with it. Are we agreed?"

Each of the three answered affirmatively. Zimmermann was the first to comment.

"What now?" he asked.

"I suppose we should have all the "i's" dotted and all the data triple checked," said Greenbaum, noting Rogers' scowl, "but I doubt that two countries would–simultaneously–come up with the same statistical error over a four-month period. We go to the President. Tomorrow. I'll just have to check the schedule and let you know when."

"The President. Good," said Rogers.

Maybe, thought Greenbaum, though he did not voice his doubts.

"And, of course, the National Security Council," he continued. "This is not just a matter of public health. That is certain."

It would be months before Arthur would tell his wife why he had insisted on suddenly inviting Harold Jonas to dinner and neglected to tell her about the two extra guests.

13

Washington, D.C.

The second President Wilson was unlike the first in most respects, but there were several intriguing parallels. Both were tall and thin, but Thomas Wilson bore a closer resemblance to John Lindsay than to the schoolmarmish and serious Woodrow Wilson. Both men shared the honor of being the only presidents in U.S. history to hold the degree of Doctor of Philosophy, but while the first President Wilson had gone directly from teaching at Princeton to the life of politics, Tom Wilson was able to ease on down the political road with the aid of television.

His progress from the faculty of Worcester Polytech to the White House was in many respects every bit as remarkable as his predecessor Carter's trek from Plains to Washington. Wilson's academic life was pleasant and comfortable–his wife, Jennifer, was the only child of a very well-to-do Hartford businessman–and had it not been for television, he almost certainly would have lived out his life teaching political science to the engineers and technocrats of the future. He was a popular professor. A good, sometimes brilliant lecturer, he was witty and thought provoking. Though more than a few of his colleagues considered him a lightweight, a raconteur rather than a teacher, no one could deny his courses were extremely popular. The year before he became a household name in western Massachusetts, the student body voted him "Professor of the Year," and cited his "clear thinking and unmatched eloquence on (sic) the podium." Professor Wilson was a very easy grader.

When WMAQ asked Wilson to be an occasional commentator on political stories, a star was born. His analyses were thoughtful and serious, but he ended almost every minilecture with the words, "But the world, my friends, goes on" and a radiant smile. All but the most horrifying events were presented with Wilson's ineffable combination of intelligence and cheer, and his viewers usually felt they had learned something important: most crises were ephemeral. The world went on.

WMAQ quickly realized it had stumbled on a hot property. Before long, Tom Wilson was anchorman on the six o'clock news. A salary of $50,000 was sufficient to seduce him away from the Worcester campus on a leave of absence, and within a year he was once again seduced by the leading Boston station to host the nightly *Newscaner 9* broadcast for a salary just under $100,000. Tom Wilson could easily have settled into a life-long career as a highly paid and much loved broadcast journalist. But Arthur Greenbaum had other plans.

"You could do it, you know," Greenbaum told the young newsman. "In eight months, you could be governor of this state. You're popular, personable, intelligent. A perfect candidate."

They were sitting in a small Beacon Hill restaurant only a few blocks from the golden dome of the statehouse. Wilson smiled pleasantly and lied when he said he had no interest in politics. He knew Arthur Greenbaum was more than another wealthy political operator; he was also *the* behind-the-scenes powerbroker for the GOP. They talked through lunch, and over coffee Tom Wilson agreed to think it over. He knew he had to give it a try, and that Greenbaum rarely picked losers. But he did not want to appear overanxious.

"Governor's vulnerable as hell, y'know. That tax package he just got through could kill him." Greenbaum flicked an imaginary bit of lint from his lapel.

"What else could he do?"

"Damned if I know, Tom, but an awful lot of people, an awful lot of *Democrats* are sick of more and more taxes every time they try to take a piss. It wouldn't hurt if you started commenting on Channel 9 about the impossible burdens of taxation. Public-spiritedly, of course."

Wilson looked shocked. "That wouldn't be fair. I can't . . ."

"Just an idea. You're not running for anything *now,* and rousing the troops with denunciations of the tax collector has been known to work a few times in the past, more than a few. When the movement begins to draft you for this high office, it could be based on your lookin' out for the little guy. Taxed to death while a bloated bureaucrat gets fat passing out money to addicts and welfare cheats. . . ."

"Pretty old-fashioned stuff."

"Oh, it'll work, Tom. You can *make* it work. You've got style, know how to phrase things so just about everyone except the governor will agree with you. Humane, but efficient. Tough minded but fair."

Tom Wilson drained his glass of red wine (his fifth, Greenbaum noted). "I'll give it thought, Arthur. Someday, maybe, but this is still a Democratic state . . ."

The older man held up his hand and leaned across the table conspiratorially. "Sure it is, probably always will be, but there are occasions. . . ." He looked around the room. "Listen, you know my reputation. I think you also know I don't bullshit people. In ten weeks, maybe a couple of months, the governor's dead anyway. It's a sure thing. Whoever's ready to move in on him can't, I repeat *cannot,* lose . . . and this could be just the beginning."

As Greenbaum chattered with the headwaiter in French about the glories of a properly prepared Soufflé Grand Marnier, Tom Wilson decided he should run for Governor of the Commonwealth of

Massachusetts. If Arthur Greenbaum thought he had a shot, maybe he did.

Tom Wilson won the primary easily, and two months before the election, his opponent was indicted on five counts of bribery. Greenbaum was right: it was a sure thing. One of the biggest corruption scandals in the history of the state, involving half a dozen legislators and the chairman of the Democratic party, swept him into office. And he gained his first bit of national exposure by bringing the Republican party into control of both houses of the state assembly. This earned him an article in *Newsweek* entitled, "The Miracle Worker." Simply winning in a normally Democratic state during the golden days of the Carter years invested him with that most magical of political words: *charisma.*

Tom Wilson was a popular Governor. Two tax cuts in as many years almost drove the citizens of the Bay State to celebrating a second Thanksgiving. Everyone praised his energy and determination–everyone, except state and municipal employees and those others dependent of necessity on the largesse of the state. The number of state employees was cut by 9 percent in just twenty months (along with a similar number in cities dependent on state aid to prop up their budgets). State and municipal employees had agreed to a very small raise and two-year contract under Wilson's disgraced predecessor, and they had agreed not to ask for an increase in Wilson's first year if he would refrain from further personnel cuts. But in Wilson's second year, the state and municipal workers had had enough. Their real income had declined and they were expected to put in longer hours for the same salary. And Governor Wilson broke his (private) promise not to lay off any more of them. His new budget called for a reduction in state personnel by another 5.5 percent.

They struck.

During the thirty-three days of the Massachusetts General Strike, Wilson appeared to all the world as a man in control. The National Guard were generally efficient in keeping public order and only a few of his closest friends, like Arthur Greenbaum, and his wife, Jennifer, knew he was struggling for control. That he was scared, almost paranoid. That he drank far too much.

But Thomas Wilson broke the strike. There were several ugly incidents including one mass demonstration of policemen which confronted several National Guard units on Boston Common. No one will ever know who fired the shot. Many of the police carried service revolvers, and the Guard was frightened. In less than a minute there were four policemen and one guardsman dead, and a score on both sides were seriously wounded. In just twenty-four hours, the Governor's popularity plunged. His determination now seemed stubbornness. His willingness to fight had seemingly led to the deaths of five men. He issued a proclamation ordering the flags to be flown at half-staff, and for the next few days said nothing.

The sanitation men caved in first. Hundreds of the unemployed turned out for the strenuous but well-paid jobs, and before long it became apparent that at least a fifth of the strikers would have no jobs to return to. The teachers capitulated next. In Boston there were thousands of highly educated, underemployed people only too willing to work in the schools. In a matter of days, labor unity shattered, the union leaders began negotiations with the Governor to beg for the jobs of those they had led out on strike. Wilson was generous in victory. Almost all who had gone out would be allowed to return to work, and the state would seek no reprisals against union officials (except for the police) who had led the walkout.

Wilson had won, and his popularity soared.

Without leaving the state, he immediately became the front-runner for the Republican nomination for President of the United States.

Jimmy Carter had been a popular President, but his personality so dominated the office that despite his efforts to support his Vice President, the Democratic party was once again adrift. Had the election been held in his seventh year of office, there could be little doubt his party would have won, but 1984 was a year of stress and crisis. The collapse of the pound and the British economy had sent the stock market into a tailspin, as cautious corporations began to retrench and lay off first thousands, then hundreds of thousands of workers. Unemployment and recession struck with a ferocity unmatched in several decades. But there was more. Carter's refusal to intervene in any way after the Communist victory in Italy alienated many Catholics, particularly after Pope Pius fled to Madrid and not very subtly alluded to those who stood by while civilization collapsed. The year saw its first 1960's-style inner city riot in St. Louis, a bloody event set off as much by six days of record heat and some mismanaged police tactics as any racial confrontation. Nevertheless, the American people were worried, troubled, and fearful.

The election was close, and the campaign bitter. But Thomas Wilson was able to eke out a narrow margin of victory. Despite all the speeches and all the debates and all the position papers, he entered the presidency much as he had the governorship: he had no idea what to do.

Even though the Washington *Post* had called him "the perfect candidate for 1984," and others had dubbed him "Plastic Man, the media creation," President Wilson very much wanted to do a good job. But while he exuded confidence in public, he and his closest associates knew him to be weak and indecisive. His election had been based, as much as anything, on his reputation for firmness and determination, and Wilson himself was quite capable of believing this masterfully contrived image, even acting out the role in the presence of those who had constructed it. The presidency, it is said, changes the man. Professional politicians know this is nonsense—a bit of national wishful thinking—but President Wilson embraced the myth wholeheartedly: the greatness he ardently sought would come to the occupant of the Oval Office with a mystical force, a kind of patriotic Holy Ghost. When things went well, he became what his creators had said he was—the confident, determined Chief Executive. When things did not go well, however, he was a different man.

As much as anyone, Arthur Greenbaum had created Wilson's public image. Greenbaum was a certifiable genius, the E. Power Biggs of the political pipe organ. Tom Wilson was his greatest discovery, and he rode the younger man's career directly into a powerful Cabinet post. Arthur Greenbaum, Secretary of Health, Education, and Welfare, friend and chief advisor to the President, the most powerful powerbroker in half a century, should have been a happy man. He was not.

Thomas Wilson bothered him. It could simply have been that Arthur Greenbaum found the man unbearably dull. He had almost choked with laughter when an aide had described Wilson as "a man of impeccable shallowness." Except for prearranged and perfectly choreographed public events, Wilson was probably the least sociable president since Coolidge. On television or before a sympathetic crowd, the Commander-in-Chief radiated self-assurance, but in private, he was vacillating. When Arthur Greenbaum had chosen him for Republican candidate for Governor, he rather liked the young anchorman; he was good looking, charming, and only a little pompous. In the White House his private charm had all but vanished, and what humility he possessed disappeared totally. In victory, the President was usually arrogant, cocky. Under pressure or facing a defeat, he typically blustered, became devious and paranoid, seeking solitude and the comfort of the bottle. In his heart, Greenbaum knew that this creation, his political "superstar," was not entirely sane, though probably only he and the First Lady understood that the pressures of the office were breaking rather than making the man. Greenbaum prayed that a true national or international crisis would not arise during the years remaining in the Wilson presidency. The result could be disastrous.

14

The White House

President Wilson strode into the Cabinet Room, smiling and nodding at the sixteen men and two women already gathered there. He had wanted to put off this meeting of the National Security Council, but Greenbaum was insistent.

"Mr. President," the HEW Secretary said, going to Wilson's side, "I would like to introduce Dr. Harold Jonas, the Director of the National Institutes of Health . . ."

"Ah, yes. We've met before. Nice to see you, Jonas." The President shook hands.

"And Dr. Eric Zimmermann, who was recently appointed to the Deputy Director's position at the Center for Disease Control . . . Dr. Simon Carey-Ross of NIH . . . and Dr. Henry Rogers, the Chief of Statistical Analysis at the Institutes." The President shook the hand of each in turn and murmured a few pleasantries. He eyed Rogers a bit suspiciously. For one thing, his grip was weak and his hand moist. Rogers had taken the trouble to have his best suit cleaned and pressed for the occasion, but he still looked disheveled and out of place among the elegantly tailored suits and uniforms in the Cabinet Room.

"Thank you for coming, Dr. Rogers," Wilson said pleasantly. "Secretary Greenbaum has outlined to me your, uh, discovery. Please, gentlemen, take your seats."

Everyone sat, and the President began in a firm voice. "The first thing I want to emphasize is the absolute necessity for keeping this matter a complete secret. Any leaks will jeopardize national security. All right, Arthur, it's your show."

Greenbaum made a few introductory remarks outlining his conversation with Sir Nicholas Rawlings in England, and the simultaneous discovery by Dr. Rogers that there was a very sudden increase in the number of cancer cases in the United States. He then introduced Zimmermann, who stood by an easel and flipped through a series of graphs and charts. He spoke uninterrupted almost twenty minutes.

"In sum, Mr. President, while we have no idea as to the cause of this outbreak, there is no longer any doubt that the situation is a grave one. With each passing day, we have more and more evidence to indicate that this is a nationwide epidemic, perhaps worldwide." He gestured toward a multicolored map of the United States. Counties with the least unusual number of cancer cases were indicated by light green; those with the most, ranged from red to purple to black. "Immediate action must be taken to undertake a huge research effort to find the cause and, one hopes, a way to stop the spread of the disease. There is very little time left."

Zimmermann sat down, and the room was silent. President Wilson rose and walked over to the map. It was mostly red. A few areas were the color of clotted blood.

"I understand you have already begun to draft plans for the research effort."

"That's correct, Mr. President," Greenbaum answered. "Code name Caduceus, after Mercury's staff and the symbol of the medical profession . . ."

"Very well, Arthur. Caduceus it is. For the time being, we can arrange virtually unlimited funding. But keep in mind that Mercury was famous for moving fast. This will be one hell of a hard secret to keep for very long."

"But sir," Rogers asked nervously, "aren't you going to tell the people? I mean, declare a state of emergency or something?"

"Certainly not," Wilson said peevishly. "What good will it do us to panic the American people?"

General McElyea, Chairman of the Joint Chiefs, cleared his throat. "Mr. President, I assume that the Pentagon and other agencies should begin working out contingency models in the event Mr., I mean Dr., Zimmermann's theory is correct?"

"It's not theory. It's fact," Zimmermann said, raising his voice. Greenbaum shot him an angry look and silenced him.

The President looked calm, but his voice trembled slightly as he spoke. "Certainly, General, but I want it limited to the smallest group possible. We can't afford any leaks. A national panic could be every bit as bad as the disease itself. It is still possible that these learned gentlemen have misinterpreted their data. Maybe the rate will slow. Maybe it will reverse itself. I repeat. This entire matter must be kept Top Secret."

Zimmermann's face was pale with anger. Williams of the CIA was about to say something, but he interrupted. "I'm very sorry if you don't believe us, sir. . . ."

"I didn't say that, Dr. Zimmermann. So don't put words in my mouth." Wilson's voice was threatening. "And don't tell me how to do my job. *I* am the President, and at the appropriate time *I* will inform the proper Congressional leaders and the public. Your group will have a free hand with research and we will immediately begin contingency planning, but I will not have an unnecessary panic in this country."

Eric's voice was controlled, and he chose his words carefully. "I understand, sir, but I must point out that, in our estimation, we will not only have a problem finding enough hospital beds to care for the victims—we won't have enough *hotel* rooms to put them in, let alone enough physicians to care for them. Unless we discover what's behind this plague, there might not be enough people left to have a decent panic!"

"Thank you, Dr. Zimmermann," Arthur Greenbaum said firmly, "we understand how serious the situation may become. In the meantime, I suggest you leave it to the President how and when he will break the news to the American people. Unless there are further questions," he paused and looked around the room, "I suggest you get going on the Caduceus project. As you pointed out, you don't have a great deal of time."

Rogers, Zimmermann, Jonas, and Carey-Ross rose and started to leave. Carey-Ross, who had said nothing during the meeting, turned. "Mr. President," he said softly, "before long you won't have to worry about leaks or the timing of the announcement." Wilson looked at him quizzically. "When thirty or forty million Americans suddenly develop cancer, I think someone is likely to notice."

The meeting of the National Security Council lasted only a few minutes after the scientists had left. Several Cabinet officers were asked to begin contingency planning, but only under very tight security. Finally, the President rose, signaling that the meeting was adjourned. He glanced at Zimmermann's map, winced, and asked Greenbaum and Bill Williams of the CIA if they could spare a few minutes alone with him.

15

The Oval Office

After the meeting ended, President Wilson led Greenbaum and Williams into the Oval Office.

"I'd like to know your personal opinions on this matter. We've taken precautions to avoid panicking the public, but I wonder if *we* are not the ones who are panicking." The President sat on a small butter-colored couch and toyed with a ballpoint, continually snapping it open and shut. He looked at the two men sitting opposite him. "I mean, what have we actually got? Cancer is on the upswing. I grant that. But it has been for years, decades, as I understand it. Now we find there's a sudden statistical jump taking place over the past four or five months, initially only a fraction of a decimal point increase, but now coming on more rapidly. Right so far?"

"Right, Mr. President," said Greenbaum.

"Now understand that I'm not trying to *minimize* the potential consequences of this trend. But at the moment we are really talking about something under twenty thousand cases above average expectations. Even that young doctor, uh, Zimmermann, admitted there's no certainty this won't stop right now at the present level.

And," he continued, "nobody can offer any explanation or even a theory to explain why this would happen."

"I see what you're driving at, sir, but keep in mind what Arthur was told in England. They seem to think this cancer thing is already out of control," said Williams.

"Right now I think the British would jump if Lichtenstein said boo. They're edgy, half-expecting the next disaster as inevitable. I half-suspect they love their troubles. Another chance to display the stiff upper lip and all that. They wallow in it, poor bastards. And that's what I'm getting at."

"Tom, Mr. President," said Greenbaum, "Rawlings is an outstanding scientist. I know him, and I very much doubt if he would overreact. What he's seen terrifies him, and he's no fool."

"No, no, you misunderstand. We've got to keep on top of this, right on top. I just think they may be overly susceptible to panic, that's all. *I'm* not going to panic. Every branch of this administration is going to be pulling on this team. But think what would happen if we tell the people there's an epidemic, a plague, and it turns out we're wrong. Just think of that. We have to marshal all our facts, all our troops. Right now it looks like a crisis, and we'll know for sure in the next few months. I just want everyone to remain calm, not to go off the deep end. . . ." He paused.

"Well, of course, we . . ." Williams began.

Wilson interrupted, "I don't want us to lose our cool. Remember that swine flu thing? Our friends at NIH looked pretty silly then. The damn thing never happened and more people were hurt from the shots than any disease. Flu is one thing, cancer is another—everybody's scared of cancer. It hits home."

"But we can't just look the other way. This has the potential of becoming the greatest crisis since the Second World War," insisted Greenbaum.

"Of course, Arthur, I'm just urging that we all keep calm. (Greenbaum thought that if Wilson told them to be calm just once more, he would scream.) A crisis of this magnitude calls for presidential leadership, and don't you worry, I will be prepared when and if the time comes to supply that leadership. Our greatest presidents have all had to face a test. A test under fire. With God's help, I can weather this storm, and lead our nation to, uh, victory over fear and panic. Americans are great people, they will respond . . ."

"Mr. President," Greenbaum interrupted brusquely, "we all have faith in the people and in your leadership. But what do we do *now?*" He punctuated the last word with a surprisingly loud thump on an end table. As Wilson had lectured about calm, he felt a sense of panic, a deep spiritual and physical nausea. Tom Wilson was already trying to run away. He had no idea what to do—he was rambling on like a stump orator trying to convince himself the situation would go away if he just sat tight.

"What we do *now,* Arthur, is fund the Caduceus Group with whatever they need to do the job." President Wilson looked annoyed.

Williams stirred uncomfortably. "I'd like to make a few suggestions, if I may." Wilson nodded. "I'm sure Caduceus will be soliciting data from a great many foreign governments, to see if this is a localized or an international problem. I don't want to interfere with this in any way, but if Dr. Zimmermann and you agree, I would suggest that the Agency could efficiently and quietly supply them with most of what they need. This would avoid letting the cat out of the bag right away."

"Good idea. Speak with them, Arthur. Explain it." Wilson sat back, smiling serenely but nervously clicking his pen. "Go on."

"Second, and I'm afraid this could be a problem of diplomacy for you, Arthur. NIH must keep extraordinarily careful records of the cancer incidence throughout the country and the rest of the world. But I'm afraid that, for the time being, they are going to have to continue to modify their weekly and monthly statistics. Same for the Center for Disease Control and any of the other Federal health agencies. Only the leadership of the Caduceus Group and, of course, the executive branch should have access to the entire picture. If we don't modify the statistics, it's only a matter of time before someone blows the whistle."

"By modify, you mean falsify, Bill," Secretary Greenbaum said quietly. "But we have no other choice. If it blows over as President Wilson thinks it may, we can adjust them with some excuse. If not . . . we can certainly justify the action in the face of a national emergency."

"Can we do that legally?" asked the President, lighting a thin black cigar. "Answer carefully, boys, everything you say is on tape." Wilson grinned his famous grin and, leaning toward the two, whispered, "I only wish it were."

Williams looked at him evenly and said, as if for the records, "Mr. President, I am not a lawyer, but in my opinion you have no choice. As far as I know, there is no legal reason why, on executive order from yourself, the DHEW statistics cannot be temporarily modified in order to prevent panic and possible civil or international chaos." Williams smiled at President Wilson. "Will that do it, Mr. President?" He knew that every conversation conducted in the Oval Office (but not in any of the other meeting rooms of the White House) was taped. This fact was, of course, a top-ultra-super-eyes-only secret, but the Director of the Central Intelligence Agency was denied few secrets. Especially with three of his own agents in the White House, including Wilson's beloved personal secretary.

"Fine, Bill, fine," Wilson said, beaming, "anything else?"

"Yes, sir. I think we will have to run intensive, but discreet, security checks on everyone associated with Caduceus. . . ."

"Oh, come now, Bill," Greenbaum interrupted, "all these people have been checked before. Cloak and dagger . . ."

"Arthur, Arthur, you misunderstand. I'm not in any way questioning the loyalty of your people. Zimmermann, Rogers, Jonas, Carey-Ross, the lot. No. I just want to make sure the staff they employ–and it will have to be a large one–is reliable. I'm sure you agree we don't want some unstable clerk or lab technician running to the press or networks with this story. I just want to make sure everyone involved at this stage is relatively stable, relatively trustworthy. I'm not looking for Russian agents . . ."

President Wilson's voice was brittle, "Why not, Bill? Why the hell not?"

"Sir?" Williams asked.

"Listen, has it occurred to anyone that this whole thing could be some plot, some conspiracy instigated by this country's enemies to panic us. . . ." Wilson's voice cracked. Embarrassed, he angrily stubbed out his cigar. Greenbaum had not seen him take a single puff.

"What I'm saying," he continued in a calmer voice, "is that we have to examine every possibility. I am astonished, Mr. Williams, that you have not considered the possibility of biological warfare against the U.S. If what Zimmermann says is true—and he certainly was convincing this afternoon—then what he describes sounds to me like some viral or chemical assault."

"I have every intention of investigating that possibility, Mr. President. Though to my knowledge the Soviets have neither the capability nor, at this time, the willingness to . . ."

"I don't want to argue," Wilson said quietly. "Even you can't know everything that goes on in the world, Bill. We have to check the Russians first, but there's the Chinese. . . ."

"Which ones? There are almost eleven countries, and the number changes every week. The civil war . . ."

"Listen, I don't need a lecture on the Far East. What I'm saying is that every avenue must be explored. *Anyone* could have launched this attack. Russian, Chinese, Italians, hell, some little scientist in Laos could have stumbled on this thing. We have many enemies in the world, Bill. . . ."

"I know, Mr. President, but . . ."

"No buts—just check it, and thoroughly. I want progress reports every couple of days."

"Yes, sir."

"I'm not paranoid, you understand," Wilson said, lighting another cigar, "but the President has to know the facts before he can act."

"I understand, sir," Williams was calm, passive. Inwardly, he raged, shouted, but nobody ever got to be Director of the CIA by telling his superiors, let alone the President of the United States, that he was a fool. "Anything else?"

"Yes," said Wilson, his voice calmer. "I very much agree with your idea to check out the NIH people. That Dr. Rogers, for example, looked, I dunno, suspicious."

"Henry Rogers has had one of the most distinguished careers in all of NIH. From what I've heard, he's a genius, a brilliant statistician as well as a medical doctor. Really, Tom, to judge a man like Rogers on his looks. . . ."

"Secretary Greenbaum," Wilson said, emphasizing the formal title, "I am simply doing my best to get to the bottom of this perplexing and, I must say, *suspicious* situation. Now from what I'm told, within the next year or so, one quarter of the American people are going to develop cancer almost overnight. Now if this is not some bio-war strike from a foreign enemy," he nodded at Williams, "then we have to explore the possibility that another government or a group within this country is trying to panic us into a hasty and embarrassing series of decisions. I can't see the purpose of the plot, but *this* president will not be rushed into rash actions."

"Mr. President," Greenbaum began.

"Let me finish. I'm just throwing this out, but I want it investigated, Bill. There could be a dozen reasons why certain groups, certain *people* could concoct this story or falsify Mr. Rogers' precious data to panic him and send him to us crying 'the sky is falling.' Are he and Zimmermann politically active? Are they Democrats?"

Williams looked sick, and Greenbaum exploded. Jumping from his chair he shouted, "Shit, Tom, the fucking country is about to go to pieces and you want to blame the Democrats. Now talk sense. This ain't Massachusetts. There are no Kennedys under the bed. You're right, this could be, and I'm sorry to say it probably will be, your baptism by fire. God help us all. But don't start looking for an easy way out. There isn't one. I only wish there were."

"Please sit down, Arthur," Wilson said, rising and touching his friend's arm. He continued calmly, "The buck will inevitably stop here, Arthur. I have to explore every possibility, every option, before I can take action; you understand that. All I was saying, just hypothetically mind you, was that a small group of people may have juggled those figures, simply to produce this result: the President, his closest advisor, the director of the CIA and, by tomorrow, man of the best minds of this government concentrating their energies o an imaginary monster. I'm not saying that's what's happening. I jus want every avenue explored. That's all."

Greenbaum looked mollified, and Wilson turned to Williams. " expect the Central Intelligence Agency, in liaison with the FBI, o course, to check out everyone associated with Caduceus. In addition I want thorough, repeat thorough, investigations of everyone wh presently knows of this so-called cancer epidemic or might hav concocted the statistics that have so upset the scientists at th Institutes. When can I have this?"

"Most of it in about a week. Perhaps ten days for the balance," said Williams.

"And the possibility of a Russian or Chinese strike?"

"A general analysis of capability within twenty-four hours Beyond that, it's hard to say. A week or two, I suppose."

"Fine, fine," Wilson said. "And I want someone on the inside."

"Inside?" Greenbaum beat Williams to the question.

"Inside Caduceus. Someone trustworthy and knowledgeable. want a man who will report directly to you, Bill. I'm sure scientist like Rogers and Zimmermann are great Americans, but I want t know what's happening as soon as they do. Scholars tend to b cautious. I know, I was one," Wilson said, smiling at the tw somber men. "They want to get all the details straight before the come up with a conclusion. Well, this may be an extraordinar event. I want to know what they're thinking. How they'r speculating—particularly. I want to know what their reports will sa before they even write them. My heart tells me this Caduceu adventure will end up as a bad joke, but my brain says it could b the greatest crisis this country's ever faced. I want to be prepared fo it. Bill, can you get someone inside?"

Williams hesitated for a moment, and said, "I'd say it's a goo possibility."

"Splendid," Wilson said, rising. He showed the two men to th door of the Oval Office. "I won't let you down," he said warmly.

"We know that, Mr. President," Williams replied. Greenbaum nodded and smiled wanly.

For a full ten minutes after they had left, the President sat and thought about what he had heard that day. He felt an unusual combination of elation and terror. He had no idea of what to do: that was the source of the terror. But the opportunity of facing his first real crisis, possibly one greater than any president had ever faced, filled him with a curious exhilaration. He crossed the room and opened an inconspicuous door that would have been thought a closet. With the door's opening, lights went on, revealing a five-foot-long room complete with an oak bar, wine racks, and two refrigerators. He paused for a moment, making up his mind, then mixed a pitcher of Manhattans.

There were no further appointments, and he had to think.

16

New York City

Francis X. Feeley did some of his best writing at Bradley's. It was not a large bar, but it was a Village institution, known for good, simple food and excellent jazz. That was at night. During the hours between 2:30 and 5:30 in the afternoon, Bradley's was deserted. Feeley would sit at the far end of the bar, his books and papers spread around him, near the only window. It gave him good light and a view of the passing scene on University Place. Village burghers, students, faded flower children now entering their mid-forties, pretty girls: all passed by. But few looked in the window, and almost none entered. The window was like Feeley's private television screen, and he spent hours staring at it when he was trying to write an especially difficult piece. On a warm day, Bradley's was cool, dark, woody and, above all, quiet. Feeley was not only comfortable there (he had once estimated that over the years he had consumed close to 2,000 bottles of Heineken sitting at that bar), but it was the only place he had credit. The owner, a quiet and pleasant man named John (Bradley and his partner, Jerry, had long since retired) willingly extended credit to his favorite customers and would let a tab ride for months before he politely, almost deferentially, mentioned the matter. Not surprisingly, John was rarely stuck with a bad debt, though he sometimes had to wait for a promised royalty statement, the sale of a canvas, or the long awaited marriage of an alimonied ex-wife.

That day, Feeley looked out the window a lot. His editor had suggested (ordered) a piece for the Sunday *News* explaining to the housewives of Queens–and their children who were looking for a good science fair project–nothing less than the mysteries of the universe.

"Make it simple, Frank," he had said, "avoid the hard stuff. People are interested in space and the future. Science fiction is all the rage. Just skim over what the physicists are thinking about, trying to figure out. Just give the *overview,*" said the editor, using his favorite word. Feeley had nodded in agreement, his heart sinking. It was an impossible assignment, but a Sunday piece was an extra three hundred dollars, money he needed badly.

Any one of the dozen science reporters at the *Times* would have carefully explained to his or her editor that the article was impossible to write and in polite, modulated tones told the editor to shove it up his ass. But Frank Feeley was not a reporter at the *Times.* He was the lowest-paid full-fledged and bylined reporter at the *Daily News,* the man who ran the science desk and was also the entire staff of the science desk. Some years before, it had been made very clear to him that the management of the *News* was not at all sure it even needed a science reporter. In status, he ranked several notches below the Inquiring Photographer and Suzy, the Decorating Tips writer.

Still, the distinct lack of interest in his work had its advantages. He had few deadlines to meet. He was not badly paid, considering the amount of work he did. He spent quite a few mornings puttering in bookstores and quite a few afternoons in bars talking with friends. An excellent writer and a fast study, Feeley had been known to whip out a good feature in longhand in the midst of an hour-long argument about baseball. The City Editor had trouble thinking of decent stories for him to cover, so fully half his pieces concerned the latest Health Department restaurant violations.

Rodent hairs, vermin, and mouse droppings littered his journalistic life.

Feeley was an accepting sort, and he admitted to himself that an easy job was better than a prestigious and demanding one. And infinitely better than no job at all. So he sat at Bradley's and tried to comprehend the secrets of quarks, pulsars, black holes, white holes, particles with "charm," particles with "lust," and now the "snark." All he could determine was that the snark acted like matter, but once it got moving, was not matter, or antimatter, for that matter. The name had come from a theoretical physicist, a lover of Lewis Carroll, who had set out to prove that such a phenomenon was impossible. It was all theory, but it seemed that a snark with a good head of steam could exceed the speed of light with ease, but when it decided to slow down it acted like matter again. Feeley poured over clippings from the *Times, Newsweek, Science Digest,* and half a dozen more scholarly publications, trying to figure out how he could describe the particle or, as *Time* had defined it, "matter that really isn't." He would have left the whole thing out except that the seeming ability of the particle to exceed the speed of light had excited a great many nonscientists, who wanted to harness the little devils and spend their next vacation out by Andromeda. Feeley cringed as he wrote that snarks had already "set Einstein spinning in his grave. There is much more to be learned about the elusive snark, but is it too great a leap of the imagination to speculate that this sounds like the beginning of intergallactic travel?" Feeley uttered an audible "yuchh," put down his pen, and looked down the bar to order another Heineken.

He was both pleased and embarrassed to see John coming toward him. Feeley hadn't paid his bill in almost three months, and not counting today's damage, it was close to three hundred dollars.

"Another, Frank?" John asked pleasantly.

"Yeah, thanks, John." John poured the beer and looked up.

"How come you're here today? Rick should be coming on now. You tryin' to save on the help?" Feeley instantly regretted bringing up the topic of money.

"He's sick," John said sadly. "Over at St. Vincent's. I saw him last night, and he said he was going to be transferred to Memorial. He looks pretty good, but lost some weight, and he's pretty weak. His spirits are good." John looked away and unnecessarily wiped a clean part of the bar.

"Memorial," Feeley said in a hushed tone, "I don't believe it. Why he's no more'n twenty-six, twenty-eight . . ."

"Twenty-five," John said. "Twenty-five next month."

"That's a shame," Feeley said sincerely, "cancer at that age." Memorial only admitted cancer patients. "What's he got?"

"It's something they usually find in kids, I think, but I may be wrong about that," John replied. "It's a kind of brain tumor. Sits on the brain stem and keeps the spinal fluid from getting to the brain. He said he was throwing up a lot most mornings. Morning sickness, he called it. Went to the doctor, then right to St. Vincent's, now Memorial. All in two weeks and a couple of days."

"Medulloblastoma," Feeley said.

"That's it. That's what Dr. Feldman called it."

"Who?"

"You know, the guy who comes in here most nights around six and has two martinis, very dry, straight up, with a twist?" John could see he was not getting through. "Silver hair. He's always trying to get everybody to read Anthony Powell."

"Got it. I didn't know he was a doctor," Feeley said.

"Well he is, and he said the same as you. I remember medulla and blast. Gotta be the same thing."

"Did they operate?" Feeley asked.

"Rick said only exploratory. Then they decided not to chance a full-scale operation. Is that bad?"

"Probably. It's probably spread, and it's a bitch to get the whole tumor out of the brain in any event. If they're not going to try to operate, and he's not real weak, my guess is they're shipping him off to Memorial for study and maybe a shot at some new cancer drug or therapy. But it doesn't sound good." Feeley looked into his glass and then began to gather his papers.

"What you're saying, Frank, is that Rick's chances are bad. That he's going to die of this thing when he's barely twenty-five. I just don't believe it. Big, healthy guy like him."

"It happens, John, believe me. But don't listen to me. I'm no doctor. He may live. . . ."

"Dr. Feldman said the same as you," John said sadly. "I just can't understand it. Guess you never know."

"Nope, you surely don't." Feeley gathered up his papers, signed the check, and left.

17

Bethesda, Maryland

Henry Rogers' career had been built on an almost mystical faith in numbers. He always remembered the words of a mathematics professor at Columbia when he was studying for his doctorate in statistical analysis: "Give me enough data, and the tools to sort them, and I can move the world." It was a metaphor, of course, but Rogers came close to accepting it as fact. Numbers were representations, compilation, symbols, which, like the dots on a pointillist painting, could be combined to show truths the senses were unable to grasp. Rogers was one of the premier statistical artists in the world. Early in his career, he demonstrated that workers who had been exposed to polyvinyl chloride at any time in their working lives ran a significant chance of contracting angiosarcoma, a relatively rare kind of liver cancer. Since workers often change jobs many times in a lifetime, and since it often took ten to fifteen years to develop into a malignancy, Rogers' discovery of the one significant variable common to all the victims was a brilliant piece of detective work. His work on diet and arthritis and patterns of bacterial resistance to antibiotics were not as conclusive, but were justly described as breakthroughs.

So, as his computer capacity grew almost daily, nourished with a surge of data from around the country and the world, Rogers intuitively believed that the answer to the cancer scourge was there to be found–if he just knew how to ask the question and where to look. The organization of the Caduceus Group was never clearly defined. Zimmermann was given overall responsibility for the effort by Secretary Greenbaum and the President. This had outraged a great many people, including Zimmermann's technical superior at CDC, but the Secretary had been firm. In addition, Zimmermann was to appoint division heads to oversee the clinical research, field studies, and data analysis. Rogers was the obvious choice for the computer work, and in an unexpected stroke of diplomacy, Eric asked Dr. Jonas to run the clinical program. Headquarters were established at the Center for Disease Control in Atlanta, largely because of its superb biohazard facilities, though a great deal of the actual research was carried on in Bethesda. Rogers had flatly refused to leave the NIH campus for an office at the Center.

"But Henry," Zimmermann had argued, "I've got it all set up."

"Then take it apart. I'm not leaving Bethesda to try and hold together some jury-rigged operation down there."

"No, no, you don't understand. I want you down there. This isn't some field station, you know. In just three weeks we've put on line bigger and better computer facilities than at NIH."

"Look," Rogers said patiently, "I've worked in this same office for over ten years. I know just where everything is. Your hardware may be bigger, but I doubt if it's better. Anyway, I can plug into everything you've got. I don't want to get down there, move into some motel, not sleep well, work with a bunch of strangers. . . ."

"You can bring your staff, Henry. . . ."

"There are at least twenty-five key people I need on call here at all times. Each of them needs at least two or three people to work with. You're talking about a mass migration. I stay here."

"Well, I'll settle for a commuter, Henry. But don't get out of earshot." Zimmermann knew he was beaten. Rogers was probably right, but Eric admitted that they worked well together, constantly commenting, crossfertilizing, hypothesizing. Rogers was as intellectually stimulating as anyone he'd ever known.

"I don't know how I can stay out of earshot, Eric. A hot line right to your office here and another at my apartment. Both fire-engine red. I feel important. If I'm not caught in traffic, you'll always be able to get me."

"You're due to get a phone in your car by the end of the week, Henry. Plugs right into the NIH switchboard. No long-distance calls, now. Except to me, of course." Eric chuckled.

"Now I *do* feel important." The two spoke for some time about the continuing upward spiral of cancer figures, and their inability after almost a month to begin to explain the phenomenon.

"It's horrible, Eric," Rogers said, "cancer incidence has now more than doubled, case-fatality-ratio is even worse. Another month, it should double again. And then again. We can fuck with the figures for as long as we want, but pretty soon somebody's going to catch on."

"And then all hell breaks loose," Eric said quietly.

As time went by, even one as faithful as Henry Rogers began to doubt he would ever find what he was looking for–a connection, a significant variable, a breakthrough. He sorted the figures, sifted them again, all but caressed them, but the answer he sought was elusive. Ironically, part of the problem was due to Caduceus itself. Millions, perhaps billions, of databits were now in the memory banks. He was swamped with information, most of which was probably useless, though there was no way of knowing that in advance. He was accustomed to finding the proverbial needle in a haystack. This was like trying to find a needle in a pin factory. He worked for weeks without success, chainsmoking his way through countless readouts and models. He was used to this feeling of impotence, the inability to ask the right question of the all-knowing but ever silent sphinx of a computer. A simple task of analysis, that he turned over to several of his assistants, involved taking the number of "basic" occupations (1,500) and correlating them, if possible, with the varieties of the disease (over 100). This easy program involved more than 150,000 databits, which, when correlated with age, sex, race, locale, ethnicity, and so forth, quickly ran into millions of fragments of information. It was nevertheless "easy" since such programs were the bread and butter of the NIH and CDC analysis and had been for years. These extensive programs revealed nothing Rogers had not already seen outlined in his original scan. The model was the same, but the figures grew worse with each passing day.

Rogers was ready to concede there was no secret to be found in the cancer statistics. For several days he worked with enormous intensity. Virtually all his staff's preliminary programs were completed, and he examined them all very carefully, only taking calls from Zimmermann and a few colleagues. He despaired of a breakthrough, or even the suggestion of one.

Until the evening of the third day.

It almost slipped by. Most of the geographical representations were based on a state-by-state, county-by-county map. A handful of counties showed a very slightly lower incidence of cancer cases, but not significantly so. Rogers had asked for a closer look at these counties, and promptly forgot about them. Tired and blurry eyed, he almost did not notice the few numbers in the columns of the printout that would prove so important. Running his index finger down the page, he paused, blinked, flipped several more pages and then dove for the terminal. It was there all right: in at least six remote districts of the United States, the incidence of cancer was normal.

He had to tell Zimmermann.

18

Atlanta

Eric Zimmermann did not answer Rogers' call. For one thing, Henry had forgotten to use the "hot line" so recently installed in his office and already half-buried under papers. For another, Eric had spent the late afternoon briefing a new and valuable addition to the Caduceus staff, Dr. Honorée Hennessey. And he spent the early evening having sex with his esteemed colleague.

He had seen her by chance that morning at CDC, and he instantly chided himself for neglecting to think of her for the staff before.

"Honorée!" he called out as she passed him in the crowded reception area for the Center's main building. "Where did you drop from? God, it must be over two years."

Initially startled, Dr. Hennessey showed genuine pleasure at seeing Eric. "Almost exactly two years, Eric. How wonderful to see you again. I've just got in, but to be honest, I'd completely forgotten you'd become a big honcho here. Congratulations. I was delighted to hear of your promotion. . . ."

"Enough of that. You may genuflect at another time." Eric's eyes twinkled as he looked at the tall, fashionably dressed woman. "What

I want to know is where you've been. What have you been doing How come you're here? Oh, hell, c'mon."

He took her arm and led her out of the crowded lobby and to hi office on the fifteenth floor. "Nice digs, Eric," she exclaimed as the entered his large, beautifuly appointed office. Two walls were floo to-ceiling glass and looked out at the distant Atlanta skyline. "Ver nice indeed. And that secretary of yours . . ."

"That secretary has a doctorate in microbiology. And m predecessor here seems to have spent a fair amount of his tim decorating this office. Now, sit and tell me where you've been hidin yourself."

Honorée chose a comfortable-looking armchair. "Well, let's se After the Milan conference, I was in Boston for a while. Then couple of grants from a variety of sources. Did quite a bit c traveling on the beneficence of said grants. I was at Cambridge las summer working with Manley on circulatory diseases. . . ."

"I thought you were in love with the pancreas," Zimmerman said.

"Still am, Eric, but it's all connected. All connected." Her voic was deep, soft, almost caressing. Though he would have been har put to explain it, Zimmermann found that her remark about it a being connected made him think of sex. For an instant, he imagine two bodies, naked and sweating, coupled in an ecstatic embrace. H cleared his throat.

"It's lucky I ran into you, Honorée," he said, blushing ever s slightly under his deep tan. "I was going to get in touch with yo anyway."

"All you good-looking guys say that." She rose and went to th window. "You never called me after Milan."

"I did. I called you in New York. Remember? We weren't able t get together."

"I'm sorry, my darling, I'd forgotten. I guess we've both bee running around and devoting ourselves to business rather tha pleasure." Honorée turned from the window and its stunning view and smiled brightly. Once again Eric pictured the naked couple, thi time engaged in oral sex.

"Honorée, I want you to work with me. And I was going to call you about it. We're onto something very big and need all the help . . ."

She cut him off. "Eric, I'd love to, but I have a grant that runs for another six months, and so far I haven't made much progress."

It was Eric's turn to interrupt. "Screw the grant. I'll fix that." He saw the look of disbelief flicker briefly in her large green eyes, and he continued in a softer tone. "Honest, kid, I can do it, and honest again, I need all the good minds I can put together. What I'm working on has the highest priority. Direct from the President. Please, I need you in Caduceus."

"In what?"

"I'll explain. If you can occupy yourself until one o'clock, we can have lunch and I can fill you in."

"No problem, Eric. I'm here to do some computer work anyway. Look, you're obviously busy. Why don't we have a drink tonight?"

"Tonight," Eric said, "you are having dinner with me."

"On orders from the President?"

"Yes, and if you refuse, I'll have you drafted." Eric grinned. After further negotiations, and consultation of their schedules, it was decided that Eric would work through lunch and get out early for a drink and then dinner. He led her out of the office, past his secretary ("Doctorate in microbiology, my ass," she whispered. "I'll explain," he said.), and past two bored-looking men in the outer office. ("Looks like something out of an old Charles Bronson movie," she murmured. "Security. I'll explain," he said.)

Eric did explain. About Caduceus. About the President. About the cancer scourge.

Honorée appeared intrigued, then shocked, and finally stunned.

"It's incredible. Doesn't make any sense at all. I believe you, Eric, but I just can't believe *it.* Of course I'll help in any way I can. You know I've no experience in cancer research."

"Neither do I. But I do know you have a variety of scientific interests. And you spent a great deal of your graduate and postgraduate years studying viral infections." He paused, toying with his drink.

"But what does that . . ."

"My personal opinion is that we've got a virus on our hands. God knows where it came from, though I wouldn't be surprised if it turns out to be someone was sloppy with their DNA research." He signaled for the check. "But that's just a hunch. We really have no leads at all. *None.*" Eric thumped the table and their dawdling waitress hurried over with the check. "It could be anything, Honorée, and we need the best minds we can come up with. Caduceus needs *you.*" She saluted solemnly, and he smiled. "And Honorée, *I* need you." Leaving the restaurant bar, they decided not to have dinner there after all. Eric pointed out that his apartment was nearby, and the food at the restaurant wasn't really very good and grossly overpriced, and anyway, he had two very fine steaks in his freezer and a microwave oven to thaw and cook them. And it was much more comfortable. Honorée said it was the best idea she'd heard in a long time.

They had met in Italy. Though Milan is more industrial than romantic, they were immediately attracted to one another. The conference they were attending was intellectually stimulating to be sure, but Eric quickly noticed that there were few female participants. He did chat with a radiantly beautiful biologist from Hungary, but it did not take him long to discover that her only passion was to serve the People and the Party. Eric did not attend such meetings to pick up young women, but he did wish he could find a good-looking woman to see whatever sights there were to see, when he was not delivering a paper or sitting on a panel. In truth, his libido rarely disrupted his professional life. Indeed, women seemed drawn to him, and ever since his midteens, he found that he was typically the object of seduction as much as the instigator. He was never callous about such affairs, though he found it difficult to become involved in more than an affectionate and mutually enjoyable sexual relationship. His work was paramount, and at the

Milan meeting, he delivered his most important paper to date on epidemiological theory and techniques. Still, after three exhilarating days of "shop talk" with colleagues from around the world, he yearned for a bit of companionship, if only to have dinner and go to La Scala. He had almost decided to invite the Hungarian when he first heard Honorée's laugh.

It is impossible to convey the sound of that laugh. It was not ladylike, but it was feminine. Intensely feminine. When Honorée was amused, truly amused, she whooped, a deep, throaty, and unintentionally sexy cry of unalloyed joy, which was virtually irresistible. Eric immediately spotted her. She was not far from him, but the cocktail party was crowded, and he had not noticed her. She wore a full-length black velvet, long-sleeved dress with a deep V-neckline, set off by a series of fine gold chain necklaces and delicate gold bracelets. He wondered how he could have missed her.

Like Eric Zimmermann, Honorée Hennessey did not attend scientific meetings to meet "eligible" men. She had only arrived that afternoon and would deliver a paper on viral analysis. But also, like Zimmermann, she had come to Italy not only for intellectual stimulation, but in the hope of spending a few days museum-hopping and exploring every tourist trap the area could provide. Like Eric, she had quickly sized up the men and decided she would do her exploring alone. Most of the males in the ballroom of the Hotel Principe were either old, married or, in a few cases, gay. Her whoop of delight was the result of a witticism delivered by a well-known Irish pathologist. He was young, to be sure, and tall—almost 6′4″—and there could be no doubt that he was heterosexual, since he regularly looked with discreet, if obvious, interest at Honorée's beautiful breasts. Alas, he was decidedly homely and horse-faced.

So when Eric moved over and introduced himself, it was convenience at first sight. To their mutual surprise, they discovered as the days went by that convenience became fondness and fondness, passion. No one could deny they made a very handsome couple. Before the conference was over, they had decided to take a few days and drive to Venice, and after two rainy days there, both cabled excuses home to the States and drove on to Rome. It was a real holiday for both of them, though both knew it would end. Theirs was one of those brief, romantic, and intensely passionate connections unique to world travellers and those who attend academic and professional meetings. Neither of them expected more than that—a brief affair—but each came to feel real affection for the other, as they drove through northern Italy, ate in small local restaurants, and slept in tiny rustic inns. When it was finally over, what they felt could have passed, for others, for love. But both had work to return to, and they parted with a kiss and sincere expressions of affection, if not love.

"I'll call you," Eric said.

"You have the number. I'll be there. Anytime."

They embraced while Eric's taxi driver fumed, and as he finally got into the cab to go to the airport, Zimmermann resolved that he would indeed call her. Honorée was something. He did not know what the feeling was that people called love, but he knew that Honorée was special.

Honorée Hennessey lay on Eric's bed and thought that this was going to be the most pleasurable assignment she had ever had. Neither promiscuous nor a prude, she had nevertheless known more than a dozen men, and she freely admitted that Eric was, without a doubt, the best lover of the lot. He was gentle, and above all, considerate. A woman would have to be an iceberg, she thought contentedly, not to get off when Eric was in charge. Which was also the problem. Eric was in charge. He went about his lovemaking in an almost calculated way. Each caress, every thrust, was designed to elicit the maximum response from his partner. It was intensely pleasurable: orgasm followed orgasm. He was good. Extraordinarily good, of that there could be no question. Still, she wondered if he ever allowed himself to let go, to selfishly give himself the brief, exquisite pleasure so many men found ideal. She despised such men, but Eric worked so damn hard. Every time, he sought to devastate his partner. Every time had to be ideal. He was even able, most of the time, to arrange that they came together. Honorée felt a little guilty as she lay in the big bed while Eric showered. She pulled the crisp sheet under her chin and scowled. The fact was that she enjoyed sex, did not wish to marry–for a while at least–and the fact was that Eric was five stars, aces, fireworks, every girl's dream. So what was wrong? What was wrong, she thought, was that Eric knew every move, every technique, and probably every reasonable position, but though he gave of himself physically, he remained emotionally distant. He was no automaton–he clearly enjoyed his work–but that was just it: he approached his work and his pleasure with the same determination, the same sense of proving he was the best. Eric was, she thought bitterly, a technician, but not the best lover. Because there was no real love involved. Fondness, to be sure, but no wild, abandoned passion. No room for error. To have sex with Eric was to receive enormous pleasure, but–that was it–not to be sure that it was as wonderful for him as it was for her. *The competitive instinct,* she thought. *Why not just enjoy it?* She could still feel the warm, relaxing tingle of their lovemaking. But Honorée wished she could play his part . . . that she could for once be in complete control . . . that she could dominate and drive him to a frenzy of sexual delight. Once that evening and several times after the Milan conference, she had tried during foreplay to take him over, and with her mouth and hand literally work on him–selflessly give him effortless pleasure. It didn't work. Every time, he would stop her, pull her to him, and of course, take over.

Eric stepped out of the bathroom and into the bedroom, a towel modestly wrapped around his hips.

"God, you're gorgeous," Honorée said sincerely.

"God, you're sexy," Eric replied, equally sincere.

He came over to her, still damp, and she caressed the hair on his stomach as he sat on the edge of the bed. *Ever ready,* she thought, noticing the gradual stiffening beneath the towel. "The phone rang when you were in the shower," she mentioned.

Eric stood up, losing his erection in a matter of seconds. "Which phone? This one?" He pointed to the receiver by the bed.

"No, the one in the living room. I didn't think it was important, or they'd call back later. Should I have . . ."

"Oh, it probably wasn't very important. You did the right thing. The one in this room is the hot line."

"Appropriate," Honorée said, stretching under the sheets and smiling.

Eric paused for a second, then returned her grin. He sat down again on the edge of the bed. Honorée once again began to stroke his chest and stomach.

"You know, Honorée, I hardly know you," he said softly. "No," he said, answering her ironic expression, "I mean it. I'd like to know more about you. You're special, Honorée: you really mean something to me, but I only know an outline of your life. No details, no . . ." Eric paused, searching for the right word.

"Databits?"

"Well, sort of. I don't know why you went into medicine, or research, for that matter. I don't know what's excited you in the past two years. . . ."

"Nothing as much as you have, baby," Honorée said, loosening the towel and stroking his genitals. "You know, Eric, you're the only uncircumcised guy I've ever known. I thought that everybody was the other way until I met you." She gently pulled back his foreskin.

"Not a matter of choice. My father believed it was unnatural. Lord knows he wasn't a flower child or a religious fanatic, but he believed men should be the way they were made. I suppose he wasn't circumcised himself, and wanted his only son to be like him. Does it bother you?"

"No way. I think it's very ... sexy." She gently moved his foreskin along the shaft of his penis. "Just unusual. But very nice, I assure you," Honorée said, smiling bewitchingly.

"Very nice indeed," she said, licking it. "Very, very nice."

Eric uttered something between a sigh and a groan. Honorée carefully examined his manhood, decided it was (like the rest of Zimmermann's body) larger than average and beautifully proportioned, and put her mouth over it. Eric allowed her to continue for a while, and then, to her mixed disappointment and delight, rolled his entire body onto the bed and for the third time that day, began to make love to her. Honorée once again felt Eric was in control. She once again was to feel his athletic body working to move her, to please her. *But this time,* she thought, *this time he really means it. This time there is more than superb technique. This time, perhaps, there is love too.*

It was no accident that Dr. Eric Zimmermann ran into Honorée Hennessey at CDC that morning. It had been arranged. The woman he was making love to, and the woman he was—to his astonishment—beginning to fall in love with, had been sent to Atlanta to fulfill the wish of President Wilson to have a "man inside." Dr. Honorée Hennessey was an employee of the National Security Agency.

19

Atlanta

Honorée Hennessey lay in Zimmermann's bed and listened to his soft, regular breathing. She was wide awake, though the iridescent dial of the digital clock read 5:00 A.M. She quietly slipped from the bed and tiptoed first to the bathroom, where she liberated a toothbrush and a mangled tube of Crest, and then to the kitchen. While she vigorously brushed, it occurred to her that there had been half a dozen extra brushes in the medicine cabinet. *The other women,* she mused. *How many have shared his bed?* She shrugged. *None of my business how many.*

Honorée made a pot of tea and sat down to think. The assignment had seemed both interesting and important, and when she had accepted it, her superior stressed that all she was to do was help Caduceus in any way possible and report any significant progress or snags directly to NSA. "You know how these things can bog down over petty disputes or personality conflicts," she had been told. "We can't allow that to happen. An independent observer was specifically requested by the President."

She sighed and lit a cigarette. She hated the taste, but for some reason Honorée felt it helped her think when she had a tough problem to solve. She sighed again and unintentionally blew a smoke ring. *So this is what you've become. Mata Hari. A spy. Spook. Bed the top guy and pump him for information while he's pumping you. Right on, sister! Let's hear it for the little lady with the Johns Hopkins degree, the doll who can actually read her own papers before scientific conclaves and be applauded! Wanna know about the pancreas? Here she is. Wanna know a man's innermost thoughts? Here she is again. Because this gal can use not only her brain, but also her body! Right on, sister!*

Honorée tasted her tea. It was cold.

She returned to the kitchen and put the kettle on the fire. No one had suggested she sleep with Eric as part of her assignment, and she very much doubted that even the NSA or CIA knew she and Zimmermann had been more than casual acquaintances. But now one of those she was supposed to be keeping an eye on shared her bed. It was a complicated situation. Honorée did not feel shame. She was, after all, working for the same government, and Eric himself had made it clear she would be of use to Caduceus. Still, she was troubled.

"You're up early."

Honorée jumped. Eric, naked, was standing next to her.

"Oh, you startled me. Sometimes I'm an early riser. Make you some tea?"

"Coffee, if you want to."

"My pleasure, handsome. Want something to eat? I can make it while you're washing up."

"No thanks. Coffee will be fine." Eric smiled and returned to the bedroom.

Honorée made the coffee and tried to push thoughts of betrayal from her mind. *Why the hell couldn't I have been a G.P.? Be like the others in my class at Hopkins?* She knew the answer. She could not stand the sight of sick people.

For Honorée Hennessey, disease could be viewed as an intellectual problem, a malfunction of the body to be analyzed, understood, and described in purely scientific terms. But disease is not an alien, abstract concept. It strikes people. It weakens them. It can bring torment, deformity, pain, and sometimes death. Honorée loved the study of medicine, but patients upset her: they were so pitiful and, well, ugly. Nor could she stand hospitals. No matter how immaculate they were, she was invariably overwhelmed by their smell—what was it? Sweat? Disinfectant? Fear? It nauseated her.

A life in pure research also held little attraction. The most "exciting" work was, almost by definition, the most plodding and painstaking, and she, like Eric, could not abide the typical administrator for whom she would have to work. When she confessed this to one of her professors he offered to call a friend at HEW. Perhaps after a few years of public health work she would be able to decide what she really wanted to do. Honorée was surprised to discover that, though her interviews were conducted at HEW headquarters on Constitution Avenue, it was quickly apparent she was not being considered for a career in public health. When she was at last offered a job with the National Security Agency (albeit with an HEW "cover"), she happily accepted. Her initial rating was high, the pay was excellent, and it was made quite clear she would never be involved in any way with covert activities or "dirty tricks."

It was a good job. Her title was "editor," and for the most part it was an accurate representation of her duties. A great deal of her work involved scanning medical journals in English, German, and Russian, searching for the first signs of any major research breakthroughs. She was consulted on the process of epidemics in foreign countries (a serious outbreak of disease could easily contribute to the discontent and toppling of fragile governments). Honorée particularly enjoyed creating speculative reports based on everything from public documents to "Top Secret" CIA reports. She won a commendation and a promotion for one paper estimating the capability of the Soviet Union for extensive biological warfare development in light of their backward computer technology. She was also encouraged to pursue her own research and attend scientific meetings.

Honorée Hennessey was not, therefore, a typical government employee or, for that matter, a typical member of the intelligence community. *I'm going to tell him.* She reconsidered. *I have a job to do.*

It's an honorable job. I won't hurt him. And anyway, one night does not a love affair make. Wait and see.

She heard Eric coming. He was dressed in jeans and a red sweater. She handed him his coffee.

"Thanks. Yet another reason it's nice to have you around here. You know, given enough warning and a good enough reason, I can whip up a damn good dinner for six in this little kitchen, but morning coffee is usually a disaster. Either I'm too impatient for the pot to boil, or I put it on when I'm in the shower and it boils away and burns the kettle. Don't laugh. I know an idiot can do it, but . . ." Honorée kissed his cheek.

"Well, it's six-thirty of a Sunday. What's the plan?"

Eric suddenly looked serious. "The plan is to go to work. Caduceus. Maybe I should've told you before you signed on that this is a seven-day-a-week operation. And most of those days are twelve to fourteen hours long."

"Seven days a week, huh?"

" 'Fraid so."

"I think I can take it."

Eric put both hands on her shoulders. "I'd hoped you'd say that."

20

The White Hou

Tom Wilson had begun to accept reality. With each passing day, i became more and more certain the cancer epidemic was not statistical fluke. It was also increasingly likely that sooner or later th public would find out about it. Some part of him knew his initia reaction had been one of panic, and he was still troubled an frightened by the implications of the crisis. But as the weeks went b and the evidence mounted, he found a previously untapped resourc of strength.

Greenbaum had helped in a way. A week after his meeting wit him and Williams, the two had returned to the Oval Office wit several initial reports. It was late in the afternoon of a particularl difficult day. The President made himself two quick stiff drink before they arrived, and when they entered the office had led them t the bar and told them to help themselves. The reports were basi enough. Williams told him that there was no initial indication of Soviet strike against the West, though it did seem they were no presently suffering from the cancer plague. But even that was i doubt and it would be several weeks before anything at all certai could be determined. Wilson nodded gravely, making only a fev brief comments. He asked them to continue their investigations.

"What I want you to do, Bill, *susseed* determining the Russians' intentions." His voice slurred, unfortunately. He spoke for several more minutes, and what he said made sense, but the damage had been done. One look at Greenbaum's eyes . . . those sad, hooded eyes betrayed pain and, worst of all, pity. CIA Director Williams' gray eyes showed absolutely nothing, but then, they never did. Tom Wilson was ashamed of himself.

They think I'm drunk, he thought. *Shit, I probably am drunk.* After they left, he thought grimly what would happen if he were to repeat the slip at a press conference. On television. He shuddered. From that day forward, he decided, he would not drink at all during the day and would ration himself to a few nightcaps before bed. The regimen worked, and he began to gain confidence that whatever happened, he would be able to meet the crises.

As he sat in his personal study trying to cope with a mass of papers and reports, President Wilson felt at peace with himself. From 5:30 to about 6:30 each afternoon was set aside on his schedule as a time for relaxation, solitary paperwork, or reading. "Quiet Time" he called it. "Happy Hour" was the description his secretary, Millie Manus, used in her report to Williams. But not anymore.

President Wilson looked up from his paperwork and stared out at the Rose Garden. It was beautiful, peaceful.

He was startled by a knock on the door; this brief bit of solitude was precious time for him, and Millie protected his peace with ferocity. "Come in," he said, and was surprised to see Colonel Andrew McKenny open the door. McKenny looked like a West Point recruiting poster. Tall, rugged, handsome, perfect posture. He had not attended the Point, but he bore a striking resemblance to Maxwell Taylor. That plus the fact that he was a fine doctor made him an ideal choice for White House physician.

"Ah, Colonel. I didn't think our checkup was for another month," Wilson said.

"I'm sorry to disturb you, Mr. President," McKenny said, his voice barely audible. "But I wanted to speak with you alone. It's a personal matter."

Wilson motioned him to a chair and looked at the grim-faced officer. "What," Wilson wondered, "does the poor bastard want?"

McKenny sat for almost a full minute, staring distractedly at his clenched hands. The President broke the silence.

"If you'll tell me what your problem is. . . ."

"I phrased that wrong, sir. I'm sorry. I meant a personal problem involving the First Family."

"Well?" Wilson leaned forward slightly and narrowed his eyes. Colonel McKenny finally looked up.

"It involves Wendy, Mr. President."

"Yes?"

"Well, I think you know that your family has regular examinations as a matter of course. Wendy's was only three months ago, and she passed with flying colors. At her age, that's what one would expect, of course. But teenage girls sometimes have certain gynecological problems and she came to me the other day and told me she hadn't had a period in over two months. So I . . ."

"She isn't pregnant!" Wilson looked incredulous. "She's only sixteen. I . . ."

McKenny cut him off. "No sir, she is *not* pregnant, though she thought it was a possibility at the time." He paused, staring at his hands once again.

"Well, that's a relief."

"Not really, Mr. President." The Colonel cleared his throat and looked directly at Wilson. "We've run a series of tests. Double-checked them. Wendy has cancer."

Wilson fell back into his chair, his jaw slack. For a moment he forgot to breathe. "Cancer? Are you sure?" His voice was a hoarse whisper.

"Yes, sir, we're sure."

"What . . . kind . . . of cancer?"

Colonel McKenny took a deep breath, sighed, and said, "Cancer of the uterus. And it's possible it's metastasized, spread." He looked at Wilson, who remained speechless. "In one so young, this is extremely rare. It's much more common around forty-five or so, and hardly ever before thirty. Still, there are cases of girls her age . . ." He paused and looked at Wilson again, who was gazing at him with vacant eyes.

"You say it's spread?" the President asked quietly.

"Well, sir, the cancer often starts at the cervix and moves back into the uterus. What we have to worry about now is whether it will metastasize into the lymphatic system and spread throughout the body. That would be disastrous. It would kill her."

"Is there any hope?"

"Mr. President, I think I can say with complete honesty that there is good reason to hope, if we move swiftly. An operation . . ."

"You mean remove it all?"

"Yes, sir."

"No, that's too much. I can't allow that. Are there other . . . techniques?"

"Well, if we'd caught it earlier. I mean, she had an examination including a pap smear just a couple of months ago, and nothing showed up. It just appeared out of nowhere. Anyway, we could use radiation. There is at least one malignant tumor, but as I said, the cancer has spread from the cervix to the uterus. The best way would be to target the site. We insert a radium-filled capsule through the vagina and uterine cavity and . . ."

Wilson groaned. "They're killing Wendy." His hands went to his face.

Colonel McKenny looked at Wilson and asked softly, "*They,* sir?"

"Nothing, go on. I take it you don't recommend radiation."

"No, sir, not in this case. Our objective has got to be to prevent the cancer from spreading further, and it seems to be very rapidly metastasizing. I recommend immediate surgery. Within twenty-four hours, if you agree. She won't be able to bear children, of course, but if we get it all, she can have an otherwise normal life. I know what a shock this must be, sir," he said sincerely. "And I wish I could tell you how much it grieves me to be the one to tell you."

"Thank you, Colonel McKenny," Wilson said, recovering his composure. "You have my permission to take any steps necessary to save Wendy's life. Move as quickly as possible."

"I took the liberty, sir, of arranging for rooms at Walter Reed, and two of the best surgeons in the country are on their way here now. We can operate tonight."

"Good. Thank you. Have you told Wendy?"

"No, Mr. President. I wanted to speak with you first." McKenny looked at his shoes.

"Well, let me think about how to handle this. We may want to explain this to her after the operation. There's no reason to frighten her to death at the outset. On the other hand . . . well, I'll see to it one way or another and let you know just how much I've told her."

"Of course, Mr. President. I understand."

"How long after the operation before you know if you got it all?"

McKenny looked at Wilson's grim but calm face and marveled at his strength. "Well, *absolute* certainty is impossible; we just have to watch her very closely. If there's no recurrence in three to five years, the odds are excellent she's in the clear."

"That's a long time, Colonel."

"Oh, we should be able to make an educated guess in a matter of days after the operation, when some tests have been run, within a couple of weeks anyway. I just wanted to emphasize that we can never be completely sure. We know very little about why cancer cells develop in some people and not in others. There could be dormant carcinomas elsewhere in the body which might take years to develop. But if we operate quickly, the odds are much improved; statistically that is certain."

"I understand." President Wilson paused thoughtfully for a moment. "I suppose the press will get wind of this."

"Well, we can try to keep it quiet, but it will be difficult to keep under wraps for very long. Your daughter is so much in the public eye in any event, and we will want to keep her in the hospital for several weeks at least."

"OK. For the time being, we will simply say that she is being admitted for the flu or a bad cold. Maybe pneumonia. Keep the cancer thing quiet for the time being. That's very important, Colonel."

"Anything you say, sir, but . . . she will have to be told at some time, and the real reason for her hospitalization will come out sooner or later." He paused and looked at the President.

"Yes, I know. I have my reasons, and that's the way I want it for the time being."

"Yes, Mr. President." McKenny stood. "The operation should begin around midnight. I will personally assist and keep you informed of every development. Please rest assured that Wendy will receive the very best care."

"Of course, and thank you." The two men looked sadly at one another for a moment, and then McKenny asked quietly, "I assume you will want to tell the First Lady."

Wilson was tempted to ask him to assume that painful duty, but he knew it was unavoidable. "Yes," he said, looking out at the Rose Garden, "I'll tell the First Lady."

As Colonel McKenny left the White House, he felt tremendous admiration for Wilson. In his professional career, he had often had to give bad, sometimes tragic, news to a variety of people. The news that a child was seriously ill was often sufficient to bring the most stoical parent to collapse. But President Wilson had shown courage. Great courage. The Colonel had not voted for Wilson, and had never liked him very much, but now he knew that the President of the United States was a strong and courageous man. McKenny felt sorry for the man, but he was also very proud of his Commander-in-Chief.

About the time the Colonel's car was pulling onto Pennsylvania Avenue, President Wilson was still sitting and looking out at the Rose Garden.

He had started on a bottle of cognac.

Tears were running down his cheeks.

"They're killing my daughter," he sobbed, again and again, his voice filled with sorrow and hate. "They're killing my Wendy."

21

Atlanta

Henry Rogers was pissed off. Very pissed off. For weeks Eric had nagged him never to be out of touch, always to be near the telephone in case of a breakthrough. And when it happened, Eric was incommunicado. Rogers was unable to reach him at CDC, and there was no answer when he had called him at home. He left messages with several of Zimmermann's assistants, but when he checked later that evening, he discovered that he had not spoken to any of them. Impulsively, he threw some underwear, socks, and a wrinkled, bulky mass of printouts into a small suitcase and caught the last plane from National Airport to Atlanta. The flight is not a particularly long one, but a chain of thunderstorms delayed landing for more than an hour, and as Henry Rogers fumed while circling thirteen thousand feet above Georgia, Eric and Honorée made love one last, sweet time, and fell asleep in one another's arms.

Rogers was tired as he sat at Zimmermann's desk while waiting for Eric to arrive. He double-checked some of his figures. He had only had three hours' sleep at the airport hotel, and his sense of personal fastidiousness was offended by what seemed to him an overwhelming odor emanating from his shirt. (He had forgotten to pack a clean one.) He was angry and annoyed, and Eric was uncharacteristically late for work.

"Why, Henry, what a nice surprise!" Eric strode into his office and offered his hand to the older man.

"Fuck you," Rogers said, ignoring the hand. He was about to begin a well-prepared tirade when he noticed that a pretty, freckled young woman was also in the room. "Pardon me," he said, "I didn't, um . . ."

"Quite all right, Dr. Rogers. We met once, some time ago. I'm Honorée Hennessey." She smiled at Rogers, who remembered he hadn't shaved that morning.

"Henry," Eric said helpfully, "you look like hell. How come you're here?"

Rogers ignored Zimmermann and rose to shake hands with Honorée. "Yes, I remember. You did that terrific work on pancreatic cell regeneration." He smiled at her and she smiled back.

"Well, I did a paper on it, but Fitzgerald did most of the basic thinking."

"You're too modest, Dr. Hennessey. Please, sit down," Rogers said.

"Henry, you're in my office," Eric said, smiling. "Please, Dr. Hennessey, take a chair. Now Henry, why are you here?" He sat on the edge of the desk.

Rogers' original excitement about the breakthrough had turned to annoyance when he was unable to reach Zimmermann. Annoyance had eventually become fury. But now that he saw the two obviously happy people before him, he felt his outrage draining away. It is said that the blind are capable of developing their senses of hearing and touch partially to compensate for their loss of sight. Rogers, who lived alone and had loved, briefly, only once, possessed a similar gift. He was sensitive to emotions, and though both Eric and Honorée did not know it, he could see that they were in love. The curmudgeon was touched.

"I assume, Eric, that you have convinced Dr. Hennessey to join the Caduceus staff. . . ."

"Yes, I have. Now tell me . . ."

"Of course, that's why I'm here. I tried to reach you last night, but there was no answer."

"Was it early? Honorée and I were out to dinner."

"Early and then around ten. But no matter."

"I must have been in the shower," Eric said truthfully.

"OK, first let me give you the bad news, and *then* the good news." Henry felt his enthusiasm returning. "The bad news is not unexpected. Time is running out as far as keeping the cancer epidemic secret. Hospitals and even individual physicians are reporting a dramatic increase in carcinomas, and before long somebody's going to add it up. Then all hell breaks loose." Zimmermann nodded but said nothing and Rogers continued. "But we knew that was bound to happen sooner or later. *Here,"* he cried, thumping the printout on Zimmermann's desk, "is the good news."

"What?" asked Eric.

"The variable. The breakthrough. Well, that's a bit strong: the beginning, I think. I hope.'

"You mean you've found the cause . . ." Honorée asked.

"No, no, certainly not. I only wish I had. But this is the start, perhaps. And that's what is so exciting."

"Go on," Zimmermann said seriously.

"Well, I almost missed it, but there are at least four groups in different regions of the country who show no signs of an increase in the incidence of cancer. An interesting sample, too. Sharecroppers in Barbour County, Alabama; poor whites in Monroe County, West Virginia; and Indians on two reservations in North Dakota and New Mexico. Oh, they're sick all right–from pellegra, rickets, malnutrition, even tuberculosis–but this is the incredible thing: there is *no* change in the rate of cancer." He looked at Eric and Honorée and beamed.

Zimmermann sighed. "Henry, the places you've spotted probably have health care that's by its very definition wretchedly poor. Probably just bad reporting. Give them a few weeks or months and you'll see it tote up to the level of everywhere else."

"That's what I thought, Eric," Rogers said. "So I had the figures checked in the field. It's a preliminary survey, I grant you, but the results have been confirmed. These are some of the most poverty-stricken counties in the country. And what's *really* interesting is that nearby counties are for the most part running the same cancer rate as the rest of the nation. It'll take some time to prove it, but it also seems that the more prosperous people in these areas are affected, while the poor are not." He looked at the two intently.

"Fascinating," Honorée said quietly.

"Well, it looks like the poor really are going to inherit the earth," Zimmermann commented dryly. "I thought you'd been unable to find any significant variables by race and economic status."

"That's right. But we really didn't look carefully at small enough units. All of these areas are rural and isolated from the mainstreams of health care, as you yourself just pointed out. Look, I know you have your doubts, but assume these indications are correct. It implies . . ."

"That these people are doing or not doing something which the rest of the population does and have protected themselves from the epidemic," Honorée said, unintentionally interrupting.

"Precisely," Rogers said, beaming.

"It could be diet, I suppose. Or maybe one of the common sicknesses has somehow rendered them immune," Zimmermann commented.

"Oh, some people are getting cancer, Eric, but just at the old rate. These people are doing something unusual. It won't be easy to find. I'm not even sure where we start to look, but these people have got to be studied and tested intensively."

"I agree, Henry. I'll assign a team to each area."

"And I've already got my people checking rural areas and urban ghettos for any variable we might have missed before," Rogers said. "I don't know if I can stand waiting for the field reports."

"We won't have to wait, Henry," Eric replied. "We'll leave tomorrow for West Virginia."

22

Hollywood, West Virginia

Monroe County, West Virginia sits squarely in the Appalachians. It contains some of the most beautiful countryside in the United States. Its hills are steep, and roads reel through the region, drunkenly swerving from one obstacle to another. Wildlife thrives in the dense forests and rushing creeks. But its beauty is deceptive; the topsoil is poor, and farming is all but impossible on the rugged hillsides. The county is home to some of the most poverty-ridden citizens of the United States.

After spending the night in Washington, Eric, Henry, and Honorée picked up several assistants from NIH and helicoptered west before sunrise. The flight did not take long, and as they clattered through the darkness, Rogers outlined his plans for the field study. In Monroe County alone, over one hundred Caduceus and military health officers would carefully monitor the residents and their habits.

They fell silent as they neared their destination. The sky had brightened and thick clouds of mist spotted the valleys and ravines below. The forest was a dark, rich green and there was no sign of human habitation, only an occasional road meandering through the hills. Honorée saw several deer bolt from a clearing as the 'copter approached. *We're like an invading army,* she thought. "Where will we land, Henry?" she asked.

"Just outside of a town called Hollywood. A real metropolis in these parts. Population, uh," he consulted some papers, "of 412 souls, and possessed of one of the few Holiday Inns in the area. That'll be our base. There's a small clinic in town which will come in handy for physicals and some of the tests. A good chunk of the county is virtually cordoned off. We told 'em there was evidence the local drinking water had been polluted and we had to check them out to see if they were poisoned. The local physician has been taken into our confidence, and there's a young public health officer, name of Richardson, we also had to let in on it. Otherwise, people are in the dark." Rogers stared out the window as the copter descended. Hollywood was a typical small town in need of a coat of paint. The marquee of the Holiday Inn said: "Have Your Next Affair Here."

"Jesus H. Christ," Zimmermann murmured. He stood unsteadily on the creaky porch of a tiny shack. A skinny dog sniffed around the rusted ruins of a Hudson sedan parked, if that was the word, a few yards from an odoriferous privy. The door to the house was open, and in the room before him were five people—two adults and three barefoot children. Something foul smelling was simmering atop a wood stove, and except for one of the children, none of the residents said a word to the tall, well-dressed stranger who had suddenly appeared in the door. They just stared and waited for him to make the first move. The scene was repeated several more times that day as he and Bill Richardson went from door to door at Dellon's Creek, pop. 61, three miles outside of Hollywood. They took blood samples, arranged for the collection of urine and feces samples, and attempted to interview each person about his habits. The populace of Dellon's Creek seemed skeptical about the polluted water story, and many were openly hostile. But their cooperation was assured by the

presence of two hulking state troopers who accompanied th
investigators on their rounds.

"You know, I thought I had some idea of what poverty was like
I mean I've been in urban ghettos, and I've read about it....
Zimmermann paused and looked down at his drink. "But I didn'
think this still existed in America. I just can't understand it." Eri
felt foolish for confessing his naiveté. Rogers and Honorée under
stood and said nothing.

"Oh, you can't get much worse than this, I guess," Bil
Richardson said, peering seriously at Eric through wire rim glasses
He was young and energetic, and at twenty-six looked barel
eighteen. "These isolated areas are by far the worst left in thi
country. The clinic down the street is only open two days a week
and the doctor," he whispered conspiratorially, "is incompetent
What these people need is education."

"What these people need," Honorée said, "is money."

"Yes, of course, but ignorance and bad health go hand in hand,
the young man persisted. Wherever they went that day, he ha
lectured the citizens of Dellon's Creek and elsewhere on the prope
way to brush their teeth (though most did not own a toothbrush)
proper nutrition and the need for a balanced diet (the average famil
income was approximately one hundred dollars per month), and th
necessity of pediatric inoculations. The mothers had nodded i
agreement, though only a few knew what a vaccination was
Richardson passed out public health pamphlets with the zeal of a
itinerant preacher distributing religious tracts. Zimmermann sai
nothing, though he doubted many of them would ever look a
them.

"One thing is clear, though," Rogers said. "All indications ar
that cancer is not out of control here, though I heard today that th
guy who manages this motel just came down with it. Wretched a
these people are, they are doing *something* to counteract the epidemi
I'd give anything to know what it is."

"Clean livin'," Eric said bitterly, and then they all laughed, eve
Richardson.

After another day in Hollywood, they all agreed they did not nee to be on hand for further examinations or interviews. With close to one hundred Caduceus and army personnel on site, their talents were wasted. Rogers put one of his best men in charge of the investigations, and after a quick inspection of a military field hospital which had been set up near Dellon's Creek, they left.

"Given enough time," Rogers said as they drove to the helicopter landing site to return to Washington, "we will ultimately figure out what it is these people are doing or not doing that's immunized them. I just don't know if we have enough time before it's too late."

They all were silent for a few minutes pondering this remark and staring out the car window at the beautiful scenery which was occasionally marred by a wretched shack. Bill Richardson once again launched into his speech about the need for education in the area to insure public health, and was met with mumbles of agreement. Eric, Rogers, and Honorée were all thinking of the work ahead of them. At last, just as they pulled up to the helicopter, their state trooper driver turned and faced Richardson. He smiled pleasantly. "You're right, young man, ab-so-lutely right. 'Course all the pamphlets you passed out won't help much: most people these parts can't read. Y'know it's damn near hopeless. If the gov'ment ever gets food stamps out this way, five'll get ya ten they try to eat them."

23

Arlington, Virginia

The Director of the Central Intelligence Agency had two offices. One was a large, tastefully decorated room used for meetings and small receptions. "Wild Bill" Williams rarely used it. His other office–his real office–was also spacious, but furnished with only a steel desk, a few chairs, numerous file cabinets and assorted communications equipment. It had no windows. Indeed, though a visitor (there were very few) might not notice it right away, the Director's office was really a vault. Its door, when shut, was eight inches of tempered steel booby trapped with an explosive charge Williams had himself designed. Only three people could open it, using a combination of a voice code and palmprint scans.

Williams hated the "Wild Bill" epithet–ironic reminiscence of his great OSS ancestor–and he hardly looked the part. He was cautious and soft spoken. He never visibly lost his temper or, for that matter, showed any emotion whatsoever. His hair was gray, his suits were gray, and his pale complexion was set off by eyes of pale, washed-out blue. He was the kind of man people never quite get around to talking to at a cocktail party. Williams liked it that way.

He was the son of a prosperous Charleston, South Carolina banker who sent him to Princeton to prepare for a life in finance. Even in college, the slight, quiet young Williams looked like a thirty-year-old loan officer. He studied hard, said little, and had few friends. When America entered W.W.II, he volunteered, and found himself in army intelligence and, before long, the OSS. It was in this period that he suddenly bloomed, rather like one of the orchards he now cultivated in his spare time (his only hobby). For young Bill Williams had an extraordinary talent: he was without a doubt the greatest concocter of dirty tricks in all of OSS. He was a master at psychological warfare, assassination, and the technology of terror, and he had an intuitive grasp of methods and operations. By 1945 his code name was, appropriately, "Dr. Death." Despite the pleas of his father to enter the banking business after the war, he stayed with the OSS as it evolved into the CIA. He had found his true vocation. His rise was steady, and his political ability to reassure the Congress without betraying the secrets of the executive eventually landed him in the Director's office. Vault, really. And the backing of the powerful senior senator from South Carolina, a close friend of his late father, had done him no harm.

Bill Williams sat in the only comfortable chair in his office and stared at a gray steel wall. He was afraid. The morning meeting of the National Security Council had been disastrous. The President was obviously under great strain, his mood alternating from near hysteria to a dazed attitude bordering on inattention. Greenbaum and Vice President Baker had taken turns keeping Wilson on the track of the agenda, but it had not been easy. Wilson began the meeting by announcing that John Keels, Secretary of Labor, had been hospitalized with cancer of the larynx. The President's speech was noticeably slurred, and though no one commented on it, even among themselves, it seemed likely the Commander-in-Chief had been drunk. At eight-thirty in the morning.

Williams picked up a file, sighed, and put it down. It was his personal opinion that at least half the presidents since Hoover had been a bit insane, and several had been quite fond of drink; but

Wilson deeply troubled him. He hadn't voted for him, of course. Like a majority of the old guard at the Agency, he was a New Deal Democrat. Years before, Williams had even found himself almost literally holding his nose as he voted for McGovern, but he dreaded the alternative. The only period of decline in his career had come when he oversaw a staff report for LBJ predicting that the "noble adventure" in Vietnam would prove a disaster. In his career, Bill Williams had devised plans for the violent destruction of scores of people, but he still thought of himself as an idealist and political liberal. He was past retirement age; perhaps now was the best time to quit.

That Tom Wilson was a Republican conservative, however, had nothing to do with Williams' sense of distaste and fear. The United States, indeed the civilized world, faced a crisis of staggering proportions, and the leader of the most powerful nation in the Free World was not in complete control of his faculties. This situation was frightening, but Williams felt a deep sense of unease because he himself was not in complete control of the situation. First, both NSA and CIA had agents in the White House, and Williams could account for almost every ounce of alcohol in the building. The President had been drinking a great deal of late, but no one saw him doing it, and he could not determine where he was getting it.

He chuckled to himself. There was a fair chance that the end of civilization, perhaps the end of mankind, was at hand, and the Director of the CIA was deeply bothered by the source of presidential booze. The reason for the cancer scourge might never be found, but the actions of an individual as closely observed as the President were knowable, and Williams was annoyed that he could not find out who supplied Wilson with his liquor.

He sighed and looked at the reports on his desk. The news was not at all good. Bonn, Tokyo, Paris, London, Rome, Caracas, Tel Aviv, Jiddah, Melbourne. The Western world, and a fair part of the underdeveloped as well, were experiencing an epidemic of the most hideous scourge known to man. But that was the good news.

". . . And Mr. Williams, I would like you to tell us what the intelligence community has discovered about the, uh, intentions of the Soviets in this matter," the President said.

"Sir?"

"Let me make the question simpler, Bill," the President sneered. "Are the Russians or for that matter any of our other enemies in the grip of this epidemic?"

"That's a very difficult question to answer with certainty right now, Mr. President. I . . ."

Wilson's fist slammed down on the table. "I want an answer, Williams. Now! You've had not days, not weeks, but *months,* and you still don't have an answer. Now what the fuck are we spending billions of dollars on intelligence for, if you can't answer a simple question?"

"If you will pardon me, sir, it is not a simple question. We do have fragmentary information that some of the Chinese governments are experiencing, at least as far as we can determine, a much higher rate of cancer, but I'm sure you will recall how much difficulty we have getting accurate information out of China."

"And the Soviets?" the President asked softly, staring at the ash on his thin black cigar.

"I do not feel we have sufficient data at this time to know for certain if the Soviet Union is presently affected."

Wilson's voice was thick with irony. "And when, pray, are you likely to have this information? When will the more than one hundred thousand employees of our esteemed intelligence community have any idea if this country has been the target of a massive biological warfare strike? *When we're all dead?*" His voice rose to a near shriek. "*When they've killed us, killed our wives, killed our children by the tens of millions? Then will you be willing to hazard an estimate, Mr. Williams?*" He paused. "Well?"

"I'm not sure how to answer that, sir, but I do believe we will have at least a preliminary picture of the Soviet situation within a week. A week at the outside, I'd say."

"So you need yet another week, Mr. Williams. In another week, ten, maybe twenty thousand Americans could be dead. Do you expect me to sit by while you . . ."

"Tom." Arthur Greenbaum's voice had a preemptory tone. "I'm sure you must understand the problems Mr. Williams has. Ever since China fell to pieces, the Russians have been close to hysteria. Eight of the ten Chinese 'republics' have more than a dozen ICBM's equipped with MIRV and MAD warheads. European Russia could be hit with A, H, or N bombs by any of them. So they're paranoid. And they are a lot harder to crack than they used to be for intelligence. It just takes longer, that's all Director Williams is saying. We've been over it before. We will know the answer soon enough. A week. Two weeks. If we can establish they've chosen to strike at us–though God only knows why–there'll be more than enough time to strike back."

"And we will," Wilson muttered grimly.

Vice President Baker adroitly turned the conversation to other matters, and Williams was off the hook. For the moment.

Williams sighed for the third time in less than ten minutes. For him it was a display of excessive emotion, even though he was alone. He had flat out lied to the President of the United States. The evidence was now clear that the Soviet Union and some of the Chinese States, like Szechuan, were unaffected, at least to the degree the rest of the world was. But then, so was Bangladesh, and parts of Portugal. And Chad and Upper Volta, or so the fragmentary information seemed to indicate. Still, Williams had to admit to himself that there was a chance, perhaps a fifty-fifty chance, that a massive biochemical attack had been launched, probably by the Russians. He could not bring himself to believe it. He should have had some warning of an attack of this magnitude. Though he somewhat overemphasized the problems of intelligence operations in Russia, there was no indication at all that the Soviets intended to strike at the West at this time. It would be a complex operation to carry out, probably involving thousands of people. And there was no hint of such Soviet plans or intentions, not a trace. Relations, while not exactly brotherly, were stable. Williams knew his duty indicated only one course: he must make every effort–even at the risk of exposing key operatives–to discover if the Soviets had attacked the United States. When and what he told President Wilson, he decided, would be up to him.

Bill Williams left his office. He pressed his palm against a faintly glowing green plastic panel and said: "Williams. Anchor. Bird. Synapse. Acupuncture." The huge door hissed shut. He decided he had better call Arthur Greenbaum the next morning and see if he was free for lunch.

24

Atlanta

"Good news, Henry!" Zimmermann burst into Rogers' temporary office at the Center for Disease Control without knocking first.

"Huh? What?"

"One of your minions just handed it to me. Young Paul DeAngelis of San Francisco does *not* have cancer." Zimmermann smiled, awaiting Rogers' expected question.

"Well, though I don't know him personally, I'm very happy to hear it. Now I've been going over some of the initial test results from West Virginia . . ."

"Hey, wait a minute," Zimmermann interrupted, "you're supposed to ask me what Paul DeAngelis' lack of cancer has to do with anything, and why it's good news."

"Yeah, I know. I've always hated knock-knock jokes. How 'bout you try telling me your good news without waiting for the appropriate liturgical responses," Rogers replied grumpily.

"OK, sorry. Look, as you know, one of the programs the CDC

computers have been spending a great deal of the taxpayers' money on is a pattern search for any indication of a group infection. And you also know, I assume, that though the machines have spit up any number of group or family patterns, none have been useful for study for half a dozen contaminating reasons, usually because by the time we have all the reports there's little hope of eliminating a multitude of potential causes of infection."

"If we are indeed dealing with an infection."

"Well, that's been my hunch all along. Only some viral mutation could possibly have spread so great a variety of carcinomas so rapidly. I think it's obvious."

"Sez you," Rogers muttered. "So what about your good news?"

"Well, it's not really mine. It's your beloved machine's. This DeAngelis kid is just what I've been looking for. First, his mother gets malignant melanoma; ten days later, her ten-year-old daughter contracts leukemia; the following week, the father is hit with lung cancer–a nonsmoker, by the way. But here's the really good part. In addition, an aunt who lives in San Diego and who stayed with them for a week less than two months ago now has Hodgkin's Disease. That leaves Paul. He's twelve, and so far seems to be perfectly healthy, at least for the moment. But don't you see, this could be our lucky break."

"Poor kid," Rogers said softly.

"Well, yes, of course. A tragedy." Zimmermann looked chagrined but then recovered his enthusiasm. "I guess I should refer to it as our opportunity. We're gonna study that kid very closely. I think whatever brought down everybody else in that family may be ready to start on him, maybe started already."

Rogers lit a cigarette, pushed his chair back from the desk, and rather carefully put up his feet atop a pile of printouts. "I see your point, Eric. But ... well, look at it this way. The odds against the disease hitting everyone in a family, including a visiting aunt from San Diego, are certainly high, but in something as widespread as this is becoming, there's almost a statistical certainty that you'll come across an occasional bunching. It is quite possible that the

DeAngelis family is just statistically unlucky. Things like this happen all the time, just like somebody tossing the dice and getting seven seven times in a row. The odds, God knows, are against it, but it can happen. It does happen."

"Sure, sure," Eric said, gesturing irritably. "Listen, if little Paul gets some form of cancer, that would make the odds even greater."

"Of course, Eric, but it's still theoretically possible for the entire Vienna Boys' Choir to contract cancer, the identical variety and all at the same time, for that matter, without it proving that there's an infection, viral or otherwise, on the loose." Rogers puffed on his cigarette and looked at Eric benignly.

"I'm not an idiot, Henry," Zimmermann spat out. "And I won't sit here and argue statistics with you. I suppose you'd say that it was not a statistical impossibility that the sun will rise in the west tomorrow."

"Rather unlikely, I grant, but not statistically impossible. I wouldn't put any money on it, though." Rogers smiled at Zimmermann. "Look Eric, I take your point. I apologize. This could be an important discovery. I just don't want you to assume too much based on one bit of data. Now," he said decisively, swinging his feet back to the floor and almost toppling the pile of printouts, "how are you proceeding?"

"Sorry to snap, Henry. And you're right to caution me." Eric took a deep breath. "First of all, the DeAngelis kid is now in the burn unit, intensive care at San Francisco General. We can keep him in complete isolation there and monitor him in sterile conditions. He's being tested constantly, 'round the clock, and under nearly ideal conditions. Don't look so sad, Henry. Maybe the kid'll be fine. And if he does develop something, we'll not only be there to try and see what's caused it, but he'll be treated by a superb medical staff before it can go any further." He paused. "Anyway, under the circumstances, he doesn't have anywhere to go as it is."

"Of course, Eric, I can't disagree. 'Course, this could lend weight to a genetic theory. . . ."

"That's bullshit."

"I agree, otherwise how come the breadth of the sudden

outbreak? Except in the few places we've found like Dellon's Creek. Still, you know there's some discussion about it, a lot of others are looking for some environmental cause, and the widespread and rapid increase in incidence inclines me to believe we're dealing with an environmental insult, not a virus."

"Look, Henry, if I were religious I'd say this cancer scourge was caused by the Almighty to punish us for our many sins. I've been convinced for some time, though, that at the root of cancer–even before this fucking plague–is a virus, perhaps a combination of viruses. Could be a slow virus, lying dormant for years, decades, waiting for just the right combination of factors to send the cells into a frenzy of reproduction. Maybe it was something in the environment that set all these slow viruses off. That's possible. But I know when we get to the bottom of this, it'll be a virus."

"Know? If you knew for sure or even had a good hunch that worked out, you'd be the most beloved man on the planet. Nobel prize for a start?" Rogers said gently.

"I'll get the prize one of these days, Henry, don't you worry. But for now, I'm going to watch what happens to this DeAngelis kid. If he gets cancer, we'll be right on the spot as it begins. If he gets cancer, I'll demand that the major effort of Caduceus will be to find the virus that caused it. Statistical possibility or no, to me it'll indicate a textbook epidemiological pattern." Zimmermann's tone was almost gloating.

"Yeah," Rogers muttered bitterly, "if little Paul DeAngelis develops cancer–especially if he dies of it–you'll be able to try and prove your point. Be a real hero around here." He butted out his cigarette. " 'Course, there's one other thing. If the kid contracts cancer, then I'd bet the family farm that it means the disease is contagious. And spreading. How long before it gets one of us?"

25

Washington, D.C./San Francisc

Wendy Wilson was resting very comfortably. Her operation ha
been a complete success, at least as far as initial tests could indicat
Her room at Walter Reed was bright and cheerful, and she receive
the best care available in the United States, perhaps the world. Bu
she did not notice the room or the nurse on duty around the cloc
or the host of attentive doctors who checked on her every hou
Wendy was dreaming about Charlie.

Charlie was a man of nineteen years, possessed of a lank
swimmer's body and a somewhat scraggly beard. She hadn't see
Charlie in several months. Their escapade in the dining room of th
Shoreham Hotel had made him *persona non grata* at the Whit
House. It was her fault, really, and she compounded the embarras
ment by saying so to a reporter from the Chicago *Tribune.* They'
had a little champagne at the House, and surreptitiously shared
joint in his car on the way to a "coming out party" for a friend. No
a friend, exactly, but a good excuse to get out with Charlie. It i
doubtful if the Secret Service men following them down the street

of the capital knew they'd been smoking, but it was clear that both young people were in high spirits. They had danced with the wild abandon and quasi-innocent lasciviousness common to people their age and had had a wonderful time. Wendy announced that she was starving, and though the ballroom had enough food to satisfy the crew of an aircraft carrier, they went to the hotel dining room, half a dozen Secret Service agents in tow.

There Charlie told her that the latest thing at Yale was to flip a pat of butter from a knife onto the ceiling of the refectory. The longer it stuck, the greater the honor, and one friend had reputedly glued one to the ceiling of the Yale dining hall which had stuck for half a day.

"Try it," Wendy had said, pushing a dish of butter to him. "Show me."

Charlie was giddy, but his mood instantly changed. "I don't think I'd better. I mean, not here."

"No balls, Charlie?" She sighed, placed a pat of butter on her knife and arched it across the Shoreham dining room. It hit the wall and fell.

Challenged, Charlie responded by carefully placing one pat of butter on top of another. "Missionary position. Difficult shot. If both stick, extra points; if they both stick while coupled, you win the Super Bowl."

Charlie won the Super Bowl for the first time in his brief career as a food flinger, but the fact that the President's daughter and her date were ejected from a Washington restaurant for misbehavior made the morning papers. Almost all were kind—the press loved Wendy—but her parents were furious. No more dates for several months, and, worst of all, no more Charlie.

Wendy dreamed of him. They danced alone in a ballroom filled with fog. They wore bikinis; Charlie's was tight. The orchestra and the surf played at equal volume. It was very romantic, and she was about to suggest he remove the bathing suit when her reverie was interrupted by a nurse who talked quietly to her, seemingly from a great distance, and pricked her thigh with a needle. After a while,

Wendy continued to dream. She did not notice two men, one plump and florid and the other slight and gray, standing near her bed and talking in hushed tones.

"She looks pretty good, considering," Greenbaum whispered to Williams. "I've passed the word to keep her comfortable for the next few days if possible."

"So I heard. Smart move. He's insisting he tell her himself, and I'm afraid that at this point he might crack when he sees her." Williams stared at the young woman sleeping in her hospital bed. She smiled slightly. "It's really something the First Lady should deal with anyway."

"Jenny'd handle it better, too," Greenbaum concurred.

"Work on that, Arthur. There's too much at stake to allow the President to confront an emotionally charged situation like this right now. We don't have much time. Press is beginning to snoop—we'll have to tell them something sooner or later. Probably in a few days. Not much time." Williams stared into space and seemed to be speaking to himself.

The two turned to leave the room. "I'll work on the President. Tom Wilson just wants to face it like a man and do his duty. I think I can convince him that this sort of thing is a mother-daughter matter. For the moment I can keep him away by saying we still have to determine whether or not her condition is contagious, though I doubt it. And there's no medical objection to keeping the girl under sedation for another couple of days. Leave it to me."

"Of course. That's my major worry, but I'm sure you can handle Wilson. As for the press . . ."

"I'm stumped there, Bill. We can hold them off for a while, but sooner or later we'll have to tell the truth. There's no way this can be covered up. When it breaks, I'm willing to bet some smart reporter is going to start poking around the cancer situation and discover what's going on. The whole thing has deteriorated badly in just the past week or two. It can't be kept under wraps much longer." Greenbaum's voice trembled slightly.

"Well, some of the most likely reporters have been taken into our confidence, and all have agreed to write nothing about it for the time being. Even they can see what could happen when the word breaks," Williams said, pushing open the door.

"All hell busts loose."

"Right, all hell busts loose."

Wendy Wilson heard none of this conversation. She lay in her bed, smiling to herself. She dreamed she and Charlie were riding two beautiful pale horses through the green Virginia countryside.

Paul DeAngelis dreamed of hypodermic needles. The narcotic haze that induced Wendy's pleasant dreams was denied him since there was (so far) nothing wrong with him in the first place, and an analgesic might prevent a symptom from being noticed immediately. If Paul had not seen for himself that he had entered San Francisco General Hospital a few days before he would have thought he'd been scooped up into a saucer to be tested by aliens, just like in a "Creature Feature" movie. His body was covered with a mass of wires and tubes. Twenty-six electrodes were patched all over his body, glued on with an acid-green jelly. Paul DeAngelis was hooked up to one of the largest medical computers in the United States; every electrical impulse in his brain, every gurgle in his stomach was instantly monitored and analyzed. A tube led into a vein in his right arm. "That's your food," a spaceman told him.

His diet was a glucose, liquid protein, and vitamin preparation specifically designed to keep potential contaminants to a minimum. Occasionally he was given a dry, flavorless cookie as a special treat and to assure that his bowels operated close to normally. Another tube was inserted in his left arm, but nobody told him what it was for. A catheter collected his urine.

Paul DeAngelis began to believe he was not in the hospital, but in a saucer after all. The spacepeople claimed to be doctors, but they could be lying. His room was circular and made of a shiny white material, floor, ceiling, and walls. The people who worked on him wore silvery plastic suits and bubblelike space helmets. Approximately every two hours, one would shuffle into his room and take a blood sample or scrape away a bit of his skin or remove his feces or urine.

"Why do you dress like that all the time?" Paul asked one.

"So you won't get sick, Paul," replied a nurse, startled by the sudden question from her usually silent patient.

"You mean I'm not already sick?"

"Well, we think you're going to be sick. That's why we're watching you so carefully. And we wear these suits so you won't pick up any of our germs."

"But I feel fine," Paul said. "How come you think I'm gonna get sick?"

"You'll just have to trust us, Paul," the nurse replied, drawing a syringeful of blood from a vein in his leg.

Paul DeAngelis did not believe the spacewoman. He knew that aside from the constant jabbing of needles and his virtual inability to move, he felt fine.

He wondered what he had done to be so cruelly punished.

26

New York City

Francis X. Feeley sat at the bar of the Four Seasons Grill, staring through the shimmering chain curtains at a summer afternoon downpour. He had long ago made it a habit to imbibe at the Grill on payday, which was every two weeks, or when he had something to celebrate. There were always some pretty women to look at, scattered like jewels among the stodgy businessmen and visiting firemen anxious to impress their friends by using the bartender's first name. Feeley had once met a real visiting fireman there, a pleasant fellow from Delaware attending a firechiefs' convention at the Waldorf. Feeley bought him a drink.

But that rainy summer's day was not payday, nor were there any particularly beautiful women about. He sat at the bar, deep in thought, convinced he was onto the biggest story of the past thirty years. He reflected on how fickle chance could be. The previous week he had almost lost his job.

"How long you been with this paper, Frank?" his editor had asked. His tone was not pleasant.

"Eight, almost nine years. Why?"

"At ten years the union says we gotta have a powerful reason for sacking you, right?" Lou Soliman was a sadist.

"Yeah, I guess so. Is anything wrong?"

"This." The editor tossed several crumpled pages onto his desk. The handwriting was crude, almost childlike, interspersed with sections of very neat mathematical symbols, most of which he was only vaguely familiar with.

"Let me save you the trouble of trying to figure it out, Frank. This here letter is from an eleven-year-old kid in Queens. He read your brilliant piece in the Sunday *News* a week ago, and the little tyke sat down and wrote a letter to the publisher—not the editor mind you, the publisher." Feeley noted that his boss' face was turning red, his voice quavering, his breath coming in short puffs. *Type A behavior,* he thought idly, *probably drop dead of a stroke before he's ninety. Only the good die young.*

"So the publisher calls me into his office and wants to know how come we do science reporting a little kid can tear to pieces. How come we got a reporter on the science desk who doesn't know a white hole from an asshole. How come he doesn't know the difference between a quark and a, a what-the-fuck-do-you call it . . ."

"Snark?" Feeley offered helpfully.

"Right." The editor was out of breath and paused for a moment. "A snark. The publisher actually had the twerp's musings checked out with some honcho at Columbia, for Christ sakes, and guess what? The kid's right; your piece was a pile of garbage. What bar'd you write that one in, Frank?"

"That's not fair," Feeley said, "it's impossible to boil down theoretical physics so every one of our readers can avoid being embarrassed next time he's invited to a cocktail party at the Institute of Advanced Study. Shit, you told me to make it simple."

"Simple, yes. Not wrong. You're paid a good salary to keep up with these things, Feeley."

"What about the letter. Gonna print it?"

"Oh, better than that, Frank. *Much* better than that." A beatific smile appeared on Lou Soliman's face and Feeley inwardly cringed.

"You, my ace science reporter, are going to do a human interest piece on this budding Einstein from Queens."

"Oh God."

"Exactly. That's how he's going to be treated. It seems our friends up at Columbia want to talk to the little turd about accelerating his education and getting a Ph.D. before he can get a hard-on. They were very impressed by his little letter, and the *News* is going to get a scoop by being the first paper to do a human interest piece on him. The publisher says it was a stroke of luck you wrote such a shitty article. The kid tore himself away from figuring out the Mysteries of Creation just to write us about your incompetence. Now, I want you to do a good job. It's a feature-length human interest, and you'll get the full fee, though why is beyond me. You got two, maybe three weeks."

"I'm in the middle of something else, Lou."

"What?"

"I'd just as soon not say right now, but it could be big. Very big," Feeley said quietly.

"You shittin' me?" Lou looked skeptical.

"No. At least I don't think so."

"Then take four weeks to do the piece on the Queens genius, but it better be good, and your little mystery project better be good too, or you'll be out on the street begging jobs from *Popular Mechanics,* not that they'd have you." The editor abruptly turned and stomped away. Feeley lit a White Owl, much to the annoyance of the Decorating Tips writer in the next cubicle, who had heard the entire altercation and enjoyed it immensely. After half an hour of reflection, he gingerly placed the hated letter from Master Billie Pockell, of Queens, New York in his drawer, and decided to forget about it, at least for the next two weeks. If he was onto what he thought he was, the publisher would kiss his ass for doing so. If not, he probably would kick his ass right out the door and onto the street, where Francis X. Feeley would indeed find himself lucky to get work freelancing articles on plastering techniques for *Popular Mechanics.*

"Another one, Mr. Feeley?"

"Oh. Yes, thank you, Jim." Feeley realized he had been deep in thought for some time, an empty glass in front of him. He watched as Jim, the world's greatest bartender, took a freshly chilled glass and carefully poured a Heineken into it. Feeley daintily nibbled a few cashews from a dish on the bar, and, taking a legal pad from his briefcase, began to write the first lines of a story which he was sure would either win him a Pulitzer Prize or a place on the unemployment lines.

For months something had nagged at him. First it was Marcia Spaguolo and his friend Joe's words, "It shunna happened." Then it was Rick at Bradley's. That shouldn't have happened either. A month before, a doctor friend of his had commented on how many cancer patients he had seen in the past few months, but Feeley paid little attention to the remark. The effect, however, was cumulative. Eventually he began to notice how many wives, friends, and colleagues themselves had recently contracted cancer. After many hours of wandering the bars, public libraries, and streets of the city, Feeley had come to the conclusion that far too many people were talking about cancer.

He made a few routine inquiries. A call to HEW elicited a promise to send all available data, but they were slow in responding, and most of the materials that arrived were publicity brochures designed to convince the taxpayer his money was well spent. A second call demanding specific cancer statistics had produced silence, and finally a batch of printouts which clearly demonstrated that the incidence of cancer was up, but only marginally.

A call to a major cancer hospital elicited a definite negative from its director, but Feeley was told that a "computer malfunction" prevented a full statistical analysis of cancer data for New York City, for the moment at least.

"When will these figures be available?" Feeley asked innocently.

"Oh, it's hard to say, Mr. Feeley. You know how troublesome these machines can be. When they're on line, they can do almost anything, but when they're down, it hits the fan. We've only been able to restore access for our immediate patient needs. Full service could be back in hours or days. It's hard to tell. But I'll get back to you as soon as anything is available."

Normally, Feeley would have believed the explanation of such a distinguished scientist, but routine calls to Columbia-Presbyterian, New York Hospital, and Bellevue all resulted in a surprising inability to supply more than the sketchiest information. Frank Feeley began to feel he was onto something.

He made a list of eighty physicians in New York and several of its immediate suburbs. Thirty were specialists in one or more varieties of cancer. The remaining fifty were general practitioners with a few gynecologists and proctologists thrown in. Then he got on the phone. He introduced himself as Mr. Lou Soliman of the City Health Service–an agency which did not exist–and took great pleasure using his editor's name for the purpose. Most of the physicians he was able to reach were willing, if not anxious, to talk.

"I tell you, Mr. Soliman," one doctor reported, "it's downright scary. It seems like every third person who comes in here has some form or at least some symptoms of the disease."

"Have you put together any statistics?" Feeley asked.

"No, not really, though I could pull them together for you if you needed them. Of course, these things go in cycles. I remember once I had a dozen patients with meningitis in less than a week. Funny how these things can catch up with you. You know, when I was a medical student . . ."

"Thank you, doctor, you've been most helpful. I'll get back to you if I need more information."

"OK. Is there an unusual incidence of cancer throughout the city? If you'd like me to be on the lookout . . ."

"Yes, fine. Do keep track. Nothing to worry about for now. I'll get back to you."

"What did you say your name was?" Feeley hung up.

It did not take many calls to determine that a lopsided majority of local physicians had diagnosed an unusually large number of cancer cases. Feeley looked at his list. He had been able to talk with sixty-six of the eighty physicians. Some had been on vacation, and others wanted to know what the City Health Service was. Of the sixty-six, fifty-eight doctors had indicated they had seen an unusual number of cancer cases, though no specific type of carcinoma was predominant. Then he carefully examined the statistics of the City Health Department and HEW. Something was fishy. Either he had by pure chance selected a list of doctors almost 90 percent of whom had simultaneously and independently noticed a remarkable surge in cancer cases, or someone was lying. He decided to take his finding to Soliman.

"Feeley, this is incredible. In the old sense of the word: I don't believe you." The editor glared first at Feeley and then at his documentation. "You make some random phone calls to a bunch of local M.D.s. You use a phoney agency as a cover. You use a phoney name ... What name'd you use?"

"Oh, different ones."

"And on the basis of *this* ..." Lou Soliman looked at Feeley's research as if he'd just found a cockroach in his fettucini. "... you want me to accuse the city, state, and federal governments of conspiracy. Beyond that you want me to believe that we are in the middle of an epidemic. An epidemic of *cancer* for Christ sakes. Say we ran this story you propose, and say it's wrong."

"I don't think it is."

"You don't *think* it is. But just suppose it is wrong. This paper will end up making the biggest editorial blunder since the *Literary Digest* predicted Landon would beat Roosevelt. And we might set off a citywide panic. The legal implications ..." Lou Soliman rolled his eyes. "Look, Frank, maybe I was a bit rough on you over that kid in Queens. We all make mistakes. But you don't have to prove yourself by trying to find the biggest medical story since the discovery of penicillin."

"Lou, I'd been on this thing for weeks before you complained about my snark piece. I know it in my bones that I'm onto something."

"In your bones ..."

"Yeah, and right in front of you on paper. Look, Lou, my job is probably on the line anyway. If you want me to do more work on the story, fine. But if you tell me to drop it, I'll have to go directly to the publisher. Whether you like it or not." Feeley spoke quietly, almost deferentially. There was a long silence. Finally, his editor picked up his papers and studied them. After ten minutes, he spoke.

"I don't know, Frank. This is hot, too hot to handle. I can't allow you to go ahead with a story based on this evidence."

"So I go to the publisher?"

"Yeah, you go to the publisher." Lou Soliman paused. "But I'll go with you."

The meeting went better than either Feeley or Soliman anticipated. Initially incredulous, the publisher examined the interview notes with great care. "Not enough here, but you may be coming up with something. You know, in the past two weeks both my mother-in-law and a first cousin have been diagnosed as having cancer. Probably just a coincidence, but go ahead, and do some more on this; use a couple of staffers for a while. See if there's indication of this going on outside the city. And try, for Christ sakes, to keep the *Times* from hearing about what you're doing." With a gesture reminiscent of a man flicking away an annoying fly, he dismissed them both.

With the help of two fulltime staff researchers, Feeley was able to interview another three hundred New York area physicians. He decided to identify himself as a *News* reporter, and found that most of the doctors he called were delighted to be interviewed by the press. Quite a few were very willing to allow attribution. He then telephoned a randomly selected list of three hundred physicians in thirty other states, including Alaska and Puerto Rico. The results were generally similar to his initial findings. HEW was totally unhelpful. Feeley was finally able to get through to an Undersecretary Samuel Potter, who cooed that everything was just fine with the health of the nation, and that an irresponsible story about an epidemic of cancer would harm millions of gullible people. He then hung up.

Finally Feeley began calling a list of several dozen of the to cancer researchers in the country. At Harvard, Stanford, Rockefelle Yale, Columbia, Texas, Sloan-Kettering, and elsewhere, every singl one could not be reached. A number were supposedly on extende vacations, and in two instances a scientific conference in the Sout was mentioned. One secretary said the meeting was in Atlanta, or s she thought. Feeley checked, and discovered there was no scientifi meeting of any size scheduled anywhere in the South at that tim nor had there been for several months.

Bit by bit, he pieced together his story, scarcely believing it implications. The evidence was by definition circumstantial, but i was nevertheless overwhelming. After three weeks of double- an triple-checking and rephoning almost 1,500 doctors around th country, he knew the story was ready. Lou Soliman and th publisher did their best to punch holes in it, but at last had to agre that it held water. "If you're right, Feeley, I'll see that we erect statue to you in the lobby of this building," his publisher sai grimly. "And if you're wrong, I promise you that you won't be abl to get a job writing dialogue for Marvel Comics. Print it."

With its usual restraint, the Sunday *News* headline went right t the point. "CANCER PLAGUE!" it screamed in huge, six-inch typ

All hell broke loose.

27

Atlanta

Francis X. Feeley's article triggered a near panic throughout the country, and at first glance it would have seemed that a riot had broken out in the biohazard facility of the Center for Disease Control. On closer examination, however, an observer would notice that the mood in the halls was one of jubilation, not fear. Placed on Eric Zimmermann's secretary's desk were two cases of cold Dom Perignon, and amid the popping of corks and outbursts of laughter, what might initially have seemed a panicked mob was in reality a riotous office party in full swing. Even the two narrow-tied security men in the outer office accepted glasses of champagne, and uncomfortably tried to make conversation with Nobel laureates and young lab assistants.

"You throw a good party, Eric," Henry Rogers said, filling a half-liter beaker almost to the brim from a magnum of Dom Perignon. He settled into a comfortable chair and lit a cigarette. "What I don't understand is how you were able to produce half a dozen cases of ice-cold champagne in under half an hour."

"Had it stashed in a dark corner of one of the autopsy coolers downstairs. It was the first or second requisition I put through when I came here." Zimmermann grinned at the half-dozen slightly drunk scientists gathered in his office. "Lucky I'm an honest guy, Henry. Old Wilson gave me a free hand to spend what I wanted, and I expected we'd have reason for a celebration one of these days."

"Or hold a good old-fashioned Irish wake," Rogers remarked dryly.

"Right," Zimmermann replied, refilling a coffee cup with champagne. "You know, I think if I put through an order for a ruby as big as a hen's egg to present to Honorée here, it would turn up in twenty-four hours."

"Not a bad idea," Honorée agreed enthusiastically, "but I prefer emeralds."

"Preference noted." Zimmermann gazed at her with obvious affection. "Preference noted," he repeated softly.

"I like a party as much as the next guy," Dr. Carey-Ross commented, "but I think we should admit that Michigan State deserves most of the credit for this one."

Zimmermann was instantly mock-serious. "You know, Simon, at last I understand why they tried to whisk you away to a posh hospital room in Bethesda, under permanent sedation." Eric pronounced the last word as "settation," and Rogers shot him an apprehensive look. "*You,* Dr. Carey-Ross, Nobel laureate, are an honest man ... and a party-pooper. Ah, what the hell ..." Zimmermann rose and held his cup aloft. "To Michigan, land of a thousand lakes. ..."

"That's Minnesota, dummy," Honorée shouted.

"You sure? OK. To Michigan, the state which gave us, ah, gave us ..."

"Diana Ross and the Supremes," said Carey-Ross confidently.

"You are one surprise after another, sir," Eric said seriously.

"To Michigan." All rose and drank the toast.

Researchers at the College of Human Medicine at Michigan State had made the most important discovery so far in the hunt for the cause of the cancer epidemic. Put simply, a fundamental shift had taken place in the gene pool. The average American, or for that matter, European or Japanese, had a very slightly different DNA configuration, a modification of only a few molecules from the previous norm. There was some evidence that though the DNA had been altered by just these few molecules, the shift was sufficient to cause some cells to begin the cancer process. What made the findings all the more exciting was the fact that samples taken from people in those areas which had not exhibited the cancer outbreak, such as Dellon's Creek, had not, for the most part, been subject to this genetic modification.

"Well," Eric said, settling back into his chair, "the celebration is certainly deserved, if premature. But I can promise you a real blowout once we isolate the virus behind this DNA modification."

"Still on the viral kick, eh, Eric?" Rogers asked.

"Oh come off it, Henry. Isn't it obvious now? We've spent months trying to find some environmental cause with your god-damned computers. You've sifted more bits of data than there're grains of sand at Coney Island. I think this Michigan State data," he held up his hand to silence Rogers, "while not proving, *per se,* the presence of a virus, surely points in that direction."

Rogers looked grim. "Maybe. Maybe not."

"Come off it again, Henry." Eric felt a surge of frustration and anger. "It could be a single viral protein, the expression of a single viral gene. Maybe a slow virus, cooking over a period of years and ultimately resulting in this . . . this scourge." Zimmermann realized he had raised his voice and that everyone in the room suddenly looked serious.

"You could be right, Eric. Of course that could be the cause. But right now you have no proof. How come your virus—a slow one or one as fast as a teenager in heat—how come it somehow avoided Dellon's Creek or some of the Indian reservations or the sharecroppers in five counties? Now wait a minute." Rogers had been fumbling through his pockets looking for a match. "I have the fucking floor."

Honorée leaned over it and lit Henry's cigarette. Taking one for herself, she ignited it and inhaled deeply. Zimmermann was surprised. He had never seen her smoke before. "OK, Henry, you got the floor. But you're just being obdurate. Stubborn."

"Who says I'm being stubborn? For the love of the Blessed Virgin in Heaven, Eric, I'm not saying you're *wrong*. You may well be right, for all I know."

"Hah," Eric interjected bitterly. Honorée silently mouthed the word "hush" at Eric and gestured to him to calm down. Zimmermann took no notice.

"Even a fundamental genetic change such as has been demonstrated by the people at Michigan could be just a symptom pointing in any number of directions," Rogers continued. "It's been demonstrated a million times that an environmental insult can take advantage of a genetic predisposition to disease, particularly, I repeat particularly, cancer."

"Thank you, professor, for your learned opinion," Eric said angrily. "Of course the years you've spent tinkering with your magical computers and away from the forefront of research uniquely equip you to tell all of us the direction our research should take."

"That's not fair, Eric," Honorée said seriously.

"Maybe not. But I'm running the show here, whether Henry likes it or not, and it's my reasoned opinion that the major thrust of the Caduceus Group effort has got to be concentrated on the search for a viral cause of this epidemic. *This,"* he crashed his fist down on his desk, "is the reason I've spent so much of my time overseeing a crash program to expand and fully equip this biohazard facility as well as the one down the road at Emory University. And don't think I don't know that you've tried to undercut this work, Rogers."

Carey-Ross spoke up. "Don't you think that is a bit paranoid, young man?"

Eric was incensed by the "young man" reference, but he tried to hold his temper in check. He failed.

"Tell them, Dr. Rogers; tell them how you've syphoned off resources for data analysis. Kept some of the best Caduceus personnel working on your programs. Subtly, insidiously, undercut my efforts to equip the Caduceus Group to investigate this virus or this whatever-it-may-be. You may look like a slob, but you're the best political infighter I've ever come across."

"I couldn't be that good, Zimmermann, could I?" Rogers retorted. "You have your labs, your biohazard facilities. All probably the best in the world. You *are* paranoid. So I've tried to keep a few people at work on the data analysis you so despise. You've let your monumental ego . . ."

"Stop it, both of you. You make me sick!" Honorée was on her feet, her eyes blazing. Eric started to say something. "Shut up!" She looked at Rogers and Zimmermann, and both seemed at least momentarily cowed. "Now, let's try to forget this argument, shall we? Particularly the *ad hominem* attacks." She glared at Eric and continued. "The question is, where do we go from here? It seems obvious to me, anyway, that Henry has to continue to gather and analyze the phenomenal amount of data we're now receiving. And it also seems to me that Eric, being in charge of Caduceus, has every right to direct the course of its research. Though he should not expect that every member of this admittedly intelligent group will automatically agree with him," Honorée said pointedly and paused.

"Now, has anyone bothered to tell Washington about the Michigan State discovery?" She looked around the room.

"I thought it a bit premature to offer them an apparent panacea to their nightmarish political problems right away. God knows we have a long way to go." Zimmermann's tone was almost sheepish. "Of course, in a week or two we can let the higherups hear about it. No way we'll have any answers by then, of course, but at least we'll be a little bit further ahead, maybe have some new leads."

Honorée honestly concurred, knowing that within the next hour she would report to her superior at NSA. She also knew that they would honor her request not to disseminate the information for a few days at the very least. NSA would be delighted. Nothing pleases an intelligence officer like a "scoop" ahead of any other agency, branch of government, or for that matter, President Wilson himself.

She felt no sense of betrayal. Eric and Henry were acting like little boys fighting in the schoolyard. There was no way either could be harmed. Besides, it was her duty.

Still, she felt guilty.

Henry Rogers and Eric Zimmermann were both very tired and more than a little drunk. The group began to break up and head for the elevators. Rogers tried to mend fences.

"Look, Eric, we're on the same side. You must know that by now, for Christ sakes. It's just that you don't have a classic epidemiological pattern to indicate a viral infection."

"Yeah, but there's no classic pattern for millions of people suddenly contracting cancer either," Eric retorted wearily.

"But don't you see, it's got to be an environmental or chemical hazard which has passed unnoticed into the whole population except for these few groups in remote areas."

"Je-*sus.*" Eric punched the down button for the elevator.

"You lack hard data. Anyway, what about that kid in San Francisco?"

"DeAngelis?"

"Right. What about him? If your theory is correct, the odds are very good that he should contract cancer. Should have already. Has he?"

"You know he hasn't," Zimmermann responded tensely. "We're moving him out to NIH day after tomorrow. Better research facilities there. I think we should do a spinal tap. . . ."

Rogers looked sick. "Oh, that poor kid. If your theory's incorrect, you'll probably torture him to death. And if you're right, and he does contract cancer, then what?"

"That should seem obvious," Eric said bitterly, "even to you!"

"In that case," Rogers said, "we should pray that you are wrong. Our DNA has been affected as well. If such a change makes an eventual predisposition to carcinoma nearly a sure thing, then by the time you develop your mythical vaccine for your mythical virus, then, my boy, *then* we'll all be dead." Rogers began to laugh to himself, quietly at first, but with increasingly uncontrollable mirth. The elevator door finally opened. Zimmermann dragged Honorée in with him and Carey-Ross followed. Rogers, however, was barely able to restrain his hysterical laughter and stayed behind.

"Fat bureaucratic asshole," Eric muttered, pushing the button for the lobby.

Just as the doors began to close he heard Rogers grumble, "fucking egomaniacal punk." Eric and Honorée said nothing as they left together and walked to his car.

28

North Druid Hills, Georgia

"Why don't you let me drive?" Honorée asked as they approached Zimmermann's car in the CDC parking lot.

"No, I'm fine. I'll be careful," he muttered.

The drive to Eric's apartment was all but devoid of conversation. Traffic was unusually light, and Eric, true to his word, drove carefully. About a mile from his apartment, Honorée asked if they had anything for dinner. Eric was silent for a moment, still lost in thought.

"Hum? No. I can stop for something if you like, though I'd be happy with some soup and a sandwich."

"Fine with me," Honorée replied. Eric carefully maneuvered the car into his parking spot, and helped her carry a bulging briefcase full of reports into his apartment. They ate in silence, though there was no evidence of hostility between them. Finally, over coffee, Honorée spoke.

"Don't you think you were a little hard on Henry? I mean I know he was, well, difficult, but . . ."

"Yeah. He just pissed me off." He paused. "Still, I shouldn't have lost my temper. I dunno, we're all tired, ready to snap, and the champagne didn't help. I thought we'd all relax for an hour or two, but that sure backfired." Eric sounded embarrassed, and Honorée was relieved his argument with Rogers would not develop into a full-fledged feud. "I'm not cut out for administration. I'm intolerant, lose my temper. Hell, for years I've been sniping at the bozos on top for giving me orders, and now that I'm there I can't brook the slightest disagreement. I think I should resign and turn the job over to someone else. Carey-Ross, maybe."

Honorée rose and began to massage his neck. The muscles were extremely tight. He closed his eyes and sighed with sincere pleasure. "That's ridiculous, Eric," she said as her fingers gently circled his temples. "I'm sure Henry feels just as foolish as you do. Why, he told me just the other day how impressed he was at the job you've been doing."

"You're kidding."

"No, it's the truth. He really respects you."

Eric sounded consoled. "Well, God knows I respect him. The man's brilliant. He's an odd duck–eccentric–I just don't know why he refused to see my point about the virus."

"Because he's a very, very cautious scientist. Maybe stodgy by your lights. You can see that he simply wants more data, more evidence, before he's willing to go along with any hypothesis. You're just so certain, and to him that certainty rests on circumstantial evidence." Honorée gently shoved him forward and worked on his shoulder blades.

"So you agree with him that I'm an arrogant young whipper-snapper?"

"Of course I do, darling," she replied. "But the great scientists usually are." She kissed his neck gently and continued. "Intuition is important, but Henry yearns for proof. You can't blame him for that."

"Sure. You're right. I'll apologize to him tomorrow. I hope he'll forgive my remarks about his being a fat slob and so forth. *Christ,"* Eric said forcefully, his voice filled with pain, "I sounded like a twelve-year-old."

"So did he, Eric. You both lost your tempers. And speaking as a scientist and not your friend and lover, I think you were probably closer to the truth than he. Henry's whole life has been one big mess of fears. He's too cautious. He could have set up practice or been tremendously successful in private research, but as soon as he could, he fled to the security of the government. He's been waiting all his life for some invisible axe to fall. He can't swim and he's afraid to learn how. He goes home every night and eats a couple of boxes of cookies and stares at the walls, afraid to ask anyone out. When he does, like to a party, he's so uncomfortable he drinks too much and then makes a fool of himself. His sex life is nil, and he saves almost every penny he earns. Though, of course, he expects to lose it all someday when the banks all fail." Honorée's voice was almost harsh.

"That's a little strong," Eric chided.

"No, really," Honorée continued. "The reason Henry Rogers is such a brilliant statistician is because in numbers, in data, he can find a degree of security, of certainty. He's only comfortable with his computer console—at least it never talks back to him—and with a handful of people he's convinced are so brilliant they are likely to be correct in their judgments. People like you, Carey-Ross, a few others. That's why your insisting that an assumption, an intuition, is fact drives him up the walls. . . ."

Eric turned and looked at Honorée, astonishment in his expression. "You should have gone into psychiatry. How, pray, do you know all about Henry's sex life? And if he's such a miser, how come the sports cars he always drives?"

"Oh, Henry and I have had some heart-to-hearts. He likes me, and I confess I do flirt with him just a little. And he's not neuter. He was engaged to a girl some years back, but she's dead."

"A shame," Eric said quietly.

"Of course it was; he'd probably be a much happier person had she lived. A stupid lab accident. It just reinforced his belief that whatever you get will eventually be taken back by a vengeful God or Fate or something. As for the cars, they're the only luxury he allows himself. All through his boyhood as well as college and medical school he travelled by streetcars, first to Boston University and then to Harvard. His family could never afford to buy him a car. His father gave him one when he graduated from B.U., but the old man died shortly after that, and Henry sold it because he felt guilty running a car when both he and his mother were so short of cash. He promised himself that someday he would have other, nicer cars, and he kept the promise. I guess it's symbolic to him that as long as he can tool around in a $30,000 machine, the world hasn't come to an end, though he penny-pinches on everything else because he really *does* expect it all to fall apart sooner or later."

"You're amazing, Honorée. I mean, you got all that out of him?"

"Well, most of it. And I'll kill you if you ever use anything I've told you on him, no matter how angry you are," she said seriously.

"I promise."

"It's just that I want you to understand what makes Henry tick, so you won't overreact and resign from Caduceus. I love Henry—I really think he's a beautiful person as well as smart. I'd do anything to keep him from being hurt. But I love you too, Eric . . . I love you very much."

Eric rose and put his arms around her. "I still say you should have been a shrink if you could get all of that out of him in just a couple of conversations." He kissed her.

Honorée closed her eyes and returned the kiss. She had had several intimate talks with Rogers, but she also had access to the psychological profiles which had been drawn up on every key member of Caduceus.

"I wonder if you know as much about the way I think?" he said, running his hands down her back and kissing her again. "Like what I'm thinking right now."

"Perhaps," she said a bit coyly.

"Well, Dr. Freud, let us continue the analysis on the couch."

"Of course," Honorée said, affecting a dreadful Viennese accent. "But firzt ve must make ze patient comfortable." She began to unbutton his shirt.

29

Scarsdale, New Yor

As any attorney specializing in malpractice would say, there i never a valid excuse for making a mistake when a patient's life o psychological well-being is at stake. This is a fact.

A second fact is that doctors are human beings, not gods, and ar every bit as capable of making an error as anyone else. Dr. Richar Lynd hardly ever made a mistake. He was careful, methodica dedicated. But for some time, Lynd's typical day had lasted well ove twelve hours, seven days a week, week after week. He recognize that he was approaching total physical exhaustion. During surgery his well-trained hands operated almost automatically, two indepen dent life forms seemingly unguided by his mind. He found i increasingly difficult to concentrate for long periods of time whil his mind raced in high gear cataloging the next consultation, th next operation, and the probable hopelessness of even attempting t halt the inundation of cancer cases at Markland Memorial.

Dr. Lynd was one of the few people not to be surprised when h read of Francis X. Feeley's exposé of a cancer epidemic and th eventual admission by the President that it was true. He had know for months that each passing day brought more cases to the hospital. He felt like a soldier in the midst of a never ending surreal battle. Every morning he awoke from a dreamless sleep unrefreshed, fatigued, ready for the next enemy assault. The image of a soldier is not inappropriate since he had already been "drafted" under a provision of the Medical Resources Allocation Act to head the surgery division of a temporary hospital being thrown together in the Bronx. In four days he would truly be in the thick of the fighting, and he forced himself to reduce the number of operations to a minimum and concentrate on clearing up all the paperwork that had accumulated in the past few weeks.

He rubbed his eyes and turned on his desk lamp. Even ignoring the non-essential forms from Blue Cross and insurance companies (God only knew how they would ever survive this), he worked steadily writing or talking into his dictaphone.

Some doctors, facing a similar situation, would have ignored paperwork altogether, but Dr. Lynd was extremely conscientious.

So it can easily be understood that as the hours dragged by, even he could make a mistake. It was an easy error to make. One file was labeled "McConnell," the other, "McCormack." Both were tumors in the left breast. He took the first file and began to examine the thermogram and mammogram. There could be no question the tumor was malignant; any medical student would have recognized it immediately. He looked at the next folder, and quickly decided that the tumor was almost certainly benign, at least when the shots had been taken several weeks before.

He realized he had to go to the bathroom, but punched the "dictate" button and said: "Carol. Please call, ah, Mrs. McConnell and tell her that there is no indication of carcinoma in her breast at this time. Tell her she definitely should have the tumor removed, but will have to wait until the present situation stabilizes. Call Mrs. McCormack and tell her that I'm sorry but there does seem to be a malignancy appearing on her shots. It's hard to tell if it has metastasized, but I am sure it's operable. Explain to her that we will do everything possible to schedule her a bed, but that it is my personal belief she should try to get into one of the New York City facilities since the turnover is a lot faster even with the present backlog. As usual," he concluded wearily, "apologize that I was unable to call myself, and tell her the survival rate is generally quite high." He pushed the "Off" button and rubbed his eyes once more.

Considering the circumstances, it was an easy mistake to make. He was exhausted. The names were similar, and so were the symptoms—a single small tumor on the left breast. Five months later, Miss Sophie McConnell, aged forty-six, would die of mammary carcinoma, from a tumor previously diagnosed as benign.

Six weeks later, Hope McCormack was in New York City anxiously awaiting a radical mastectomy that she did not need.

30

Washington, D.C.

A nondescript black sedan swung out of the main exit of Central Intelligence Agency and crawled down Route 123 toward Chain Bridge and across the Potomac. Bill Williams drove himself, as was his habit. Every morning, the same black Ford would pull up to his house in Alexandria. A distinguished, silver-haired gentleman sat comfortably in the back, and a young bodyguard was invariably in the right front seat. The car would cruise quietly into his driveway, and Williams was invariably waiting for them.

The Director was by no means a timid man, but a profound sense of caution and anonymity had been the hallmark of his successful career as an intelligence officer. One could never be too careful. The head of the CIA received death threats the way a politician gets Christmas cards. Few were serious, and even fewer had the will to carry them out. But Williams also knew there were several terrorist groups with good reason to want to kill him; hence, the "dummy" in the rear of the car. A serious attempt at assassination would probably take them all out, and a professional killer would instantly recognize him behind the wheel. But Bill Williams believed in improving the odds whenever possible, and terrorist suicide squads usually made up for a lack of brains with an excess of courage. The "dummy" did not mind. The assignment was not a difficult one, and every morning he carefully checked the loaded, high-velocity submachine gun which lay on the floor by his feet.

The car swung onto K Street and headed toward the Soviet Embassy on 16th Street in Northwest Washington. On that evening, Williams dispensed with his surrogate in the back of the car and paid little attention to the chatter of his bodyguard, a man he had hand-picked primarily because he looked and acted like a car salesman, not a Federal agent.

He paid little attention to the traffic. The meeting ahead of him with Anatol Semenov occupied his thoughts entirely.

"Sir, you just ran a stop sign," the guard commented.

"Huh? Oh, sorry," Williams apologized unnecessarily.

Normally, Bill Williams got along with the Russians very nicely. Once, as an unofficial member of the SALT IV negotiating team, his blunt, though fair, conversations with Soviet intelligence officers had helped with the drafting of a mutually acceptable treaty. On another occasion, he had negotiated a secret agreement to limit the activities of "killer" satellites. Though Williams definitely considered the Russians to be the primary enemy of the United States, he had always found it comparatively easy to deal with them. They were such complete cynics, he could usually understand their motivations and, in a way, see their point of view. And the Russians would compromise, if necessary.

His dealings with the Chinese had not been as satisfactory. They never seemed to understand that diplomacy is at least partially a game. Clutching their copies of Mao (Old Testament) and Tung (New Testament), they would lecture their opponents rather than negotiate with them. Williams had had experience with a majority of the Chinese Republics, and he felt he understood what it would have been like debating with Oliver Cromwell.

Or President Thomas Wilson.

His last meeting with the President had left him deeply disturbed. Wilson was hardly able to control his emotions. Occasionally, he seemed giddy, manic. More often, however, his mood was dark. Despite Arthur Greenbaum's effort to keep him under control, Wilson was obviously drinking heavily.

"It's not the political pressure," Arthur Greenbaum had told him after one particularly rancorous meeting of the National Security Council. "The speech he gave last week was one of the most brilliant performances I've ever seen."

"I have to agree," Williams said.

"He kept the people calm, explained at least the outlines of the crisis and the effort being made to cope with it. It mean when you consider what's going on, it's a wonder people aren't marching in the streets."

"The epidemic apparently has a long way to go, Arthur. He didn't mention Henry Rogers' figure of fifty million cancer cases. He minimized the situation. And that line about every patient having the best medical care available–you know as well as I do that within a month there probably won't be any available hospital beds. Then what?"

Greenbaum looked perplexed. "A nationwide panic wouldn't do us any good, and you damn well know that. What happens will happen. We've simply bought a little time. Maybe not enough, but what with the Michigan State results . . ." Williams showed surprise. "Oh yes, Bill, I know, and I can see that you do too. So you got your man on the inside, eh? Well, let's say I have a few sources myself." The two men smiled at one another.

"I can see your talents are wasted at HEW, Greenbaum," Williams commented dryly. He became serious. "Will the Presidential Powers Act pass Congress?"

"Definitely," Greenbaum said confidently.

"And what do you make of that line in Wilson's speech about 'seeking out and confronting those who are responsible?' Make anything of that?" Williams asked quietly.

"Most commentators assumed he was referring to the big stink about the surprise element. The 'coverup' of the crisis. Which of course we were, are, all involved in. Justifiably, of course."

"Fuck the commentators," Williams exploded with uncharacteristic obscenity. "I want to know what you thought he meant. It wasn't in your original draft."

"How do you . . . oh, of course. Well, I have my own idea on that score. But I'd like to hear you first," Secretary Greenbaum said.

"Very well. I think it is obvious President Wilson was referring to the Soviet Union."

"And?"

"And the President is under great psychological strain. He could snap at any time. Perhaps he already has. Clearly, he's lost a grip on himself. He blames the Kremlin for his daughter's illness. He's been drinking heavily and steadily. Even talks to himself when he thinks he's alone. The man is dangerous."

Arthur Greenbaum said nothing for several moments. "The man," he said carefully, "is the President of the United States. And I thought you had a reputation for being taciturn. You've just all but admitted that you have the President bugged, and you obviously don't think he's fit for office. *And* you're telling this to me, one of his closest friends, probably the closest. Why?"

Williams colored slightly, and minutely examined his fingernails. "Because–" He paused. "Because I think this crisis can only get worse, for the short term at least. And because I am afraid the circumstantial evidence points to a biological attack from the Soviet Union. . . ."

"And you of all people don't think the Russians would do such a thing?"

"Oh, at least some of the leadership are capable of it, but there are a dozen reasons why it can't be the answer. It's the wrong time. Our relations are cool, but hardly critical. If they were to hit anyone, it would be the Chinese. They're scared silly of them. Additionally, leaving aside the fact that every bit of intelligence indicates they are presently incapable of successfully launching such an attack, if you're going to wipe out an enemy, you do just that. Boom. Airborn anthrax or botulism strains or a host of other agents which act fairly fast and are far more deadly than a mixed bag of cancers. It's just too subtle. Very un-Russian. And on top of that it's stupid to release some kind of bug and sit back for several years while your enemy is slowly being decimated, all the while showing no ill effects yourself. It just doesn't wash."

"And you're worried that Tom Wilson will get us into a war?" Greenbaum's voice was flat.

"Yes, I think he might. At this point I think the odds are in favor of it. You've heard my arguments before, and you've also heard the President. I'm being candid with you because I think you can be trusted and because you know Wilson better than I do. Now, I've spilled my guts. You said you would give me your opinion. . . ."

Greenbaum looked directly into the pale blue eyes of the CIA Director. "I agree with every single word you've said. My only disagreement is with your judgment that Tom Wilson is likely to react with an act of war, let alone nuclear war. It's possible. But he can be controlled. Take my word for it. You've been honest, so, I will too. I made Wilson president, and he knows it. For better or worse, I'm his Dr. Frankenstein. He does what I say when I choose to tell him what to do. He's pretty ragged right now, I admit. The strain must be crushing. But I can keep him in line. I know it."

"I hope you're right," Williams said evenly. "I hope to God you're right."

The car swung into the driveway of the Russian embassy and stopped at a massive iron gate. A guard took a quick look at Williams' identification and face and gestured him forward. "You're expected," he said, in perfect, unaccented English.

For the first time in more than two decades, it crossed his mind that he should have been the banker his father had wanted him to be. He sighed audibly and got out of the sedan. Williams had been sent to deliver an unofficial ultimatum to the Soviet Union.

31

New York City

Francis X. Feeley should have been a happy man. He had been given a raise which almost doubled his salary. His superiors regularly solicited his opinion, and Lou Soliman prophesied a Pulitzer Prize for both Feeley and the *News.* Most wondrous, his puny expense account had been transformed into a blank check. "Go out and spend, Frank," Lou had said. "Get in with the doctors and politicians. Find out what the little people are thinking. Spend whatever you need to cover this story." Feeley should have been very happy, and he did bask in the praise and attention. But he was miserable.

He hated the assignment, and in more than a month he came up with only four tentative stories. He spent most of his time covering the better bars of Manhattan and avoiding any discussion of cancer.

"Let me go to the West Coast, Lou," he had pleaded. "That's where the wildest stories are. New York is like an armed camp, like some medieval village during the Black Plague. It's too depressing."

Lou Soliman looked hurt, then angry. "This paper covers New York. We can get all the looney stories we need off the wire services.

So one group in L.A. says that beating off causes cancer and another claims it prevents it. That's not the story we're after—group masturbation for Christ sakes." He looked disgusted. "Or any of the religious zanies either."

"Come *on,* Lou, what about those thirty people in New Mexico who *volunteered* to be crucified, and were allowed to go through with it? What about the guy in Marin County selling mud by the ton claiming it has medicinal properties, and people lining up to eat it. To eat dirt. Or . . ."

Soliman cut him off. "Feeley, you surprise me. You're supposed to be the *science* reporter for this paper, not the human interest editor. I want you in this city or in Washington, if you think you can break through to somebody in the government. And I want you to cover the progress being made in finding the cure for this plague."

"There is none. Believe me. No progress—no cure," Feeley said.

"Well, then report that. But you should be out talking to the scientists anyway. Find out what they're thinking. And if you do come across a human interest story, it had better be in this city. No mass crucifixions unless they're in Central Park."

"I can't wait," Feeley muttered, and headed for the Four Seasons Grill. Jim smiled and poured him a Heineken without being asked. He began to read the latest HEW reports, but tossed them aside with a curse and pulled out an old collection of Irwin Shaw stories. He had settled in for the afternoon.

Of the four pieces Feeley attempted, none was ever printed. First, he interviewed the Chief of Staff at City Hospital. This distinguished gentleman explained that the city's medical resources were all but drained. A huge supply train of analgesics was on its way from an army base in the south, but it only travelled a few dozen miles a day (never at night) under a very heavy guard of more than five hundred troops. The security was commendable, but it would take another ten days to reach New York, and drugs were in short supply.

"How are you able to treat so many people?" Feeley asked.

The doctor looked very thoughtful. "Off the record?" he asked.

"If you insist."

"I do. The centralization of care in dozens of hospitals and an equal number of temporary medical facilities such as Rockefeller Center, Roosevelt Island, Co-op City, and elsewhere has helped a lot. Bellevue and New York Hospital, for example, are among those which handle cancer cases exclusively. But people still get sick, still have babies, still have accidents; so other facilities, like St. Vincent's in the Village or Bronx General concentrate on general medicine. That way we're able to concentrate all the cancer treatment for the city in a few dozen large facilities. It's much more efficient." He leaned back, lit a pipe and looked content, almost smug.

Feeley thought his explanation sounded rehearsed; the doctor had probably had a great deal of practice discussing it.

"I hear you're not treating the elderly," Feeley said quietly, being careful to note the doctor's reaction.

"Where did you hear that?" He'd hit home: the man was obviously flustered.

"I get around."

"Look, do I have your word this conversation is off the record?"

Feeley feigned sincerity. "Let's just say it's on deep background."

The doctor hesitated, then asked, "Have you ever heard the word *triage?*"

"Sure, comes from the First World War. When too many casualties came into the field hospitals, they were divided into three groups. The ones who seemed mortally or very seriously wounded were made comfortable, but allowed to die. Those with slight wounds were made to wait or were dismissed. The medical care went to those who had serious wounds but a good chance of survival." Feeley knew his history.

"Precisely. Well, off the record mind you, we have had to adopt a slightly similar procedure."

Feeley looked curious. "How slightly?"

The Chief of Staff sighed. "To some degree you are correct about the elderly, though it is not an official policy, let me stress that. If a patient is admitted who is sixty-five or over and has any serious form of carcinoma, he is given a generous supply of pain-killers and sent home. If he is unable to leave, then we keep him in the wards and try to make him comfortable."

"So the cutoff is sixty-five?" Feeley asked casually.

"Well, if it's serious and there are any other complicating factors, heart disease, say, sixty is a closer estimate. We do everything possible to keep them comfortable, you understand."

"Of course," Feeley agreed.

"Then there's the children . . ."

"You mean you don't treat children?"

"Good God no! Children have the highest priority after physicians and health workers themselves. It's just that we have a very distinct, uh, problem with very small children. I'm sure you must understand that there are relatively few pediatric surgeons available, and babies, children, require specialized medical care. A high percentage of them are not surviving, whatever is done for them. But believe me, they get the highest priority." He looked worried but sincere.

"I believe you, doctor."

"I hope you do, Mr. Feeley. I hope you do. The physicians here and all over the city have been working twelve-, thirteen-, fourteen-hour days for over 120 consecutive days. Even some of the young men have suffered heart attacks or nervous collapse. We're doing our best to save everyone who can be saved. Believe me."

"I believe you, doctor."

That night, Feeley lay awake trying to decide whether or not to do the story. It would make the front page; there was no question of that. But what good would it do? Deep background simply meant he could not ethically give his source, though he doubted that the doctor at City Hospital understood the distinction. He decided not to file the story.

The next week, Feeley interviewed a Department of Health official who explained that there was a severe shortage of coffins in New York because of the sudden increase in the death rate. The city was going to open up a "temporary potters' field" for both the indigent

and those unable to find any other burial site. "It will be done wit
dignity," the official insisted, noting that they would be able t
"handle" a thousand burials a day within a week. The mass grave
were to be located at Crookes Point on Staten Island. When h
checked his map that night, Feeley discovered that Crookes Poin
was actually part of Great Kills Park, a former landfill area. He toye
with the idea of a headline reading: GREAT KILLS: NEW
YORKERS TO BE USED AS LANDFILL, but decided correctl
that it would sound flippant. The story appeared as a small item o
page thirty of the *News.*

Then there was the mammoth "Festival of Life," which was bette
known as the "Fuck-In." What had begun as a city-organized "Nev
Yorkers Together Day" evolved into a bizarre fiesta even befor
sunset. Feeley had always prided himself on having a raunch
imagination, but as he wandered around Central Park that night, h
was simultaneously aroused, disgusted, astonished, and terrified
Close to twenty thousand of his fellow citizens of all ages from th
barely pubescent to definitely geriatric coupled, fondled, and flaile
in every version of the sex act he had ever seen or imagined. As h
walked around the periphery of the "Festival" on the Central Par
West side, a well-dressed middle-aged man approached him.

"Pardon me, sir," he said politely.

Feeley regarded the man. He was the epitome of the Paul Stuart
accoutred, well-barbered Wall Streeter. "Yes, can I help you?" Feele
asked.

"Yes, I think you can," the man said confidently. "I would like t
give you a blow job."

Feeley pushed him away, and started to leave the park. A fa
woman in her forties or fifties lurched at him from the bushes. "Hey
you," she said in a commanding tone. Feeley paused.

"Yes?"

"You look like an Irish face to me, an' I only fuck with Irishme
or people who look like it. Whatsha say?" She lifted her caftan

revealing a fat and ugly body. Feeley, saying nothing, began to run.

He circled back to the main event in Sheep Meadow and watched with wide eyes the coupling, if that was the word, of male-female, male-male, female-female, human-animal. From his perspective, the mostly white bodies roiling before his eyes looked like spaghetti boiling in a pot. Fortunately he was not in the immediate vicinity of the shots.

One, perhaps two–the police were never sure–religious zealots marred the festivities by opening fire with automatic weapons. Four killed, Feeley wrote, hours later, six wounded. At a certain point he ceased being a reporter. He wandered about, observing, making no notes, trying to comprehend the scale of it all. He was Pierre on a battlefield of sex. As he staggered across the Sheep Meadow, trying to get home, he found himself trying not to look at the naked bodies gamboling despite the chilly weather. If he had remained on the scene, he would have witnessed the counterdemonstration of some Penitent Christians, who joyfully crucified three of their group in the foliage around Bethesda fountain, and violently resisted police efforts to tear down the crosses and help the voluntary Christs to the hospital.

The Festival of Life continued until sunrise, and finally was cleared from the park by mounted police.

Frank Feeley worked hard on his story, incorporating some of his own experiences with his professional observations. It was one of the best pieces of journalism he had ever done. Vivid but fair. Realistic but impressionistic.

He filed the story, but Lou decided to use the one submitted by the theater critic.

Finally, he flew to Washington for an interview with Arthur Greenbaum. Because the Secretary had to testify before a Senate Committee that afternoon, Feeley was shunted off to Undersecretary Potter. The interview lasted for over an hour, but Potter said nothing not already available in HEW handouts. On the shuttle back to LaGuardia, Feeley looked at his notes. He flipped through the pages hoping to find some angle for a story. It was hopeless. Potter's last quoted words were: "It's a difficult situation at present. Of that there can be no doubt. But in the long run, we have nothing to worry about." Feeley stared at his typewriter for over an hour that evening, trying to write a story based on these words. Men like Potter had always set his teeth on edge, and he thought he could make something of the comment that there was nothing to worry about when New York City alone admitted close to two hundred thousand cases of cancer. He filed the story mostly to show he had not completely wasted his time in Washington, though he did not expect it to run. It never did.

32

Washington, D.C.

Bill Williams was escorted to a comfortable room of the Soviet Embassy. The young woman who showed him in offered tea, but he declined and walked to the fire. She politely assured him the Ambassador would be with him immediately. He nodded, and looked around. He expected to wait fifteen to twenty minutes. There is an unwritten protocol determining the length of time an ambassador keeps a visitor waiting, varying with the rank of the caller and the nature of the call. Williams eyed a comfortable chair by the fire, but decided to remain standing. He was certain he was being watched, and did not want to appear too informal.

The room was filled with books neatly arranged by author. He noticed that a great many were by American writers, not a few of whom were forbidden to the Russian people. He smiled when he noticed several volumes of Solzhenitsyn, and wondered if an alarm would go off if he were to remove one from the shelf.

Ambassador Semenov and a dour, heavy-set man were watching Williams through a two-way mirror. Both noticed the slight smile across his face, though they could not see its cause and to both of them he looked perfectly at ease. He was not. He could not remember a time when he had been so nervous. He glanced at a beautiful nineteenth-century clock which told him he had been waiting under four minutes. It had seemed much longer.

Williams was pleasantly surprised when the door to the library burst open and Semenov charged across the room, his hand extended. "Mr. Williams. I hope you have not been waiting long . . ."

"No sir, I just arrived a minute ago. Thank you for agreeing to see me."

The Russian smiled. "But *of course* I would see you: a distinguished and, shall we say, *unusual* visitor to the Soviet Embassy! I don't suppose," Semenov said in a hushed tone, "that you've decided to defect?" He paused, and burst into a hearty laugh.

Williams smiled slightly, against his will. The Ambassador was charming, but then, that was his job when the occasion called for it. The smile disappeared when he noticed to his astonishment the other man in the room, Nikolai Krylenko, was trying–and failing–to look pleasant. He offered Williams his hand.

"It is a pleasure to meet you again, Mr. Williams. It has been many years since Salt IV. I hope you are well." Krylenko smiled again, exposing bad teeth. He was a silver-haired, moon-faced man who could have passed for a minister or a small-town businessman. He was the head of the KGB.

Williams tried not to look surprised. "I did not know you were visiting us, Mr. Krylenko. . . ."

"Nikolai arrived just this morning, Mr. Williams," Ambassador Semenov interrupted, "and he will be leaving for Moscow the day after tomorrow. Since I am unable to leave Washington at the moment, he was kind enough to come all this way to consult with me about the crisis presently affecting so much of the world. I assumed you would have no objection to his presence at this meeting, though if you do . . ."

"No, Mr. Krylenko may stay. My message is a brief one." Williams looked for a moment at the KGB man. He had survived

Stalin and Beria, kept a low profile under Khrushchev, and ultimately clawed his way to the top of the Soviet intelligence establishment. He was one of perhaps half a dozen people in Russia who held real power, and Williams was furious he had not known of his arrival in Washington. The Ambassador offered him a seat, but Williams refused.

"As you know, I have a message for the Soviet government from the President of the United States. At this time, we felt that an informal statement of our views would be more appropriate than a diplomatic note, but I want to emphasize that we have carefully considered our position. Lacking what we consider an appropriate response from your government, we will be compelled to consider a course of action which could lead to a conflict between our nations."

Ambassador Semenov nodded gravely. Krylenko's cold gray eyes betrayed nothing. Williams took a sheet of paper from his coat pocket and continued.

"Gentlemen. We have reason to believe that the Soviet Union has surreptitiously and without provocation launched an insidious biological attack against the United States and its allies." The two Russians exchanged glances. "Unless action is immediately taken on the part of the Soviet government to provide a vaccine which we have reason to believe you have in your possession, the consequences for both our nations will be extremely grave. If you comply with this demand, the matter of reparations will be taken up at another time, but there is no reason to risk a nuclear exchange if you will cooperate. That is the message from my government, and I thank you for your attention."

Williams folded the sheet of paper and returned it to his pocket. He was ready to leave, but Semenov blocked his way and took his arm. "I understand that you do not agree with the contents of the message, Mr. Williams," he said softly.

"You assume too much, Mr. Ambassador," Williams replied, glancing at the silent but attentive Krylenko.

"Ah, no, my friend, I do not owe this information to your rival Nikolai, but to Mr. Norman Douglas, your Secretary of State. Mr.

Douglas also gave me the, ah, gist of your message almost two days ago, which is the primary reason Mr. Krylenko is here. Please. Do take a chair."

Williams looked stunned. Almost without thinking, he sat. "I don't believe you, Ambassador Semenov. I don't see what you expect to gain by . . ."

"I will explain." Semenov crossed the room and opened the door. The young woman who had shown Williams in appeared in a matter of seconds. "We would like some drinks. Our guest will have a gin and tonic."

"Rum and tonic," Krylenko stated.

"Ah, yes, of course, that is your drink, is it not, Mr. Williams?"

"My compliments to Mr. Krylenko, and I will have a short drink with you if you insist. . . ." Williams' mind was racing. Had the KGB penetrated the Department of State? Perhaps even the Secretary of State? ". . . but I'll have what you have."

Semenov smiled. "Ever cautious. Well, I understand." He turned to the young woman. "Bring us ice, tonic, and one bottle of rum. We will all drink with you, Mr. Williams. You may mix and I'll be the first taster. Is that satisfactory?" The Ambassador's tone was sardonic. The bottles appeared quickly, and Williams did indeed mix the drinks, pouring himself a very light one. He returned to his chair.

"About your claim that Secretary Douglas . . ."

"Fact, not claim," Semonov said quietly. "I had no intention of springing one surprise after another on you, Mr. Williams. None of us likes surprises. Mr. Douglas told me he was going to call you before this meeting and explain."

"I've been unavailable most of the day," Williams said.

"Then there is one more surprise, I'm afraid. Secretary Douglas will resign his position tomorrow. By now, he has already informed President Wilson of his decision. I will leave it to him to give you the details, but you do know that he opposed this ultimatum and refused to deliver the message you just read."

"Go on," Williams said.

"As Mr. Douglas had informed the President, his resignation will be for 'reasons of health,' which, sad to say, is common enough these days. Secretary Douglas will not be a party to your President's belief that the Russian people are the cause of the disaster which has befallen so much of the world. Though I do not expect you to believe me, I would also resign my position if my government were ever to contemplate such a genocidal policy."

Williams said nothing, and Semenov continued.

"We are willing to offer the entire medical research resources of the USSR and also additional funding for these institutes of approximately five billion dollars in an effort to find the cause of this plague of cancer. They are at your disposal, your scientists, and even your CIA." Krylenko shot a look at Semenov, but he took no notice.

"Then you admit that the USSR has been unaffected while this scourge is otherwise worldwide?"

"Yes, I do, for the most part at least. Oh, calm down, Nikolai." The Ambassador petulantly dismissed the expression of his KGB superior, who was now flushing a deep red. "Candor is essential. Would you have our country and much of this planet destroyed because of a fantasy of the President and some of his generals?"

Williams stared for several moments at a life-size plaster bust of Lenin directly across the room from his chair. Lenin stared back. Williams did not like his looks.

"Then how do you explain the fact that your country has been spared?"

Semenov took a long pull on his drink. "I don't know. Our best biologists don't know. If we weren't a nation of atheists, I'd say that God had singled us out, but perhaps your Divinity has singled us out for destruction in another way."

Krylenko spoke at last. "Enough of theology. Mr. Williams. Do you have any, I repeat any, evidence that my country has launched the biological attack your message mentions? Other than the circumstantial fact that, so far, we have been largely unaffected?"

"No."

"Do you believe we have the capability for such an attack? Or, rather, an attack of this kind?"

"Probably not."

"If the Soviet Union did possess this capability, would you expect us to use it against you and much of the rest of the world indiscriminately or against another power?"

"China."

"Precisely." Krylenko smiled, exposing his bad teeth once again. "Thank you for your honesty. Can you give us any reason why the Soviet Union would launch a strike at this time, even if it had the capability?"

"No, I cannot. But I am not privy to your policy meetings."

"You are too modest, Mr. Williams. We all know that you are not what an American would call a 'fan' of the Soviet Union or Communism. But you are an intelligent man. You have access to a great deal of information. We have, I hope, our secrets from you. But this is not one of them. You cannot believe my government would do such a thing!" Semenov's voice was loud.

"What I believe is of little consequence," Williams said carefully. "Since we will have to assume that God has not intervened in this matter, the fact that the Russian people are not falling victim to this plague when most of the rest of the world is, is highly significant."

"You are not making sense, Williams," Krylenko said, a hint of anger in his voice.

"The sudden appearance of millions of cases of cancer does not make sense either. If this is not the work of the government of the USSR, then I would suggest you look for a Dr. Strangelove."

"Pardon?"

"A lunatic or a small group in the military who for some insane reason launched this attack."

Ambassador Semenov jumped to his feet. "There is *no* attack. There is *no* vaccine. Don't you *understand?* Your demands are impossible. Demand to see any of our military or civilian research sites, and we will agree. But we cannot produce something we do not have!"

Williams believed the man. "I'm sorry, but that is not in my hands," he said softly. He rose to go.

Semenov appeared to be near tears. "Then you must convince the

President that there is nothing to this fantasy. You have to do something, Mr. Williams. You have to."

Williams shook his head almost imperceptibly. "I'm sorry. As of two hours ago, the armed forces of the United States have been on alert, condition four-red. The Soviet Union has two weeks to act on this, ahm, ultimatum." He quickly made for the door, leaving the two Russians staring at his back. Semenov caught up with him at his car. "Do something, Williams. Will you destroy the civilized world because of a *mistake?*"

Williams slid behind the wheel and closed the car door. He wanted to answer Semenov, but he knew that the truth of the matter was "Yes, we will very likely do just that." He looked at the Ambassador and then at Nikolai Krylenko, who stood several yards away, framed in the bright light of the embassy doorway. His expression was impassive, but his cold gray eyes betrayed anger, frustration, and hatred. Williams said nothing, put the car in gear, and drove off into the Washington night.

33

Washington, D.C.

Calvin T. Cook sat on the edge of his bed and stared at his wife. It had been several weeks since she had slept through the night, and he wondered if the medicine his son had given him was working after all. Loretta turned on her side, sighed, but remained sleeping. He noticed that her eyelids were flickering, and remembered he had read somewhere that this meant a person was dreaming. *What's she dreaming about?,* he wondered. *Heaven?* As if on cue, Loretta smiled in her sleep.

Calvin pulled on his bathrobe and padded into the kitchen. He put on the water for coffee and set about washing the dishes from the previous night's dinner. *That's the surest sign it's real bad.* They had been married for forty-three years, and he could never remember a time she'd left dirty dishes to sit in the sink. He rinsed the last plate, made a cup of instant and stood sipping it at the kitchen counter; he wondered how long she had. It had never occurred to him than he might outlive his wife, and the thought of spending his last years alone chilled him. Jim had said there was a chance it wasn't serious, but when his Guard unit had been activated for duty in Baltimore, he had given his father a bottle of pills and a prescription.

"What're these for, Jimmy?"

"For the pain."

"Yes, but why the pain?" Calvin stared at his son, who avoided his eyes. "It's the cancer, isn't it?"

"It's hard to tell, Pa, without a lot more tests, and you know how busy the hospitals are these days. I'll see if I can get her into Kennedy Municipal, but there's bound to be a wait. Look, it could be ulcers, colitis, any number of less serious things."

"Now I know why there's so few black doctors," Calvin muttered.

"Huh?"

" 'Cause they don't know shit! Can't tell a person's got cancer or ulcers. Sweet Jesus, *Doctor* James, what'd you do all those years in medical school? Chase nurses?"

The young man rose and walked across the room. He stared out the window at nothing in particular, and without turning said, "I gotta go in a few minutes, Pa. I've written down some instructions about the pills and what Ma should eat. Beyond that there's nothing more I can do besides give you the name of a friend of mine at the hospital who may be able to get you some stronger medication when these aren't enough. Technically, I could be court-martialled for swiping these from military supplies." Neither man said anything for a long minute. Calvin Cook touched his son's elbow and saw his eyes were moist.

"Thanks, Jimmy. Thanks." They embraced, and then his son was gone. That had been three weeks before, and now Jim was somewhere in Baltimore and there were only a few pills remaining.

It's not fair, he thought, tossing the last few sips of coffee into the sink and rinsing out his cup. All his life he had worked, saving his money until he was able to buy his own cab; then driving ten, twelve hours a day, six days a week so his family could eat well and dress decently. And Loretta. Down on her hands and knees scrubbing floors at the vets' hospital, emptying bedpans, helping people walk, changing soiled linen. Years of hard labor so he children could be better off—a doctor, an accountant, two teachers And now that they were able to take it easier, enjoy their saving maybe even travel a little, now she was stricken by a painful, wastin disease.

"Watcha thinkin' about, darlin'?"

Startled, Calvin Cook jumped. "Ah! You scared me. Wasn' thinking about anything special. How you feel?"

"*Much* better. I think that medicine is finally beginning to work. She smiled and Calvin smiled back. He thought how old she ha suddenly become. Loretta had always been a trifle plump, but in jus the past two months she had lost close to twenty-five pounds, an her face was taut and deeply lined.

"Well, if you feel up to it, then I think we'd best go up to th hospital and get some more medicine. Jimmy gave me a prescriptio and the name of a doctor friend who'll get it for us."

Loretta looked pleased at the prospect of a trip and immediatel began to bustle about. She bathed, and after almost an hour o selecting and discarding clothes which seemed too big for her, finall settled on a handsome gray suit and a dark blue coat and hat.

Calvin grinned when she presented herself for inspection. "Lord Lori, we're just goin' to pick up some medicine, not attending th church supper."

"And how would you know 'bout church suppers, Calvin Cook? think I got you to church five times in all these years! Anyway there's no harm in looking respectable when you go to see th doctor. 'Specially one of Jimmy's friends."

Calvin said nothing but nodded and went to get his cab.

Loretta sat in the front with him. She commented briefly on th likelihood of rain, but otherwise seemed lost in thought. Calvi drove through the light Saturday morning traffic hardly noticing th troops guarding virtually every key intersection. The parking lot a Kennedy Municipal was crowded, so he cruised around the bloc and finally risked a ticket by parking a few feet too close to hydrant. Loretta's enthusiasm for the trip had clearly waned, an though she did not complain, he could see that she was very tired

He took her arm and slowly walked toward the entrance of the glittering new hospital.

For all its exterior appearances of modernity and efficiency, one had only to walk through Kennedy's front door to comprehend the chaos within. For one thing, it smelled. Sweat, disinfectant, smoke, vomit, and urine combined to produce an almost palpable impact on everyone who entered. Calvin and Loretta stopped and looked about uncertainly at the scores, perhaps hundreds, of people milling around the lobby. Many were seeking information about patients, while others were trying to gain admission for themselves or loved ones. Calvin found his wife a seat and after a half-hour wait, at last worked his way to the front of the crowd around the information desk.

"Where can I find Dr. Mitgang?" he asked a harassed nurse.

"Appointment?"

"I beg your pardon?"

The nurse's voice had an edge to it. "I said do you have an appointment?"

"Ah, no. It's a personal matter. He's a friend of my son, and . . ."

"Then I suggest you try to reach the doctor at his home or write him, sir. All the doctors here are extremely busy." She started to turn to the next supplicant.

"No wait. Please. Dr. Mitgang is a friend of my son, Dr. Cook. James Cook. He did his residency here and was on the staff until his Guard unit was activated. You know him? Dr. Mitgang has something for me he promised my son. If you'll just check with him, I'm sure he'll confirm that." Calvin paused, unable to think of what else to say.

The nurse brushed a strand of hair from her brow and eyed him suspiciously for several long seconds. Then she flipped through a batch of mimeographed sheets on a clipboard. "You're in the wrong wing. Dr. Mitgang's in Wing C, fifth floor. Follow the yellow line on the right all the way to the end, then take the elevator to five." She scribbled on a small piece of paper. "Here's a pass. Next."

Calvin took the pass and went to get Loretta. She was leaning forward in her chair, hands over her face.

"What's wrong, honey? Pain again?"

Loretta looked up and tried to smile. "Oh, it comes and goes. That was a bad one, though. It's like a thin, red-hot knife carving away from the inside. But it's letting up. You find the doctor?"

"He's in another part of the hospital. Do you want to wait awhile until you feel better?" Loretta shook her head and pulled herself to her feet. Calvin noticed she was using his arm for support as they slowly headed for Wing C. On several occasions, they were stopped by armed security guards who demanded their pass. The yellow line seemed to stretch for miles, and all along the corridor were beds, cots, and stretchers occupied by postoperative patients. Many were groaning in agony, and the stench of excrement and corruption was overpowering. Calvin glanced at his wife, fearing her reaction to the sight, but she seemed not to notice. Loretta just stared at the yellow stripe on the floor, concentrating on each step.

Finally, they reached the elevators. "How you doin', honey?"

Loretta smiled brightly. "Not bad. No pain to speak of, but that surely was a long hike. Tired me right out." The elevator door opened and Calvin pushed 5.

Once again, Calvin Cook waited patiently before a crowded reception desk. Fortunately, Dr. Mitgang was still on duty, and though they had to wait almost an hour, the nurse's assurance that he would be able to see them was good news. Calvin was surprised when a smiling, slightly plump and middle-aged physician approached.

"I'm Dr. Mitgang. It's such a pleasure to meet you both. Jim has talked of you so often, I feel I know you." Loretta beamed.

"Jim said you were good friends ..." Calvin was still surprised that Mitgang was not closer to his son's age.

"Yes indeed. I taught him at one time, though I wouldn't be surprised if he'll be teaching me before much longer. A brilliant young man. And a delightful colleague." They chatted for a few more minutes, and though Loretta said very little, both men could see how proud she was to hear her youngest son praised. She smiled brilliantly, and her eyes glistened.

"Now, Mr. Cook, if you'll just come with me I'll give you some new pills for Jim's mother. You just make yourself comfortable, Mrs. Cook. I wish I had more time to talk, but it's very busy today. I hope we'll meet again." Mitgang shook hands with Loretta and led Calvin down a corridor and into a tiny, book-filled office. He was no longer smiling.

"How's she been?"

"Not too good. The pills Jimmy gave me don't seem as effective as before. He said you'd be able to give me something stronger."

The doctor sighed and seemed to crumple into a chair. "Yes, Jim expected this. A real shame." He seemed at a loss for words.

"She has cancer, doesn't she?"

"Yes, almost certainly. Stomach cancer. Jim's familiar with the symptoms, and he did make a few tests after he examined your wife. If we could take her in, there's a possibility that with major surgery she could be saved, but that's impossible, sad to say."

Calvin jumped to his feet. "You mean she can't come to this hospital if she gets *worse!* Even though Jim is a doctor here and has friends on the staff?" His voice cracked with anger.

"Please, sit down, Mr. Cook. It's impossible. With the backlog of cases we already have, it'd be at least a month before we could operate, and then it would probably be too late. And it's just not allowed for us to perform major surgery on anyone over sixty, let alone someone who's sixty-seven. It's a cruel thing—and I don't endorse it—but I couldn't get my own mother into this hospital. No matter what. There's just too many cases and too few surgeons. They're trying to save those in the prime of life. All we can do for the seniors is try to make them comfortable." Mitgang's words rang hollow. He felt profound pity for the older man who stared at him with a look of horror and despair. Opening his desk drawer, he removed a large brown bottle filled to the brim with tiny tablets.

"These are about the most potent analgesic I could get. One every eight hours or so should keep Mrs. Cook from feeling much pain." He passed them across the desk, and Calvin silently accepted them. "Now if Jim's diagnosis was correct, in about six weeks, maybe eight, these will seem to begin losing their effectiveness. You may very gradually increase the dosage to four, then five a day. That'll work for a while, but toward the end, they'll only mute the pain."

"The end," Calvin murmured softly.

"Yes, I'm sorry to say it, but the end will likely come in the next three or four months." Dr. Mitgang had recently seen more suffering and death than he could comprehend, and he had been able to maintain a professional distance. But now, seeing the bleak sadness in Calvin's eyes, he suddenly felt the urge to weep, to howl at whatever god or force had concocted this nightmare. He got hold of himself and cleared his throat. "I sincerely wish I could do something more, Mr. Cook," he said quietly.

Calvin rose and took the doctor's proffered hand.

"I know. And you've been very kind. Very kind. You're a good friend." He turned to go.

"Mr. Cook. There's one thing I think you should know." Mitgang hesitated for a moment and then plunged ahead. "Near the end, even with these pills, your wife's pain will be tremendous. They're a powerful new opiate, and more than five tablets in twenty-four hours could be fatal. I . . . I don't know if I should say this, but if the pain becomes too great . . . four or five taken all at once will hasten the inevitable. Five would be a certainty."

Calvin stared at Dr. Mitgang for several seconds and then took his hand once again. "Thanks. You're a good man."

On the drive home, Loretta was as cheerful as he had seen her in several months. She was still glowing after Dr. Mitgang's remarks concerning Jim, and how blessed they were to have four such successful children. Calvin did his best to sound equally enthusiastic, and as he helped her from the car, she impulsively kissed him hard on the lips.

"Well, now. What brought that on?" he asked, grinning.

"That's just 'cause I love you, Cal. And because I'm proud of the kids. It all makes me happy, is all. We're lucky, you know. We're very, very lucky."

That night, after Loretta had fallen into a peaceful, medicated sleep, Calvin Cook sat at the dining room table and counted out the tiny white pills. There were more than enough. *Five would be a certainty,* he remembered Dr. Mitgang saying. He returned most of the tablets to the bottle, making sure to leave ten aside.

34

New York City

Francis X. Feeley had several hours to kill before the press conference, so he took a leisurely stroll down Fifth Avenue. It was Sunday and the weather was sunny and pleasant. The street was jammed with happy crowds enjoying life and spending their savings as fast as they could. He sat by the pool at the Steuben Glass building and watched a knot of tourists bustle by, laden with a dozen large packages. Christmas was weeks behind, but cancer, he mused, had proved a boon for business. Except for Tiffany's, which held to an ancient tradition of refusing to open on Sunday, all the stores were jammed with mobs of people determined to buy and enjoy while they could.

Feeley thought about brunch—a couple of Bloody Marys and some nice Eggs Benedict, maybe the Rainbow Room down the street—but dismissed the idea. All the restaurants would be jammed. He sauntered down the avenue and bought a hot dog at Rockefeller Center. Sitting at the feet of Atlas, he munched and watched the crowd across the street that had spilled out of St. Patrick's. A vigil of prayer and penance was now in its third week of twenty-four-hour-a-day supplication to the Almighty. He'd read that even in the small hours of the morning, the huge cathedral was packed. Feeley grunted and headed for the subway. Business was good for the churches as well as the stores.

He would be at least ninety minutes early for the City Hall press conference, but this was an important one—a televised one—and he should get there early and lay claim to a good seat. Lou Soliman had long since ceased predicting a Pulitzer Prize for him, and had even muttered that the publisher was curious why, after so many expensive lunches and dinners, Feeley had yet to come up with a decent lead story.

"Start asking the tough ones, Frank," Soliman had said, putting his arm around Feeley's shoulders and doing his best to seem paternal. "Don't let the wire service guys or those creeps from the *Times* ask all the questions. Get right in there and hammer away." Lou emphasized this point with a friendly squeeze on Feeley's arm that would leave bruises for over a week.

"Right, Lou, right. Not to worry," Frank said, pulling away. "I'll be in there swinging."

"Good boy!" Soliman slapped him on the back. "Go get 'em!" He slapped his back again, and Feeley tried not to wince. As he rode the subway down to City Hall, he wondered what boyhood sin he had committed to result in his working for the Vince Lombardi of American journalism. Lou was about as fatherly as Himmler.

Mayor Goldin looked terrible. He was near exhaustion after months of trying to manage a city quite literally under siege. New York now had at least 250,000 diagnosed cases of cancer, and even with Federal and State help and the comforting (if suspect) news from HEW that the rate of new cases was beginning to slow, he doubted either he or the city could hold together much longer. Goldin himself was disfigured by fibrosarcoma, which formed a large purple blotch on the left side of his face. He tried to keep his right side to the cameras, but he knew the television producers continually chose the left. More dramatic.

As the conference dragged on, Goldin found it more and more difficult to keep his temper. That bastard Feeley had been needling him for close on to an hour, and it was with great relief that the Mayor noticed that in just ten minutes he would be able to introduce Dr. Zimmermann and sit down. For a third time he was asked about the seizure of several major hotels for use as emergency hospitals.

"I've already answered that question," he said wearily.

"Try again," somebody muttered, "maybe you'll get it right this time." Was that Feeley?

Goldin glared at the *Daily News* reporter, who smiled beatifically, and then explained that such measures were necessary for public health and safety and that everyone who had been inconvenienced would be fully recompensed. He defended for the third time the use of force to evict the Roosevelt and Ward's Island protesters.

"Do you know of any plans to evacuate the city?" called out a young man from *Newsday.*

"Where the hell to? Conditions in New York are no worse than anywhere else in the country, and the care facilities, as I have already explained, are excellent and concentrated in a few selected locales." He glanced at the clock. Five minutes to go. Actually, Manhattan had the highest incidence of cancer in the country, though it was a fact that it was bad everywhere else. But that information was Top Secret, and Goldin had not been told.

Gabe Pressman, who had retired just a year before but was back at Channel 5 rose and asked the Mayor if some hospitals were being allowed to use heroin as a painkiller.

Goldin hesitated, and glanced at the clock once again. "Well, yes Gabe, we have been allowing the use of this drug in some circumstances. You probably know that it was originally developed over half a century ago as an analgesic—a painkiller—and when used carefully, it is one of the best there is. Since there is a nationwide and citywide shortage of these necessary drugs, we have supplied various treatment centers with heroin accumulated by the police over the past few years. But please let me make it clear that this is being very carefully regulated and is in the hands of physicians." He paused and saw Pressman was about to ask a followup, almost certainly a statement that he had heard the city was purchasing large amounts of heroin and other drugs from organized crime leaders at very high prices.

The Mayor held up his hand. "I'm sorry, sorry, but my time is up, and as you know, Public Television is going to patch in for the words of the man I am very pleased to introduce. Dr. Eric Zimmermann has been in New York for the past two days consulting with several of our finest medical minds at Sloan-Kettering, Columbia, and elsewhere. You all know him as the leader of the Caduceus Project, and I would personally like to thank him for taking the time out to come here and answer a few questions. Dr. Zimmermann . . ." Eric rose and shook hands with the Mayor, who smiled broadly and almost collapsed into a chair. There was scattered applause.

Eric's handsome face beamed calm reassurance into the cameras and millions of living rooms in the metropolitan area. "The worst is over," he said, knowing he was certainly exaggerating and probably lying. It was true the most recent HEW statistics had shown a leveling off of the incidence of new cases—Rogers had predicted just that; the rate could not go up forever—but it was still at a very high level, and Henry's original estimate of close to fifty million cases in the U.S. alone seemed close to the mark unless there was a very sudden change for the better. Zimmermann fielded the reporters' questions with ease; he had heard most of them before. But he was uncomfortable in the role of government spokesman.

Arthur Greenbaum had persuaded him to appear to help quell some of the ugly rumors sweeping the country. Not surprisingly, the suicide rate was at an all-time high, and violent crimes skyrocketed. End-of-the-World prophets who once had trouble convincing half a dozen people to listen to their streetcorner harangues now were interviewed on national television, and it was to be expected that a large number of people now believed the End was only a matter of time. Some used this as an excuse for public displays of hedonism, like the Festival of Life, while others turned to religion. On the whole, the citizens of the United States and the rest of the world held up with remarkable calm and courage, particularly in Japan and Holland. But there had been violent riots in Paris and Munich, and outright revolution in Spain and Australia, whose governments slid from centrist to radical left to neofascist in a matter of months. It was as if all the people of the world were barely repressing screams of horror. All of this concerned Eric, but several recent incidents had convinced him more must be done to keep the public calm while Caduceus desperately pushed forward with its research.

For one thing, there was the Salem Incident. For reasons never fully understood, the Pacific Northwest was swept with rumors that cancer was contagious. Victims were at first shunned, and as their numbers grew, many municipalities set up New York-style cancer treatment centers, ultimately making it mandatory for anyone diagnosed as having the disease to turn himself in. Only those who were completely cured were allowed to return home. When it was announced that it was impossible to locate all cancer patients in isolated rural areas, a group of about fifty people in Salem, Oregon attacked a municipal hospital and burned it to the ground. Three hundred people died in the flames.

Then there was REAL (the Revolutionary Environmental Action League), a radical terrorist group which maintained that all cancer was caused by environmental pollution. Despite FBI arrests of suspected members, REAL struck again and again. A Dow Chemical plant was dynamited. A toxic gas was released into the air conditioning system of the Union Carbide building in New York. The president and chairman-of-the-board of DuPont were machine-gunned to death as they left for work one morning. An Esso tanker burned and sank in the San Diego harbor. When the John Birch Society announced that REAL was a front for the Peking government, three Chinese were lynched in a suburb of Minneapolis. Clearly, the nation was on the edge of anarchy. So Eric had agreed to say a few words at the conclusion of his trip to New York. He beamed confidence.

"I think I can say that we have made a great deal of progress in just the past few weeks. The Caduceus Group, in cooperation with WHO and research centers around the world, is close, I believe, to a significant breakthrough." He was lying, but the reporters seemed to believe him.

"Does this cooperation include the Soviet Union?" a reporter from *Newsweek* asked.

"All countries are involved in this campaign to . . ."

"Then how do you explain President Wilson's statement in an interview with our Washington editor this morning that the Russians are unaffected by this plague, and may well be behind it?" There was a stunned silence in the room. Zimmermann flushed and then replied, a edge of anger in his voice.

"I find this assertion very hard to believe. I'm sure the President has been misunderstood or misquoted."

The reporter looked hostile. "No, I have his exact . . ."

Eric interrupted. "Listen, there are a dozen paranoid rumors floating around every day. All I can tell you is that at no time, I repeat at no time, have I heard anything about the Russians being behind the outbreak of cancer all over the world. The idea is ridiculous on the face of it." The *Newsweek* man and several others continued to press, but Zimmermann was firm: he had heard nothing about this prior to the press conference. Which was true, but he was seething with anger. His queries to colleagues at the Soviet Academy of Science had gone unanswered, and when he persisted, Secretary Greenbaum told him to make further inquiries through the State Department. Greenbaum had been vague, evasive, and as the press conference drew to a close, Eric resolved to get some straight answers right away.

His momentary preoccupation with this question was probably the cause of the only discordant note in the otherwise flawless presentation. Feeley of the *News* jumped to his feet and asked in a loud voice if the isolation of so many of the city's cancer patients in

"island pest houses" was due to a suspicion that the disease was o
could be contagious.

"That," Zimmermann said, banging his fist on the podium, "i
nonsense. There is not one shred of evidence for that theory, and i
is the kind of thinking that can lead to another Salem Incident!" H
glared at Feeley, who looked, and was, chagrined. At least Lou woul
be off his back for the time being. "The concentration of medica
care, whether it's on an island, or in a single hospital or hote
reserved for that purpose is an excellent idea. Everyone knows ther
are only so many qualified surgeons available, and these are cuttin
day and night."

There were no further questions.

35

Washington, D.C.

"No, Sara, it's nothing that can't wait. A personal matter. Just tell him when he comes in to see me first thing in the morning. Only wanted to chat," he said cheerfully. President Wilson put down the phone and scowled. He had to talk with Greenbaum: Arthur was about the only person he could trust these days. He rose from his chair and moved a little unsteadily across the Oval Sitting Room on the second floor of the White House. He stubbed his toe on the foot of a velvet-covered Victorian armchair and cursed: he was wearing slippers.

The room was dark. Heavy, lined drapes were drawn across the windows, allowing none of the last rays of dusk to enter. Several White House staffers referred to the room as "The Cave" because the drapes were never opened and the President spent an increasing amount of time in its dark, almost gloomy recesses alone with his thoughts. Only the light on his desk was burning.

Wilson started to make himself a vodka and soda, then paused. He had already had three—or was it four—and was just beginning to feel their effects. He pulled a bottle of white wine from the refrigerator under the bar and filled a tumbler. *Better take it easy,* he thought. *Something important in the works.* He recrossed the room, avoiding the chair, and once again picked up the phone: he dialed a twelve-digit number. It only rang once.

"Williams here."

"Wilson here." He grinned and waited.

"Mr. President?"

"Yes, Bill, Mr. President. There's something I want you to do for me." Tom Wilson took a sip of his wine and listened intently. He did not trust the CIA Director, and he prided himself on his knack of reading inflections with unfailing accuracy.

"Yes, sir?" Williams' voice was flat, but slightly curious.

"I'm concerned about the Norman Douglas defection," Wilson said slowly, carefully choosing his words.

"It is a difficult time to lose the Secretary of State. I assume there've been no leaks about his reasons for resigning?" Williams also chose his words carefully.

"No. None. And I'm well rid of the bastard. I never did trust him. There's more to this than meets the eye, I'm willing to bet. I want him watched." Wilson listened intently for Williams' reply. The line was silent save for the faint buzz of the scrambler.

"Watched." The CIA Director simply stated the word as if he was reading it from a list. "What, uh, do you suspect, Mr. President? Mr. Douglas has had a distinguished career in the State Department. Surely you can't believe that he . . ."

"Damn it! Alger Hiss had a distinguished career too! I want Douglas watched, tailed. I want to know who he sees and who he calls. He's been all too concerned for the tender feelings of our Soviet friends, and, well, maybe I'm wrong, but I think he knows more than he's let on." The President's voice had an edge of hysteria, and he quickly calmed himself. "Think you can handle it, Bill?" he asked a bit ironically.

"Wouldn't the FBI be more . . . appropriate for the job?"

"No, they're boobs, and you know it. Anyway, Greeley doesn't have my full confidence. I'm sorry I held him over from the Carter administration. I don't trust his judgment."

"I see." Williams paused. "Well, the Agency can certainly handle the job. My only hesitation is about the matter of the, uh, legality of such an operation."

"Yes, Bill, I understand. Strictly speaking, it would be an FBI matter, but there's no problem now the Emergency Powers Act is in force. I'll have Arthur Greenbaum call you in the morning. He was in on the drafting of the bill. Any other questions?"

"No, sir. I can start work on getting a team together tonight. They can be in place by morning. And I would appreciate talking with Arthur. This is a delicate matter, and I trust you understand my concern about the propriety of the Agency being involved . . ."

"Then we're agreed?"

"Of course, Mr. President. Anything you say."

Wilson's voice was pleasant, soothing. "Thanks, Bill. Thanks. I appreciate your help. And don't worry about a thing. Goodbye."

"Goodbye, Mr. President."

Wilson put down the receiver, lit a thin black cigar and stared at a heavy brass paperweight representing the presidential seal. It had gone well. He smiled slightly and drew on his cigar. There really was an art to statecraft, but the rules never changed. He knew, of course, that Williams was out to get him, but he also knew he would obey a presidential order. There was a certain elegance to the maneuver. It pleased Tom Wilson to use one of his enemies to destroy another. Later there would be plenty of time to get rid of Williams.

Everyone agreed. Wendy Wilson had changed. She was still capable of an outrageous prank or a deflating remark, but the President's only daughter had come close to heroism in her struggle to help cancer victims. After her mother had told her the truth about the operation, she sank into a deep depression. Her parents had even allowed Charlie to visit the White House again, but she refused to see him. Though she had announced to her startled family at the age of thirteen that she never intended to have children, now she felt maimed. Like an amputee.

Wendy's recovery was rapid, and after a few weeks she felt hardly any pain. But the depression persisted. She would burst into tears unexpectedly and she avoided everyone except her parents. Finally, it was her mother who snapped her out of it.

"When are you going to get off your ass and help, Wendy?" the First Lady asked calmly. Wendy was stunned. She had never heard her mother swear or even say "hell."

"What?"

"I know it's been terrible, dear, but there are many thousands of people, millions perhaps, who are worse off than you. You can help them. Arthur Greenbaum told me the other day that many people think it's the end of the world and won't even seek medical attention. You could speak to them. Think about it." With that, the First Lady swept from Wendy's room, leaving the door open behind her. Wendy sat on her bed and thought for almost an hour. It was true. She could help. She knew she could.

So began a nationwide crusade which bore the name "Survive!" Wendy crisscrossed the country, appearing at hospitals, speaking before groups, and submitting to countless local radio and television interviews. She was candid about her operation and her sense of loss, but she also stressed the will to survive and the need for everyone to fight the disease and help those who had it.

Before long, she had become one of the most beloved people in America. Even the *Times,* a powerful enemy of Wilson's administration, went so far as to compare her to St. Joan, a teenage girl who led her people to victory. It was an exaggeration, but Wendy offered one of the few glimmers of hope available to a stunned nation. There was just one thing that bothered her.

"It's father," she told the First Lady one night after she had returned from a speech in Delaware. "He avoids me."

"Don't be silly, Wendy. We all had dinner tonight, didn't we?"

"Yes, for the first time in over a week."

Jennifer Wilson touched her daughter's hand. "Do I have to tell you how preoccupied your father is with this crisis? Surely you must understand that, darling."

"I do, Mom, really. It's just that he avoids looking at me. And when he does, he always looks like he's going to cry. His eyes are so sad. Sometimes they even look angry. Ever since the surgery, he's been unable to say more than how-are-you-I'm-fine-see-you-later."

"He loves you, Wendy. Give him time. He was hit hard by what . . . what happened to you. And he's under tremendous pressure. Be patient." Jennifer Wilson kissed her daughter and walked down the East Hall of the Family Quarters toward her bedroom directly across from the Oval Sitting Room. She paused outside the door for a moment, and thought about knocking. She raised her hand, hesitated, and crossed the center hall to her bedroom. She had reassured her daughter, but what Wendy said was true. Tom was always polite, even deferential, but he spent most of his evenings alone. For months, he had said little to her, and for months he had not asked her to his bed.

"How long are you going to let this go on?" Henry Rogers stood with Eric Zimmermann in the intensive care wing of the main hospital of the NIH campus. They peered through a small window at a dimly lit white room. Paul DeAngelis was sleeping naked on a sheetless plastic bed. Dozens of tubes ran into and out of his small body.

"As long as I have to," Eric Zimmermann replied. "I know what you think, Henry, and I thought we'd have some indication of carcinoma by now, but the tests have got to continue. Even if he doesn't develop cancer, maybe this intensive monitoring will give us a clue as to *why* not."

Rogers peered again through the thick glass, his mouth drawn downward with annoyance. "Kid looks like a fuckin' puppet," he muttered, and stomped off.

"There is always the possibility of remission." The young Navy doctor looked almost cheerfully at Arthur Greenbaum.

"How long have I got?" Greenbaum asked softly.

"That's difficult to say. Radiation will help a little, but I don't think we should overdo it in this case. We've made tremendous strides with chemotherapy in the past couple of years, even in just the past month."

"But it's inoperable. Spread too far."

"I don't think surgery is called for in this case."

"In this case," Greenbaum said reflectively as if he were trying to find a synonym for a crossword puzzle. "How long have I got?" he repeated.

"It's really very hard to say . . ."

Arthur Greenbaum sprang from his chair. His face was less than six inches from the startled doctor's. "I'm not asking you to give me the date," he said, struggling to control his anger. "Just give me an idea. No bullshit." He sank back into his seat.

"Yes, well, barring some new discovery by Caduceus or another group, and without a remission, I'd say you have at least a month or two of full activity–probably more like six months. After that, it's hard to say, but I've seen a number of similar cases who with proper treatment have survived for over two years."

Greenbaum looked calm. He rose and pulled on his topcoat. The young doctor jumped up. "Sir! There's a great deal more I have to tell you about this. . . ." Greenbaum paused at the door and smiled slightly. "Thank you, doctor, but it will have to wait. I'm busy right now." He closed the door on the startled doctor and headed for the elevator.

Greenbaum told his driver to drive to Annapolis. "What address, Mr. Secretary?" he asked, annoyed that he would be hours late for dinner.

"Hum? Oh, no address. Just drive there and back. I want to think. Maybe we can stop and have some ice cream. Yes, I'd like that. Strawberry," he said aloud, as though to himself. He did not notice that the driver slammed his door with more force than usual.

On the way back from Annapolis, he had decided. If it had to be done, he should be the one to do it. He did not fear death overmuch. Life had been good to him, and his family would be comfortable for the rest of their lives. Once he had decided he knew he could do it. If necessary. But only if he could get Bill Williams to help.

36

New York City

It was one of the great views in the world. Hope McCormack stood quietly and looked at an unusually beautiful sunset tinting the sky behind Manhattan's spectacular towers. Her dormitory room on Roosevelt Island was comfortable despite the four other patients she had to share it with, and she spent much of her waking time looking at the seemingly normal city only a few hundred yards away.

On close examination, of course, she could have noticed that several stories of New York Hospital, which was almost directly across from her, were boarded up and charred. The first Drug Riot (and last, now the National Guard was on duty) had been fought in and around the huge hospital when a rumor swept the city that there was only a three-day supply of painkilling drugs left in New York, as well as shortages of almost every other pharmaceutical. New York Hospital was erroneously reported to be the repository of these drugs for the entire city, and with black market morphine selling on the street for more than one hundred dollars a shot, the largely unguarded hospital was a tempting target for a carefully assembled mob of street hustlers, criminals, and pushers. Their "raid," involving close to one hundred troops, had been a fine tactical success until it was discovered that the hospital did not, contrary to the rumors, store all its drugs in one location. A hit-and-run score turned into a pitched battle, with patients and staff trying to dodge automatic weapons' fire, as nervous police shot at anything that moved. It was an ugly incident. Four police dead, eight seriously wounded; nineteen raiders dead, twenty-four wounded; four patients and three staff dead, half a dozen of each seriously wounded. The *Times* especially noted the death of Dr. Richard Lynd, recently arrived from duty in the Bronx, and one of the best cancer surgeons available in the beleaguered city.

Hope did not look at New York Hospital. It was back to normal, and most of its lights were already blazing. Indeed, everything looked absolutely normal from her fifteenth-floor room. The skyline twinkled, and traffic was heavy on the FDR Drive. But even through her preoperative demerol haze she knew that nothing could be further from the truth. She and almost twelve thousand others were prisoners: prisoners of the disease which afflicted them all . . . prisoners of the authorities who refused to let them leave the island without medical authorization. The famous cable car across the East River had been "temporarily out of service" for months, and the only escape was across a small bridge on the Queens side of the island. It was manned by armed guards.

To keep drug raiders out? To keep those cursed with this new leprosy in? She did not know, and didn't care. She was a lucky one. It took solid political pull to get her into the Roosevelt Island Treatment Center, reputed to be one of the two best facilities in the city or anywhere else.

"It wasn't easy," Jim had said proudly, "but Irv has a good contact through a judge right up to the Governor's office."

Hope tried to look pleased, even though she felt Jim was a bit too cheerful about it. Presumably Louis XVI had been kept in quite comfortable quarters before he was executed. But that was unfair, she told herself. With luck she would survive this plague, while thousands of others in far worse condition were unable to get a hospital bed reservation at all. She felt she should be grateful. She was a lucky one. She should be happy, and the preoperative drugs she had been given almost succeeded in making her happy. Almost but not quite.

She watched a tanker steam slowly up the river, and wondered where it was going. She wondered why Jim only called every couple of days and then had almost nothing to say. He was fine. The children were fine. Everything was just peachy. Hope knew he was trying to be positive, upbeat, but though she could hardly admit it to herself, she wanted pity. She yearned for him to say, "Darling, you sure got a shitty deal, and I feel guilty as hell that I'm not about to have my balls cut off instead. You're such a nice person, yet God is giving it to you and a whole lot of other innocent people for no good reason. It's a damned shame. It's outrageous. A crime."

One of her roommates, Mrs. Lieberman, swished into the room and interrupted her reverie.

"Nice sunset."

"Yes, it's very pretty tonight," Hope replied absently.

"I hear you're going down tonight," Mrs. Lieberman stated. "Well, I envy you, dear," she continued. "I can't wait to get it over with. Charlie told me it can make a big difference in the recovery time the longer a person has to wait." Charlie, her husband, was a professor of biochemistry at NYU. "The sooner the better, as far as I'm concerned," she said. "You're only losing one. As for me, both of them go. One swoop and shazaam! the titless wonder."

Martha Lieberman chuckled at her own joke, and Hope had to smile. She had probably put a fair dent in the good professor's bank account preparing for her stay on Roosevelt Island. Hope had never seen her in the same nightgown, dress, or dressing gown in the ten days they had shared the suite. Or the same pair of shoes, for that matter. All from Bergdorf's or Bonwit's, maybe some of the cheaper items from Bloomingdale's. For five days, Hope could not stand her. Mrs. Lieberman seemed to be trying out for the part of a middle-aged "It" girl. Lots of oomph, razz-mataz, good humor, a cheerleader lacking only her pom-poms. Suddenly she thought that the cheerful Mrs. Lieberman would soon be denied her pom-poms for life. She felt guilty, and then decided that the older woman was okay.

"Look, honey," Mrs. Lieberman said gently, "I know how tough this must be for you. I mean, I'm an old lady who looks back on menopause as one of the highlights of recent years, and you're still young. But, listen, you have a lot ahead of you, and you know damned well that you'll survive, you'll cope, and before long, you'll be enjoying life as always. You've *got* to believe that, Hope." She waved a ruffled arm.

"You're very nice . . ."

"I'm just telling the truth, honey."

"In four and a half hours, I'm scheduled to have the operation. That's bad, but I can deal with it. Honest. It's just the recovery, and not knowing what Jim will think," she stopped Mrs. Lieberman's comment with a gesture, "I mean *really* think when he finally sees me. Assuming, of course, they get it all." Hope looked at her watch. "I wish I could go downstairs right now and get it over with."

"I know, dear, me too."

Hope looked around the room. The forcible evacuation of the Island must have been done very quickly since all the furnishings had been left. There was a deep, wine-colored carpet. Comfortable sofas were surrounded by walls of books. Hope had always been a complusive reader, but though she had started half a dozen titles, she was never able to read beyond the first fifty pages. It was difficult to concentrate.

"Look at that. Sweet Jesus, look at that," Mrs. Lieberman cried, pointing out the window.

"What?"

"The joggers." Martha pointed at the tiny figures trotting alongside the East River. "They're out there trying to stay healthy by running through the fumes of bumper-to-bumper traffic." She cupped her hands as if to shout across the river. "Keep it up, fellas, and you'll jog right over here!"

Hope smiled. "I read somewhere that a California doctor has a theory that the more you exercise and the better shape you're in, the less chance you have of getting cancer."

"That's bullshit," Mrs. Lieberman stated authoritatively. "Every crackpot in the country, doctor or otherwise, has a theory. And they're *all* bullshit. I know this assistant professor in Charlie's department. A real athlete. A body to make Apollo jealous, and he got cancer of the colon, of all things. What a shame–such a waste." She sighed.

"What happened to him?" Hope asked.

"Who?"

"The young professor with the great body."

"I really don't know. I heard about it just after I got my diagnosis. I guess they operated. Don't know if he survived," she said abstractedly.

"Oh." Hope jumped when the doorbell rang, a courtesy since all locks had long since been removed. She started for the door, but another of her roommates, Jane Who-Never-Said-Anything, answered first. Jane stood back and said nothing as a nurse and a burly male attendant entered.

"Mrs. McCormack," the nurse cried out, as if calling the roll.

"That's me," Hope said.

"They're ready for you downstairs."

"Are you sure? I'm not scheduled for another four hours," Hope said.

The nurse looked unimpressed. "Well, the schedules are pretty vague. Something to shoot for. I guess they are running a little ahead today." She spoke as if describing the pace of an assembly line, which in a way she was. She referred to an index card. "You may still have some time to kill. You're to report to Dr., I mean Mr., Powers on the third floor, room 306."

"All right, I'll come right down," Hope replied.

"We'll wait," said the nurse. The attendant shifted uncomfortably and looked at his feet. Hope realized they were there to insure her cooperation. She wondered how many patients had to be dragged kicking and screaming to surgery and why they would use force when so many people were desperate to get into the hospital in the first place.

"Okay, I'm ready," she said calmly. She felt Martha Lieberman's hand on her arm, and turned to face her. The older woman's eyes glistened despite her broad smile. "Now look, honey, you just take it easy. Maybe I'll see you in the postop ward, but if not you've got

our number and address–Irving Place–and in a couple of week
we'll get together and trade stories about our operations like two ol
ladies at a bridge game."

Hope forced a smile. "Thanks, I'll take you up on that. I'll brin
the bourbon." She left with the nurse, and was halfway down th
corridor when Martha called out, her voice cracking, "Good luck
Hope. Good luck. And make that scotch. I hate bourbon." Hop
waved, gave the thumbs-up signal and forced another smile. She fel
like vomiting.

She was afraid, very afraid.

For three hours, Hope McCormack sat on an uncomfortable meta
folding chair outside room 306. Typewriters chattered in several o
the converted apartments and scores of people hurried up and dow
the corridor on a variety of errands. Once, a doctor ambled by he
and entered 307 without knocking. His tunic was spattered wit
blood.

"Mrs. McCormack?" a secretary asked, without waiting for a
answer. "We haven't forgotten you. Mr. Powers will be with yo
shortly. Please make yourself comfortable."

Another hour passed.

Hope felt decidedly uncomfortable. The chair was hard, and th
scheduled hour for her operation came and went. She felt silly sittin
in the hall in her robe while everyone else who came and went wa
fully dressed. Not that anyone seemed to notice her. Finally, she go
up and knocked on the door. There was no answer. She pushed i
open.

At the far end of the room, a large man sat hunched over som
papers on his desk. He faced the window which looked out at th
river, and did not hear her enter.

Hope cleared her throat. The man continued to concentrate o
the papers. "Excuse me," she said. He jumped, startled, and turne
to look at her. "Are you Mr. Powers?"

Powers looked at the slight, pretty woman standing uncertainl
by the door. "Yes, I am. And who are you?" he asked, more than
trace of annoyance in his voice.

"I'm Mrs. McCormack, Hope McCormack." He looked mystified. "From Suite 1504. I was told to see you before my . . . my operation today. That was four hours ago. I've been waiting . . ."

Powers jumped up from his chair and charged across the room. He was enormous, at least 6′3″, 230 pounds, and sported a full, shaggy beard. Hope was not sure if he was going to eject her physically from his sanctum, but he extended his hand and smiled broadly.

"Of course, of course. Mrs. McCormack. I'm so sorry. I'm sure you can imagine what a madhouse this place is. I completely forgot about you."

"Your secretary said . . ."

"An idiot. She can hardly remember her name. But it's damned hard to get really qualified people out here. It seems that a lot of people don't want to be surrounded by so much illness. Then there's the worry that the cancer epidemic might in some way be contagious. Nonsense, of course, but there it is." He held his hands out palms up. "Now, please have a seat. There, by the desk."

Powers sat down behind his desk and began shuffling piles of papers and file folders. Hope sat opposite him, her hands in her lap. For some reason she felt as if she had been caught playing hookey and was about to be chewed out by her school principal.

"Ah, here we are," he said at last, selecting a file with her name on it. "It's really most extraordinary."

"What?" Hope asked nervously.

"Well, I'm sure you remember Dr. Lynd. . . ."

"Yes, of course."

". . . And you know, I suppose, that he was a victim of the rioting over at New York Hospital. A tragedy," he stated sadly.

"Yes, I read about it at the time. A real loss."

"Quite. Well, that all happened some weeks ago. What you probably do not know is that his wife is, or I should say, *was* a highly trained registered nurse who had assisted him in his speciality before they were married." Powers looked pleased with himself as he imparted this tidbit.

"No, I didn't know," Hope replied. "What does that have to do with me?"

"You see, after Dr. Lynd's death, Mrs. Lynd set about getting his records in order. Not just personal affairs, but all the medical paperwork he had been unable to take care of due to the crisis. She's really a very talented person, but it was only by accident that she happened to glance at your file before putting it away."

"And?"

"Well, I'm sure you can understand the kind of pressure Dr. Lynd was under. He was a very dedicated man, and put in superhuman hours for months on end." He paused and Hope nodded in agreement. He coughed. "Under this pressure, anyone can make a mistake and . . . well, what Mrs. Lynd discovered was that he had accidentally confused you with another woman who had a similar name and almost identical symptoms. She double-checked the lab records at Markland Memorial and consulted with another physician there before starting to track you down. You see . . ."

"Are you telling me that he made a mistake?" Hope asked, her voice piping like a small child's.

"Yes, that's just it. We got the call this morning. There can be no doubt of it."

"And his diagnosis was wrong. I do *not* have cancer."

Mr. Powers beamed at her, his eyes twinkling. "Precisely. It was a mistaken diagnosis. These things can happen even under normal circumstances. You look pale. Can I get you some water?"

Hope sat in her chair, gripping its arms. She stared, unblinking, at Powers for a long time. "A mistake," she whispered. "A mistake." She stood up unsteadily, and Powers came around the desk and took her arm.

"I know what a shock this must be, but at least it's a pleasant one. Good news. If Mrs. Lynd hadn't been qualified to spot the error . . . or if she hadn't done so before today, well . . ." He gestured again with his hands palms up. "You are a very fortunate young woman, Mrs. McCormack. Very, very lucky," he chuckled.

Mr. Powers smiled broadly and was astonished when, with all her strength, Hope McCormack slapped his face and knocked him down.

37

Atlanta

When Eric Zimmermann arrived in Atlanta he was in a dark mood. The press conference in New York had been upsetting, especially after the now-confirmed statement by President Wilson that there was at least a possibility the cancer scourge was the result of a biological attack from the Communist bloc. It seemed incredible, and Eric was outraged he had not been informed that it was even a possibility. On the flight that morning, he decided the time had come to use some muscle with Greenbaum. Either Caduceus had all available information, or he would resign.

A car met him at the airport, and on the short ride to the Center, he absently chewed his lip and thought about the emergency meeting of all division heads he had called for that evening. Eric prayed that a real breakthrough was possible in the near future. Clearly, time was running out. After he was settled in his office, he was incensed to discover that several key personnel were spending the day briefing a congressional delegation. "We're in the middle of a plague and you're running a circus," he screamed at the CDC public relations officer. "I want those politicians out of here. If your staff can't give 'em the guided tour, I damn well don't want research people wasting their time on them." He slammed down the phone and stared at two fat folders of paperwork that had accumulated over the past three days. He shoved the file aside and tried to call Greenbaum's office in Washington. The Secretary was not in, he was told, but he was expected any minute. Would Eric like to call back later? He slammed down the receiver and swore to himself. It was going to be a rough day.

Eric's mood had not improved by the time of the meeting. For one thing, Greenbaum had been "unavailable" for the entire day, and by the time he finished all the paperwork, Zimmermann was ready to scream with frustration. He sat grimly in the conference room, flicking through some reports and occasionally glancing at his watch. Henry Rogers, as usual, was late.

"You're late," he snarled, as Rogers bustled into the room ten minutes after the meeting was supposed to start.

"Sorry," Rogers said sheepishly, "I wanted to double-check some figures."

Zimmermann ignored the excuse and turned to address the fifteen Caduceus division heads. "All right, we have a lot to cover, and I think it's time we try to see exactly where we stand. I hope I don't have to emphasize to all of you how serious the problem has become. Dr. Rogers seems to have detected a slight slackening of the rate of cancer, though it remains extraordinarily high, with thousands of new cases reported every day."

Rogers cleared his throat. "Yes, I've just been going over the latest data, and it would seem . . ."

Zimmermann cut him off. "We'll get to that later, Henry, in just a minute. But the first thing I want the group to consider is the possibility that we've been looking, or rather, barking up the wrong tree for all these months."

"How so, Eric?" Carey-Ross asked.

"I'm referring to the statement made little more than a day ago by the President that there is reason to suspect the cancer plague could be the result of biowarfare initiated by the Russians or one of the Chinese republics. I've been on the phone all day trying to get through to Secretary Greenbaum to find out if there is any possibility of this being the case. If it is, then we've been given virtually no help from our friends in the military who supposedly follow these matters. And if it is, we've wasted a great deal of time looking for a seemingly innocuous source for the outbreak."

"The Chinese have certainly been unstable for the past few years," Carey-Ross said reflectively.

"No, no, don't be ridiculous, Simon," Honorée said. "I very much doubt if the Soviets have the capability to produce such a generalized outbreak, but for the Chinese it would represent a tremendous breakthrough. And they're incapable of putting together an effective delivery system. It's out of the question."

Eric looked disgusted. "And how, little lady, do you become such an authority on the Chinese biochemical warfare capability?" he sneered.

Honorée was furious, not only because her comment was so cavalierly dismissed, but also because Eric uncharacteristically chose to do so in a sexist manner. "Little lady, eh? Listen, buster, I've spent close to three years of my life studying the Chinese program, and they, I can assure you, are still tinkering with good old-fashioned anthrax and botulism strains . . ." Honorée suddenly stopped and flushed. Everyone in the room was staring at her. Zimmermann's mouth was slightly open, an expression of disbelief on his face. Henry Rogers hastily lit a cigarette even though one was already burning in the ashtray in front of him.

"I, uh, I mean . . ." Honorée began.

"I think I get the picture, Honorée," Eric said abruptly. "We'll come back to your area of . . . expertise . . . later in the meeting." He stared at her for a moment, then turned his gaze on Rogers.

"Well, Henry, what do your numbers tell us?"

Rogers stubbed out one of his cigarettes and cleared his throat. "For one thing, I think we can say with some certainty that the rate of reported cases has levelled out, though at a very high rate. This is particularly true in the U.S., but we are beginning to get similar data from England and Japan. *Why* this has happened is beyond me, but we're not out of the woods. Worldwide, we could easily reach a billion cases, though the WHO stats are fragmentary and occasionally contradictory. I've highlighted the apparent anomalies in a report that's being typed right now. It does seem, though, that there is a positive correlation between extreme poverty and a greatly reduced incidence of cancer—at least by present standards."

"Are most of these poverty-stricken areas rather remote?" Eric asked.

"Yes. For the most part, and I know what you're driving at in terms of a viral theory. I don't deny the possibility, and you are in charge of this effort. But I suspect it's some sort of environmental insult we're dealing with. I mean, it could be anything commonly used or consumed—an ingredient in aspirin, or bread, or gasoline, or a beef hormone or something in the air or water. Any of tens of thousands of chemicals needed to manufacture the hundreds of thousands of products consumed or used in this country or around the world."

Zimmermann looked at Rogers and smiled. "We're not going to have another argument, Henry. You may well be right . . . though I still have my own theory." Zimmermann asked for each division leader to report, but after nearly two hours of discussion it was clear that though a great deal of work had been done and many possible explanations suggested, the fundamental questions as to the cause of the epidemic remained unanswered. Honorée, seemingly lost in thought, said little. Finally, Eric looked at a few notes and addressed the group.

"Very well. Two things present themselves to me. First of all, despite the application of enough brainpower to levitate this building, we are not at the breakthrough stage. Second, this discussion has been fruitful, and I think each of us has learned something he or she didn't know." He looked pointedly at Honorée and continued. "In one week's time, I want us to meet for the entire day. As I see it, each division has been working on one part of the picture with too little concern for the entire canvas, so to speak. Next week, each of you is to prepare a brief report of no more than five pages—you can bring documentation with you if you like, but no more than five pages—summarizing what progress you've made, where you expect to go in the immediate future, and throw in some speculations. These can be thoughtful or crazy, but try to use your intuition."

"Why wait a week, Eric?" Carey-Ross asked quietly. "I think we can pull that together in a day or two."

"I understand. But at that time, I also want to have before us additional material summarizing our knowledge on six points. I'm afraid a good deal of this falls on your shoulders, Henry . . ."

"Shoot," Rogers said, grabbing a pen and paper.

"Well, the first task is for me and Drs. Zachheim and Michaels to answer. We've made an intensive effort to isolate a virus. So far, we've made little progress. Our task will be to outline our experimental models and future research plans, particularly in the short term. This will be thrown out for discussion by the entire group."

Rogers grunted but said nothing more.

"Second, I want the intensive study of those groups not affected by the genetic mutation along with what these diverse peoples have in common."

Rogers looked up. "That's impossible to do with any certainty, Eric. We're dealing with people from Singapore to Sardinia. There's too great a margin for error to come up with . . ."

"Tough shit, Henry. This country, this world for that matter, is about to come apart at the seams. We don't have the luxury of time necessary to dot every 'i' and cross every 't.' You'll just have to go with what you've got as of next week and pray that something is suggestive."

Zimmermann raised his hand and silenced the objections Rogers and Dr. Schwartz were about to make. "Just do it. Third, I will report on what information we have gathered on those who have exhibited the genetic change and whose families have suffered a severe death/disease ratio but who have not themselves shown any effects. So far at least. We have several dozen individuals under intense scrutiny, and so far we have nothing concrete to go on. At that time we can discuss whether to continue or abandon the program."

Henry Rogers, who had been writing furiously, looked up, smiled, and winked. Eric showed no sign of noticing.

"Fourth. Dr. Rogers is to complete a new computer model to determine whether this disease appears to be contagious, at least in the classic epidemiological pattern. We should now have sufficient data to know one way or another."

Eric glanced at his notes. "Fifth, an up-to-date analysis by age, sex, occupation, personal habits, type of carcinoma, and so on for all those on whom we have information who've contracted the disease within the past year, both in this country and elsewhere."

"Maybe we should try to levitate the building after all, Eric," Carey-Ross said cheerfully. "Probably be easier."

"There's one other thing," Eric said unsmiling. "We are going to demand that the CIA and other intelligence services cooperate in discussions aimed at determining if the cancer epidemic is the result of a Russian or Chinese strike. If so, we will require access to all secret research these agencies have conducted which might be of help." He paused. "I trust you can handle that, Honorée?"

Before she could reply, the telephone rang. "I told them not to interrupt . . ." Eric muttered. Honorée, who was closest to it, picked up the receiver. A few of the group chatted quietly, but soon everyone fell silent when they saw her look of horror. Honorée said nothing except "OK, thanks." She gently returned the receiver to its cradle and struggled to find the words.

"What is it?" Dr. Schwartz asked.

Her voice was hoarse, almost raspy. "We've got to get out of here."

"What? Why? What's happening?" Several Caduceus members were on their feet and all spoke at once.

"We've got to get out of here," she repeated. "The city's burning, and there's a mob on its way here."

38

Atlanta

Francis X. Feeley sighed with contentment and luxuriated in the comfort of his first-class seat. The cabin was nearly empty, and two attractive stewardesses seemed to take great pleasure in offering him magazines, martinis, wine, and cigars. Feeley reflected that though the world might be going to hell, the only way to go was still First Class.

"May I get you another brandy, sir?" asked one of National Airlines' Finest. "We won't be landing for another thirty minutes," she added helpfully.

Feeley feigned a thoughtful expression, then nodded judiciously. "Yes, I think that would be quite nice. Thank you." As the young woman hurried off, he wondered if he should ask for her telephone number. He knew several reporters who murmured delicious things about the stewardesses they had met on short flights such as this one. But after the attractive brunette returned and asked if there was anything else she could do for him, Feeley just smiled and shook his head. He sighed wistfully and looked out the window at the strands of tiny lights gliding beneath him. Sipping his brandy, he tried to estimate the chances of getting a decent story out of the CDC and Caduceus bureaucrats in Atlanta. *Nil,* he thought and sighed again. But Lou Soliman had been insistent.

"You were great, Frank, su-*perb* at that Zimmermann press conference! *That's* what I've been trying to get you to do–be aggressive, ask the tough questions. We got two great headlines out of that conference and moved a lot of papers." Feeley tried to look pleased.

"I'm sending you down to Atlanta. Stay as long as you want. Hang around the Caduceus people and try to catch Zimmermann or one of the others off guard. There's a lot of rumors that they've found the reason for the cancer epidemic, and maybe even the cure."

"Dr. Zimmermann won't want to talk with me, Lou . . ."

"Then talk to his girlfriend or his secretary or his cleaning lady! I don't give a shit *who* you officially interview. Let the *Times* get the official handouts; I want you to find out what's really going on. They call it a 'scoop,' Frank."

Feeley looked pained. "But Lou . . ."

"No arguments. Just *go.*" Soliman thrust a thick manila envelope into his hands and stalked away without another word. In it was a ticket to Atlanta for a flight that evening, a suggested itinerary, including the name of a stringer who would meet him at the airport, a batch of expense account forms and three thousand dollars in cash. Feeley shrugged and headed for the door.

The jet was beginning its descent, and he had just fastened his seatbelt when the captain's calm and authoritative voice crackled through a loudspeaker above his head.

"Ladies and gentlemen. We have begun our descent into Hartsfield International Airport and should be landing in approximately ten minutes. The temperature is sixty-three degrees and it should be a clear evening. We have received word from the traffic controller that there is some sort of disturbance in downtown Atlanta, and passengers are advised to remain at the airport at least until we know the details. I've been assured there is no cause for alarm, but if you are requested to remain at Hartsfield for more than an hour or two, we will be happy to help you find accommodations at one of the hotels in the immediate area. . . . Thank you for flying National."

A number of passengers moaned and several called out to the stewardesses for more information, but the plane was swinging into its final approach, and the attendants were themselves seated and buckled in. Feeley peered out his window and thought for a moment that he saw a flash and a flicker of reddish light on the horizon, but it lasted only an instant and was swallowed up in the darkness.

For over an hour, Feeley mingled with the airport crowds trying to find out what was going on in the city. He never heard the same story twice. There were no taxis or buses running into town, and his promised car and driver were nowhere to be found. Finally, in frustration, he stood in line for a pay phone and put through a call to his editor's home in the suburbs of New York. The idea of waking Soliman from a sound sleep didn't exactly thrill him, but he had to know what was happening. Soliman was wide awake.

"As of this moment, Feeley, consider yourself ninety percent fired. If you weren't the only fucking reporter we had in the area, you would be a hundred-fifty percent fired." There was a brief pause while Lou panted with rage and Feeley meditated on Type-A behavior and heart attacks. Soliman recovered first.

"I just can't believe that even *you* would call me up and ask me what's happening in Atlanta. *You are in Atlanta!*"

"Lou, I'm not in Atlanta; I'm stuck out at the goddamn airport. Nobody can get out of here into the city. The radio reports are vague, maybe censored, I dunno. In any case, nobody out here knows what's going on or why. The last person I asked said it was the work of the angel Gabriel. There's some kind of civil disturbance, right?"

"Very good, Feeley," Soliman said quietly. "Very good. Last word we've got says half the city is in flames, Federal troops are on the way or already there, thousands of people are rioting in the streets and you've somehow gathered that there's some sort of 'civi disturbance!' " Feeley listened to several more moments of heav breathing on the other end of the line and was surprised to hea Soliman's tone change abruptly.

"Now, Frank. Maybe I was a bit hasty. I lost my temper. Yo know how it is. There's very little solid information coming out o Atlanta the last couple of hours, and I hoped you'd be able to tel me what the story was. Forgive me. What I said about your bein fired was just my rotten temper. You *know* I'd never do that." H paused, waiting for a reply. Hearing none, he continued.

"Frank, you've got to find a way to get into the downtown area That stringer who was supposed to meet you–Honan's his name– I'm sure he'll show up. And if not, buy a car, bribe a cop, buy horse, whatever it takes to cover this story. This is the biggest thin in years if our initial reports are accurate. Frank, I *know* you can d it," Soliman cooed.

Feeley paused for a moment and made an angry face at a teenage who was rapping on the glass of the telephone booth. "Be a hell of story if I can get to it, wouldn't it, Lou?"

"For sure. What with your other coverage of the cancer plague, think a definite Pulitzer, Frank . . ."

"Or a bullet in the head, Lou, old chum. You're telling me tha thousands of people are rioting and burning a city to the ground an the U.S. Army is coming in. I'd say some people are going to ge shot, Lou."

"Well, I suppose so. And I want you to be very careful Frank . . ."

"Oh, I will, Lou, I will." Feeley paused for a moment. "Ok, here' the deal. If, I repeat *if,* I can get into the city, then I will get as clos to whatever action there is without getting killed or arrested . . ."

"Of course, Frank."

"And if in my judgment, I repeat *my* judgment, I get you th whole story in all its glorious and gory detail, then I want a bonus Five thousand bucks, Lou."

"Are you trying to *blackmail* me, Feeley?" Soliman's voice began to crack.

"Nope. It's just a part of the deal. If I'm going into combat, I want combat pay. It's not for me. I got this friend, a fireman; lost his wife to cancer a while ago, and now he's met a good woman. But whenever he's around his old house all he can think of is his dead wife. It's messing him up. I want him to go off to some nice island somewhere with this lady, courtesy of the *News*. . . . Are you still there, Lou?"

"Yeah."

"Is it a deal?"

"A deal, but the stuff better be good."

"We'll see. And as for myself . . ."

"I'll kill you, Feeley. I promise you I will personally smash your windpipe. When I'm through with you . . ."

"You'll give yourself a heart attack, Lou. All I want is a letter of agreement saying I can't be fired for the next eighteen months, and after that period, I quit. Rate we're going, it's only a matter of time for all of us anyway. And as you said, I'm the only guy you've got down here. Do we have a deal? Do I get the next plane out? Do I call the *Post* or the *Times* and ask them if they'd like to hire me for the job?" Feeley listened to a long silence and then Soliman replied wearily, "It's a deal."

Francis X. Feeley grinned fiendishly and said, "OK, I'm on my way. But hold the line, Lou, there's someone here who wants to talk to you." He threw open the door of the booth and handed the phone to the pimply teenager who had been impatiently tapping on the glass throughout most of his conversation. "Here. It's for you. It's your mother."

He ran for the parking lot.

Feeley found his driver with remarkable ease. Honan was pacing back and forth on the sidewalk in front of the terminal with a large sign inscribed with the word *Feeley*.

"You're looking for me," Feeley said, pointing to the sign.

The gangly young man only stared at him for a moment and finally replied, "Maybe, maybe not."

"Huh?"

"Look, mister, it's not the world's most unusual name, and there's half a dozen people who've claimed to be the person I'm trying to find, since they assume I have a car and I'm meeting this Feeley person. Not much transportation in or out of the airport right now, so . . ."

"I gotcha. I'm Francis X. Feeley, ace reporter for the New York *Daily News.* Your name is Honan, right?"

"Wrong. Name's Wentz. Hamilton Hayward Wentz. Honan couldn't make it. Pleased to meet you, Mr. Feeley. I'm the ace gopher for the Atlanta *Constitution."* He stuck out a bony hand and Feeley grasped it. "Got any other bags?" Wentz gestured to Frank's single small suitcase.

"Nope. That's it. How do we get out of here?"

"Follow me."

They set off across the airport parking lot until they at last came to a gate marked "Airport Security. Authorized Personnel Only." Wentz pushed the gate open, entered the empty guardhouse and lifted some keys from a pegboard. "Don't worry, Mr. Feeley," he said cheerily, "I got an uncle who works here. I thought this'd be the best place to stash the car. Just wait here. I'll only be a minute." He sprinted off into the murky recesses of a small hangar some twenty yards away.

Feeley sat a bit nervously in the empty guardhouse, and in a few minutes an enormous Lincoln limousine emerged from the hangar and stopped next to him. Wentz dashed around from the driver's side and opened the back door with a flourish. "I'll be damned," Feeley muttered as he got in. "You sure this is your car, kid?" he asked suspiciously.

"I wish. Honan told me to meet you no matter what, but all the *Constitution* cars were out. So I borrowed this one from another uncle of mine. Biggest undertaker in Atlanta," he said a trifle proudly.

"Undertaker, huh?" Feeley muttered.

"Yeah. Needless to say, business has been terrific lately. He's added a dozen new limos in just the past few months. Where to, boss?"

Feeley scratched the bridge of his nose and realized he had no idea. "Well, I think I have to leave it up to you, kid. Close to the action, I guess."

"That won't be hard. From what I heard, the shit's hit the fan in half a dozen parts of town."

"Center of town?"

"Yeah. 'Specially there."

"Okay, that's where we'll go. But keep in mind we're reporters, not combat troops. So be careful."

"Yes, *sir!*" The car lurched forward, throwing Feeley back onto his comfortable seat. It squealed down several dark access roads and finally pulled onto Route 75 heading north. Ahead of them, the sky had an eerie pink glow. There was very little traffic. As they roared along the almost deserted highway, Hamilton Wentz explained what he knew about the circumstances of the rioting: the seemingly spontaneous outpouring of violence and sniping in all sections of the city, black and white, rich and poor. He had just finished reporting the rumored breakout of several hundred inmates from the U.S. Penitentiary when Feeley noticed that the car was equipped with a bar, telephone, and television set.

"Hey, kid. You said you got this limo from your uncle the undertaker?"

"Yeah. Right."

"Since when do funeral cars have bars and TV's?"

"It's the latest thing. It costs more, you understand, but the bereaved can get snockered on the way to the cemetery and not miss an installment of *The Edge of Night.* Car's not hot, honest."

"Sure, sure. Just wondering." Feeley poured himself a shot of Glenlivet and noticed a sign indicating the Atlanta Stadium exit in one mile. "Better slow down, kid. We're getting near the thick of it if what you said is true."

"Nah, the first incidents started near the stadium, but the action's moved on by now."

"Ah, the confidence of youth. Now see here, Hamilton Hayward Wentz, I'm the boss, and *I* say there's no need to go hurtling into a fire fight at eighty-five miles an hour. So slow the hell down."

"Yes *sir,* Mr. boss-man Feeley!" Wentz took his foot from the accelerator and turned to flash a brilliant smile combined with a jaunty little salute.

Feeley wasn't sure at first what had happened. He heard an odd "pop," followed by a faint but audible "thud." The smile on Wentz's face froze, and his eyes remained locked on Feeley's as the car continued to lose speed. The young man's hand dropped from the steering wheel, but his posture remained rigid. For several long seconds, Hamilton Hayward Wentz continued to grin, and then he slid slowly to his right and onto the front seat.

Feeley was speechless as he watched the huge car slowly drift to the right, just miss a bridge abutment and plow into a mass of wisteria and honeysuckle by the side of the highway. At contact, they were going barely twenty miles an hour, but he was hurled to the floor. Miraculously, he didn't have a scratch, and the car seemed undamaged. Keeping low, he crawled out and opened the right front door.

For many months to come, Francis X. Feeley would awake in the middle of the night moaning, sometimes screaming, as the sight that greeted him when he wrenched open that door forced itself once again into his consciousness. Wentz's head was only a few inches from Feeley's face. He was still grinning boyishly, but now his expression seemed to have been contorted into a hideous grimace. He was dead. A small dark hole, hardly noticeable, had appeared just below his left ear, and a somewhat larger one had fragmented a piece of his skull almost at the top of his head.

Feeley fought back the urge to vomit as he carefully took Wentz's hand and checked for a pulse. He observed with clinical calm that there was almost no blood coming from either side of the wound. A small-caliber rifle. Someone crouching low on the other side of the highway, or perhaps on the divider. He was trying to figure out how the bullet could have entered and exited in such an odd fashion—perhaps it was a ricochet—when his hand, which had been resting on the seat as he crouched by the boy, felt something warm. He pulled it away but forced himself to look. It was the size of a quarter. It was a fragment of brain.

Feeley puked.

He rose from his knees, gasping, trying to make his mind work. Trying to figure out if the sniper was nearby. Trying to make himself go back to the car.

He fainted.

39

Atlanta

A full thirty-six hours before the services were due to begin, lines started to form at Atlanta's Omni Coliseum. Dr. Jimmy Grand, the elder statesman of American evangelists, could always count on a full house, but this was to be something special. For months, he had watched in anguish as millions suffered and died, and he prayed intensively, hoping for a sign, an indication of how he could help. At last, he decided to end his self-imposed retirement and preach his Final Crusade. His call for a day of prayer, fasting, and penance met with huge response. Grand knew this would probably be his last sermon, and he wanted it to be the highpoint of his career. He worked for hours on his message. The plague, the scourge, was not the work of God, but of Satan, the result of man's overwhelming corruption and sin. Dr. Grand thought grimly that he was going to really "let 'em have it," in the hellfire and damnation style of a Jonathan Edwards. *Sinners in the Hands of an Angry God.* But that was only part of the message, because he deeply believed that there was still time, still hope. Hope in Jesus Christ. Man was being taught a bitter lesson in the manner of the Old Testament, but if people could be brought back to the faith, he believed, there was no question God would be merciful.

The Omni was sold out within hours, and still the lines grew until the police feared that even the god-fearing could be driven to violence if prevented from seeing Grand. They had come from all over the South and all over America. Several thousand even flew in from Europe and Canada. The Mayor quickly arranged for the use of the Atlanta Stadium for the overflow, and the Grand organization swung into action and set up six huge screens to carry the event live. By the time the services began, the Stadium was filled to capacity and thousands more milled in the streets in front of the Omni listening to loudspeakers and hoping for a chance to get in.

It was an emotional evening.

As usual, associate ministers warmed up the crowd for several hours before Grand appeared. There was very little preaching, *per se,* and most of the time was spent in well-known political and theatrical personalities' testifying to the joy of finding Christ in troubled times. One person after another described how prayer and faith had healed their cancers. A chorus of close to a thousand voices boomed out hymns and traditional spirituals, and the choir of the Ebenezer Baptist Church sang gently, and then fiercely of the power and glory of the Lord. By the time Dr. Grand was about to speak, even the policemen struggling to prevent the crowd from surging onto the stage had joined in the singing. Some were openly weeping.

And then he appeared. Quite suddenly, Dr. Jimmy Grand was standing at the pulpit, his hands resting on the edge of the lectern, a broad smile on his face. The crowd, which had been near hysteria only moments before, began to cheer but was instantly silenced by a quick gesture from the man they had come to hear. Jimmy Grand had not appeared in public for almost two years, but he had changed little in the past decade. He was somewhat thinner, but he still stood ramrod straight. His face was almost boyish, though he was old enough to collect Social Security, and he seemed to radiate confidence and energy. Those who sat closest to him, however, could see that he had lost a great deal of weight and while his expression was serene, his eyes betrayed an infinite weariness. What no one knew—though he planned to tell the crowd at the conclusion of his sermon—was that Jimmy Grand was in tremendous pain. His hands did not rest lightly on the lectern—they clutched it for support. His body was ravaged by leukemia, and despite therapy, he was given no more than six additional months of life.

For Jimmy Grand, this was the greatest opportunity of his ministry. Now he could personally demonstrate the true meaning of faith in Jesus and the joy of embracing the life to come. He desperately wanted this to be the greatest sermon of his career, and without consulting his doctors he had stopped taking all medication for the previous twenty-four hours so his mind and enunciation would be sharp. The pain was intense, and he paused for a long minute for it to diminish. It did not, but when he began his sermon, he was suffused by a surge of joyful energy. The time had come for a real Great Awakening, and though every cell in his body was howling with agony, he hardly noticed.

He gazed out at the huge crowd. They were hushed and intent, and his first word made many of them jump. "WHAT," he shouted, "has happened to us?" Grand's voice dropped. He looked around the coliseum. "What has happened to us? What has happened to us? What . . . has . . . happened . . . to . . . *us?*" His voice was almost a whisper, and many of his auditors leaned forward in their seats, anxious lest they miss a word. Grand reared back from the pulpit as if he had been administered an electric shock.

"I'll *tell* you what. But you may not like to hear the truth. . . ." He paused and glared at his audience. "WE ARE GETTING WHAT WE DESERVE!" Several people gasped, while a number of others murmured agreement. The first twenty minutes of Grand's sermon were electrifying. Cotton Mather or John Knox could not have done better. Fire and brimstone poured forth, and hundreds and then thousands who listened were sobbing, knowing how loathesome they must appear to their Creator. Others sat stunned, pressed back in their seats as if by the physical force of his passionate oratory.

There were two parts to the sermon. First, a vision of evil and death; then, a message of hope. God was still merciful, infinitely merciful, and willing to comfort and help anyone, no matter how bad, who had faith in Him and His mercy. As Grand began to reach the crescendo of his denunciation of mankind's wickedness, he felt the pain begin to grow once again. He fought it, tried to push it back, knowing that if he could just complete this speech, he would be able to die happy. He was angry at the pain, and he struggled with it; holding tight to the podium, he leaned forward on his elbows and rasped out the final words of Part One.

"There are rumors. Oh, yes, there are rumors that there is some secret withheld from us. A secret cure to this cancer that has invaded our bodies. Well, I can tell you I know for sure that there *is* a secret, and that it is there for anyone who wants to go and get it." The pain grew, almost overwhelming him, but he continued. "But know this one thing. We are not seeing the cancer of our bodies. This is the cancer of our *souls.* It is not the work of God, however disappointed in us He may be. . . . This is nothing less than THE WORK OF THE DEVIL!" Grand raised his arms above his head and pain exploded in every part of his body.

He collapsed.

The crowds from the Omni and Atlanta Stadium dispersed very slowly. Grand's emotional jeremiad remained in their minds despite the attempts of assistant ministers to deliver the second, most important part of the message. Sadness, despair, and anger were the typical emotions, and at least half those attending the Crusade drifted out before the final benediction.

The hub of downtown Atlanta consists of huge skyscrapers, modern hotels, and well-tended parks. But sprinkled along the side streets of this glittering area are the bars, massage parlors, and topless dancer joints common to every major city in America. Few of those who had waited so patiently to get into the Crusade had taken any notice of these seedy establishments, but to at least a few who left after Jimmy Grand's collapse they now seemed to symbolize the corruption and evil he had so furiously denounced.

Someone threw a rock, and the grimy plateglass of the Dixie Topless Nightclub exploded into the sidewalk. A fight broke out, and within minutes, a full-scale riot was set in motion. Some groups attacked "sinful" businesses–bars, liquor stores, and nightclubs. The dozen only mildly aroused patrons of a small movie house who were watching the concluding minutes of *Teenage Wet Dream* were astonished when a handful of zealots broke into the theater and began smashing the projection equipment. The entire incident took only minutes and everybody fled into the street before anybody could notice that sparks from a short circuit in the smashed projection room had started a fire. By the time smoke was billowing out of the theater's lobby and an alarm sounded, the Atlanta fire department was already fighting half a dozen blazes in the downtown area, though history was to record that the Great Atlanta Fire began in the Cavalier Adult Cinema.

The handful of religious zealots who started attacking disreputable establishments were soon joined by many others whose motives were less "pure." For every person intent on smashing a liquor store, there were scores who preferred to loot one. Clothing and hi-fi shops were soon overrun, and the outnumbered police fell back and called for reinforcements as the mob rampaged out of control on Peachtree Street. Word of the riot spread with astonishing speed, and in half a dozen areas of the city, looters–white and black, children and adults–began to sack their neighborhoods.

For weeks, rumors had swept Atlanta that a cancer cure had been found, but that supplies of the vaccine were being reserved for the powerful and wealthy. Even Jimmy Grand, it seemed, had referred to the "secret" before he was struck down, some said assassinated. As fires began to spread in three sections of the city and harried police fell back to defend public buildings and key intersections, a mob began to gather spontaneously. Some were on foot, and others drove, but all who headed for the Center for Disease Control were determined to have the secret vaccine for themselves, their loved ones or, in some cases, to sell on the black market. It was a desperate mob that poured onto the Emory University campus and attacked the frail defenses of CDC. They were not going to be denied the most valuable prize: the prize of life.

Eric and Honorée were among the last to get away. As they ran through the lobby of the CDC headquarters building, lugging cartons of documents and reports, they heard the angry cries of the mob and the sound of shots. Somewhere nearby windows were shattering.

"Back way!" Eric shouted, throwing down the carton he was carrying. "Leave the papers." Honorée hesitated, and he pushed the box out of her arms and grabbed her hand. "C'mon!"

They raced through the empty halls. Behind them they heard screams and more shots. Closer this time. Eric threw himself against the metal door of an emergency exit, and they ran for the parking lot. Honorée's eyes were wide and Eric muttered, "Jesus Christ!" as they raced for the car. In the west, the sky flickered pink as fires began to burn out of control in downtown Atlanta. Behind them, several nearby buildings on the Emory campus were already in flames.

Eric fumbled for a few seconds with his car keys, unlocked the door, and slid across the seat to let Honorée in. He slammed the car into reverse and squealed toward the exit.

"There! Look out!" Honorée shouted. Eric spun the wheel and narrowly missed a crowd charging into the CDC parking lot. He gunned the small Toyota onto a sidewalk, over a lawn, and onto the street. "What's going on?" she asked as they barrelled away from the CDC campus.

"They must be after the so-called secret cure we're supposed to be hiding from them," Eric said grimly, hurtling down a deserted suburban side street.

"Eric, are you heading the right way?"

Out of nowhere, a rock struck the windshield on Honorée's side, spider-webbing the glass. Eric floored the accelerator. "If I go north toward home, we're almost certain to run into that mob. I'm heading for the city if I can just find Dekalb or Memorial Drive!" Eric shouted.

"The city! Are you crazy? The goddamn city's on fire! That's the *last* place we'll be safe."

Eric swung the car onto Dekalb Avenue. Traffic was heavy going out of town. "Look Honorée, maybe, *maybe* we could've skirted around the crowd at Emory and CDC, though I don't know how many there are or where they're coming from. But I *do* know we can be at the State Capitol in five minutes with a little luck."

"Why? You want to pay a call on the governor?" There was an edge of hysteria in Honorée's voice.

"Think. No matter what happens the police are sure to defend the Capitol. If we can just get there and get behind their lines, we'll be safe." Eric swerved to avoid a pickup speeding directly at them in the right-hand lane. "Shit!" he cursed, narrowly missing a telephone pole. "And you're forgetting something. We're doctors. Maybe we haven't seen a broken arm since medical school, but we're going to be needed if this thing's as bad as it looks."

Honorée was silent for a moment and then said simply, "Okay."

The car sped past Oakland Cemetery and the King Memorial. Few people were on the streets and traffic was surprisingly light. Less than a quarter-mile away, flames shot out of the Hyatt Regency and Peachtree Center. "Oh, my God!" Zimmermann slammed on the brakes and the car screeched to a halt. Only a few yards in front of them lay the bodies of three men, one a police officer. Directly ahead was the Georgia State Capitol, surrounded by state and city police who crouched behind their cars and fired at snipers. An automatic weapon chattered and a stray bullet pinged on the Toyota's grill. Somewhere behind them there was the thump of an explosion.

"So much for the Schweitzer routine," Eric said with grim humor, turning the car into a side street. "We're getting out of here." The streets of the business district were almost deserted. Once, he had to swerve to avoid hitting a teenager who charged the car with, of all things, a golf putter. "Next one, I run down," he muttered. The streets were filled with shards of glass and Eric prayed he wouldn't get a flat.

"Where'd everybody go to?" Honorée asked, scanning the vacant streets.

"Dunno. Guess the pickings are better somewhere else right now. Glad we weren't here an hour ago, though." Eric leaned forward and pushed the car up to fifty, hoping someone else wasn't doing the same thing coming into the blind intersections he sped through.

As they were passing the Colony Square Hotel, Eric sighed and said, "I think we're almost out of it." Just then a gas line exploded, demolishing the front of the skyscraper and spewing glass and flaming rubble all around them. The small car suddenly took flight, hung for a second in the air, and crashed to the street. Huge tongues of flame spurted from the wreckage immediately behind them. "You all right?" Eric shouted, wiping a bit of blood from a cut on his lip.

Honorée was shaken, but unharmed. She nodded and then shuddered. "Let's get out of here, Eric. Please. Now."

Eric tried to start the car. Nothing happened. "Car's dead," he said quietly. "We'll have to run for it. Stay close to me." Honorée's lip trembled, but she nodded and took his hand. They ran down the block, keeping close to the buildings. "If we can't find the cops, we'll look for a place to hide and . . ."

They were both blown off their feet and slammed onto the sidewalk. A massive secondary explosion shattered the core of the Colony Square. The Toyota they had abandoned just a minute before exploded and burned. Eric helped Honorée to her feet. They were both scratched and bruised but otherwise unharmed. "Nine lives," he said cryptically. Honorée was staring at the burning Toyota.

"Oh, my God, I just remembered . . ."

"Later. We've got to try to make it to St. Joseph's Hospital. It's not far from here, assuming it's still in one piece." He grabbed her arm and pulled her into the side street. Twice they avoided a crowd of looters. They had obviously raided a sporting goods store since each of them carried a powerful hunting rifle and several handguns. Eric and Honorée crouched in an alley and watched them pass. Oddly, they ignored the pickings in several stores as they crept down the street. They seemed to be hunting something. Or someone.

Eric and Honorée ran, keeping off the main streets, occasionally getting lost and finding themselves back where they had started fifteen minutes before. "Baker Street," Eric said joyfully. "I know where we are. St. Joe's is just a couple of blocks from here." They dashed down the street and paused only when they came to the intersection of Peachtree and West Peachtree Streets. They looked downtown and saw nothing but a mass of flames gutting the splendid towers which had been the city's pride. The air was acrid and smoke hung like a thick fog around them. Through the smoke they saw figures running in the street, silhouetted by the dark red of the buildings blazing all around them. A constant chatter of gunfire sputtered and they saw one figure jerk, throw his arms in the air, and fall.

"Run!" Eric cried. They dashed across Peachtree Street. Both thought they heard bullets behind them, but both thought they were imagining it. St. Joseph's Hospital was only a block away.

"Well, the hospital's not on fire anyway," Eric said, breathing heavily. "C'mon." They ran, crouched over, occasionally looking behind them.

"Right *there!*" a voice called out. "Freeze or you're dead!" They froze, and found themselves looking down the barrel of an M-17 held shakily in the hands of a perspiring and very nervous soldier.

Eric and Honorée were treated for their cuts and given some tranquilizers at St. Joseph's. Their offers to help were dismissed. They were obviously near exhaustion. They sat in the doctors' lounge and listened to a transistor report that National Guard units had been supplemented by troops from Dobbins AFB and Fort McPherson. Much of the city was in flames and a large part of the CDC and Emory University had been destroyed, but by 3:00 A.M., the situation was said to be "under control."

As they sat silently in the back of a state police car taking them to Eric's apartment in North Druid Hills, they both found it difficult to believe that only a few hours before they had been in the middle of a conference in Eric's office.

"The car," Honorée said softly. "The car."

"I can get another, darling. I'm just glad we're both still alive."

"No, Eric. I didn't mean that," Honorée said. "I only thought of it when I saw your car on fire in the street . . ."

"Thought of what?"

Honorée stared at him, her eyes welling with tears. "Henry's car. I saw it when we were trying to get away from the Center parking lot. The little Mercedes. It was on fire. Henry Rogers didn't get away."

40

North Druid Hills, Georgia

Eric and Honorée were exhausted, but too keyed-up to sleep. They thanked the officer who drove them home, and as they stood in the entry hall of Zimmermann's apartment, she looked at him closely and announced that he looked like hell.

Eric smiled wanly and studied her from head to toe: "My dearest, you look like something even the cat wouldn't drag in." They both laughed ruefully and went into the living room. "Who hits the showers first, coach?" she asked.

"You go ahead," Eric answered. "Maybe I will later. I'm pretty tired, though. You may have to sleep with a filthy scientist tonight."

Honorée looked disgusted, held her nose, and marched to the bathroom. She had just finished drying herself and was pulling on a robe when Eric knocked lightly on the door. "Puff?" he asked, holding out a long, tapering joint.

"Hum. Smells good. We haven't indulged since that time in Italy."

"We deserve a break today," Eric replied cheerfully.

For a while they sat quietly on the living room sofa, smoking and relaxing. "I'm so worried about Henry. He . . ."

"Hush. There's nothing we can do. He's a slippery old fox. He got away. I'm sure of it."

"But the car," she persisted. "It was burning. He couldn't . . ."

"Hush, I say again. Let's just try to forget all that for just a few hours. Tomorrow will be one hell of a day. Here. Your toke." He handed her the joint and rose. "I am starving," he announced. "You?"

"Yes, come to think of it."

"Then the chef will see what is easy and delicious in the kitchen." Eric headed in that direction.

"Anything will do," Honorée called out.

He stuck his head out of the kitchen and smiled. "Don't worry. Anything will be just what the chef will prepare."

After what seemed like a very long time, Eric returned with a huge tray. There were liverwurst sandwiches, frozen egg rolls, leftover chili, and frozen donuts.

"Magnificent," Honorée said sincerely. She opened a bottle of Bordeaux and lit a log in the fireplace. "It's not really very cold tonight, but still . . ."

"Good idea," Eric said, watching the kindling catch. "Now come and eat."

They dug in, and quickly devoured Zimmermann's eclectic meal. Eric refilled Honorée's glass, unbuttoned the first few buttons on his shirt, and sat back. "Well, do you really work for the CIA? Or does some branch of Defense fund your research into the Chinese biowarfare capability?"

Honorée grimaced, but Eric's tone was not hostile. "National Security Agency. And I suppose I could be described as a spy."

Eric looked thoughtful. "I thought our meeting so fortuitously was too good to be true," he stated calmly.

Honorée put down her glass and turned to face him directly. "Listen, Eric. We're both on the same side. I've worked very hard on the Caduceus project. I almost got myself killed tonight. I'm a trained scientist, and I'm useful to the group. The same government that pays for Caduceus wanted to be sure they weren't being left out in the cold while a bunch of woolly-brained scientists played research politics with unlimited government funds. You must understand that." She looked at him hopefully.

"I understand one thing very clearly . . ." he began.

"No, let me finish. If you think I was chosen because I'd slept with you a few years ago, then forget it. I never told anyone about that. And it was my decision to sleep with you again. For *my* reasons, not the Agency's. Yes, you've had a 'spy,' as you call it, in your midst. But has it occurred to you that you've been given an astonishingly small amount of shit from HEW? I happen to agree with your viral theory. And I happen to think you're the only man–person–who can hold this research program together. Still, I'm sorry you've got to have doubts about my loyalty to you. You have to take my word for it that I've done nothing but good for Caduceus, and for you." Honorée paused. She swirled the wine in her glass. "I hope you'll forgive me," she said in a very small voice.

Eric's laughter filled the room. "Yes. Yes, I forgive you. I sort of suspected it all along." He chuckled and stared at the fire. "You know," he said, almost to himself, "it would have been awkward, but I don't think it would make any difference if you worked for the KGB. You see . . ." He took a sip of wine and cleared his throat. "You see, I think I love you, Honorée. I can't be totally sure since I've never really been in love before. Not really. But, well, I, us . . ."

Zimmermann never finished the sentence. He gently stroked her hair and she began to caress him.

"Ah, lady," Eric said wearily, "the spirit is willing, but the old flesh is much too weak. It's been a hell of a night, and I'm really so tired I don't think I have the strength to make it to the bedroom, let alone satisfy a sexy woman like you."

"Shut up, dummy," Honorée said lovingly, "tonight's lady's night. Woman's liberation. Now just sit back and enjoy yourself for once. You can make the earth move for me some other time." Honorée continued to caress him. She unfastened the remaining buttons on his shirt and loosened his belt buckle. Her hand ran along the inside of his thigh. She slid to her knees, and slowly removed his pants and briefs. She looked up at him and smiled.

"Really, Honorée, you don't have to . . ."

"I thought I told you to keep still," she said. "And don't believe all the reports about your flesh being so weak." She toyed with his erect penis for a few moments, then gently and methodically took him in her mouth. Eric sighed delightedly and leaned back on the couch. He groaned with pleasure when he climaxed, and after a few loving words to Honorée, he promptly fell asleep.

She sat watching him for several minutes. Once again it occurred to her what a splendid body he had. In the flickering reddish light by the fireplace, his half-clothed torso reminded her of a Greek—or was it Roman—statue. The Gladiator, she thought it was called. He was well muscled, lean, and beautifully proportioned. But in sleep, Eric's face resembled a child's, an innocent little boy's, she thought. He looked so comfortable, she decided not to move him.

Honorée rose and quietly padded to the bathroom. As she was looking for some toothpaste, she realized that she was humming happily: she had never felt so deeply in love. She smiled and glanced in the mirror. She froze. A thin trickle of blood ran from the left side of her mouth and down to her chin. She touched it tentatively, questioningly.

Then she hastily returned to the living room. Eric had not moved and was snoring softly. She hesitated for a moment, and then looked. Honorée's heart sank when she found what she had prayed she wouldn't, an ulceration on the underside of Eric's penis. She shuddered, and realized she was about to vomit. She barely made it back to the bathroom in time.

For hours, Honorée sat and stared out the window until the pink glow in the western sky from Atlanta's fires was superseded by the gray-pink light of sunrise in the east. She was exhausted, but she knew that sleep would be impossible. All she could think about was how she was going to tell Eric what she had discovered.

41

Atlanta

Feeley was unsure how long he had been unconscious. He groaned and raised himself on one elbow. It was still dark and the moon was high in the sky. A glance at his watch showed he had fainted perhaps fifteen minutes before, and yet he felt he had been in a deep, narcotic sleep for hours, even days. Pulling himself to his feet, he lurched to the car and rested his hands on the fender. He was anesthetized; his limbs moved when he willed them to, but in a jerky, robotlike way. He stood by the open door of the limousine and stared for a long minute at the still grinning face of Hamilton Hayward Wentz.

"Poor kid," he murmured, and pulled the sprawling corpse from behind the steering wheel. He gently propped it up and then got in on the driver's side. He half-expected the car would no longer function, but when he flicked the ignition key back and forth two or three times, the engine sputtered, then roared to life. Feeley calculated that whoever shot Wentz had done so only about half a mile back; but other cars, seemingly unscathed, still passed occasionally on Route 75. If someone was circling around to creep up on him, then all the more reason to get going.

He put it into reverse, and the big Lincoln growled and then burst through the foliage, down a small embankment, and onto the highway. Feeley threw it into drive and floored the accelerator. Before him, he could see clearly several skyscrapers wreathed in flames. Atlanta's stadium was ahead on the right, but Wentz had been correct in his judgment that the rioting had moved away from its immediate vicinity. Feeley's first thought was to find a way to turn around and head back for the airport, but a combination of numbness, curiosity, and the fear that the anonymous sniper was waiting behind him, kept him heading for the center of Atlanta. Finally, he chose an exit at random and crept down Georgia Avenue. At Hill Street he slammed on his brakes to avoid hitting an ostrich.

Feeley blinked, rubbed his eyes, and wondered if he had lost his mind. The enormous bird pranced daintily through the crosswalk and disappeared into the night. Feeley sat very still for a moment and then noticed a sign indicating that the Grant Park Zoo was just ahead. Had that one ridiculous bird escaped alone or had some lunatic released other, more dangerous animals? He didn't wait to find out. He took a left, then a right and then a left again. Less than a mile away, tremendous explosions were detonating, and the howl of sirens filled the soft night air. Surprisingly, the streets Feeley chose were almost deserted. He changed his course several more times at random, hoping to find a place of safety.

He turned again and found himself driving through the ranks of a regular army regiment. Too late Feeley realized he was surrounded, and he slowed to a crawl, desperately trying to extricate himself from the ragged troop column. On all sides were nervous young soldiers, who looked surprised and then angry to find him in their midst. Some of the troops kicked the car as it passed while others thumped on its sides. "Get the fuck outta here!" a short but mean-looking lieutenant bellowed at him. Feeley buzzed the window down and tried to explain, but the officer darted off to shout at several enlisted men who had stopped to admire some watches scattered on the sidewalk in front of an inefficiently looted jewelry store.

At last he found a hole in the line of march and pulled ahead, only to be stopped again by a group of grim marines. An army general darted out from the cover of a makeshift barricade and ran to the car. "Who in hell are you?" he asked incredulously, staring at the huge car, its driver, and the corpse sitting next to him. Before he could answer, Feeley heard the voice of the short lieutenant screaming perhaps fifty feet away.

"Left! Left! We turn here, for Christ sakes. Left!"

Feeley was once again surrounded. He pulled himself together and faced the general's furious glare. "My name is Francis X. Feeley. I'm a reporter for the New York *Daily News* and the News Syndicate . . ."

The general's features softened slightly. "Ah. I recognize you. Saw you on some talk show or something. But what on earth are you doing here? I advise you to get the hell out of here."

"Easier said than done, sir. We were ambushed coming into the city, and I, uh, gather things are still pretty hot all around us. Where are you bound?"

"State Capitol. It's only a couple of dozen blocks away, but it's not all that far from some of the worst fighting in the area."

"But who's doing the fighting? Why is this happening?" Feeley asked almost plaintively.

"Just 'bout every loony group within fifty miles of here, from the KKK and Minute Men to REAL terrorists and religious fanatics. And a whole bunch of people who've been so scared by the cancer thing, they're ready to go off the deep end anyway. Some pretty ugly racial incidents too. It's all happened so fast. There've been some lynchings on the fringe of one black part of town, and some pretty nasty things perpetrated by blacks in white sections. But it's not really a racial conflict. Looters run into some vigilantes and shooting starts; you drive down some streets in expensive neighborhoods and some guy is layin' in the bushes popping off rounds at anyone who comes near his hundred-thousand-dollar house. And, as I say, all the crazies are out either to raise hell or exorcise the devil." The general paused and looked tired. "And just about all of them shoot at us. It'll probably be sunset tomorrow before the whole city's pacified."

By this time, most of the troops had passed Feeley's car, and General Meade—or so his badge said—suddenly looked up.

"Gotta go, Mr. Feeley . . ."

"If you don't mind, I'll attach myself to your unit, General. Probably safer in the thick of it with you guys than wandering around by myself. Maybe I'll be able to help . . ."

"Suit yourself, Feeley. But we can't be responsible for you."

"I understand. Can I give you a lift?" General Meade looked tempted but then noticed Wentz's body.

"No thanks. I'll hoof it. Stay with the column; and please, Mr. Feeley, try to keep out of the way. I'm sure you understand."

Feeley nodded, and within seconds of the general's departure, a massive explosion went off some distance away. The big Lincoln shook, and he put it in gear and fell in at the rear of the battalion.

At last, the ragged column, which gave every appearance of being lost, found its way to the State Capitol grounds. Feeley eased his car among the army transports and finally found a parking place in what, only hours before, had been a flower bed.

"Mr. Feeley?"

"That's me."

A young lieutenant saluted and took his arm. "General Meade ordered me to help you in any way which does not endanger you. . . ."

"Don't trouble yourself about me, Lieutenant. If you'd just spare me a few minutes of your time, I'd like to know how this situation . . ." At that moment, a mortar round fell perhaps fifty yards away, leaving a crater in Mitchell Street and spraying the area with rubble. A chunk of asphalt shattered the windshield of Feeley's car.

"Looks like you're getting a baptism of fire, Mr. Feeley," the lieutenant muttered, helping him up. "I guess your limo has had it for the time being at least."

"Well, it got me here. Oh, there's a young man in the car. My driver. Dead, I'm afraid. If someone could take care of the body, I'd

like to be sure it's properly identified so the poor kid's family wil
know what . . ." Feeley's voice began to crack.

"I'll see to it, sir. Please, come with me to the command post, anc
I'll take down your information. Then you can ask me any question:
you have." They entered a large tent hastily set up along the side o
the Capitol Building. Feeley told what little he knew abou
Hamilton Hayward Wentz, and the young officer took it down
Finally, Feeley sat up straight and blinked.

"That was a goddamned artillery shell back there!"

"Mortar round, to be precise."

"Yeah well, who the hell is firing on us with weapons like that?"

"Oh, it could be one of those paramilitary groups, I suppose
More likely it was fired accidentally or inaccurately by some half-wi
in a National Guard unit. There's some pretty heavy fighting in th
Underground."

Feeley looked mystified.

"Underground Atlanta. Tourist area only a couple of blocks fron
here. There's a lot of shops and bars and stuff below street level, anc
when the rioting started, a lot of people decided it'd be a good plac
for some serious looting. When the first substantial units of loca
and state police got here in big numbers, they sealed it off. Why th
fuckers didn't just surrender is beyond me, but they're still shootin
down there. It's funny–I don't know where they got enoug
weapons and ammo to go on this long, unless they got hold of on
of our supply vehicles."

"So you think that's the area of the heaviest fighting?"

"Oh, no sir. That's just a mop-up operation. Come to think of it
that round probably came from fighting somewhere else. A littl
while ago there was one *hell* of a pitched battle around Rich'
department store. He gestured in a more or less westerly direction
" 'Bout six or eight blocks from here. And there's supposed to b
some *really* bad stuff going down around the Morehouse-Spellma
campuses. Some white punks went on a shooting spree and wipe
out maybe a dozen blacks in that area including three or four young
girls and an old lady. It took an hour or two for the word to ge
around, but now there's a hell of a lot of pissed-off people shooting

at one another as well as any whites they see. Some black kids got in *their* cars and shot up a mostly white neighborhood. God knows where it'll end, but we *are* beginning to organize a thorough sweep, and in a few hours I'd say most of the city will be pacified." He smiled confidently.

Only a few dozen feet from the tent, several automatic rifles began firing. The noise was deafening, and both Feeley and the lieutenant threw themselves to the ground. After half a minute of continuous shooting, the guns were silent, and the young officer crawled out of the tent, gesturing to Feeley to stay behind. He returned shortly, flashing a V-For-Victory sign.

"Sniper in a building 'cross the street. It's OK now; we got 'im."

"Do you think I'll be able to see General Meade for a quick interview?" Feeley asked, getting up and brushing off his now filthy three-piece suit.

"He just left. I'm sorry to say that I'll have to leave you, too. We're moving out in maybe half an hour to keep one of the Interstates open. I have to admit I'm glad we're going north. To the south, there's still a lot of prisoners on the loose from the Federal pen. And some lunatic let out the animals from the zoo. I heard 'bout one guy was chewed up real bad by a goddamn tiger, if you can believe it!"

"Yeah. I saw an ostrich on my way here. Look, can I come with your unit? I promise to stay out from under foot . . ."

"I'm very sorry, sir," the lieutenant answered quickly, "but I can't allow that. General Meade told me to keep you safe, and now that I've got orders to move, I couldn't be responsible. Anyway, if you stay here you'll hear about everything and still be out of danger. OK?"

"Sure, Lieutenant. And good luck." They shook hands seriously and then grinned at one another. "The name's Holler, H-o-l-l-e-r. Jim Holler. Feel free to make me famous." The young officer saluted and hurried off. They never met again, and only days later did Francis X. Feeley learn that a bullet had shattered Jim Holler's elbow and necessitated the amputation of his right arm.

When Feeley left the tent and began wandering around the

grounds of the Capitol and the park immediately abutting it, he suddenly realized how dazed he had been for the past few hours. The pleasant, almost balmy night air stank with smoke, and only a few blocks away, immense fires blazed out of control despite the efforts of hundreds of firefighters. The flames tinted the sky an ugly Halloween black-orange, and through a satanic symphony of sirens, shouting men, roaring trucks, and even screams of pain, he heard the distant but incessant rattle of rifle and machinegun fire. Lieutenant Holler had thoughtfully provided him with a helmet and a pass, and Feeley aroused minimal attention as he roamed the hastily constructed military base. Only slowly did he begin to comprehend the magnitude of the destruction Atlanta was suffering.

Still within the perimeter of the makeshift camp, he picked his way through streets jammed with all manner of military and civilian vehicles ranging from tanks and armored troop carriers to civilian cars and ambulances. Occasionally he stopped to interview a weary policeman or soldier, but all he could gather was that much of the city was burning, thousands were dead, and thousands more under arrest. There was also some evidence that the forces of–quite literally–law and order were beginning to gain control of much of Atlanta, though in perhaps half a dozen areas looting and fierce fighting continued unabated. Feeley was drawn to a parking lot lit by the harsh blue glare of several dozen large arc lamps. He walked a few paces and then stopped.

Hundreds of men, perhaps as many as a thousand, lay in confusion all around him. Many were civilians, and the others wore a variety of uniforms: army, marines, state police, National Guard, and several colorful varieties he had never seen before, including that of a Confederate cavalry general. Feeley approached the activity around one of the floodlights, and realized too late that the parking lot had been converted into an emergency operating theater. A surgeon, his hands and operating gown drenched in blood, muttered an oath and turned away from the body before him. It was covered with a sheet and hastily removed. He pulled off his mask and looked up at the sky; then he surveyed the dozens of stretchers surrounding him. He looked away, sighed, and rubbed his eyes, smearing his face with blood. He was obviously exhausted. Digging into his pocket, he extracted a cigar and strode a few yards away from the brilliant light. He cursed again and, seeing Feeley, called out. "Hey. You got a goddamned match?"

Feeley pulled out a lighter and watched as the surgeon sucked deeply on the cigar. "Tried to give 'em up. Pure death if you inhale. Before tonight, I'd stopped for almost a year . . ." Though he was looking directly at Feeley, he seemed to be talking to himself. A nurse appeared at his side and murmured something. "In a minute," he said testily, eyeing a wounded officer being prepared for surgery. "Even a colonel can wait once in a while. 'Specially with a flesh wound like his." He took another drag on the cigar and seemed to see Feeley for the first time. "Well? What're you staring at?"

"My name's Feeley. I'm a reporter for the New York *Daily News.* I didn't mean to stare, but this . . ." he waved his arm, "scene is a lot to comprehend, if you know what I mean." He shuffled his feet nervously while the surgeon glared at him.

"Reporter, huh? Ever in Vietnam?"

"Uh, no. Why?"

"Nothing. Just that this 'scene,' as you call it, wouldn't be so awe-inspiring if you'd been at a field hospital in the Central Highlands during Tet." He paused and studied the glowing tip of his cigar. "Though God knows we had better facilities there than we've got tonight." He drew in another mouthful of pungent smoke.

"Have you had many serious cases?"

"Some. Just lost one a minute ago. Thank God most of 'em are taken to one of the city hospitals. This is just a field station, Frawley, so in theory we should be treating minor wounds. But sometimes," he threw his cigar down and ground it out, "we get critical cases. And we lose most of 'em. Put *that* in your fuckin' newspaper." The doctor turned and strode away; then he took a few steps back toward Feeley. "Sorry. Been a rough night. Thanks for the light, and take care of yourself. My ESP tells me there's a lot of trigger-happy people roaming the streets tonight." He suddenly grinned and, before the startled Feeley could reply, was gone.

Francis X. Feeley stood for a moment among the hundreds of mangled bodies and then hastily headed back toward the Capitol grounds. He was almost there when he noticed two sweating soldiers struggling to unload a crate of ammunition from the back of a pickup.

"Need a hand?"

One of the soldiers looked up gratefully. "Thanks, mister. Could use one." Feeley and the two pulled off the last dozen crates and piled them on the sidewalk. "Thanks for the help. My name's Hull, and the strong silent type here is Corporal Mayer." The three men shook hands all around, and then Private Hull spoke.

"Funny thing. We been hauling those crates all night. They all look 'bout the same, but after the first hundred, they get heavier and heavier. C'mon up to the cab. We got some beer." Feeley sat in the pickup and shared a quart of Schlitz with the two weary enlisted men. They explained they had been transporting ammunition to various parts of the city from a dump on the grounds of the Piedmont Park Golf Course, where several transport copters had landed.

"We're almost done," Private Hull said cheerfully. "Maybe three more runs and that'll be it."

"Why don't I tag along?" Feeley asked.

"Would'ja? Sure could use some help," Hull said hopefully.

"Against regulations," Corporal Mayer muttered sadly.

"Fuck regulations," Hull replied. "You know as well as I do we can use an extra man. There's only three or four guys guarding the ammo back at Piedmont, and there's been a lot of trouble out by the Emory campus. And that's only a few miles away. You know what Captain Snyder says: 'When you've got a tough job to do, then use your initiative. Otherwise, you're dead.' "

"OK, OK, let's go," the corporal said wearily.

The pickup eased into traffic, and after crawling along for three blocks, swung onto Interstate 75-85 heading north. Mayer floored it, and they were soon cruising at a comfortable ninety miles an hour. In what seemed only a few minutes, they pulled up before the clubhouse at Piedmont Park and began to load the pickup. They had it more than half-filled when an angry sergeant came running toward them.

"Where the fuck have you two been? And who's *this* guy?" he asked.

"This is Mr. Feeley. ghte's a reporter, and he's helping us with the loading. A volunteer," Corporal Mayer said quietly.

"Oh. Captain Snyder wouldn't . . ."

"Captain Snyder's always said we should use our initiative, Sergeant Moldow, and this gentleman volunteered even though he knew the risks, and . . ."

"Hey," Moldow interrupted, "there's a bunch of empty beer bottles up front. Do you know the penalty for drinking while . . ."

"Those are mine, sergeant," Feeley said.

"You mean to tell me you drank six quarts of beer since you met up with these two?" Sergeant Moldow looked dubious.

"I drink a lot."

The sergeant looked thoughtful for a long moment, then brightened. "Ah, the hell with it. We've all been working our asses off. Now, I want you to start unloading the ammo and . . ."

"*Un*-loading!" Hull cried incredulously. "We're already behind schedule. These are for General Meade's headquarters down at the Civic Center."

"Calm down, Private," Moldow said quietly. "The captain got a call just ten minutes ago, and he's given orders that every man is to stay at his post and defend this position. There's a possibility that some nuts who've just wiped out the Disease Center and a lot of Emory know we're here, and they'd like nothing better than to get hold of the weapons and ammunition we've got. We can't take a chance of being short-handed in the event of an attack."

"But General Meade . . ."

"He'll have to wait. The captain was most specific. You stay. Now unload the stuff."

"Excuse me," Feeley said, almost humbly.

"Huh?"

"I was just thinking, sergeant, that I could make the run with the supplies–if you could give me directions–and then bring the truck back. . . ."

"Sure," Private Hull said, "that's a great idea. That way we get no flak from either the captain *or* headquarters. The Civic Center's maybe two miles from here. It's like a ten-, fifteen-minute trip. I can tell ya how to get there."

"I dunno," Sergeant Moldow said thoughtfully. "This is government property, and damned dangerous stuff to be letting a civilian have his hands on. Nothing personal, Mr. Feeley, but could I see your credentials?" Feeley gave him his press pass, driver's license, and Master Charge card. "Well, looks all right to me, but please, get there and back as fast as you can. There's plenty of troops to help with the unloading at the Civic Center. . . . C'mon you guys, load up the rest of them crates. . . . And don't worry about the ammo going off, Feeley. It's packed for rough transportation. Nothing to worry about. And the roads are clear around here, so you shouldn't have any problems. But be careful too. . . ."

"Don't worry," Feeley said, smiling. "I can do it and I *will* do it!" He saluted, and Sergeant Moldow beamed and slapped him on the back. Moldow tried to think of further instructions, but the mission was a simple one, and he was unsure as to how to give orders to a civilian. The pickup was quickly loaded, and Feeley looked over the directions to the Civic Center. Private Hull shook his hand and wished him luck.

"Not to worry, Mr. Feeley."

"Frank."

"Oh yeah. I'm Mel and the Corporal is Edgar. Really, it's a piece of cake. Keep in mind there's some nice cold beer back here at the old clubhouse, and I think even Moldow would let us have a Heineken when you get back."

"Sounds good. Take care, you guys."

Feeley took one more look at the map Private Hull had sketched for him, waved, and backed out of the country club parking lot.

Despite the sergeant's assurances, he kept his speed around twenty, and involuntarily winced every time he hit a bump. "Packed for rough transportation," he reminded himself. But why take a chance when you're carrying a ton or two of live ammunition.

Before long, he pulled up at the entrance to the Civic Center. Hundreds of troops were milling around, and it took him several minutes to find one who could direct him to the ammo dump. To his surprise, there were few if any guards around the piles of weapons and explosives, and only a portly master sergeant seemed to know what was leaving and what was arriving. Feeley hopped out of the cab and explained his situation.

"Just pull 'er up anywhere over there," the master sergeant mumbled, gesturing to his left with an enormous, beefy hand. "I'll send a couple a guys over to help you in just a few minutes." Feeley maneuvered through the crowds of soldiers and scattered supplies. Finally, he pulled up at what he hoped was the right location. He lit a cigarette and leaned against the pickup's grimy fender. To his surprise, Feeley discovered he was humming cheerfully. The sky was still stained an orange-pink, but the fires were clearly being brought under control. The colors were muted, and he noted that dawn was probably only half an hour away. After a brief wait, two soldiers arrived to help with the unloading, and the task was quickly completed.

A jeep pulled up. "It would seem you've joined the army, Mr. Feeley." It was General Meade.

"Yessir, I suppose you could say that. Are things under control yet?"

"Let's say much improved. Still some really bad fires, and we have some sniping in several parts of town. But on the whole, I'd say things'll be back to normal in another five or six hours. By noon, anyway." General Meade smiled, and Feeley wondered what his definition of "normal" was.

"Can you spare me fifteen minutes for a short interview? I could ride along with you if . . ."

Meade glanced at his watch. "I'm afraid not. Check with me tomorrow. There's still a lot to be done." He started to turn to his driver, then stopped. "You sure do get around, Feeley. I wouldn't be surprised if you knew more about what's going on than I do. We *will* talk tomorrow, and I'll see to it you get a citation for pitching in and helping instead of walking around with a tape recorder." He flashed another smile, tapped his driver's shoulder, and was gone.

Feeley sighed, climbed into the truck, and began picking his way down the streets around the Civic Center. He made a wrong turn and was momentarily lost, but after a few course changes he was heading back the way he had come. He looked forward to the promised Heineken and made a mental note to try to call Lou Soliman from the clubhouse. Lou would be right by the telephone, waiting for the first-hand report, the "scoop" for a *News* "Extra."

Francis X. Feeley grinned, then began to chuckle. He imagined Soliman pacing a path in his living room carpet, alternately wishing him in hell and praying he hadn't been blown to pieces. No Feeley, no scoop. He felt the surge of elation he'd once read combat soldiers experience when they realize they have come through a battle unharmed. Then he thought of Hamilton Hayward Wentz and the hundreds of bodies he had seen at the dressing station and his laughter abruptly ceased. He increased his speed and soon pulled up to the front entrance of the Piedmont Park clubhouse.

Something was wrong.

For several minutes he stood uncertainly by the truck, trying to figure out what was the matter. Everything looked the same. Some military vehicles were in the parking lot. And the lights were still on in several of the clubhouse's ground-floor rooms. Just as before.

Feeley punched the horn, and its blare sounded hollow in the perfectly still dawn.

That was it. No birds chirping, no sounds at all. And no troops. The thought crossed his mind that the soldiers must have moved out, but their transport was still there. Feeley took a deep breath, and headed for the clubhouse. It was deserted.

He circled the building, instinctively trying to be as quiet as possible. Floodlights still blazed, though the sun was already bright in the morning sky. He saw the body near the first tee. Feeley ran up and stopped a few feet away. The man had a crimson stain completely covering his chest. He was dead.

Feeley shuddered and moved quickly away from the corpse. Then he stopped again. Within a radius of twenty yards there were half a dozen bodies. He saw Private Hull, whose throat had been cut; near him was the body of Corporal Mayer, who had been shot at least five times at close range. Feeley jogged back toward the front of the clubhouse, avoiding several other corpses. He stopped by Sergeant Moldow. One side of his face was a bloody pulp, but he was twitching slightly. Feeley paused and quickly determined Moldow was beyond help. For the first time in twenty years, he murmured a prayer.

Frank Feeley stood by the now-still body of Sergeant Moldow and forced himself to think. He had been gone for ninety minutes, maybe two hours. There were no signs of the attackers and, strangely, no nonmilitary corpses. It must have been an ambush—it had to have happened very recently—and they might still be around. He rose very slowly and peered into the nearby trees. There was no sign of activity, but, he noted once again, the birds were still silent. Moving quickly and quietly, he headed for the front of the clubhouse and the pickup. He was passing a small shed when he saw it.

A half-naked body was hanging from a limb of a chestnut tree. Its feet were barely six inches from the ground.

It had been mutilated.

Feeley wanted to run, but he could not move. The horror was only five or six feet away, swinging very slowly from left to right. Feeley stared, trying to take it all in. The face was a puffy, purplish hue, and the tongue dangled ludicrously almost to its chin. Feeley tore his gaze from the staring, bulging eyes and noticed that the man wore the tunic of an army captain. Captain Snyder, probably.

The lower half of the torso was naked. Feeley stared, terrified and sickened. Where the genitals should have been was a gaping, bloody wound. Captain Snyder had been castrated.

Feeley felt it coming, and tried desperately to resist. *They could still be around. Keep your head. Don't panic. Easy. Easy.* He panted, trying to keep control. Finally, it burst. He screamed . . . screamed at the top of his lungs . . . a scream swelling louder and louder until he fell to his knees from weakness.

Then he ran.

A Georgia State Policeman found him pulled to the side of Route 16, ninety miles past Macon and almost halfway to Savannah and the sea. He was sound asleep and, when awakened, had no recollection of how he had got there.

42

The White House

The atmosphere in the Cabinet Room was decidedly tense as the members of the National Security Council awaited the arrival of the President. He was fifteen minutes late, and several of those sitting around the huge, highly polished mahogany table were visibly nervous. Vice President Baker was tapping his fingers on the table and staring at a massive grandfather clock at the far end of the room. Several of the Joint Chiefs were murmuring quietly among themselves, and Arthur Greenbaum was intently doodling on a large yellow legal pad. Only Bill Williams of the CIA seemed completely at ease as he stared impassively at the heavy, forest-green drapes closed tight against the brilliant morning sun.

The President burst into the room, smiling and nodding. "Gentlemen, sorry to keep you waiting." He was followed by John Acton, his press secretary, and Jerome Rotrosen, Assistant Secretary of the Treasury. President Wilson gestured for everyone to sit down and he took his chair at the center of the table.

"We have a great deal to cover, as I'm sure you all know. But I first want to announce that I have just asked for and received

Secretary McCauley's resignation. Though it will be up to the Senate to confirm the appointment, I will be nominating Jerry Rotrosen to take the job at the Treasury. I trust no one will have any objections to his attending this meeting."

Everyone was silent. Arthur Greenbaum looked up from his doodling and asked, "May we know why you saw fit to fire Secretary McCauley, Mr. President?"

Wilson was no longer smiling. "Yes, uh, I've been able to ascertain that McCauley was in constant communication with former Secretary Douglas. They speak almost daily and have coincidentally been guests at no fewer than four dinner parties over the past couple of weeks. Where they doubtless conspired at length. Mr. McCauley no longer enjoys my confidence. I believe he was secretly working to oppose my policies for this government." He paused and looked at each person in the room. "Jack Acton will make the announcement this afternoon that the Secretary of the Treasury is forced to leave office because of pressing personal matters. McCauley will go along with the story." A quick grin flashed across the President's face. "He'd better."

General McElyea cleared his throat, but otherwise the only sound was the quiet ticking of the grandfather clock. Arthur Greenbaum stared at Tom Wilson and decided he looked terrible. The President had lost weight, and his face was puffy and haggard. He slouched in his chair as he pored over several papers he had brought with him. Finally, Wilson looked up and stared at the FBI Director.

"Well, Greeley, why don't you lead off by giving us a rundown of the Atlanta situation."

"Yes, sir. As you know from my report of last Tuesday, the city is now completely pacified. Regular army and National Guard units will be kept on duty for an indefinite period, and their presence supplemented by approximately one hundred Georgia State Police. There was sporadic looting up until a few days ago, and damage was extremely heavy in the downtown area and in the vicinity of Emory University and the CDC. For now, though, everything is quiet."

Wilson giggled suddenly. "Only thing they were missing was Clark Gable and Vivien Leigh! Maybe we should organize something similar in Plains and give old Jimmy something to think about." He laughed at his own joke, hardly noticing that only Press Secretary Acton joined in. Most of the others in the Cabinet Room smiled nervously and were relieved when Wilson suddenly became more serious.

"General McElyea."

"Mr. President?"

"Both the FBI and CIA have reported to me that despite our best efforts to squelch the rumor of a secret anticancer vaccine, it and a dozen other crazy theories propagated by groups ranging from REAL terrorists to Jesus Freaks and Satanists are stirring up the American people. In many cities the situation is nearly out of control. May I assume the armed forces will be able to handle any domestic, uh, uprisings?"

General McElyea coughed and grimaced. "Our own sources in military intelligence indicate much the same situation, sir. The Atlanta episode could be only the first." He paused and looked at Director Williams, who nodded in agreement. "Our forces are stretched pretty thin at the moment, what with the Red Alert and military medical aid in several dozen major cities. In sum, I would say that we could handle any given two or three Atlanta-style incidents that might happen simultaneously, providing the local police can contain the situation for at least four hours. Should more than six major civil disturbances break out at one time . . . I have to admit the situation would likely be out of control."

President Wilson looked grim. Everyone watched him carefully. After his initial inappropriate giddiness, he had once again become a careful, probing chief executive.

"Arthur, what progress has our Caduceus Group been making? Not much it seems to me." Wilson looked intently at Greenbaum.

"Mr. President, it has never been a sure thing that we would ever be able to find a cure, a vaccine, for this cancer epidemic. As you know, the disease has been studied for a century with only some glimmers of understanding after billions spent in research." Wilson grunted, but Arthur Greenbaum continued. "Dr. Zimmermann has been taken ill and will not be back on duty in Atlanta for at least two more weeks. In the meantime, I have asked Dr. Rogers of NIH to take his place. . . ."

"Not that guy," Wilson groaned.

"He is a brilliant scientist, Mr. President. Anyway, Zimmermann will be back in a matter of weeks. I've been pressuring Caduceus for a thorough explanation of what progress they have made to date as well as the likelihood of a significant breakthrough. Zimmermann had promised to have it to me by the end of this week, and Dr. Rogers has guaranteed it would be on my desk no later than next Monday morning. I think I should add that even if the Caduceus Group gets lucky and discovers the cause of this plague, they probably will not have anything concrete for a year at the very least. The rate of new cancer cases being reported has begun to drop—nobody knows why—but Dr. Rogers assured me that within a year we will have an absolute minimum of twenty-eight million cases of cancer in the U.S. alone, and more likely closer to thirty-eight million."

"That's enough for now, Arthur. Thanks, and let me have that report on Monday," the President said. "Anything else?"

"Yes, sir. The supply of analgesics is close to the critical level. Even using our stocks of heroin seized over the years by various agencies, we are likely to have a serious shortfall. As you know, there has been a persistent rumor that the drug manufacturers are deliberately keeping supplies tight and dealing on the black market or secretly selling supplies overseas."

"May I interrupt, Arthur?" Director Greeley asked.

"Of course."

"The Bureau has investigated this with extreme thoroughness, and our conclusion is that there is no basis to the rumor. Recently, a bomb was found at one of Merck's major plants in Ohio, presumably planted by REAL or another fanatic group."

Greenbaum nodded in agreement and addressed the President. "The biggest bottleneck is due to our own high standards for drug purity. The sudden demand for painkillers has caught everyone off guard, and the production of large quantities of pure drugs takes time."

"Any suggestions?" Wilson asked.

"Yes. I've been assured by the chief executives of several of the largest manufacturers that they could speed up production if they are allowed to cut some corners with the absolute safety of their products. They're loath to do this without a guarantee from us that they will not be liable to lawsuits which might arise from people who are harmed by the drugs so produced."

"Tell them to go ahead. I'll speak to Senator Broadbent about it this afternoon. No problem. What about 'Project Nightcap'?"

Greenbaum sighed. "We've had to be very discreet about this, but our estimate is that roughly one hundred million doses of a painless suicide tablet could be produced in ten days to two weeks. Distribution would take almost as long."

Greenbaum's voice was soft, but as he spoke, his bones seemed to be on fire. The pain came and went in waves, despite the drugs he had been given. He struggled to maintain his composure, though he knew he was sweating profusely.

"God save us all," Vice President Baker murmured.

President Wilson leaned back in his chair and glared at the CIA Director. His eyes, which had seemed intelligent and thoughtful only minutes before, now blazed with fury. "Well, Director Williams, will you too have us rely on the Almighty, or do you have any information for the Council concerning the Soviet Union's role in this disaster?" Wilson's voice cracked, but Williams did not seem to notice.

"There is nothing significant to add to the Agency report we sent to the Oval Office yesterday, Mr. President. If you haven't had a chance to read it yet, I can . . ."

"Bullshit! I've read it. What the hell do you think the American people pay me to do? What I want from *you,* Williams, are some straight answers. Your so-called report," the President's voice was rich with contempt, "is a pile of shit."

"Sir, I . . ."

Wilson's fists came down on the table. "Shut up!"

"Easy Tom," Greenbaum said, lightly touching the President's arm. "Easy."

"Keep out of this, Arthur. If you are about to tell me that Mr. Williams has a fine record and all of that, don't bother. I'm quite familiar with his record. But there is nothing, *nothing* in the CIA report that even hints at the Russian role in this crisis. If I didn't know that Bill Williams was a loyal American, I'd suspect his motives."

Arthur Greenbaum noticed that Tom Wilson's fists were so tightly clenched his knuckles were white. The President glared at his CIA Director. "Do you have anything to add to your report?"

Williams showed no emotion. He blinked twice and then spoke. "No sir, not really. There is no doubt that the general population of the Soviet Union remains unaffected by any significant increase in cancer cases. But we have excellent sources in the Kremlin. Deep sources. And it is clear the Moscow regime is as much in the dark as we are. What is most significant is that those Russians who have travelled extensively in the West, including a high percentage of their diplomatic corps, as well as those who've had contact with westerners–and I include several dissidents and agents of ours–have been contracting some form of the disease at an accelerated rate."

"Another mystery, Bill?" Wilson asked rhetorically.

"Yes, I'm afraid it is. As much a mystery to them as to us. We've had several approaches from Soviet intelligence officers offering unheard-of cooperation. Frankly, they're scared. Their forces are on alert, and they're terrified we are going to make a hostile move on the basis of this circumstantial evidence."

"Has it occurred to you, sir," press secretary Acton said, "that even granting that the Russians may not have attacked us, they almost certainly do have some form of vaccine or immunization program to protect their people while the rest of us are dying like flies? Their denying us this information has cost thousands of lives. That in itself could constitute an act of war!"

A flicker of contempt crossed Williams' face. "Yes. It had occurred to me, Mr. Acton. There is no intelligence whatsoever to indicate this is the truth. I only deal with reality."

"*Fuck* your reality." Wilson's fists smashed onto the table again. "You're dead, Williams. You've been sitting on your butt at Langley too many years." Everyone was silent. "You're out as of now. We won't announce it, and I'm sorry I shot my bolt on McCauley today. Some of your Kennedy and Carter friends will try to make hay with this, but we're going to wait a few weeks before the axe *formally* falls. You keep your mouth shut, or things will get very rough. Very rough. Remember that. Clear out your office and don't go back. Is that understood? Is *that* bit of intelligence clear enough to get through to you?" President Wilson was screaming.

"It's quite clear, Mr. President. Shall I leave now?"

"Yes. We don't need you any longer." Wilson glanced at Arthur Greenbaum, who was intently studying his folded hands. Bill Williams gathered up his papers and quietly left.

President Wilson coughed and suddenly seemed almost placid. He glanced at his watch. "I'm sorry, gentlemen, that we've used valuable time on this squabble. In your briefing books some of you will find an envelope marked SUPRA. You are hereby ordered to keep this envelope in the most secure place your agency has. In nine days, no earlier than 9:00 A.M., you may open the envelope. It will contain all the information you and your people will need to know. All I can tell you at this time is that we are going to give the Russians one more chance. People like former Director Williams have been giving them the impression, I'm afraid, that we're weak. We're going to show them just how tough we can be unless they come around. This meeting is adjourned." President Wilson stalked from the room.

Arthur Greenbaum followed Tom Wilson down the hall and into the Oval Office. Acton was hovering nearby, but the older man grabbed his arm and shoved the press secretary toward the door with one word: "Out." Wilson nodded, and Acton left, shooting a look of pure hatred in Greenbaum's direction. The President was in his closet bar, pouring himself a waterglassfull of chilled Manhattan.

The President's voice was trembling. "I'm not going to stand for this anymore, Arthur. People either work with me on this or they're out. Williams has no balls. He's an old, gray man. And people like Douglas and McCauley: it's not just that I distrust their loyalty to me. I distrust their loyalty to this country." He drained the glass and poured another, larger drink. "The time has come for real strength, real power to be thrown around. I've got the guts to do it, don't you doubt that!"

"Of course you do, Tom. I know that better than anyone else. You're a great leader. Only a fool wouldn't agree with that. Tell me. What happens if the Russians don't come through on the ultimatum?"

"You mean, am I going to push the famous button?"

"Yes. I guess that's what I wanted to know," Greenbaum said.

"Nothing of the kind, Arthur. You'll see. We're just going to start turning the screws on them the way they've been turning them on us. You'll see soon enough. THEY'RE NOT GOING TO PUSH ME AROUND ANY LONGER!" President Wilson shrieked.

Greenbaum saw that though Tom Wilson was grinning, tears were running from his eyes and down his cheeks. "Of course not, Tom. Of course not." He left the Oval Office and headed for the men's room.

Greenbaum sat in a stall in the lavatory just off the press room and opened the envelope marked SUPRA. He was a bit pleased that the President had trusted him with more details than an HEW chief would have to know. The operation's code name was to be "Terrible Swift Sword." If the Soviet Union persisted in refusing to give up the necessary information to end the cancer plague, then the United States would launch a gradual and limited biowarfare attack. First, Vladivostok. Then Odessa. Then Kiev. The pressure was to escalate until the Soviets revealed how they had immunized their population against the plague. It was also noted, gratuitously, that the Soviet military knew that the United States possessed a dramatic edge in nuclear capability, and that any action against the North American mainland or Europe would be met with massive retaliation.

He crumbled up the envelope and its contents, and was about to flush it down the toilet when a tremendous wave of pain hit him. He lurched forward, banging his head against the stall door. The painkiller he had been given was obviously not working; he'd have to get something stronger that afternoon. Greenbaum felt his bones coming apart, disintegrating as he sat there, unable to move. At last, the pain receded, and almost disappeared entirely. He glanced at his watch and realized he had been in the stall for over half an hour. Hastily, he pulled up his pants, and leaned against the partition. Greenbaum noticed the crumbled envelope and papers on the floor; he took out his cigarette lighter, ignited and then flushed them.

As he left the White House, he felt much better. He had to talk with General McElyea and he had to talk with Bill Williams. He had finally made up his mind what had to be done.

43

Atlanta

Henry Rogers was deeply depressed. When Honorée had announced that a mob was marching on the Center for Disease Control, he had bolted from the room. Not to save his life. To save the computer. He raced for the elevators, but they were tied up with CDC employees evacuating the building. His office was on the ground floor, and most of the computer equipment was concentrated in a climate-controlled area in the first basement. If there were a sizable crowd about to attack the building, these would be vulnerable–months of work could be destroyed.

Rogers danced with impatience waiting for the elevator to come to the fifteenth floor. He had not run in almost thirty years, and it was fortunate he had to go down rather than up. Even so, when he reached the ground floor, he sagged against a wall and listened to his heart smash against his ribcage. He panted and wondered if he was going to have a heart attack. But the pain in his chest receded and he lurched unsteadily down the hall to his office. The corridor was deserted, though he could hear distant shouts and feet running through the main lobby behind him. He paused at his door and looked at its plastic nameplate: "Dr. Rogers. Director of Information Retrieval." He tried to pry the sign from the door with his fingers, but it would not budge. Running into his office, he threw a few papers into a small safe he never used and whose combination he had forgotten and slammed the door. Then he froze.

The noise was distant, though he could not explain how he could be so certain, never having heard gunfire before. The shots were still far away, he estimated (inaccurately as it turned out). Rogers wheeled and threw open his desk drawer. Removing a letter opener, he returned to the office door and pried the plate off, trying not to damage the wood. Then back to the office, where he frantically tore through a filing cabinet and then his desk. At last he found them: a small collection of signs he had picked up from the trash or stolen outright, intending some day to use them for a long-forgotten practical joke. He chose two. One was a poorly printed cardboard but nevertheless ominous. It read: "POISONOUS SNAKES KEEP OUT." The other was metal and smaller, reading: "HIGH RADIATION LAB: STERILITY RESEARCH CENTER." He then grabbed a white plastic bottle of Elmer's Glue and after biting off the residue around its cap, methodically pasted both warnings on the door. He stood back to admire his work and even managed a smile when he heard a brick smash through the plateglass of the main lobby. For the first time in an incredible fifteen minutes, he was afraid. Quickly, he double-locked the door and headed for the basement. There he was satisfied to see that the emergency system had worked. Massive steel doors sealed off access to the computers; it would take dynamite to get through them. As he raced up to the main level, he found himself part of the mob.

Henry Rogers was saved by his appearance. The frantic activity of the previous half-hour had left him as disheveled as any asylum inmate, and his clothing and bearing quickly established him as a member of the crowd rather than one of the scientists they were so ardently tracking. Henry Rogers may have been slovenly, but he was far from dumb. He quickly joined in, charging down the hall with a group of drunken zealots until he made his way outside and got away.

A few CDC personnel were not so lucky. Several had been caught and killed. One was tortured to death with a Bunsen burner without giving up the "secret" of the cancer cure. Guards were able to secure the upper floors of the building by shutting down the elevators and shooting anyone who came up the stairs, but by the time sufficient police arrived to disperse the crowd, the main building of the CDC was all but destroyed on its first six stories, and a number of smaller structures in the complex burned to the ground.

For some reason, Rogers' office was untouched.

But Henry Rogers was deeply depressed. With Zimmermann's hospitalization, the weight of organizing and directing the Caduceus effort had fallen on him. Carey-Ross had refused it and threatened to resign if his friend was not appointed. Eric had not won any popularity contests at CDC, or in Caduceus, for that matter, but his energy and ability had kept the HEW bureaucrats—who demanded an immediate cancer cure—at bay or at least off guard. Rogers missed him. He mourned for him.

Now, at the end of an eleven-hour day and almost eight straight hours of data analysis, he rubbed his eyes and looked around the dank room he had risked his life to preserve. To the untutored eye, the office looked as if a mob had not only run through but spent the weekend there. Rogers scanned the heaps of paper surrounding him: printouts leaned unsteadily against two walls; file folders were everywhere, spilling from his desk and onto the floor; articles, journals, magazines, newspaper clippings everywhere. His office was a wreck.

Rogers sighed, and wished aloud that paper had never been invented. He started to read a twenty-one page summary of cancer data from Japan. The only significant fact was on page two: the rate on Hokkaido, the northernmost major island in the Japanese archipelago, was significantly lower than that on the more densely populated areas of Honshu. He read on. The remainder of the document consisted of medical jargon and bureaucratic ass-covering.

Rogers swore a mighty oath and flung the file across the room, where it started an avalanche of papers from the top of his filing cabinets. He sighed and thought about calling it a day. He sincerely wished he had never learned how to read, and turned for consolation to his computer console.

His fingers tapped out the code for display of all statistical anomalies by region. A map of North America flickered onto the screen, and almost immediately a rash of red dots were overlayed. These represented pockets of resistance to the cancer epidemic, scattered from above the Arctic Circle to the Mexican border. More than eighty such locales had been discovered, and a number were under intensive study, but so far only one positive correlation had been found. *Every one was wretchedly poor.* Rogers punched a few numbers and looked at a similar map of the world. Nothing there suggested an answer, save for the persistent mystery of the words NOT AVAILABLE which labeled the Soviet Union and China.

Rogers typed ENDIT and scratched his head. The rural sharecroppers, Indians, Eskimos, chicanos, and others were doing something right that the urban poor, who had an almost normally high cancer rate, were not. He lit a cigarette and thought of what Carey-Ross had called Heisenberg's Curse. Recently, the residents of those unaffected areas subjected to the most intense study, like Monroe County in West Virginia, had begun to exhibit a gradual increase in cancer incidence. Carey-Ross had alluded to the Heisenberg Uncertainty Principle, which postulated that the test results were often affected by the very act of testing. Rogers butted out his cigarette and began to type again.

This time, he asked the machine to generalize for the single most common variable in all the groups of unaffected rural poor. The screen was blank for several seconds, and then it balked. The word UNAVAILABLE flashed onto the screen.

Rogers was annoyed. He thought there had to be a #1 on the Hit Parade of rural miseries. He recoded the request in a somewhat different way, but the reply was the same: UNAVAILABLE. Rogers pursed his lips with frustration, and tried again. And again. The computer seemed to anticipate him, and each time he had hardly finished punching out the question when the same UNAVAILABLE popped up. Furious, he typed, THINK YOU IDIOT.

There was a noticeable pause, and then the screen filled with columns of figures. Above them was the headline DATA OVERLOAD SELECTIVE STATISTICS RANDOM CHOICE. Rogers scanned the readout and realized that he had indeed asked for too much. The NIH and Caduceus computers now had access to figures from all over the world, and the best the machine could do to answer him was to make a random selection. It had pulled out six variables: infant mortality rate, minimal sanitation, illiteracy, substandard housing, excessive chronic illness, and alcoholism, for nine groups ranging from Mississippi to Sicily. He grinned when he read the sentence which flickered along the bottom of the screen: CAN'T YOU READ TURKEY.

Henry Rogers did not believe in machine intelligence. Clearly, the linkup of dozens of large computers from around the country and the world was the source of the message. Someone, probably in a university, had programmed his computer to react when it was repeatedly asked an impossible or poorly phrased question. He scanned the columns of figures again. No single factor dominated with any continuity. All were above the +50 percentile. All or none could be the key to resistance to the epidemic, or it could just as easily be a factor not even deemed worthy of inclusion in the databank. He chuckled aloud at the question at the bottom of the screen and raised his hand to turn off the console's power.

He stopped. For a full ten seconds his hand hovered over the switch as he stared straight ahead, hardly daring to breathe.

And then he shuddered. Rogers shook his head and looked around the room. Very suddenly, through pure intuition, he knew he had found the answer. He *knew* what was at the root of the cancer plague. Rather, he now knew where to begin.

44

Georgetown

Arthur Greenbaum and General Peter "Mac" McElyea could not have been cast from more dissimilar molds: where Greenbaum was sallow and plump, McElyea was ruddy and trim; Greenbaum was elegant, dapper, and soft spoken, while McElyea was flamboyant and impulsive. For some reason though, they trusted one another. So when Secretary Greenbaum called him at the Pentagon and asked his friend to meet for a drink at a small Chinese restaurant in Georgetown *and* to come in civilian clothes, the general agreed without asking any questions.

The restaurant, Ling Fat, was one of the worst Cantonese establishments in Washington, and was consequently popular with university undergraduates in the nearby dorms. It was not frequented by Washington insiders or the press and was, therefore, a perfect place for the President's most trusted advisor and the Chairman of the Joint Chiefs to have a private conversation.

Arthur Greenbaum sat at a booth near the back, and waved when McElyea entered. It was barely five o'clock, so there were only a few other customers wolfing down combination plates. None of them looked up as the well-dressed bear of a man strode by. Greenbaum thought he looked like a successful prizefighter turned out for a date with a socialite. He smiled and half-rose to shake McElyea's hand.

"Good of you to come, Mac. Drink?"

"That's what you said we were here for. Scotch. Dewars and water." Greenbaum flagged a passing waiter and ordered two scotches. He ignored the glass of white wine he had earlier pushed aside after one sip. Neither said anything until the waiter brought the drinks and went into the kitchen.

General McElyea raised his glass. "Cheers, Mr. Secretary." He looked around the shabby restaurant. "Much as I enjoy your company, I have to say that this is not the most elegant saloon I've ever visited. Sort of place I'd expect you to negotiate with the Mafia in. Or Bill Williams, of course." He smiled.

"Director Williams and I are planning to attempt to eat dinner here in approximately one hour, Mac. I wanted to talk to both of you separately tonight about the Security Council meeting this morning."

General McElyea looked serious. "I see. OK, shoot."

Greenbaum took a sip from his glass and very gently put it down on his napkin. "You really aren't going to do it, are you, Mac?"

"Do what?" McElyea asked, a hint of irritation in his voice.

"Terrible Swift Sword, or TSS as it is referred to in the material I was given this morning."

"Ah, so you opened the envelope. The President would not be pleased to hear you disobeyed his explicit instructions."

"The President," Greenbaum hissed, "is insane." He studied the ruddy face across the table from him. "The President is likely to launch this insane operation at any time; maybe tonight if he dips too deeply into the brandy bottle. You saw him this morning. Now I want you to give it to me straight. Are you going to do it? I want to know *now.* Yes or no."

General McElyea looked angry and was about to speak when a waiter returned. "More drink?"

"No," Greenbaum snapped.

"Yes," McElyea commanded, "a double." The waiter scurried away.

"Now look here, Art," McElyea began, recovering his composure. "I've been in the military all my life. You haven't, so I'll spell this out. The President of the United States, no matter what I may think of him personally, is the Commander-in-Chief. That means when he says spit, I spit. No argument. That's the way it has to be. You must see that."

"I do. But this TSS is the creation of a madman. I assume, by the way, that you too opened your envelope. . . ."

"No need to. The operation was devised by the Pentagon as a contingency option several years ago. We refined it somewhat and I personally delivered it to the President just yesterday."

"Good God," Greenbaum murmured.

"Look, Art," McElyea said in a conciliating tone of voice, "Terrible Swift Sword is not going to be used. The Russians may give in or Wilson may change his mind. I know it's an extreme step, but I think the Russians will see the light and tell us what they know. . . ."

Greenbaum exploded. "They don't know a *fucking thing!*" he shouted, his hand thumping the formica table and spilling a bit of his drink. An elderly woman paused, an egg roll halfway to her mouth, and glared across the room at Greenbaum. He lowered his voice. "You know that every bit of intelligence clearly shows that there is no evidence the Soviets have *anything* to do with this plague. If there was one fragment of a fact that they had attacked the United States or were withholding the solution to this cancer problem, I wouldn't object so strongly to this. But this is an outright attack, not a counterattack."

"Look, I tend to agree with you," General McElyea said grimly, "though I still wouldn't be surprised to find one of our enemies at the bottom of this whole mess. No, wait, let me finish. But I am goddamned sure that TSS will not be set in motion."

"And how come you're so sure?" Greenbaum asked.

"I just feel it in my bones."

"Your bones." Greenbaum looked disgusted. The pain was starting again, but he pushed it aside.

"No, honest . . ."

Arthur Greenbaum glared at McElyea and then his expression softened. "Well, maybe your bones are right, Mac," he said very quietly, "because it's not going to happen. And that's a fact."

"I agree. But why do you sound so sure?"

"Because if it comes down to it . . . I'll warn the Russians."

Silence.

"That would be treason, Arthur. Treason."

"Perhaps. And I don't know if I could do it, to tell you the truth. There's at least a chance the USSR would respond to the warning by launching a preemptive attack. But the end result would be the same in any event: thermonuclear war, possibly starting as 'limited,' but soon escalating into a world war. I don't doubt that, and I think you're far too intelligent not to see it as well." Greenbaum paused.

"Maybe," McElyea replied, stirring the ice in the drink with his finger. "Maybe."

"No maybe, Mac. A sure thing." Greenbaum sighed. "Look, I know Tom Wilson as well as his wife does, in some ways better. Without my help, he probably would still be doing the six o'clock news in Boston. He's not an evil man, Mac. But he *is* over the brink. Paranoid. Drunk. Violent. Maybe I feel guilty for putting him in the Oval Office, but I do know that I will not stand by while a petulant child causes the slaughter of innocent millions. Maybe it's just because I'm a Jew and I can remember the slaughter of millions of other innocents, but I don't think that's it, Mac . . ."

"Oh, Art . . ." General McElyea began sadly.

"Listen, I don't think I have the nerve to tell the Russians and risk a war which will start in any event. But, Mac . . ." Greenbaum who was usually an unemotional man, reached across the table and placed both his hands over McElyea's. "We can't let this happen."

"There's little I can do, Art."

"Please. Take my word for it. The President is no longer sane. Maybe what I'm proposing *is* mutiny, but it's certainly not treason to disobey the orders of an alcoholic madman! If Tom Wilson orders you to execute Terrible Swift Sword you have got to refuse to carry out that order." Arthur Greenbaum's eyes filled with tears, and McElyea finally had to look away. "Well?"

General McElyea got to his feet and looked for a long moment at his friend. He said nothing and turned to go. After a few steps, he returned to the table. "I'll think about it, Art. That's all I can promise. I'll think about it." McElyea touched his friend's shoulder and said softly, "Stay well," and quickly left the restaurant.

The meeting with Director Williams was much more successful. After McElyea had left, Arthur Greenbaum went to the men's room and took the new painkiller he'd been given that afternoon. His doctor had warned him it could affect his mood and he could swing from elation to depression and back again whenever he took it. But the pain was eliminated by a warm surge of well-being suffusing his entire body. He had also been told the medication would affect his appetite, and he was both astonished and appalled to discover that he was gobbling up shrimp with lobster sauce and moo-shu pork with the same relish he normally reserved for the finest Beef Wellington or the perfect Sacher Torte.

Director Williams toyed with his food and said little. At last he spoke. "You seem to have a good appetite, Mr. Secretary."

"It's the dope they're giving me. Said it'd play tricks with my eating habits. It's amazing, but I think I could go out and have a Big Mac for dessert. You finished?"

"Yes. Help yourself." Bill Williams slid a virtually untouched platter of chow mein across the table. "Ah, how long have they given you, Arthur?"

"Doctors never give you a straight answer, Bill. They say I'll be 'active' for at least a couple of months more, whatever that means. Six months at the outside. Dead in a year, probably," Greenbaum said almost cheerily, wolfing down Williams' chow mein. He looked up and wiped his lips with a napkin. "In any case, I've made my decision."

"Are you sure?" Williams asked in a hushed voice.

"Yes, definitely."

"You know, I assume, that I can prove that I am not here but in the middle of a final late meeting back at Langley right now."

"Deniability, eh? Can't blame you." Greenbaum suddenly felt sad and wondered if the drug was affecting his mood. "You don't have to worry, Bill. I can keep a secret. What've you got, a double?"

"Sort of. Uh, something like that. Ah, are you sure you've made the right decision? I mean, we've been talking in a sort of code for the most part, but I know what you have in mind. We're both, especially you, still in the clear. You can go home and curl up in bed . . ."

"And die," Greenbaum said bitterly.

"That's not what I meant."

"No, I know—of course not. I think it's this medication. But I do know this: I have made up my mind what I have to do. And whatever happens, you have my word you will not be involved. I promise." Arthur Greenbaum paused and stared at the gray man whose icy, pale eyes bore into him. "Well, my stomach's likely to rebel just at the thought, but that was a delicious meal. I've gotta go," he said pleasantly. "You got the package for me, Bill?"

Director Williams slid a thick business-size envelope across the table, and got up to leave.

"Stay for dessert?" Greenbaum asked, already knowing the answer.

"No, Arthur, I have to be on my way." The Director of the CIA stood by the table and looked uncertain. "I just want to say . . . uh, that, well, you are one of the few truly great Americans I've ever known. I'll always remember you. God bless you, Arthur Greenbaum."

Once again, Greenbaum was left alone at the table. He stuffed the envelope into his pocket and waved for the check. It arrived along with a fortune cookie. He left a twenty-dollar bill, which covered the entire dinner and a generous tip, and started to slide across the red vinyl banquet. On impulse, he stopped and cracked open the cookie.

It was empty.

45

Atlanta

Henry Rogers' brilliant intuitive leap was based at least partially on some facts he had previously noticed but discarded as unimportant. Some of his earliest statistical studies showed that professionals and the better-educated were being particularly hard hit by the cancer scourge. But Rogers had assumed that since the cities had a slightly higher incidence of diagnosed carcinoma and since professional people tend to be concentrated in urban areas, it was unlikely to be a fruitful research project. But that was where scientific intuition came in. Dr. Rogers had always disagreed with Zimmermann's theory that the epidemic was the result of a virus. There was a mass of theoretical work suggesting this, but no one had ever been able to isolate one. And there was an absolute certainty that any number of chemicals and pollutants ranging from tobacco to asbestos did, for a certainty, cause cancer.

His search for a contaminant was not an easy one. Thousands of chemical compounds were invented every year and used for tens of thousands of purposes, and unless these were intended to be a food or drug, the government did not require any tests as to their long-term safety. What was clear, however, was that the contaminant had to be so broadly distributed that it affected the genetic structure of virtually everyone in the population.

It was just a hunch, but Henry Rogers was quickly able to determine that the correlation between illiteracy and a lack of genetic damage and the resulting susceptibility to cancer was very high. He had impulsively called several staff members on the evening of his conversation with the computer and insisted they drop everything and come to the CDC.

"Look, it's just a hunch. That's all. But I want you to run programs tonight on the correlation of illiteracy and cancer incidence. And, for that matter, the level of literacy of those who have contracted the disease in the past two years." Henry Rogers looked at the six Caduceus staffers who stood glumly around his desk. It was obvious they thought he was crazy.

One spoke up at last. "Dr. Rogers, I don't see why we have to do this tonight. I mean, it will probably take five or six hours to do the entire run. Can't it . . ."

"No," Rogers said, raising his voice. "It can't wait until tomorrow. Just do it." He lit a cigarette, and sat down at his computer terminal, ignoring the stares of his unhappy assistants. He flicked on the console's power and turned in his chair. "That's all. Now *move!*"

By four in the morning, he had the information he wanted. But it just didn't make sense. Illiteracy was a common enough corollary of the poverty found in the known unaffected areas. But what was stunning was the remarkably high percentage of literacy-to-cancer. Even the staffers began to sense they were onto something as the data began to roll in. Every person with diagnosed cancer in the past six months had been extensively tested and interviewed. The Caduceus computers could supply data on every aspect of their lives from eye color to automobile ownership to the regularity of sexual intercourse. And the degree of intellectual attainment. The computer "knew" all along that literacy was a virtual necessity for developing the disease—close to 90 percent—and the converse was almost as certain. No one had even thought to ask the right question. Until Rogers.

"What do you make of it?" Henry Rogers asked his blurry-eyed but elated staff. The sky was pearl gray; soon the sun would be streaming through his window. Most of the Caduceus people sat on the floor or leaned against the wall since Dr. Rogers' spare chair and his couch were piled high with books and papers. All agreed that they were onto something, but nobody could understand what.

"It's paper," Rogers said finally. "There's something in paper. Look around heie," he urged, waving his arms at the piles of paper surrounding him. "This is a goddamned paper civilization: just think of the amount of paper the average person handles every day, whether it's a printout, a book, a newspaper, or a note from mom. Any other guesses? At least for tonight?" The room was silent. "Okay. Let's sleep on it. I want all of you back here no later than noon today. We'll meet here. If any of you have any further thoughts, no matter how wacky, please bring them up at that time." He looked around the room and smiled. "If I were President Wilson, I'd give you all the Medal of Honor for your work tonight and over the past months. I can't thank you enough." Rogers smiled again and everyone left, tired but happy.

He considered driving back to his apartment, but he suddenly felt as if he'd been up for three straight nights. Rogers looked around his office, and then strode across the room and shoved an avalanche of books and reports off the couch. He realized that Molly Duffy, his secretary, would raise hell about it, but he curled up on the sofa and was content. A year before he had read a book called *How to Be Assertive, But Loved,* but it hadn't done a thing for him. As he slipped into a deep sleep, he was pleased with himself. At last he had been able to be assertive and liked, perhaps even loved. Best of all, he was sure he had found the cause of the cancer epidemic.

It was a dead end.

Henry Rogers sat uncomfortably on the edge of a chair next to Eric Zimmermann's hospital bed.

"Cheer up, Henry. You're still on the right trail. Are you sure the tests were thoroughly done?" Eric sat propped up by three pillows. He looked remarkably cheerful considering what he had been through.

"Well, there are a lot more to be made, of course, and something may still turn up, Eric, but I'm discouraged. For one thing, there're only a handful of compounds which've been introduced to the processing of paper in the last fifteen years, and even fewer show up as minimal traces in the final product. Of those, the analyses show no substantive effect on DNA or immediate carcinogenic results in test animals. It's very frustrating." Rogers folded his hands in his lap and looked at his shoes.

"Rogers, you should be forbidden to visit anyone in the hospital. You all but take the will to live out of a guy. I mean, you weren't rushed in here not knowing whether you'd ever see your cock again or not."

"Oh, Eric, I'm sorry. I know how gloomy I must seem. Tell me, how are you doing?"

"The prognosis is pretty good. We won't know for sure for years, of course, but it seems they got it. Anyway, it makes me a full-fledged, typical American boy. Circumsized and all. Though I confess I now wish my parents had thought of it some years ago; hurts like hell sometimes, and the most optimistic physician here says it'll be two months at the very least before I can do anything except be a warm body in bed.

"But I have a lot to be thankful for. After all, Wendy Wilson has made carcinoma almost a national duty, and the prognosis in my case is quite good. Though I must say that cancer of the goddamned penis is one of the more, uh, embarrassing ways to be laid low, so to speak." Zimmermann's cheerfulness had little effect on Rogers, whose mind was obviously elsewhere.

"Um. Yes. Not very pleasant."

"Well, I'll be up and around in another couple of days, and I should be back on the job in two weeks or so. I was just thinking this morning how lucky I am. . . ."

"You mean catching it in time?" Rogers asked.

"Yes, that of course. No, I was thinking I might have developed a serious case of cancer of the prostate. One of the techniques for treatment is an orchiectomy."

"Orchi–?"

"The surgical removal of the testes: castration. Get you in good form for the heavenly choir."

"Oh," Rogers replied, not knowing quite what else to say. He blushed slightly and both men were silent for several long moments.

"What about the ink?"

"Huh?" Rogers asked.

"The ink on all that paper you seem to think is wiping out the better part of the Western World. Checked it out?" Zimmermann stared at Henry Rogers and watched his expression change from depression to curiosity to thoughtfulness to elation: all in a matter of less than a minute.

"Of course," Rogers said aloud, but really to himself. "Of course."

"It seems to me, Henry . . ." Zimmermann started. He stopped; Rogers was already almost out the door.

"Good thought, Eric. Don't know why I missed it. Good thought." Rogers rushed from the room and only stopped halfway down the hall. He ran back to Zimmermann's room and pushed open the door. "Sorry to rush out like that. Listen, take good care, don't give the doctors too much grief, and you'll be back on the fifteen-hour day before you know it. Take care. Take care."

Before Zimmermann could reply, Rogers had once again darted out of the room, leaving the door flapping in his wake.

Zimmermann was right. It was the ink. Though it took several months for confirming evidence to be found, and years before the actual chemical reaction was understood, it was only five days later that the agent was found: PEC-4.

PEC-4 was a remarkable compound developed by a French firm

during the mid-1970s. After a series of tests, it was released on the world market, but with the shakiness of the European economy the patent was sold to an American conglomerate for $500,000 cash. The basic structure of PEC-4, a coal tar derivative, had been known for over a decade, but the French engineers had discovered that in combination with other chemicals it had several remarkable properties. Most particularly, it allowed for the extremely rapid drying of ink as well as a sharper resolution of type and, in most processes, printed images.

Within a few years of its introduction, PEC-4 had become a standard ingredient in virtually all printing ink. Books, newspapers, advertisements, photocopies, typewriter ribbons, ballpoint pens: just about everything which was printed or written—all contained PEC-4. Commercially, the compound was a solid success.

Of course, it also caused cancer.

46

Washington, D.C.

Secretary Greenbaum's limousine pulled up at the barricade and stopped. A young marine and a Secret Service man peered in at him, then waved the car through. It cruised a few yards and halted at the dock, where the presidential yacht lay at anchor, lights ablaze.

"Wait for me, Jerry," he said casually. Ignoring the disappointed look on his driver's face, he headed for the gangplank where he was met by another Secret Service agent.

"I'm afraid I have to take a look inside, Mr. Secretary," the agent said, pointing at his briefcase. Greenbaum snapped it open, and looked bored while the agent quickly poked through the bag. It was empty save for some HEW reports and an unopened bottle of Hennessey XO. The Secret Service man registered no expression, clicked the case shut, and stood aside.

"Funny, but I've never been searched before," Greenbaum said pleasantly.

"I'm sorry, Mr. Secretary. The world situation being what it is . . . uh, the President ordered that everyone meeting with him be checked out. He didn't mention any exceptions." The agent looked chagrined.

"Quite right. Good idea. Will you want to 'frisk' me as well?" Greenbaum seemed amused.

"No, sir. No need. Please. Go right ahead."

Arthur Greenbaum shuffled up the gangplank. The medication was working well, and he felt no pain, though his body was daily becoming weaker. He took his time, knowing that he was being automatically scanned by a variety of electronic devices and metal detectors. Bill Williams had told him not to worry about these security measures, and he heard no alarms as a steward greeted him and led him to the main salon.

"We'll be weighing anchor shortly, Mr. Secretary," the steward said, opening the cabin door and standing aside. "The President will be with you in just a few minutes. May I get you anything?"

"No thanks," Greenbaum said, sinking into a comfortable armchair. "Ah, how many are there aboard tonight?"

"Just you and Mr. Acton, sir."

"And the crew?"

The steward blinked. "Oh. Twelve, I guess. The galley crew is off duty, but I can get you anything you wish. . . ."

"No, son, I'm fine. Thanks."

The steward silently closed the door and left Greenbaum with his thoughts. Twelve men. He sighed and thought of the steward's handsome young face. The pain started again, first in his lower back, then spreading to his limbs. He rose and went to the bar, where he downed two orange capsules and a glass of water. In a few minutes, the mild discomfort would, he knew, disappear. But he also knew it was still there, hidden under a blanket of narcotics. His body was riddled with cancer, and eventually even the strongest painkiller would be inadequate. It was like a fire blazing in a tightly sealed room: eventually the blaze would explode through the defenses and rage uncontrollably until it burned itself out. Greenbaum crossed the room, took the bottle from his briefcase, and poured himself a drink. The pain was already diminishing, but he knew he had just days before he would have to be hospitalized.

That morning he had awakened screaming. The symbolism of the dream was obvious, but terrifying nevertheless. He was in a dark, fetid pit. There was almost no light, and for a while he staggered around, trying to find a way out. He lurched toward the source of a curious sound, a sort of clicking, tapping sound, like millions of tiny clocks chattering somewhere nearby. Finally, the chasm seemed to brighten a little and he looked around. He was naked. He looked at his hands and then his legs, and stared in horrified disbelief. He was completely covered by a layer of tiny crabs, none of them larger than a centimeter or two. The clicking sound he had heard was the snipping of millions of their tiny pincers as they tore at tiny bits of flesh. One mass had bored into his belly, hollowing out the stomach cavity. He wanted to run, but was paralyzed with fear. At last, he opened his mouth to scream, and thousands of the creatures instantly streamed into his mouth and down his throat, choking him, gagging him ...

"Arthur! Hello!" President Wilson strode into the room, followed by Jack Acton. Wilson seemed ebullient as he grabbed Greenbaum's hand and pumped it. "Aha. Some cognac. You didn't even wait for me." Wilson grinned and poured himself a stiff shot. He looked more closely at Greenbaum and the smile left his face. "Arthur, you look terrible. Are you ill?"

"No, no. Overwork, I guess. I've been having some trouble sleeping lately."

The President took his friend by the arm and led him to an overstuffed leather sofa. "You've got to take better care of yourself, Art. You're about the only person left I can trust." Acton shifted uneasily, unsure whether to sit or leave. "Well, Jack," Wilson said testily, "is there anything else?"

"No sir. I just thought ..."

"Thanks, Jack. I'll call if I need you." Wilson dismissed him with a gesture.

After Acton had left, Wilson spoke quietly to Greenbaum, "You know, Arthur, I don't entirely trust that guy. He's ambitious, loyal for the moment. But I think he'd sell his mother into the white slave trade if it would help get him to the top."

Greenbaum smiled noncommittally.

"Anyway," Wilson continued cheerfully, "I'm glad I finally succeeded in getting you out for a cruise after all this time."

"It's a splendid boat," Greenbaum agreed, looking around at the richly decorated room. "I'm surprised Carter was willing to part with it."

"A populist gesture. I think if he knew how relaxing a run up the Potomac could be, he would have kept it. I'm glad you were able to get it donated back to the government."

"It made a good deduction. Ah, Tom, there's something I wanted to talk with you about in complete privacy."

"Well, this is the place," Wilson said, pouring himself another drink. "You know, except for some of the furnishings, this ship has been almost unchanged since FDR's day?" Below decks, a powerful engine murmured as the *Boston* slipped away from its dock.

"Tom . . ."

"I really feel happy when I'm aboard. It's comfortable and cozy. Not like that goddamned fishbowl at the White House."

"Mr. President, I want to talk with you about Terrible Swift Sword," Greenbaum stated tonelessly.

"Peeked in your envelope, did you? Well, I'm not surprised. Your curiosity has always been one of your greatest strengths."

"In slightly more than forty-eight hours, according to the plan, the United States will launch an attack against a Soviet city . . ."

"And I suppose you want me to extend the deadline; give 'em more time? No way, Art. This time the chips are down, and they know it. I'm not going to be the one to back down. Kennedy stood up to them and won. The stakes are a lot higher this time–quite literally our national survival." Wilson's voice was sharp.

"You can't do it, Tom."

"Oh yes, I goddamned well can! They're cowards. Under pressure they'll crack. You'll see." The President's breath was short; his eyes blazed ferociously. He jumped up and began to pace the room. "I've got the balls even if weak sisters like Bill Williams don't. When the showdown comes, *I will not flinch!"* He stopped and suddenly giggled. "Good line, that. Remember it for your memoirs, Arthur: 'I will not flinch.' Good line."

"You can't be serious. I still can't believe it."

Wilson charged across the room and roughly seized Greenbaum's arm. "Now listen to me, you old fucker. You're either with me one hundred percent or you're off the team. You'll be back in Boston in twenty-four hours doing your money-changing routine again. But don't think it'll be so easy unless I'm on your side, Arthur. You've cut a few corners over the years that the IRS and SEC might be interested to hear about," Wilson rasped. His face was contorted by a twisted smile.

"I really don't care," Greenbaum said sadly.

President Wilson suddenly seemed contrite. "Oh, Arthur. Arthur. I wasn't serious. You're the best friend I have in the world. Almost everyone else has turned on me, and I'm edgy. Here, have some more brandy." Wilson sloshed a generous serving of XO into Greenbaum's almost untouched snifter. He stared at his friend and advisor and was moved and then angered to see tears welling in Greenbaum's eyes. "For Christ's sake, Arthur, pull yourself together. I thought you had more guts."

Greenbaum said nothing and lit a cigar.

Wilson began to pace the room once again. "They're not going to get away with this," he muttered.

"Tom, you have no hard evidence the Russians are in any way involved . . ."

"Oh, *shit,*" Wilson sneered, "come *off* it. I've listened to that crap for too long. Maybe thousands of Americans would still be alive if I hadn't listened to our so-called intelligence reports about how innocent the Russians are. Christ, if I know two people are locked together in a room and I hear a shot and run in and find one of them standing over the body of the other with a gun in his hand, I don't need any first-hand proof to know what happened. Don't you worry, they'll back down. If they don't, they'll get what they deserve." He glared at Greenbaum. "And no one's going to stop me. No one."

While the President was speaking, Arthur Greenbaum took an envelope from his pocket and unwrapped a small packet of what looked like pie dough. It was the color of a corpse. "I'm sorry, Tom. More sorry than you will ever know. You do have to be stopped. For the good of the country. Maybe for the survival of the world. More than anybody else I got you the presidency. So it's up to me to stop you myself."

Wilson giggled bitterly. "*You?* You senile coward. You couldn't stop a toilet." Wilson giggled at his witticism. He sneered at Greenbaum and started to say something, when he noticed the oblong chunk of dough Greenbaum gently placed on an antique rosewood table directly in front of him. "Ah, what the hell is that?"

Greenbaum flicked the ash from his cigar and blew on its tip. "It's a high explosive, Tom. A kind of plastique, I believe, but far more powerful. This little lump is supposed to be more than sufficient to blow the boat to pieces."

"You'd try to blackmail me?" President Wilson asked, his voice filled with disbelief. "Traitor!" he screamed, and hurling his glass to the floor, lunged across the room toward Greenbaum.

"Stop," Greenbaum commanded and Wilson did.

"That you'd blackmail me . . ."

Tears ran down Arthur Greenbaum's cheeks. "I'm not going to blackmail you, Tom. I'm going to kill you."

The Secret Service man stationed outside the door had heard Wilson's glass shatter, and pressed his ear to the door. Something was wrong. He burst into the cabin, his gun drawn.

"Shoot him!" Wilson screamed.

The agent hesitated for a moment and looked at the weeping Cabinet officer.

"I'm very sorry," Arthur Greenbaum said to him. He touched the putty with his cigar.

The explosion was heard in downtown Washington, almost three miles away.

47

Atlanta

Air Force One turned and made its final descent to Hartsfield International Airport. The presidential plane was actually one of three bearing that designation, and it was almost filled with nearly fifty members of the Caduceus Group. Eric Zimmermann peered out the window at Atlanta's scarred landscape. Parts of the city looked as though they had been bombed.

"Look," he said, touching Honorée's arm. "It's still hard to believe, let alone that we survived it."

Honorée nodded in agreement, and Henry Rogers, who sat in a seat opposite them, responded with a loud snore. Around his neck was a large gold medal hung from a red, white, and blue ribbon. Rogers was sound asleep and drooling just a bit on the colorful decoration. Honorée sighed, and turned to Eric.

"What are we going to do about that guy?" she asked petulantly.

"Well, he's a hero, now. Winner of the Medal of Freedom. And I think you've done a terrific job refurbishing his wardrobe. Henry's never looked more dapper." Rogers snored again and stirred in his seat.

"Dapper is an exaggeration, Eric, but I think that a little mothering has helped just a bit."

Rogers suddenly opened both eyes and glared at the two. "Bullshit. I would've bought some new clothes for the occasion. That's the story of my life–people taking credit for my ideas." He was about to launch into a denunciation of his colleagues when a steward came by and asked them to fasten their seatbelts.

The big plane landed gently, and they headed for the parking lot. Simon Carey-Ross hurried behind them and called out, "Party still on at your place tonight, Eric?"

Zimmermann waved. "Definitely. Wanna come with us now and get a head start?" Carey-Ross smiled and nodded. He caught up just as Rogers started to flag a cab.

"Hold it, Henry. Your car's over here," Zimmermann said, taking his friend's arm and leading him to a two-door Mercedes sedan. Its convertible top was down.

"Lovely," Rogers murmured. "Not mine though."

"It most certainly is. The gift of a grateful people. Took a special act of Congress to vote the funds to replace your last car, but it passed easily. I should add, however," Zimmermann grinned, "that the bill was pushed through as a rider to a very lengthy revenue package, and nobody took much notice of it." He handed the keys to Rogers, who looked like a child receiving the ultimate Christmas present. The four of them piled in and headed for Eric's apartment in North Druid Hills.

As they drove through the city, bulldozers and heavy machinery seemed to be at work everywhere. The burned-out buildings were mostly cleared away, and new foundations were being dug. Atlanta would rise yet again.

"Amazing, isn't it," Carey-Ross commented. "A city almost destroyed. Hundreds of thousands dead. Hundreds of millions around the world–over thirty million in this country alone–struck down. All because of a relatively simple ingredient in ink. It's hard to believe. You know, I still don't believe it."

Rogers swung onto I-285 and headed north. "I guess something like it had to happen sooner or later, Simon. PEC-4 was a particularly talented chemical. For one thing, it's remarkably easy to absorb through the skin. Just about anyone who touched anything printed was bound to pick it up. Its effect is probably cumulative, though it'll take years to find out the specific dosage necessary to cause the genetic mutation." Rogers brushed his hair out of his eyes. "Who knows, Eric, we may find a virus hanging around and helping it out after all."

"Go ahead, rub it in," Zimmermann muttered softly.

"But it's such a great opportunity!" Carey-Ross cried, his eyes shining. "PEC-4 does not cause cancer. It allows it to happen. Think of it. A few segments of the DNA strand seem to be involved in the normal immunological resistance to the development and growth of cancerous cells. But this leads us to the astonishing discovery that unless a person is really hit hard with active carcinogens, only those with a genetic predisposition are likely to be afflicted."

Rogers pulled into the driveway of Zimmermann's building, and they all entered his apartment. While Eric opened a bottle of champagne, Honorée turned on some Mozart. "All well and good," Rogers said, accepting a glass, "but I still don't understand one thing."

"What's that?" Honorée asked.

"The babies. Infants don't read, but their rate was almost as high as the adults'."

Honorée shook her head. "Henry, I know you're a bachelor, but as a doctor you should know what the first thing every hospital does to each newborn." Rogers looked blank.

"Footprints, dummy. Fingerprints. *Ink!*"

"Of course."

"In any case," Carey-Ross said enthusiastically, "the result of this tragedy is bittersweet. The ingredient in the ink simply cocked a genetic trigger. Those who were likely to develop cancer in their lifetimes got it right away, and many, alas, died. But those without the predisposition are safe unless they come in contact with some powerful biological insult. Since as far as we can now understand, the genetic modification passed along through the germ cells to most offspring, it seems that within the next generation cancer will become a relatively rare disease."

"That's one hellish dose of Darwin," Zimmermann commented dryly. "A hell of a price to pay."

"Of course, Eric," Carey-Ross said sheepishly. "Forgive me. Please believe that my enthusiasm was only due to the new research aspects this opens. Why, three months ago, I would have said the whole thing was impossible. Absurd. It's like having the law of gravity repealed. But a terrible price *was* paid."

Everyone was quiet for several long moments, staring vacantly, listening to the music.

"What about the Russians?" Honorée asked, breaking the silence. "I mean, they've been a big help in the past couple of months with contributions of drugs and medical equipment. Will they have to go into isolation?"

"In a way," Eric replied. "Their embargo of certain industrial commodities has gone on for quite a number of years, and saved them from the effects of PEC-4 and the cancer plague. But now they, and everyone else in the world—or in this country—who have not been in contact with the contaminant will have to avoid it. As Simon has said, in purely scientific terms this is the most stunning breakthrough we've ever had in understanding the mechanism of the disease or the cell itself. Maybe now we will be able to find a cure for it. Certainly it will be imperative for the Russians to do so, and I think we'll be able to help."

Rogers spilled a few drops of champagne on his medal.

"Henry, will you take that goddamned thing off before you ruin it entirely?" Zimmermann scolded him.

Rogers sheepishly removed the ribbon from around his neck and gently put it on the mantel. "Hey!" Honorée cried, "the news is on. Quick, maybe we'll see ourselves."

Eric switched on his portable Sony, and there they all were, being praised by President Baker and receiving their awards.

"Ugh. I look terrible," Rogers muttered.

"You look wonderful, Henry." Honorée said, kissing him on the cheek. They all began to talk again, but stopped when the commentator reported that administration sources had confirmed that Eric Zimmermann would be President Baker's nominee to fill the vacant post of Director of HEW.

"Eric!" Rogers shouted, throwing a bear hug around Zimmermann and actually lifting him a few centimeters off the floor. "Is this true?"

"Yes, it is. Though I wanted to tell you myself. This calls for more celebration." Zimmermann poured around some more champagne. "Baker asked me this morning, and I accepted. Though why I want to join the ranks of the bureaucracy is beyond me." He smiled. "Unless it's to have the power to make appointments, or at least suggest them. You should all know that I hereby endorse cronyism. You're all going to be even biggershots than you were before. I have a particularly tough assignment for you, Henry."

"Oh?"

"Well, I'll want you to continue as before at NIH. You're the best numbers man around. But I'd like you to take some time to help me with administration . . ."

"I dunno, Eric. I appreciate it but . . ."

"Don't worry, you won't be tied up in endless meetings. You'll have staff for that. I thought I'd give you Sam Potter to oversee. You know, make sure he's on the ball and everything."

Rogers smiled broadly. "I think I may be able to serve my country after all," he said.

The conversation stopped for a few moments and they listened to the latest bulletin concerning the manhunt for the REAL leaders who had masterminded the assassination of President Wilson and Secretary Greenbaum. CIA Director Williams speculated they had fled the country and vowed he would make every effort to track them down, though they had seemingly disappeared into thin air.

The next item concerned the awarding of the Pulitzer Prize to Charles W. Elton of the New York *Times* and Francis X. Feeley of the *Daily News,* but Eric flicked off the set.

"I want to propose a toast," Eric said. "To you, my good friends who've come through so much with me. And most of all to Caduceus."

"To Caduceus!" the four called out. Henry Rogers circulated with a new bottle and, weaving slightly, proposed his own toast.

"To Eric Zimmermann. Our fearless leader. Who gave his all . . . well, part of his all (Honorée giggled) for the cause. It was a tough fight but we made it. And remember, Eric, the Nobel nominations are due to be made next week."

They all silently raised their glasses and grinned.

Late that night, Honorée raised herself on one elbow and looked at Eric, who was dozing peacefully. "Hey, wake up," she whispered softly.

"Humm? What is it, darling?"

"You said we'd all be big shots in Washington now."

"You betcha."

"Well, you talked to over a dozen people tonight about different HEW posts, but you never said what you had in mind for me."

"Not to worry, Honorée. You too will be a bureaucrat, though you'll have to turn in your cloak and dagger." He looked at her affectionately. "But for you, Ms. Hennessey, I have something very, very special in mind." Eric smiled. Honorée smiled. They kissed.